KT-151-413

... **ntosh** was born in ... ... north for a number of years, and ... resides in ... central Florida with her husband. She's a proud ... mama to three grown children, loves tea, crafting, animals (except reptiles!), bacon, and the ocean. She believes in the power of romance to heal, inspire, and provide hope in our complex world.

... **an Carlisle**'s love affair with books began when ... made a bad grade in mathematics. Not allowed to ... ch TV until the grade had improved, she filled her ... with books. Now, having turned her love of reading int... a love for writing romance, she pens hot Medicals. S... ves castles, travelling, afternoon tea, reading v... ...usly, and hearing from her readers. Join her ... ...etter at SusanCarlisle.com.

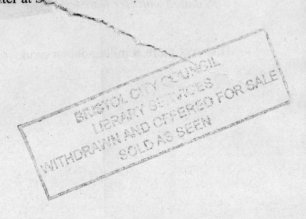

Discover more at millsandboon.co.uk.

ISLAND FLING
WITH THE SURGEON

ANN McINTOSH

TAMING THE
HOT-SHOT DOC

SUSAN CARLISLE

MILLS & BOON

Published in Great Britain 2021
by Mills & Boon, an imprint of HarperCollins*Publishers* Ltd,
1 London Bridge Street, London, SE1 9GF

www.harpercollins.co.uk

HarperCollins*Publishers*
1st Floor, Watermarque Building,
Ringsend Road, Dublin 4, Ireland

Island Fling with the Surgeon © 2021 by Ann McIntosh

Taming the Hot-Shot Doc © 2021 by Susan Carlisle

ISBN: 978-0-263-29770-6

07/21

MIX
Paper from
responsible sources
FSC™ C007454

Printed and bound in Spain
by CPI, Barcelona

ISLAND FLING WITH THE SURGEON

ANN McINTOSH

MILLS & BOON

Dedicated to my long-time friends
Renee, Odette and June.
Good fren betta dan pocket money.
Miss yuh, and mi soon come!

CHAPTER ONE

THE FIRST TIME Dr. Genevieve Broussard operated with the assistance of surgical nurse Zachary Lewin she was cautious, as was normal when working with new personnel. But the main difference, in that circumstance, was how aware she was of him. His presence alone put her on high alert in a way she didn't imagine she'd be if he were a woman.

Of course, it was hard *not* to be aware of Zach. Although he wasn't exceptionally tall—perhaps three or four inches above her own five foot six—he was barrel-chested and solid; the muscles in his arms and legs seemed set to tear open the seams of his scrubs.

He was also very good-looking, his skin the color of café au lait with a sprinkle of light freckles across his nose and cheeks, making her wonder if he had any elsewhere. Not conventionally handsome by any means, but striking in a serious, no-nonsense type of way. The lovely British accent didn't hurt either, adding a rather exotic flair to an already interesting package.

And he had a direct, interrogative way of looking at her, as though his dark brown gaze was trying to ferret out her every secret.

He was also quiet and—she later came to learn—

rather solitary, with an air of distance that forestalled any impertinence or overtures of friendship.

Not that, at the time, she was considering fostering any kind of camaraderie. She hadn't come to St. Eustace to make friends, especially of the male persuasion. All she needed to know was whether he was competent in the operating room or not. Especially since the anesthesiologist she'd been assigned was one of the new doctors who'd traveled to St. Eustace to gain extra experience.

She'd been assured the young anesthesiologist was capable, and all she had to do was keep an eye on him and write a report afterward, but the teenage patient on her operation table was her first concern. Kingston Matthews had been stuck by a car in downtown Port Michael and suffered life-threatening internal injuries. As trauma surgeon on duty when he came in, Gen had gotten him into the operating room as quickly as possible.

He'd needed a partial splenectomy, and ahead lay the surgical splinting of a couple of severely fractured ribs, but that had to wait until she was able to stop all the internal bleeding.

"Suction," she said, realizing as the word left her lips that the tube was already almost in place, Zach anticipating her request.

Blood trickled back into view.

She waited for an update on BP and O-sat from the anesthesiologist, as she carefully retracted the exposed organs, looking for the bleeder, but it was Zach who supplied the information.

Glancing up, Gen was just in time to see the anesthesiologist give the nurse a glare, but when he glanced her way and she raised her brows, all the doctor did was look away.

Even being very new—to the hospital, and to his duties—she'd expected better. This called for a talk with him later, to make sure he recognized the importance of communicating necessary information.

Kingston Matthews's blood pressure had risen since the splenectomy and the repair to a damaged minor artery, but it still wasn't up to where it should be. And wouldn't get there until she found the other bleed.

She'd already checked the liver and stomach for damage, surprisingly not finding any, but maybe she'd missed something?

The suction tube appeared again and, as she watched, Zach moved it slowly, clearing away the blood and revealing where the first trickle reappeared.

It was at that point she realized the extent of his experience and knowledge.

There were some surgical nurses who actively, if unobtrusively, used know-how gained over many years to be a surgeon's other pair of eyes and hands.

Some surgeons pretended it didn't happen, or feigned being oblivious, but Gen wasn't one of them. When the life of the patient was on the line, she'd take every advantage she could get to keep them alive, and be grateful.

"Thank you," she said. "I see it."

As she was about to cauterize the small blood vessel, the vision in her left eye blurred slightly.

Dammit.

She was usually more aware of when her eye was becoming dry, but she'd been so intent on finding the source of the bleeding, she'd left the mitigating exercise too long.

Her eye problem was a lasting effect of the Bell's palsy she'd suffered just after qualifying as a surgeon, causing the lid to noticeably droop. Unfortunately, the nerve damage also meant that her left eye didn't blink as efficiently as the right. At first, she'd been terrified that it would scotch her career, especially when it became clear she'd never fully recover, but over time she'd learned how to live with it and still operate.

"One second," she said, using the muscles above her eyebrow to force the offending eye closed, allowing lacrimal fluid to lubricate the eyeball. At any other time, she'd have simply used her finger to manipulate the eyelid, but she'd had to develop a different method of dealing with it when at work.

Especially in the sterile environment of the operating room.

After getting her eye open, she looked up, blinking to make sure her vision was clear, and caught Zach watching her.

In the past, it would have made her angry, or exacerbated the embarrassment that had followed her for a long time. Even now, she felt a rush of heat rise into her face, but she lifted her chin, daring him to say anything.

But those dark eyes just surveyed her, seemingly impassive and infinitely patient.

When she was studying, one of her instructors had told the class, "A surgeon must exhibit complete confidence at all times. You're like the captain of a ship. Everyone is looking to you to steer through the rocks and make safe harbor."

Bearing that in mind, she said briskly, "Okay. Here we go." She heard the defensiveness in her own voice, but hoped no one else did.

Zach simply nodded, but before he turned his attention back to the patient, she thought she'd seen a flash of something in his eyes, although she wasn't sure what it was.

All she knew was that it filled her with a different kind of warmth. One that had lasted the rest of the successful operation and even carried over for a couple of days.

Now, five months later, as she sat in the doctor's lounge with her fingers pushed into her hair, distractedly pulling at the short strands, she was sure it was then she'd told her mother the whopper.

The biggest, silliest lie of her life, which now had her contemplating whether it was too late to apply for another job.

Maybe in Nepal, or somewhere like that?

Far, far away.

Too far for her mother to fly to from New Orleans.

"Coo-calloo-calloo," she muttered to herself, using the expression she'd made up when she was eight, right after her father washed her mouth out with soap for cursing.

"What was that?"

The amused question from the doorway had Gen straightening to see orthopedic surgeon Mina Haraldson coming into the room. The grin on the other woman's face had Gen smiling too, although she felt anything but amused by her predicament.

"It's the strongest curse word I know. I made it up myself, so I could use it in front of my parents and not get in trouble," she admitted, making Mina laugh.

"Now, what on earth has you cursing so horribly?" the other woman asked, once she'd stopped chuckling.

Even though she liked Mina, and they'd developed a nice rapport, Gen hesitated. After what had happened with her so-called best friend, Loren, she'd gotten out of the habit of confiding in others.

Not that she expected everyone in her life to be a back-stabber, but the experience, although occurring years before, had left her cautious.

So instead, as she watched Mina pour herself a cup of coffee, she asked, "Is that a new prosthesis?"

Mina shot her a sideways glance, before looking back to reach for the creamer. "Yes. Arrived two days ago. I'm still getting used to it, but I have to admit it's pretty badass."

They'd spoken about Mina's accident, when she'd lost her hand, and her previous resistance to getting a prosthesis. It had seemed a waste of time getting one, she said, when it wouldn't enable her to operate on patients. But eventually she'd come around, realizing she could do so much more with one. And, once the prosthetic company she'd approached about making the hand for her realized the possibilities, they'd asked her to become one of their main testers.

"It looks it," Gen replied, admiring the realistic appearance and the movement of the fingers as Mina picked up her cup with it, while stirring the coffee with her right.

As she walked over to the table and sat across from Gen, Mina replied, "The action is unbelievably smooth. Almost as smooth as that change of subject you just did."

Gen couldn't help the little groan that escaped her throat, even though the other woman's comment made her smile too.

"Clearly not smooth enough," she replied, letting amusement color her words.

Mina held up her hand. "Hey, I'm not trying to pry, but you sounded pretty upset. I'm here, if you need an ear."

She was smiling as she spoke, but Gen saw how serious Mina's eyes were, and a pang of loneliness made her chest ache. Suddenly, she went from reticent to wanting to tell the other woman the whole sorry story.

Hopefully, Mina wouldn't think her nuts.

"My younger sister called to warn me that Mom is planning to come to St. Eustace in a couple of weeks to surprise me."

Mina's gaze sharpened. "Warn you?"

Something in her tone had Gen hurrying to continue, not wanting to give the wrong impression.

"Mom's amazing, and I can't wait to see her, but…" She realized she was pressing the knuckle of her index finger into the numb space at the left-hand corner of her lips, and forced herself to stop.

Mina took a sip of her coffee, obviously giving Gen a chance to continue. When the silence stretched on, she said, "But?"

Embarrassed, Gen dropped her chin to her chest for a moment, then sighed as heat rose into her cheeks.

Best to just get it over with.

"I went through a rough patch after I got sick, and it threw Mom into hyper-nurture mode, and she hasn't come out of it since. It's really only seemed to get worse once I decided to come to St. Eustace."

She shook her head, not wanting to go into details about the Bell's palsy, and her then-fiancé's painful defection, which Gen would be the first to admit she hadn't handled very well. And now how hard it was, knowing her mother was fretting about Gen's mental and emotional health, and that she was too far away to do anything, should her daughter need her.

Meeting Mina's sympathetic gaze gave her the impetus to continue.

"Mom's hell-bent on my going back to New Orleans.

She seems to think I'm here hiding, not getting on with what she calls my 'real life.' So, I spontaneously came up with an idea to make her feel I was having a great time here and was extremely happy."

"Oh?" Mina's eyebrows went up. "What did you tell her?"

Taking a deep breath, Gen replied on a rushed exhale, "That I was seeing someone. Then, to make it worse, I built an elaborate fantasy about the guy and our relationship."

"Uh-oh." Mina put her cup on the table and actually leaned forward, as though in anticipation. "What are you going to do?"

"I don't know." She tried to sound adult, but the ridiculousness of it was hard to ignore. "It sounds so juvenile when I say it out loud—like when a teenager tells their friends they do so have a boyfriend, but he goes to a different school."

Mina's eyes were wide as she said, "Yeah, but that's when you're a kid and you lie to your friends. This is your mom, and if she's anything like mine, heads could roll."

"Tell me about it," Gen said, the words coming out more like a groan. "She'll kill me if she finds out."

"If?" The skepticism in Mina's voice was unmistakable. "How could she not?"

Gen just dropped her head back into her hand, unwilling to answer the question, or even tell Mina the rest of the story.

She hadn't just told her mother she was seeing *someone*; she'd said she was seeing Zachary Lewin.

Named him, specifically.

And Marielle Broussard was no shrinking violet. Even if Gen told her the relationship hadn't worked out, she'd want to know why. And she'd be on the lookout for the man in question the entire time she was on St. Eustace, inclined to glare, or outright ask what had gone wrong.

Not to mention, Gen would be right back where she started, with her mother all up in her business and pushing for her to go back to the States.

"I have two choices," she muttered toward the floor. "Pretend to have broken up with the man, or set up a fake relationship well enough to fool my mother."

Mina blew out a breath, then asked, "What was that word you used, when I walked into the room?"

"Coo-calloo-calloo."

"Yeah," Mina replied in a rueful tone. "Coo-calloo-calloo."

Zach Lewin closed his locker, then snapped the padlock into place, but instead of heading straight out the door as he usually would, he stood there a little longer, lost in thought.

Normally he easily compartmentalized work, and once he was finished a shift rarely let his thoughts stray back to anything to do with the hospital. But today was different, and it wasn't a patient he was worried about, but one of the surgeons.

Dr. Genevieve Broussard.

They'd worked together earlier in the day, operating on a patient who'd come in with volvulus. While Dr. Broussard had performed with her usual calm competence, Zach was sure he sensed a difference in the way she'd spoken and behaved toward him. A certain coolness that hadn't been present the umpteen other times they'd worked together.

He wasn't given to flights of fancy. In fact, he'd been

described as unimaginative and detached. If memory served, *daft* and *oblivious* had been tossed about too, but who was counting? Yet, he was sure he'd sensed something strange in Dr. Broussard's manner during and after the operation.

And it irked him.

He admired her skill as a surgeon. They'd always got on well, and had a cordial relationship. She had an effervescent personality, although mixed with firm professionalism. It was a combination that worked well for her, as he hadn't heard one murmur of complaint about her the entire time he'd been at the hospital. She seemed universally liked and never appeared to have any problems with anyone, which made her change in attitude toward him all the more noticeable.

Normally he'd brush it off and leave it alone. His time in the military and as a nurse had taught him not to expect everyone to like him and, if someone didn't, not to take it to heart or even care. But the sudden shift in their previously easy working relationship gave him pause, and made him want to know if it was because of something he'd done. If he'd inadvertently caused the change, it made complete sense to make it right, since they'd be working together for at least the foreseeable future.

Another thing he'd learned was to nip problems that had the potential to become career threatening in the bud. While unsure whether this could be classified that way or not, he wasn't willing to take the chance.

He'd come to St. Eustace to get away for a while and get his head on straight. Although he didn't plan on staying forever, this was, after all, his father's homeland, and he wanted to maintain the family's good name while he was here.

Yet, did it make sense to bring it up at all, at this early stage? Maybe she'd just been having a bad day, and he'd presented an easy target?

He bent to pick up his kit bag, still unsure of what to do but leaning toward letting things remain as they were, just to see what would happen when next they worked together. That wouldn't be for at least three days, what with their overlapping days off.

Right, then.

Decision made, Zach headed out of the changing room, only to see the object of his ruminations standing just down the hall, looking at her phone. She was still in her scrubs, but her bag was on the bench next to her, and he knew from the schedule that, barring emergencies, she was now off duty.

So, why was she hanging about?

And, even with the decision he'd only just made, he was tempted to stop and speak to her about what had happened earlier. In fact, he found himself heading right toward her, but before he'd taken more than two strides, a door on his right opened and Dr. Kiah Langdon stepped out.

Kiah immediately stopped and said, "Hey, cuz. On your way to the gym?"

From the corner of his eye Zach saw Dr. Broussard turn her head toward them, before he gave his full attention to Kiah.

"Going down to Coconut Beach for a run," he replied.

"How's the house coming?"

Kiah knew Zach was refurbishing his grandfather's home, which had sat mostly empty since the old man died, and always took a moment to ask about the progress being made.

"Good. Finished the veranda and just about to start upgrading the kitchen."

And by the time they'd finished chatting, Genevieve Broussard was gone, leaving him no option but to revert to his prior plan of letting things ride and seeing what would happen.

The drive over to Coconut Beach took only about fifteen minutes, but Zach found his thoughts repeatedly going back to Genevieve, no matter how he tried to keep them on other matters. So much so that, on turning into the car park next to the beach, he thought perhaps his eyes, following the lead of his brain, were playing tricks on him.

That couldn't be Dr. Broussard sitting on the bonnet of her car waving to him, as he pulled into a nearby space, could it?

It most certainly was, and as she hopped down from her perch and made her way toward his car, bemusement had the muscles in his neck tightening.

What the heck was going on?

He had hardly closed the car door behind him before she started speaking.

"Hey, I'm sorry to stalk you like this, but I really needed to talk to you, and the hospital wasn't the best place to do it…"

Although she stopped to take a breath, Zach didn't have a chance to utter even one word before she asked, "Would you be my boyfriend?"

CHAPTER TWO

GEN HADN'T MEANT to blurt it out like that, but she was so nervous her palms were sweating, her knees were weak and the words just tumbled out of her mouth. The look of shock on Zach's face just made it all worse. Heat climbed the back of her neck, and she rubbed at it, trying to dispel the prickling sensation.

"I'm sorry?" he said, his voice clipped and terribly precise, sharp enough to cut. "I beg your pardon?"

"Oof," she replied, then wished she could pull the inarticulate sound back into her mouth, especially when his eyebrows contracted into a fierce scowl. Who would have thought she'd won prizes for elocution in the past, if that was the best she could come up with? "No, *I'm* sorry. I know it sounds crazy, but will you give me a chance to explain?"

He was still wearing that scowl, and the searching nature of his gaze made her wonder if he thought she was nuts.

She was wondering the same thing herself and couldn't blame him if he were!

"I'm waiting with bated breath for you to do just that," he said with a hint of sarcasm overlaying the words.

She rubbed at her nape again and tried to regain some hint of composure.

"I'm not propositioning you, although I know it sounds like it." The urge to start babbling again had her stopping and taking a deep breath. After blowing it out, she continued. "The truth is, I lied to my mother and told her you and I were involved in a relationship."

"You *what*?"

He said it softly, but he couldn't have sounded any more dangerous if he'd shouted.

Gen held up her hands. "I know. I know. It was stupid, but Mom is always on at me about not having a social life, and one night I just couldn't take it anymore. So, I made up a story to get her off my back."

Not the entire truth, but close enough under the circumstances.

"Why me?"

Now she could hear curiosity warring with his outrage, and it made her embarrassment deepen, if that were at all possible.

"I don't know for sure," she replied, trying to be honest. "I think it was because you'd just arrived, and I'd worked with you in the OR for the first time, so your name just popped into my head."

Zach shook his head slowly, still giving her a suspicious glare.

"And now—?"

"Now Mom's coming to visit, and I can't let her know I lied."

His nostrils flared slightly, as he drew in a harsh breath. "Just tell her it didn't work out, and we're not friendly anymore. Wouldn't that solve the problem?"

"No!" Yikes, now she was barking at him. She had to

get a grip. "It would make it worse—for me anyway—because then the whole cycle would start again."

His gaze made her feel like a recalcitrant child, and now her entire body flushed hot. Looking around, she spied a small gazebo farther along the beach and gestured toward it.

"Can we sit down and talk about it?" Yeah, she was pleading, but although it felt weird, she was willing to do whatever it took to get Zach on board with her plan, no matter how crazy it was.

He didn't reply for such a long interval she was absolutely sure he was going to tell her to get lost, but finally he nodded and waved his hand in the direction of the hut.

"After you."

"Thank you," she said as they started walking that way. "I really appreciate it."

"Don't thank me yet," he said in that cool, cutting tone. "I haven't agreed to anything."

"You agreed to at least hear me out," she pointed out, perhaps more sharply than she should, all things considered.

That earned her a stern, sidelong glance, but he was gracious enough to say, "That's fair."

By the time they sat across from each other at the shaded table, she was struggling with what she was going to say. It had sounded, if not sensible, at least reasonable when she'd rehearsed it all in her head, but now all that she'd planned to say fled in the face of that interrogatory gaze.

"Well?" he said, not breaking eye contact. "What do you have to say for yourself?"

She was suddenly catapulted back in time to the principal's office, where she was supposed to explain how one of her many escapades had gone awry and the sensations were still the same.

Embarrassment.

Shame.

But also the unmistakable high of an adventure unfolding.

The last made her smile, and Zach's scowl grew even more ferocious.

"The fact is," she started quickly, before he could cuss her out the way he seemed set to do. "My mother thinks that I'm suffering ongoing psychological effects from my bout of Bell's, and I'm trying my hardest to reassure her that isn't the case."

"Are you sure you aren't, though?" he asked, no longer looking as fierce as he had a moment before.

"No." She shook her head in emphasis. "I'll freely admit it was a setback I wasn't anticipating—not that anyone anticipates a situation like that—but my main concern, really, was whether it was going to destroy my career. Once I got to the stage where I knew I could still operate, I was okay with what had happened."

Again, not the full story, but enough for him to get the gist without exposing her private issues too much.

He looked skeptical, but only said, "So, if you're okay, why the deception? Wouldn't it be better to just tell your mother the truth, instead of lying to her?"

"I've tried repeatedly, believe me, but she's unrelenting." Gen rubbed at her eye, which was getting a little dry, but stopped when Zach's gaze followed the motion of her finger. She quickly continued, "I know she just wants to see me happy, but the stress of her constant worrying was wearing me out. Telling her I was in a relationship at least allayed some of her fears."

Zach pondered her words in silence, and Gen wondered what was going on in his head. There was more to it, of course, but she wasn't willing to tell him about Johan abandoning her after the Bell's palsy, or the shock of him marrying Loren immediately thereafter. The aftereffects of her illness were nothing in comparison to the pain of the betrayal. If anything was holding her back from moving forward in life and considering getting involved with a man again, it was that.

"So, what exactly did you tell your mother about our imaginary relationship?"

Gen gave him her most winning smile, aware that it was a lot more lopsided than it had been when she used it on her teachers, parents and any others she wanted to impress. Hopefully it would still do the trick.

"I told her that you're fabulously good-looking and had a body to die for. And, because my mom is big on excellence, I also told her you're the best surgical nurse I've ever worked with."

His lips twitched, ever so slightly, at the corners.

"In other words, you've compounded the original lie several times over."

She wrinkled her nose and shook her head. "Not one of those statements is a lie. You are extremely handsome, and you obviously work hard to stay fit, so I don't know why you wouldn't just admit your body is amazing. Plus, you actually are one of the best, if not *the* best surgical nurse I've had in the operating room."

He gave what could only be classified as a snort and said, "Now I know you're just buttering me up. What else did you tell her?"

His modesty made her smile. Who knew that humbleness could be so attractive and tempting? His brushing aside her honest compliments made her want to push, to see what it would take to make him really self-conscious.

"I told her your father was originally from St. Eustace, but you were born in England and had a sexy English accent." She paused, thinking back to the conversations she'd had with her mother, then added, "And that although you're ridiculously cute, you're not flashy in any way."

He rubbed the side of his hand across his lips, and Gen saw a little rush of color stain his cheeks for an instant.

"Good grief. I meant, what did you tell her about the progress of this mythical relationship of ours? Such as, what we were supposedly doing over the last few months? Have we got serious or anything ridiculous like that?"

For some reason, hearing him talk about them getting serious as "ridiculous" kinda hurt. Was there something about her that made him think her unfit to be serious girl-friend, or even wife, material?

Realizing she was pushing at the corner of her mouth, she dropped her hand back onto the table and replied, "Well, I told her you were getting over a really bad breakup and weren't interested in getting too involved too soon, and that slowed her down some."

His demeanor changed so quickly it was shocking, going from slightly amused to cold and intense in a blink.

"Who told you that?"

There was that soft, dangerous voice again, coupled with a narrow-eyed stare. It should have sent alarm bells ringing like crazy, but instead Gen felt a tingle of unmis-takable excitement rush through her veins.

"No one told me anything," she replied, trying for a conciliatory tone and wondering if she'd touched a nerve. "I made it up, remember?"

His response was to swing his leg over the bench and get up so abruptly she was left looking up at him, bemused.

"Listen, this is just bonkers," he said. Pausing, he rubbed a hand across his mouth again. "I can't even digest this right now. I'm going for a run. If you're here when I get back, I'll try again to listen to what you have to say, but I can't right now."

Then he took off at a blistering pace, leaving her with a mouthwatering view of a whole lot of hard-bodied man in motion.

As she watched his long muscular legs and amazing butt disappear along the shoreline, Gen shook her head, wondering why her heart was pounding so hard. And she couldn't help asking herself if it was worth waiting for him to come back. Who knew how long he'd be, or if he'd have run off the snarky attitude?

Getting up, she picked up her car keys, then just stood there, stupidly poised between staying and going, unable to make up her mind about what to do.

Looking to where Zach was just disappearing around a bluff was like watching her grand, brilliant plan disappear into the sunset.

"Coo-calloo-calloo," she muttered. "Coo-calloo-ca-cock-a-doodle-do."

Zach pushed himself hard for the first two hundred meters of his run, then, when his muscles started reminding him that he hadn't done his usual warm-up routine, he slowed.

It felt, strangely enough, as though he was running for his life, from a woman who was in turns amusing, infuriating and—curiously—beguiling. He'd seen Gen

Broussard in work mode, but hadn't spent much time in casual conversation with her, so he hadn't known what it would be like to be the recipient of her full attention. Or that she had all the impish charm of a pixie.

Those dark twinkling eyes that seemed to be perpetually laughing at herself and the world, coupled with her beautiful, asymmetrical grin, had made it hard for him to truly take in what she was saying.

What she was asking of him.

And when she said she'd told her mother he'd had a bad breakup, he'd been shocked. So much so that the hurt, which he'd assiduously pushed to the back of his mind, was as sharp as the day his very real relationship imploded. The wave of embarrassment that had inundated him almost knocked him off his seat and made him wonder if the entire island knew his sorry story.

Hence the quick retreat, which he refused to think of as running away, although clearly it rather was.

She'd said she'd made it up so, clearly, she hadn't actually heard how he'd been used by Moira, then discarded like a piece of chewed gum. Now, remembering the honesty he'd heard in her tone filled him with relief. He'd come to the island to get away from the embarrassment, and the thought of once again being the recipient of pity, sympathy or unkind amusement made him cringe.

That aside, even now he found it impossible to believe Genevieve had told her mother they were involved. If an hour ago someone had asked him to describe Dr. Broussard, he'd have used words like sensible, and steady. That was her persona in the hospital, and definitely when she was in the operating theater, so this whole switch to troublemaker and spinner of tales had thrown him for a loop.

How on earth was he supposed to respond to her crazy scheme?

It would be better, easier, to make her tell her mother the truth, yet there was a part of him that absolutely understood where she was coming from.

His parents weren't the type to pry, but he was always aware of their gentle probing whenever they called.

Dad would ask about the progress of the house and whether he'd been to visit any of the cousins who lived on the other side of the island. Invariably he'd ask if Zach had seen Kiah or spent time with him, reminiscing a bit about how he and Kiah's father had been both second cousins and the best of friends. And always there was the undercurrent of wanting to know Zach hadn't locked himself away from the world, but was enjoying his time in St. Eustace.

Mum would ask about work, and they'd talk about things like his newly discovered love of gardening, but all the while he was hearing the subtle subtext of concern. The worry she felt, knowing how hurt he'd been by the events that led him to abandon his life in London and move to the Caribbean.

He was honest enough to admit that when speaking to his parents he'd donned a facade of cheerfulness and talked as though life was busy and fun, when it was anything but. When in reality he'd withdrawn into a solitary existence. One that gave him far too much time to brood.

Was that very different from what Gen Broussard had done, when she'd tried to placate her mother?

Slowing to a jog, he approached the path he usually took away from the beach and through a wildlife area, which would extend his run for a few more miles over diverse terrain. At the spot where the sand ended, he stopped and carefully considered what she'd said.

She claimed it wasn't the effects of the Bell's palsy holding her back from having a relationship, and he hoped that was true. Yes, the physical effects were noticeable, as soon as one saw her for the first time, but did little, if anything, to lessen her attractiveness.

At least, as far as he was concerned.

While this was the first time he'd been exposed to her quirkier side, he'd been very aware of her beauty and the energetic charisma that made her a favorite among the hospital staff. Although it really was none of his business, he couldn't help wondering why she was still single. Not that being single and wanting to remain that way was a bad thing. Just that she seemed the type who would have men buzzing about like bees and would bring a great deal of happiness into a man's life.

Which made her mother's worries, and Gen's desire to assuage them, understandable.

Besides, he couldn't help being amused, not only by her way of dealing with her mother, but also by the nerve it must have taken to approach him with her crazy plan. Doing so spoke to an adventurous spirit, which was something he once upon a time would have claimed to share. The younger Zachary had been spontaneous and fun loving, until Moira had told him his "antics," as she called them, were embarrassing.

Now he envied Genevieve her audacity and wished he'd retained some of his own.

But maybe he had, since he found himself wondering what it would hurt to hear her out and perhaps even help?

If nothing else, it would get him out of his self-imposed shell and add a bit of sparkle to his life.

There was, after all, no need to feel this deep trepidation. He'd seen combat and lived to tell the tale. Pretending to be involved with a beautiful woman should be a walk in the park.

And it wasn't as though she were really interested in him, as a man or potential partner. She was a surgeon, and he'd already learned the hard way not to do what his father called "flying above his nest." If and when she settled down, he had no doubt it would be with someone far more talented and ambitious than him—another doctor, or a lawyer perhaps.

Not an ex-soldier and RN, who was completely content with his lot.

And since the scheme was hers, and they'd be keeping it totally platonic, it wouldn't affect their work life either.

A truncated bark of laughter forced its way past his throat, and Zach shook his head as he turned and started jogging back. Genevieve Broussard might just be the catalyst he needed to get his life out of the doldrums, and he realized he'd already made the decision.

If she was still at the gazebo and hadn't chosen to abandon her crazy plan, he'd hear her out and, more likely than not, agree to help.

Somehow, he wasn't at all surprised to round the headland and see her in the distance, right where he'd left her but facing the other way so she could see him coming. And when he got closer, he noticed the jelly coconuts on the table, the tops already lopped off, hers with a paper straw in it.

"I got you some coconut water," she said, giving

him another of those impish smiles. "Still in the original container."

"Thanks."

He knew he sounded grumpy but didn't do anything to mitigate it. In the back of his mind he still thought she was barking mad to have come up with the scheme, and he was just as crazy to be considering going along with it.

Sitting across from her—and even though it felt as if he was making a colossal mistake—as he unwrapped his straw he looked at her and said, "So, how do you want to proceed?"

And her grin of delight once more almost knocked him off his seat.

CHAPTER THREE

GEN CHECKED HER GPS again, as the road she was driving along narrowed to the point where she wondered if another vehicle could pass going in the opposite direction. Zach had warned her he lived out in the "country," although it was only about fifteen minutes away from the hospital. Before they'd left the beach the day before, he'd made her program his address into her phone and checked to make sure the directions were accurate.

"Sometimes, once you get outside of the city, the smaller roads don't appear," he'd said, looking at her phone. "But this looks right."

Now, as she was directed to take the next right, she couldn't help wondering whether the darn app was actually working properly. As far as she could see, the right-hand side of the road was cliff face without even a track in sight.

Just as she was about to find a spot to squeeze over into and call him, she rounded a corner and saw an even narrower road branching off from the main.

"This cycle track he lives on better not scratch my car," she groused aloud, perhaps in an attempt to quell the nervous flutters in her belly.

She still couldn't believe he'd agreed to her harebrained idea. But somehow, and she wasn't at all sure why, he'd given in and invited her up to his place the following evening for supper. She wasn't even sure what he meant by supper since, to her, any meal after six in the evening would be dinner.

Was supper just another way to say dinner, or a completely different type of meal?

Would she have to stop and get a burger on her way home, after being given crackers and cheese or something similar?

Realizing she was thinking like that so as not to dwell too much on the craziness of what she was doing, she chuckled to herself. It didn't matter, really, what he fed her, although she was quite hungry. The important thing was to firm up their plans.

But she knew he had some deep reservations.

"How on earth are we going to fool your mother into believing we've had a months-long relationship, when we don't even really know each other?" he'd asked the day before at the beach.

She'd already given that some thought.

"We each write a list of things a partner would know about us after about five months. A dossier, if you like. That way we can at least talk about stuff together when she's around and make it sound good."

He'd looked extremely skeptical. "What kinds of things?"

"Whatever you think necessary," she'd replied, because she didn't know *exactly* what to tell him. "Pertinent information."

Since he'd worked the morning shift, he probably hadn't even gotten to it, while she'd labored over putting her list together, the chore taking up most of the day.

It had been surprisingly difficult. People thought she was gregarious and outgoing, and she was, to a point. Beyond the superficial, though, she liked to play her cards close to her chest. Figuring out just how much information was enough had been hard. There were things she wouldn't share with anyone right now, much less a stranger she was roping into what amounted to a performance.

She was traveling uphill, along a road that was surprisingly smooth, although it seemed no wider than a deer track through the woods. The wild vegetation that had bordered the main road gave way to banana trees on one side and some sort of citrus grove on the other. In the distance, and farther up the road, she caught a glimpse of a roofline behind the hill, but couldn't see the house although, according to the GPS, she was within mere yards of it.

Then, as she rounded another corner, she came upon a pair of gateposts and, as she turned in, got her first view of the house.

Instinctively easing off the gas, she took in the lovely, if slightly dilapidated, sight, set at the top of a hill above her position.

The base was of irregularly cut stones, stacked perfectly, above which rose the second story's wooden walls, topped with a steep pitched roof decorated with gingerbread trim. To make it even more perfect, there was a wraparound veranda outside the second story with a colonnade below.

"Whoa," she breathed, absolutely enchanted. She'd always had a soft spot for older, characterful houses, and this one was adorable.

Making her way slowly up the curved driveway, she

could see where the bushes alongside had been trimmed back and were bright with yellow flowers. Other parts of the terraced garden seemed rather wild, but there were spots where grass had been cut away, revealing freestanding trees and bushes.

While there was a gravel parking area on one side, Zach had told her to drive around to the back, and Gen admired the rest of the house as she did. The land at the back was flatter and had what looked like a well-tended vegetable garden, along with a small gazebo under which was a table and four chairs.

Pulling in beside Zach's SUV, she took a moment to admire the house once more while she put the car in Park. Just as she was wondering whether to text him or toot her horn to let him know she was there, the back door opened, and Zach stepped out onto the stoop.

For a moment, she froze, as though seeing him for the first time. Wearing cargo shorts and a T-shirt, he was barefoot and casually yummy. The thought that she'd chosen well, if she wanted to impress and reassure her mother, made her grin, and she saw his lips quirk upward in return.

Grabbing her tote from the seat beside her, she got out, just as he walked down the path toward her car.

"What a glorious house," she said before closing her car door. "Is it yours? How did you find it?"

His smile got a little wider, and Gen realized she'd never heard this man laugh. Not once in five, almost six, months. And suddenly, she wanted to be the one to make that happen.

"It was my grandfather's family home," he replied, meeting her at the end of the path and turning back to gaze up at the house with her. "The family farmed here for generations, but my father and his siblings left the island to live abroad, so there was no one here to take over when Grandad died."

"That's a shame," she said. "But at least the house is still in the family."

"Yeah." He put his hand lightly on the small of her back, saying, "Come on in. Grandad left the property to all his children—four in total—but only my father was thinking of coming back here after he retires, so they split the fifty or so acres up. Dad took the house and five acres, while the rest was doled out between his siblings."

"And you're fixing it up?" she asked, sure she'd heard Kiah say something to that effect the day before at the hospital.

"It definitely needs some work," he replied as she went through the double doors and into a hallway. "Parts of the veranda upstairs weren't safe, and I had some windows replaced, as well as started on painting the outside. I'm trying to work up the stamina to redo the kitchen."

He'd slipped past her and started up a wooden staircase on the left side of the corridor, making her wonder where he was going.

"What's up here?" she asked, even as she had one foot already on the first tread.

He glanced back at her. "It's an upside-down house. All the bedrooms are on the ground floor, where, because of the thick stone walls, it's cooler, and the living spaces are upstairs."

"An upside-down house? I've never heard that expression before. Is that what they call it in England?" Halfway up the steps, she caught the scent of something delicious cooking, which allayed her fears of being starved.

He threw her an amused look over his shoulder. "I thought that was what it was called everywhere."

That made her chuckle, but her laughter died when she got to the top of the staircase and found herself in a huge, square kitchen with doors on both sides, opening onto the veranda and...

"What an amazing view!"

As though drawn by the spell of the verdant land and distant ocean, she moved toward the doors. From its position at the top of the hill, there was a clear view through a valley, which opened up to the sea.

"They really knew how to build back in the day. Excuse me," he added, coming up behind her and then slipping past to go to a cupboard. He left behind a warm, masculine scent that somehow went straight to her head. "The house not only catches the prevailing winds but also has stellar views of sunrise and sunset."

Gen tore herself away from the sight of the sun dipping toward the horizon and, instead, walked over to the table, setting her bag down on one of the chairs.

She wasn't here to drool over the house, the view or Zachary Lewin. She was on a mission.

Pulling out her dossier, she pulled out a chair and sat down.

"I know you probably haven't had a chance to put anything together yet, since you worked today, but here's my information."

"Mine is there," he replied, pointing to a sheaf of papers on the table next to her.

"Oh." Surprised, she picked up the pages and started reading.

"You were in the army?" That certainly explained that straight-backed, solid posture and his level of fitness.

"Yes, for almost ten years."

"What was your rank?"

"Captain."

She giggled. "That'll impress Mom."

He made a noncommittal sound, but when she glanced up at him, he had his back to her, leaving her with no clue what it meant. So, she went back to the list.

He'd thought of almost everything, even things she'd missed, like favorite TV shows and book genres.

"*Doctor Who* fan, huh?"

He was at the stove now, stirring something, and she saw the wide shoulders shrug.

"It's one of the few shows that have stood the test of time. Have you watched it?"

"Some," she admitted absently, still reading. "But not the entire thing."

"Great binge-watching show, if you ever have a year or so to spare."

His dry comment made her snort. "Yeah, right. I count myself lucky when I get two full days off in a row. Or I did, before I came here."

"You worked as a trauma surgeon only, back home?"

"Yes, and unfortunately was kept far busier than I liked." Working in a large central hospital had meant they got more than their fair share of trauma victims, and she'd gotten way too close to burnout. The night she'd found herself sobbing uncontrollably in the ladies' room, having been unable to save the life of a young victim of a drive-by shooting, she'd known it was time for a change.

"How do you find it here?" There was nothing but genuine curiosity in his voice. "It must be a lot different from what you're used to."

"I like it, a lot," she said. Then she had to admit, "At

first, I wasn't sure how it would work out. I wasn't used to what felt like a far more leisurely work schedule and had to get back into doing more general and elective surgeries. But after a while, I realized I'd been running on adrenaline for years, and it had taken its toll."

He'd turned to face her while she was talking, leaning casually against the counter, and he nodded.

"It takes a while to get out of flight-or-fight mode, once you've been in it for a while. After I came back from a war zone, it would take me months to come down off high alert."

"Yes," she said, not sure why she was willing—no, eager—to tell him what she'd experienced. "It took me ages to actually sleep straight through the night, without startling awake, sure my phone was ringing and I was being called to the hospital."

He didn't reply but nodded gently, his expression one of complete understanding, and Gen had to look away, back to the papers in front of her, almost in tears.

"Anyway," she said hurriedly, "What else do we have here?"

Zach cleared his throat, the sound unusual enough to have her looking back up at him. He was wearing a rueful smile, but all hints of compassion were gone.

"It's a little late to ask if you like fish, since that's what I cooked. If you don't, I'll take you out somewhere to eat."

She laughed, relieved to have gotten past the awkward moment without making a fool of herself.

"I'm from New Orleans," she reassured him. "If I didn't like seafood, I'd be disowned."

Still no laugh from him, but she did get something close to a grin.

"It's just some steamed fish with okra, onion and carrot, served with brown rice."

"Perfect. And can we eat out on the veranda, so I can watch the sunset?"

Now there was a full-on grin, and it transformed his face from handsome to stunning, making Gen's heart do a funny little flip.

"I already set the table out there," he replied, before turning back to the stove. "It's my favorite place to eat in the evenings."

Suddenly uninterested in what he'd written about himself and more intent on food and more natural conversation, she got up and tapped the pages in her hand into a neat pile.

"Come on then," she said, putting the paper on the table. "What can I carry out for you?"

"If you could grab those trivets, I'll bring out the food," he said, pointing to a couple of wooden hot pads on the counter.

Doing as he bid, she asked, "So, you're related to Kiah Langdon? How? And do you have any more family still here?"

As they went out onto the veranda and sat down to the delicious meal, she was aware of being—perhaps for the first time in a long time—fully engaged. Interested and relaxed in a way unusual for the life she'd been living.

And the little pang of melancholy she experienced, as she realized it was all too temporary, had to be forced aside.

CHAPTER FOUR

ON THE DAY after his supper with Gen Broussard, Zach woke up just before sunrise, as was his habit. With his cup of tea in hand, he went downstairs and out into the back garden, taking a deep breath of the morning air.

He'd hardly slept the night before, having spent much of the wee hours poring over Gen's biographical information and trying to sort out in his own mind just who *exactly* Genevieve Broussard was.

Having worked with her for months, he'd thought he had some kind of handle on her personality, but the more time he spent with her outside of the hospital the more he realized he had no clue. Turning to her own words—to the things she considered important for him to know—was another effort to figure her out.

The dossier was factual, with one or two surprises, like the information she'd been a contestant in a number of beauty pageants and her talent had been dancing.

But as interesting as her listed information was, the hours they'd spent together the evening before were even more illuminating.

Her avid curiosity, coupled with a mind that flitted unerringly from subject to subject with the precision of a hummingbird, left him slightly shell-shocked trying to keep up. But despite the mental gymnastics she'd put him through, Zach realized it was the best night he'd had in a long, long time.

Yet, after she'd left to go home, Zach realized that while he'd thought she'd been gregarious and outgoing, he'd actually learned very little about her personally.

She'd ferreted a whack more information out of him than she'd revealed about herself by asking him myriad questions and jumping to another topic before he could ask her anything in turn.

It made him wonder what she had to hide, and unfortunately, her dossier didn't offer any answers on that point.

Taking a sip of his tea and admiring the way the treetops were starting to glow with clear golden light, he came to the conclusion that Gen was a master at deflection. If they were to present themselves as a couple, as she wanted, he was going to have to pin her down over certain things. It was all well and good to know where she went to school, that she graduated summa cum laude and where she did her residency, but there was no intimacy to the knowledge.

Zach sighed. So many questions brought up by her sparkling, yet rather mysterious persona.

But he was out of practice in getting women to open up. Out of practice in being a working part of a relationship. Since Moira dumped him, he'd had ample time to reflect on the last few years they'd been together, and all the signs of deterioration had been there. Unfortunately, he'd missed or ignored them and, in some cases, just accepted her assurance that everything was fine when, in reality, it was going down the drain.

The truth was she'd already had one foot out the door

and was just making sure she was set career-wise before leaving.

"We've grown apart," she'd said. "It's not the same anymore."

"I've been away for most of the time and have hardly had a chance to settle back into civilian life." Gobsmacked by the sudden turn of events, it was all he could think of to say. Surely Moira would realize this new phase of their relationship needed a chance to work out? With him no longer in the army, her finally being certified as a barrister and them actually living together full-time, everything had changed. "We can make it work. Things are finally more settled—"

"You just don't get it, do you?" The veneer of sadness and regret she'd worn fell away, revealing the cold, hard surface beneath. "I've outgrown you. You'll never be in my league, and I won't be embarrassed by you anymore. I'm moving up in the world, and you'll always be just a boy from Brixton, without ambition or drive."

It was only later, after it was all over, that he'd realized how she'd used him, and how many of his so-called friends knew.

The familiar weight of shame and anger settled on his shoulders, but this time Zach refused to give in to the impulse pushing him toward melancholy. Instead, he took another deep breath and walked over to the gazebo to put his cup on the table. Then he made his way across to his vegetable patch.

Since coming to the island, he'd discovered an interest in and a knack for gardening, aided by Mr. Alexander—or Mass Alex, as he was called—the elderly gentleman who lived down the road. Mass Alex, now in his eighties, had looked after the garden before and after

Grandad had died, cutting back as much of the bush as he could manage. Under his tutelage, Zach had started bringing the landscaping back to life and was growing a lot of his own veg.

The tranquility of the land first thing in the morning was one of his favorite things, and as he walked through the neat rows, bending occasionally to pull a weed, he let that peace flow over him.

Yet, his brain wouldn't stop ticking over, thinking about Gen.

Then he realized he was smiling, thinking about her and the crazy scheme he'd signed up for. It was an adventure. A little fun in the midst of a life he'd allowed to grow a bit stale and flat.

Why not just enjoy it?

They'd agreed to meet for lunch so as to be seen together outside of the hospital, setting the stage for the performance to come.

And if Genevieve wanted a boyfriend, that was what Zach would give her.

Hopefully she was fully prepared.

It was only after he'd unhooked the hose from the side of the concrete water tank that he realized he was whistling, and that made him chuckle out loud.

Watch out, Dr. Broussard. Here comes your English lover-man.

Gen slept in, sleepily rolling out of bed just after eight thirty, glad to have the chance for a lazy morning. By nature she wasn't a morning person, and years of having to get up early hadn't changed that, just made her adapt to whatever schedule she was on. So, it was nice to sleep in for a change.

As she sat on the edge of the mattress, her first thought was of Zach Lewin and the evening they'd spent together.

He was a dream, if imaginary, boyfriend, and she couldn't help patting herself on the back for having chosen him—and having gotten him to agree to the farce.

There was no doubt in her mind that her mother would be impressed with Zach. He was nice, respectful and—despite being so good-looking—somehow perfectly ordinary, in an extraordinary way. It had been lovely to simply sit and talk, without worrying about whether he'd try to take advantage of the situation or was somehow judging her.

She was honest enough to admit her past dating life hadn't been as relaxing and fun as last night. With most men she'd been hyperaware of each of her quirks, constantly reminding herself not to talk too much or ask too many questions, but with Zach she could just be herself.

It was a nice change to realize he didn't seem to mind the way she jumped from subject to subject.

He definitely wasn't like the men Gen had dated in the past, but that was probably all for the good. Mom hadn't been terribly impressed with any of them anyway, especially Gen's ex-fiancé.

"Johan was too smooth," she'd said, when she heard about the breakup. "I'd go so far as to say smarmy, considering how things have turned out."

Gen had wanted to argue but couldn't in good conscience disagree. In hindsight she'd realized Johan was more enthralled with the idea of being able to tell people his fiancée was a beauty queen than he'd been enamored with her. Not even her credentials as a surgeon were as important to him as being seen with what he considered a beautiful woman on his arm.

As soon as it became clear the nerve damage was permanent, he'd dropped her faster than a red-hot coal, as though her looks were all she had to recommend her.

Then turned around and married her supposed best friend and fellow pageant contestant.

The hurt had taken her to a dark, dark place. One she'd fought hard to escape. At heart, she was an optimist, and she'd taken to counting her blessings as a way to remind herself how much she had going for her.

A family who had rallied to her side.

A job she loved and believed in and had been able to continue, even after the Bell's palsy.

This new, quieter and more relaxing life on St. Eustace.

Yet, she'd been screwed so tight by everything that had happened and the effort to push it all to the deep recesses of her mind that the stress had almost cost her everything anyway.

Funny to realize that thinking about it now didn't bring the same deep emotional response as usual. Maybe she was actually getting over it all?

Smiling, she hopped out of bed to put on the coffee maker before heading into the bathroom to shower. Just as she'd finished getting dressed and was pouring her first, much needed coffee of the day, her phone rang, causing her to scamper back into the bedroom to find it.

The hospital.

"Hello, Dr. Broussard," said the voice on the other end after Gen had identified herself. "Sorry to bother you, but Director Hamilton asked me to call. We have a patient coming off the cruise ship that's in port, and the ship's doctor suspects a ruptured appendix with possible complications. Dr. Langdon is on the other side of the island, and Dr. Goulding is performing back surgery. Can you come in?"

"Of course," Gen said, pushing aside a spurt of annoyance and regret. She was supposed to meet up with Zach for lunch and, depending on how bad the patient was, she might not be able to make it. "I'll be there in about fifteen minutes."

Ruefully, she poured her highly anticipated coffee into a travel mug, then found Zach's number as she headed into the bedroom to change into scrubs. Might as well be prepared, rather than have to change again when she got to the hospital.

"Hey there," she said when he picked up. "I might have to cancel lunch. I've been called in to the hospital."

"I have too," he replied, and she heard a car door slam. "One of the surgical nurses called in sick."

"Oh." Knowing they might be operating together shouldn't bring that little tingle of pleasure. "Well then, I'll see you there."

"Yes," he said, and for some reason it sounded as though he were smiling too. "See you in a few."

Her townhouse wasn't very far from the hospital, so she was there within the time range she'd specified.

As she was heading down the hallway from the staff entrance, she saw Director Hamilton farther along and stopped when he said, "I'm sorry to call you in on your day off, Genevieve, but you're the most experienced surgeon we have available right now."

"No problem." She gave him a smile, knowing that with Kiah and John unavailable, it was either her or one of the younger doctors who'd have to operate. And coming from an area where tourism was important too, Gen knew the director would be nervous about having one of the visitors to the island operated on in their hospital. "I don't mind."

"Thank you. I appreciate it very much. The patient is on her way by ambulance from the port and should be here within minutes."

As the director patted her shoulder, Gen heard the outside door open behind her and footsteps approaching. Even without turning, she knew it was Zach, but glanced back anyway.

He was smiling, and something about that grin had her brain scrambling and goose bumps rushing across her torso and arms.

"Morning, Director," he said when he was still a couple of paces away. Then he turned his dark, somehow mischievous gaze on Gen, and she froze.

"Morning, Zach…"

The director's words trailed away as Zach paused and, bending his head, kissed Gen on her cheek, leaving a warm, electrically charged spot on her skin.

"Morning, love," he murmured, and Gen swore she heard barely suppressed laughter in his deep, soft tone. "Sleep well?"

"Y…yes, thank you," was all she could get out past the lump of mingled horror and laughter clogging her throat. "You?"

"Never better," he replied.

Then he strolled away as casual as could be, leaving Gen biting the inside of her cheek, hardly daring to look at Director Hamilton. When she finally risked a glance, the other man, thankfully, was gaping at Zach's retreating figure.

By the time the director turned his startled gaze her

way, Gen had some semblance of control over herself, and she gave him one of her best smiles.

"Well, I better get ready for when the patient arrives. See you later, Director."

Quick walking for all she was worth, she almost caught up to Zach near the staff changing rooms, but he swerved into the nurses' lounge, leaving her high and dry in the walkway.

"What the hell?" she muttered to the now empty corridor. She still couldn't make up her mind whether to laugh or be angry. Neither seemed exactly appropriate, but what else *to* feel? "What the coo-calloo-calloo?"

Then she heard the wail of the approaching ambulance and shook her head, pushing all of it aside, as she hurried toward emerge.

She'd deal with Zachary Lewin later.

Oh, yes. She would.

CHAPTER FIVE

MRS. BATTEN, THE patient from the cruise ship, was in extreme pain and already running a high fever by the time she arrived at the hospital. After taking a history and examining the patient, Gen agreed with the cruise ship doctor's prognosis. Further tests pointed not just to a ruptured appendix, but also peritonitis.

"It's my first cruise, and I didn't want to miss it," Mrs. Batten said in between groans.

She admitted to having pain before she boarded the ship, but convinced herself that it was nothing more than nerves and excitement. As the severity increased, she'd finally sought medical attention on board.

"Unfortunately, you're going to miss the rest of the cruise," Gen told her gently. "I'm going to operate to remove the appendix and clean up any infected tissue, but you'll be here in the hospital for at least a few days."

"I don't even care anymore," her patient said, her eyes closed. "I just want the pain to go away."

It was up to Gen to explain to the woman's worried husband just how serious his wife's situation was.

"I'll have a better idea of how severe her condition is when I operate, but she may have to be in hospital for a while," she told Mr. Batten.

"Do whatever you need to," the man said, his eyes misty, although he was making a valiant effort to hold himself together. "Just make her well, please. We were celebrating our third wedding anniversary, and I really want to make it to thirty at least with her."

Entering the presurgery meeting with the team, Gen gave Zach a sour look and then put him and his foolishness aside, running down her findings and her expectations.

"From her T cell count and the scans, I suspect this will be a long one, folks."

Her pronouncement was greeted with a murmur, and then it was all hands on deck.

The operating room was already set up, and Gen went to scrub in while the patient was transported from emergency.

As it turned out, she'd been right in her assessment. Removing the ruptured appendix and all infected tissue was a long, painstaking job, and it was almost one in the afternoon before Gen was able to close.

Once Mrs. Batten was in the recovery room, the surgical team handed over to the ICU staff, and Gen, Zach and the other surgical nurse, Monica, started walking back toward the desk.

Gen decided, with Monica as witness, this was as good a time as any to get back at Zach for his earlier mischief.

"Hey," she said in the most casual tone ever. "Are we still on for lunch? I'm starved."

From the corner of her eye, she saw Monica do a double take and had to bite her lip not to giggle.

But Zach didn't sound at all fazed as he replied, "Sure. Do you mind swinging by the house first, though? I left in such a hurry I didn't pack a change of clothes."

"I didn't either," she answered, making her voice light and airy. "How about we meet somewhere? I have to go and update Mr. Batten, and then I can leave."

"How about Nectar on the Beach?" he asked. By now, Monica wasn't even pretending not to listen but was avidly soaking in the entire conversation.

"Perfect." She gave him a dazzling, beauty queen smile, suddenly wishing it were as bright and symmetrical as it used to be. "Meet you there in about forty minutes?"

And, as soon as he agreed, she strode off, chuckling to herself.

He was surely in for a grilling from the rest of the nursing staff, and it served him darn well right.

She wasted no time taking him to task too, when they met up at the seaside restaurant, getting right on his case as soon as she sat across from him at the table overlooking the rolling surf.

"What got into you this morning?" she demanded, giving him a glare, although she really wanted to laugh.

Maybe he saw the amusement in her eyes, because his lips twitched upward slightly before he said, "Hey, just setting the scene."

"But in front of the director? Really?"

Zach shrugged. "I saw him there and realized that if it gets back to him that we're dating, he might worry about our ability to work together. The operation today was already scheduled, and we both know what we're doing won't make a difference to our jobs, so it was a good way to get ahead of any concerns he might have."

Gen thought it through for a moment and then couldn't help the smile forcing its way onto her mouth.

"Okay, I have to admit that's genius."

He smiled back, but the rest of the conversation was put on hold by the waiter coming to take their drink order and give them menus. Once they'd chosen their meals and ordered, the conversation became more general, as they discussed the various restaurants they'd visited since coming to the island.

Only after they'd eaten some of their meal did Gen jump to a subject she found interesting and wanted to know more about.

"How did you end up in the army?"

Zach didn't look up right away, but she saw his eyebrows twitch upward for an instant.

His voice was calm and factual, though, as he replied, "My parents wanted me to go to uni after I finished comprehensive, and I started but realized it wasn't for me."

"What do you mean?"

He met her gaze then, and she was at a loss as to what it was she was seeing in his expression.

"Well, firstly, I was tired of sitting in classrooms all the time, although I didn't mind the studying. Secondly, I realized how much it was going to end up costing for me to stay in uni and opted for military training instead."

"What did your parents think about that?" she asked before taking a bite of her delicious fish taco.

"Mum was fine with it, but Dad was a bit disappointed. He was banking on me being the first in the family to graduate from university. I did point out to them that I still planned to get a degree, just not in the way they expected. Besides, my younger sister is the true brains in the family, so it was better they concentrate on her going on to higher education."

"Did she get a degree?"

He smiled slightly. "Two, actually."

"Did you ever consider becoming a doctor instead of a nurse?"

Now the glance he threw her was truly unfathomable, but it made the back of her neck prickle for some reason.

"Didn't really want to spend the time necessary," he replied in the kind of laconic tone people use when they don't want to continue the conversation.

"I think you'd have been excellent at it," she said honestly. "But having gone through the slog myself, I can completely understand."

"I'm happy with what I've achieved," he said in an even more quelling voice, which only served to pique her curiosity and make her want to dig deeper.

"Oh, but—"

He held up his hand, stopping her midsentence. "No. My turn to ask some questions. How did you get into pageants?"

A little taken aback at the quick change of subject, which was usually her modus operandi, Gen shrugged.

"I was one of those kids who couldn't keep still, so my parents put me in dance class. One of the other students' mother was into pageant organization and talked my mother into letting me enter one to see how I'd like it, and I just kept doing it."

In reality, she'd kept doing it because it had given her a chance to spend more time with Loren, whose mother had gotten her involved, and she would have sworn her friend felt the same way. It was only years later she realized that in Loren's mind they'd been competing, not just for titles and crowns but for Loren's mother's attention.

And eventually, for men.

Hopefully Loren was content with the big win, and Johan was making her happy, although Gen knew that sometimes what you consider a prize turns out to be not one at all.

She pushed the unhappy thoughts aside as Zach asked, "Did you keep on because you enjoyed it, or was there some other reason?"

She considered how to answer, unwilling to bring up Loren, as she ate the last bite of her meal.

"I did enjoy it," she finally said. "I was mostly involved in charity pageants, and that was satisfying in itself. And I know people think there're all fluff, with the contestants wanting to cat fight all the time, but it isn't really like that at all. It can be quite empowering, if you go into it with the right attitude. Besides, I got to see places I probably wouldn't otherwise, and build some really solid relationships with other women." Sending him a teasing smile, she added, "And I got to wear clothing I never would have in any other setting."

His lips quirked at that, although she got the feeling he saw through her attempt at humor. Talking about that time of her life was still both pleasure and pain, although now she could look back at it with a bit more equanimity.

"So, why did you give it up?"

Startled, she gave him a long, searching look, before answering, "I stopped when I was doing my residency because that was, of course, most important. Then, when I was considering doing one more..."

She touched the corner of her mouth. The immobile part that had effectively scotched any hopes she might have had of winning one of the major pageants.

He didn't reply at once but lifted his hand to get the waiter's attention. When the man came over, Zach said, "Do you have the bread pudding on the menu today?"

"Yes, sir," the waiter replied with a grin. "Can I get you one?"

"Two," came the immediate reply.

"Right away, sir."

"Bread pudding?" Gen questioned with eyebrows raised.

"You won't regret it," he said. "I promise. They make it with dark chocolate and a rum sauce that's absolutely splendid."

She gave a little giggle. "I get such a kick out of some of the things you say. 'Absolutely splendid' is up there with my favorites."

"You're a fine one to talk. What was that I heard you say today in theater when you realized just how badly infected Mrs. Batten was?"

Warmth spread up into her cheeks. "Yeah, it's a cuss-word I made up long ago, and sometimes it slips out."

Was that a chuckle issuing from Zach's throat? It was so brief Gen couldn't even be sure, and before she could say anything more the waiter was back with their dessert.

"Oh, my, goodness." She stared at the confection on her plate and inhaled the glorious scent rising up to tease her nostrils.

"I told you," he said, reaching for his fork. But then he paused with it hovering over the plate and said, "I think you should have entered that last pageant if you'd really wanted to."

Startled, she shook her head. "Not after the Bell's, I couldn't."

His brow creased, and his eyes narrowed slightly. "You're still beautiful. And a well-respected surgeon. Think of all the little girls you'd have inspired if you'd put yourself out there again."

The wave of surprised pleasure his words gave her made heat rise up her chest and into her face, and she wanted to look away, but the intensity of his gaze kept hers snared.

For a long moment she forgot.

Forgot this was just a farce and the handsome man looking at her with such surety from across the table wasn't a love interest. Not even really a friend, although she hoped they were on the way there.

Instead, her body grew warm with pleasure and something far too close to desire to be comfortable, and she had to force her thoughts away from wondering if he really meant it or was just being kind.

But she got herself back under control and gave him what would have been an award-winning smile back in the days when her smile was considered one of her best assets.

"I would never consider doing another pageant," she said truthfully, but with all the amusement she could muster in her voice.

The furrows in his brow deepened. "Why not?"

"Because I'd have to forgo pleasures like this bread pudding, and I'm no longer willing to make those kinds of terrible, if noble, sacrifices."

Zach laughed.

There was no mistaking it.

Not a chuckle, but a full-on laugh, and now the pleasure she felt before was magnified until it filled her to the brim, and she laughed along with him.

Zach watched Gen eat the bread pudding and couldn't help smiling to himself. She treated it as though it were a gift from the gods, each bite to be savored with a little hum of enjoyment.

She even gazed with what looked like longing at her empty plate and scooped the last of the sauce into her mouth with the side of her fork.

"That was…decadent," she sighed, placing the fork back on her plate. "Thank you for ordering it."

"I'm glad you enjoyed it," he replied. "It suddenly occurred to me that I should have asked you if you wanted it." He shrugged ruefully. "I've been told I'm too take-charge at times."

Actually, what he'd been accused of was making arrogant assumptions, which still hurt, since all he'd ever tried to do was make Moira happy with little gestures and gifts he thought she'd like.

He'd been completely wrong about that.

"Well, if I didn't want it, I'd have canceled the order," Gen said in a serene tone. "Believe me, I'd have no problem doing that."

"Good," he said. "Tell me if you think I'm overstepping my bounds."

"Will do."

She was smiling as she said it, making him wonder what she was thinking, but before he could ask she got down to business.

"So, since you've set the scene at the hospital, there are a few things we should discuss if we're going to make this work in front of my mother."

"What kinds of things?"

"Well, like how affectionate we should be toward each other in public," she replied, straight-faced. "Especially around my mom."

For some reason, her words made a tingle run up his spine, but he tried to match her matter-of-fact attitude.

"How will she expect us to act?"

He hadn't even thought about that aspect of things and was genuinely surprised that it didn't make him feel in the slightest bit uncomfortable.

In fact, being honest with himself, he was rather looking forward to seeing how far she expected them to go.

"Well, she knows I'm pretty affectionate by nature," Gen said slowly. "So, she'll expect us to touch each other, although—you know—respectfully, in front of her."

The tingling settled low in his back, and he had to resist the urge to shift in his seat.

Clearly there needed to be some other, clear-cut rules put in place.

Not for Gen, who seemed completely sanguine about the entire thing. But he was suddenly having to push aside some pretty risqué imaginings.

"It'll be like performing a play, yeah? We're just playing the parts your mum expects us to, so we have to learn our lines and coordinate our actions to make it believable."

Gen's face lit up with one of her beaming, beguiling smiles.

"Yes!" she exclaimed, as though he'd made a profound pronouncement. "That's it exactly. And we'll have a bit of time to practice, so it'll be perfect."

Somehow that did nothing to dispel the idea forming at the back of his mind that he was in beyond his depth.

But all he said in reply was, "All the world's a stage, and all the men and women merely players."

"And he knows Shakespeare too." Gen beamed at him across the table. "Mom's gonna *love* you!"

CHAPTER SIX

FROM HIS TONE when she suggested it, Gen wasn't sure
Zach was too enthused by the thought of them practic-
ing to behave like a couple in love. Yet, after a few days,
he seemed to be totally into the role.

He was completely professional at work, but when
they met up afterward, as they did almost every evening,
anyone seeing them together would absolutely believe
they were a couple.

Holding her hand or putting his palm on the small of
her back to guide her up the stairs.

Whispering into her ear, even though what he was
saying was usually something prosaic, and totally un-
lover-like.

Smiling at her, as though she were everything and a
bucket of chicken.

He even took her out to a club one Friday night, and
danced with her to a couple of smoochy slow songs.

Gen reminded herself it was all make-believe, but had
to admit that being held tenderly in Zach's arms was the
sort of memory a woman could cling to forever.

His muscular body against hers had been thrilling and
had made her feel feminine in a way she couldn't recall
feeling before.

Not even when dressed in eveningwear with a tiara on her head.

All in all, besides the feeling that perhaps she'd bitten off more than she could chew, she was pleased with the progress of their deception.

The only person who took her to task about it was Mina, and even though she did it in a pretty gentle way, Gen was still left feeling a bit like a worm.

"Zach Lewin?" Mina asked her, having cornered her in the doctor's lounge where, thankfully, it was just the two of them at the time. "Gen, what are you thinking? And how on earth did you rope him into your crazy plan?" Then her face got stern. "It is part of your crazy plan, isn't it? You aren't just leading him on to get your mom off your back, are you?"

"What? No." Gen was quick to tell her, feeling unaccountably hurt that Mina would think her capable of that kind of underhanded behavior. "I explained what I'd done to him, and he agreed to help me out. He's a great guy."

"He is," Mina said, still not looking too happy about the whole affair. "And that's why I'm worried."

"What are you talking about?" It sounded as if there was a story there, and Gen's curiosity was piqued.

"Just that I don't want to see him get into anything that might make life hard for him. He's been through enough."

But when Gen tried to get her to elaborate, Mina was stubbornly silent, only adding, "Don't hurt him."

Gen didn't know why Mina was so worried. As Zach himself had said, they were just playing roles for a little while, and once her mom went back to New Orleans, things would go back to how they'd been before.

"Mom finally called and told me she's coming," she

told Zach a week before her mother was due to arrive. "I had to act surprised and delighted."

They were outside in his "veg patch," as he called it, Gen sitting under the gazebo, watching him weed and water and pick some greens to go with their dinner.

He sent her a teasing glance. "You're not delighted that your mother is coming to visit? I thought you liked her."

Looking around for something to toss at him, she came up empty and had to be satisfied with sticking out her tongue.

"You know what I mean."

Zach just laughed and went back to his gardening.

Strange to think how badly she'd wanted to make him laugh before, and now it was a reoccurring event whenever they were together.

Somehow that warmed her heart in a way she probably shouldn't allow but couldn't seem to control.

A rustling from the bushes nearby had her half out of her chair, until she spotted a pair of yellow, feline eyes staring out at her, and she relaxed again.

"Holy cow, your cat scared me half to death," she told Zach, who straightened from where he'd been uprooting a stalk of scallion. "I didn't know what was going to spring out of the bushes at me."

"There aren't any big predators here in St. Eustace," he said. "So, no need to worry on that score. And, for the record, I don't have a cat."

As he was speaking, the feline in question slunk out of the bushes, giving Gen a sideways, somehow disapproving look, and headed straight for the man who'd just disavowed it. Once it got up to Zach, it proceeded to twine around his ankles in a rather seductive fashion, pausing to meow plaintively.

"Are you sure about that?" Gen asked, giggling at Zach's baffled expression. "It sure looks like you do."

"I don't even like cats," he said, promptly belying that by bending to scratch behind the cat's ears in what was, apparently, the perfect way.

The ginger beast melted onto its back on the path, gazing up with sloe-eyed adoration when Zach switched to rubbing its belly.

"Well, whether you like them or not seems a moot point to me, right now."

"It must be one of the cats from the farm." Zach straightened, which had the kitty jumping to its feet to resume its previous ankle dance. "But although she doesn't look malnourished, I can feel her bones."

Gen didn't comment on how concerned he seemed over a cat he didn't own, but said, "Well, clearly it needs some fattening up, and it's decided you're the man for the job."

That gained her a shrug, but she wasn't at all surprised when, before they ate, he took a bowl of water and a tin of tuna down to the cat, who'd taken up residence on one of the chairs under the gazebo.

While they were eating, she broached a subject she'd been dreading a bit.

"Did you notice that we only worked together once this week? Do you think that was by design?"

The last thing she wanted was for their "relationship" to affect their work life.

But Zach shook his head. "That's happened before," he pointed out. "And the operation we worked on together was a tricky one. If anyone had any doubts about our ability to work together, they wouldn't have us working on the most intricate surgery of the week."

"True," she said. "I just don't want either of us to be sidelined in any way because of what I've gotten us into."

Zach laughed.

"I worked twelve hours on Wednesday, and I know you slept at the hospital after that little girl's esophageal surgery, so I don't think either of us can complain about being underutilized."

"True," she agreed, relaxing with relief. "I didn't think of it that way."

"What time is your mother coming in?"

The change of subject was welcome, and Gen jumped on it.

"Five o'clock on the twelfth. And she'll be here for ten days. I'm going to try to take some time off to spend with her, but I told her I can't take ten days off from work. I'm lucky if they let me have any at all, since I haven't even been here for a year."

"I've been working at the hospital even less time, so I'm afraid I can't take any vacation days."

Gen waved her hand. "That's fine. Mom can't expect us to be able to drop everything to entertain her while she's here, especially when she decides to 'surprise' me."

Zach smiled. "Luckily for me, my parents are scrupulous planners. They'd never turn up here out of the blue. It took them five years of planning to go to Portugal. Mind you, it took them that long to save up for it too."

Gen nodded, recognizing how privileged her family really was but not willing to say so. "There are studies that say the anticipation of a vacation induces as much pleasure as the vacation itself. Sometimes even more."

He gave her an amused glance. "I'm glad to report that they enjoyed the trip so much that Mum has consistently tried to encourage Dad to retire there instead of here."

"Is your mother from St. Eustace too?"

That was one of the few things he hadn't covered in his dossier.

"No. She was born in Glasgow. Dad met her after he moved to England. Hang on," he added, getting up. "I have a picture of my family I can show you."

He went inside, and she heard him going down the steps to the ground floor. In short order he was back, with a silver-colored frame in hand.

"My mother gave this to me when I was going to university, so it's old," he said, putting it in her hand.

It showed a smiling group, shaded from his dark-skinned father to his very fair mother and their four children, who ranged in every hue in between. She could see Zach got his broad chest and stature from his father, but the shape of his face, nose and eyes came from his mother.

Bending over her shoulder, he pointed out the various members. His breath brushed her cheek, making her entire face tingle. "My dad, mum, Cameron, Catriona and Benjamin."

"And you," she added, smiling at the young, grinning Zach. "Your mother is a redhead," she added. "That explains your freckles, I guess?"

He chuckled, still leaning over her, causing her heart to pound and goose bumps to fan out across her chest and arms. "Actually, although she's a redhead, she doesn't have freckles. Those come from my father's family."

"Funny how that works, isn't it?" she replied, sounding a little breathless even to herself. "I like your names too."

It was the only thing she could think of to say with his lovely fresh scent filling her head and the heat of his chest warming her nape.

He straightened as she handed him back the photo, leaving her with a sense of loss that was inexplicable.

"We're all named after relatives. Thankfully Mum refused to name me Zachariah, after my grandfather, and got Dad to agree to Zachary. Cameron and Catriona are named after Mum's parents, while Ben is named after Kiah Langdon's father. His father and mine were best friends growing up."

"Wow, so much history," she said, finding some equilibrium now he had retreated to the other side of the table again. "I love that."

"Kiah got the short end of the stick," he said with a chuckle. "He's Hezekiah, named after my father."

And being able to laugh with him dispelled the last vestiges of her tingles, and her heart rate slowed down to a normal pace once more.

Zach leaned back as the deepening shadows cast Gen's face into a mysterious, gorgeous study in gray scale. They were sharing companionable silence, while she watched the final colors of the setting sun fade from the sky, and he found himself equally enthralled by her profile. The more time he spent with her, the more fascinated he found himself becoming.

It was all well and good to say they were play-acting in an effort to fool the people around them, but he knew, for him, the acting was starting to feel far too real.

Leaning over her earlier, he'd realized he was tempted to kiss the top of her head or her cheek.

It had been a long time since he'd felt drawn to another person the way he was to Gen. He could spend hours with her and never feel bored or uncomfortable—

except when his body reacted to hers in untoward ways, like when they'd danced together.

Whew.

That had been far too real for comfort.

She'd moved like silk in his arms, her lush body swaying in perfect time with his. It had been easy to imagine they really were a couple, and all he had to do was dip his head and she'd lift hers for a kiss.

Which was something he'd been thinking about way too often.

Kissing Gen.

It had crossed his mind repeatedly that kissing her on her cheek when her mother was around would seem highly unusual. After all, they were supposedly in the midst of a monthslong relationship. Wouldn't it be more natural for them to greet each other with a kiss on the lips?

But that was a direction he was chary of going in, since he wasn't sure he was ready to take such a step.

It seemed far too dangerous to go down that path, especially with his heightened awareness of the attraction building toward the beautiful woman across from him.

What he was beginning to feel for her was way too close to desire to be entirely comfortable, despite the fact it would make his performance all the more realistic.

Shaking the thoughts away, he got up to turn on the lights in the house and catch his breath.

"Would you like some pudding?" he asked, as a way to distract himself. "I have some stewed local plums and ice cream."

The sound of her little chuckle made him smile too.

"That's not pudding. That's fruit and ice cream. But no, thank you." Her chair creaked as he watched her get up. "I'm going to head home. I'm operating early tomorrow morning."

As she spoke, she came into the kitchen, blinking at the brightness of the light. When she rubbed her left eyelid, he realized she was probably more tired than she was letting on.

"Okay," he said, his brain unerringly going back to his previous thoughts about kissing. "Drive carefully, and let me know when you get home."

"Will do," she replied, taking up her handbag. "And why don't you come by my place tomorrow evening for a change. I'm so in love with your house, I keep coming here, making you cook for me. It's time I returned the favor."

He chuckled. "I don't mind. I like cooking."

And he liked having her there. She brought new life to the house, blowing away the cobwebs of his previous funk.

"And I very much like eating your cooking," she agreed serenely, as they walked to the stairs. "But come by anyway. I have a hankering for steak, done on the grill."

"I'd like that," he admitted, and it was no lie. He'd only glimpsed the inside of her townhouse when he'd gone to pick her up for one of their excursions. It would be nice to get a more intimate look. "You need me to bring anything?"

"Nope."

They were at the foot of the steps when she paused, looking up at him, and something in her expression froze him in place.

"Zach," she said softly, coming a little closer. "I'm

going to kiss you. If you have any objections, now's the time to voice them."

His throat was suddenly so tight it rendered him unable to voice anything at all. So instead, he opened his arms to her, reminding himself it was all just playacting, even as his body hardened and his heart rate went into overdrive.

She smiled slightly, but it had an uncertain edge to it, and he saw the color staining her cheeks just before she stepped into his arms.

And even though he tried to hold back, he couldn't resist moving his mouth against hers, deepening the kiss in minute increments until he felt the tip of her tongue touch his lower lip.

Then all bets were off.

CHAPTER SEVEN

GEN WASN'T SURE how she made it home in one piece after the kisses she'd shared with Zach the night before.

All she knew was that by the time they broke apart, her insides felt like jelly, and desire was raging like a wildfire through her veins.

Coo-calloo-calloo, that man could *kiss*.

It had come to her as she sat across from him, listening to him talk about his family and watching his mouth move, that they were going to have to get used to kissing, at least enough to fool her mom. Convincing herself it was one more part of their performance that needed to be rehearsed was easy, but she hadn't been able to figure out how to broach the subject with him. So, in her typical jump-in-with-both-feet style, she decided to just go for it.

Well, she'd gotten a heck of a lot more than she'd planned.

It was seared into her brain—his taste, the sensation of his body against hers, the heat inundating her, the way she'd plastered herself to him, wanting to get closer and closer.

The latter memory made her bury her head beneath her pillow and groan in distress.

Or was that a moan of desire?

Hard to tell, since her body still thrummed and tingled, reminding her how sexy Zach really was and how much she'd like to find out if he was as skilled a lover as he was a kisser.

Dragging herself out of an exceptionally rumpled bed, she took a cold shower to help her wake up and squelch the need shimmering under her skin.

Luckily, Zach was off that day. She wasn't ready to see him just yet. Later, when he came by for dinner, was soon enough.

Putting the memories aside was easier once she was immersed in the hospital atmosphere, and her scheduled operations went as planned, although she was worried about one patient, who had clotting issues. She ran out after her shift to pick up what she planned to cook that evening, but swung by the hospital one more time to make sure the night shift nurses were fully apprised of the situation before heading home.

It was only after she was driving away from the hospital for the second time that she remembered she hadn't put in for time off. Between operating and the distraction of kissing Zach the night before, it had slipped her mind. It would have to wait until she was back at work in two days. Hopefully the director would be able to accommodate her request.

After quickly showering, she found herself slathering on some of her favorite vanilla-scented lotion. She hadn't used it since coming to St. Eustace, and the realization that she was doing so now because it made her feel lovely and desirable gave her pause.

What on earth was she doing?

Here Zach was, trying to do her a favor, and she was

in the process of trying to make it all more complex by beginning to fall for him.

She deserved a kick in the pants!

Putting the bottle back down on the shelf with a snap, she marched out into her bedroom and pulled on a T-shirt and dungaree shorts.

There, she thought, looking at herself in the mirror. There was no less seductive outfit in the world, unless she switched the dungarees for a stretched-out pair of sweats.

And, she told herself sternly while putting the steaks to marinate, there would be no more of that kissing business, unless they had to up their game in front of her mother.

That determination lasted until she opened her front door and saw Zach standing on the stoop.

"Hey," she said, battling the urge to grab the hunk of scrumptiousness standing there. "Come on in."

He wasn't smiling this evening, and as she led the way toward her covered patio, she wondered if she'd messed everything up with her actions the night before.

But when they got partway through her living room, she felt him touch her arm and paused.

And when he pulled her into his arms, she did nothing at all to resist.

In fact, she was immediately pliant and willing.

Way too willing, she thought hazily as his mouth found hers.

Then she couldn't think anymore.

Just feel.

And want.

"I doubt this is a good idea." His voice was deliciously raspy, and still only a millimeter away from hers. "And

I know it wasn't a part of the act, but you taste so delicious, I can't resist."

"Then don't," she replied, before pulling his head back down for another long, drugging kiss.

When they finally pulled apart, she was glad to note she wasn't the only one having a hard time breathing.

"Sorry," he said, although he looked anything but repentant. "But I spent almost all of last night and today wanting to do that."

She rubbed at the corner of her eye, still a bit dazed, wondering if she should admit it had been the same for her, but finally deciding discretion was the better part of valor.

Clearing her throat, she said, "Well, you didn't see me objecting, did you?"

"No," he agreed, still stern-faced. "But it's probably not something we should do much more of. I'll be honest and tell you it could lead to complications neither of us are ready for."

Contemplating his words, she realized what he was trying to oh, so politely say.

He might be tempted to sleep with her, but wasn't interested in a relationship.

That shouldn't hurt, but it did and, in a way she was glad, since it threw a nice bucketful of cold water on her raging lust.

"Understood," she said, finding a smile from somewhere deep inside. "Come on outside so I can fire up the grill. If I don't get it going soon, we'll be eating in the middle of the night."

Then she walked away, glad to have her back to him so he couldn't see her expression.

With some effort, she was able to find the wherewithal

to fall back into the easy companionship they'd shared up to that point. In fact, it was easier than she thought it would be, but a lot of that had to do with Zach, who acted as though those kisses had never happened.

"Bagged salad?" he teased, when he wandered into the kitchen as she was putting the rest of the meal together. "You're in the Caribbean, where you can get the freshest veg you could ever want, and you buy a bag of salad?"

She sent him a baleful look. "Hey, not everyone has a veggie garden outside their back door. Besides, for one, this is local produce, just prepackaged." Emphasizing the words with an upheld finger, she added another to make her next point. "And two, because I've been eating at your house so often, I had to toss out a bunch of stuff that had gone off. Don't judge."

He chuckled. "Okay, but next time, just let me bring the veg, yeah?"

The steaks came out perfectly, and for once she timed it just right, so the baked potatoes were done at the same time as the meat.

"This is something I'd never cook at home with my parents," she explained. "We eat a lot more rice and, for some reason, my father dislikes baked potatoes. I didn't learn how to bake a potato until I went to college. Isn't that funny?"

"It really isn't until you leave home that you realize the deficiencies in your real-life education," he agreed. "Mum made sure all of her children knew how to cook and clean, but somehow I missed the lessons on laundry." He chuckled. "Well, to be honest, I was the messiest of all her children and she got tired of waiting for me to do my laundry, so she kept doing it. Probably afraid I'd just wear the dirty clothes."

Gen laughed. "I can't even imagine that. Your place is always immaculate."

"The military very quickly breaks you of those kinds of bad habits."

"Ah, yes. I can see how it would."

They resolutely kept the atmosphere light, the conversation flitting across a bunch of subjects, but Gen couldn't shake the desire shivering in her belly each time she looked at him.

So she was relieved when, as he was leaving, Zach made no move to kiss her again.

Relieved, and severely disappointed.

They'd agreed to go to the beach together the next day as they were both off from work. So the next morning found Gen standing, coffee in hand, looking at the bathing suits she'd laid out on the bed.

Bikini or one-piece?

Taking a sip of her morning wake-up juice, she contemplated her motivations for even giving it this much thought.

She'd always tried to be scrupulously honest with herself and knew she was prone to impulsive, ill-conceived ideas. For all the control she had to exert in her job, she'd never outgrown the habit of doing things outside of work others would consider outlandish. Even outrageous.

Case in point—Zachary Lewin and her roping him into a fake relationship.

One she now was thinking she'd like to make real. Or at the very least, physical.

There was something about him she found infinitely attractive. Not just his looks, although no red-blooded woman would disagree those on their own weren't enough. But he had other, less quantifiable characteristics that she found terribly appealing.

His steadiness, and how easy it was to be with him just hanging out and talking. The way he'd figured out how to rein her in when she'd been inclined to bulldoze through a conversation, doing it in a way she couldn't take offence to or that made her self-conscious.

That intent, focused way he looked at her when she spoke, which told her he was completely there, concentrating on what she was saying. Listening, not planning what he wanted to say when she was through.

And, she'd finally admitted—actually out loud to herself in the shower—that she wanted him, physically.

Okay, she wasn't really the affair kind of woman. When others in college had been sowing wild oats, Gen had had a couple of long-term relationships. It had never felt comfortable to just sleep with a guy because of a physical urge. Her head, at the very least, had to be engaged too.

Not necessarily her heart though, right?

She knew, without a doubt, Zach wasn't interested in a relationship with her. Although he hadn't come right out and said it, she could read between the lines. So, if she was going to get in any deeper with him, she had to keep that in mind. It did no good to take the pie-in-the-sky approach.

An optimist she might be, but not an idiot.

If she put herself out there, and he didn't take her up on the offer, she'd be the only one embarrassed, right? So why not at least try?

"Bikini it is."

Not the skimpiest of them. That would be too obvious. But she had one in a light blue, batik-inspired print that fit her to a tee and showcased the new and improved curves she'd acquired since giving up pageants.

Curves she'd grown to like a lot and enjoy. In contests they were expected to maintain a slim figure, without any exaggerated physical features, and Gen had been able to keep her size down because she was, at the time, so active. After the Bell's palsy she'd concentrated on maintaining a healthy weight and getting enough exercise to keep strong without overdoing any of it.

Looking into the mirror, she couldn't help giving herself a little smirk. If Zach found her even slightly attractive, and his kisses said he did, this swimsuit should only increase his interest.

"You're a bad, bad girl," she told her reflection, but the smile on her lips said, *I don't care.*

She put on a rather shapeless terry cloth cover-up, just before Zach knocked on the door to pick her up.

"Good morning," she trilled, giving him a wide smile as she closed her front door and locked it. "Perfect day for the beach."

"It is," he said. "Did you bring sunscreen?"

She gave him a sidelong glance as they walked to the car. "I did, and I put some on already. Did you?"

He opened her door for her and had the nerve to smile as he replied, "No, I forgot."

She'd have taken him to task, but he'd already closed her door, and she had the pleasure of watching him walk around the front of the car. By the time he'd gotten to the driver's side, she was completely distracted and forgot.

The beach wasn't very full, since it was a weekday, so they had their choice of spots to set up the umbrella Zach had brought and spread Gen's beach blanket beneath it. Although it was blazing hot, the sea breeze kept the temperature bearable, and Gen had to admit the sea view was one of the loveliest she'd ever seen. The sky was like a cerulean bowl above their heads, and the water, aquamarine near the dazzling sandy shore and ultramarine where the seabed fell away, was capped by little hits of white froth.

"I'm going in," Zach said after he'd arranged the cooler and towels to his specifications and adjusted the umbrella for maximum shade. When he pulled off his shirt, Gen bit back a groan of pleasure, seeing his bare torso in all its glory for the first time. "Are you coming?"

"Sure," Gen said, her heart going into overdrive as she stood up and unzipped her cover-up, aware of Zach standing just a step or two away, waiting for her.

Oh, she hoped he felt the same way looking at her as she did at the sight of those magnificent pecs and his firm, ridged abdomen.

She didn't look at him as she shrugged the sleeveless dress off her arms and stepped out of it, before bending to pick it up and fold it carefully.

Then, with the long strides she'd learned during her pageant days, she walked past him toward the surf.

He wasn't beside her as she ran the last few steps into the water before doing a shallow dive beneath an incoming wave.

When she came up and turned back toward the beach, wiping the salt water from her face, he was still standing where she'd left him. When their gazes collided, despite the distance between them a shiver of longing ran up her spine.

Then he was in motion, not running but following her with decisive, intentional strides. He didn't dive into the water, but kept wading until he was standing just inches from where she was bobbing in the water.

"You're trying to drive me bonkers, aren't you?"

It was little better than a growl, and her nipples tightened at his tone, while her core turned molten and needy.

"Is it working?" she asked, holding his gaze, trying to figure out if the gleam there was anger, annoyance or something else entirely.

"Yes," he snapped. "But this…" He waved his hand between them. "This is supposed to be make-believe."

She shrugged lightly. "It doesn't have to be. I'm horribly attracted to you, so if you want to change the rules, we can negotiate."

"Consider this my opening bid," he said, pulling her close, placing his hands on either side of her face and kissing her as though he'd never stop.

CHAPTER EIGHT

IT WAS A short trip to the beach.

Far shorter than Zach could ever have anticipated.

Having Gen in his arms in the water—her long legs wrapped around his waist, those beautiful breasts pressed against his chest—made him ravenous.

Almost unbearably so.

And the yummy little sounds she made as they kissed didn't help his growing need.

Eventually he had to gently disengage, and he held her until she found her footing in the water.

"Wow," she said, her tongue peeking out to touch her lower lips. "Oh, wow."

"Yeah," he said, watching her, wanting her so much it hurt.

She blinked a couple of times, then said, "Can we leave now?"

Her eagerness filled him with almost obscene pleasure and made him chuckle roughly.

"You're going to have to give me a few minutes. I can't walk out of the water like this."

She blushed and shook her head.

"Okay. Want to venture out a bit? Then we can at least say with all honesty that we went swimming."

He laughed and agreed, and they spent about a half hour in the surf, diving and swimming, keeping the conversation light. But beneath the chatter was the knowledge that when they left, it would be to go somewhere private and make love.

Even knowing the situation, he couldn't think of it as having sex. What he wanted from Gen felt so much more than a mechanical slaking of lust.

Although what, exactly, he wanted from the upcoming encounter—or her—he didn't dare consider too closely.

"Your place or mine?" she asked, after they left the water and packed up their kit.

"Mine, if that's okay with you?" He wanted her in his room, in his bed, with an almost primitive hunger.

And the smile she gave him made him want to grab her for another kiss, but he restrained himself.

They didn't speak much on the drive to his house, or even when they pulled up and he parked.

In fact, the silence was thick, lying between them like smoke.

Then she said, "If you want to change your mind, this is the time to say so."

As if he were going to do any such thing.

"I'll say the same to you," he replied, not wanting to give her the out, but determined to do the right thing as best he could with desire riding him like a beast.

Her reply was to throw him a glance that smoldered with promise, open her door and step out.

Hastening to join her, he was by her side as they walked up the path to the back door. Puss meowed at them from the box he'd put out for her on the porch, but didn't come over to greet him the way she usually did.

Maybe even the cat could feel the shimmering tension between them and wanted none of it.

When they got inside, she said, "I'd love to rinse off the salt."

"Sure," he replied, immediately imagining her under the shower, water sluicing over all that luscious flesh he'd seen and felt earlier, and his body hardened even more.

He led her along the corridor to the bathroom, stopping at the airing cupboard to get her a towel, suddenly aware of how threadbare they all were. His grandad hadn't replaced any of his linens after Gran died, and Zach felt self-conscious, wishing he'd thought to buy some new.

But Gen took it without hesitation, and with a thank-you.

As she followed him to the bathroom, he wondered what she'd think of the old fixtures and fittings. She'd only ever used the powder room upstairs, which was considerably newer than the rest of the house, having been put in twenty years before. Nothing else had been touched, he thought, since maybe the fifties. Perhaps even earlier than that.

"Here it is," he said, seeing the room as though through her eyes and fighting a wave of embarrassment.

The old cast-iron tub and stained sink. A toilet that belonged in the previous century by a number of decades. A vanity with wonky doors and peeling paint. The mirror so old some of the backing had come off, leaving it opaque in spots, brown-speckled in others.

From her own place, even though it was rented, he knew she was used to far more luxurious surroundings, and he wanted to apologize for the facilities.

Even while hating himself for the impulse.

He looked at her and found her staring back, not looking with distaste at the room.

Then she smiled, and whispered, "Wash my back?"

And suddenly the condition of the towel, the room, the house and even the entire blooming world could go hang.

No one had ever touched her body as gently as Zach did, with tenderness akin to reverence. Gen found herself stretching and almost preening beneath the intensity of his gaze, even as her body thrummed and tingled with ever-growing desire.

The sheer eroticism of standing under the fitful stream of water coming from the showerhead and having him slowly, carefully slick soap over her skin turned her knees to jelly. Need built inside, short-circuiting her brain, even though he only lightly touched her as he anointed each spot with the sudsy washcloth in his hand.

And she knew he wasn't unmoved by the experience. Not only was he marvelously erect, but his face was tight, the skin taut across the bones, giving him an almost predatory air, and his hands trembled, ever so slightly.

When she touched him, letting her fingers trace the hard muscles of arms and chest and abdomen, letting them fall to his thigh, the air hissed through his lips, as though each contact burned.

She knew how he felt. She was aflame, her flesh so sensitive each soft touch drove through nerves and blood and bone, until they all collected and collided in her core, driving her to lust-filled madness.

Yet, although strung tight as a bowstring, with urgency trying to take precedence—telling her to force him to hurry, do something to make him lose control—she let him take the lead. And the almost leisurely pace he set was, she knew instinctively, designed for maximum effect.

"Turn around."

His voice was raw, demanding, so in contrast to the tenderness of his ministrations it pulled a moan of pleasure from her throat.

She faced the tiled wall, felt the cloth slick over her shoulders and back, go lower, to her bottom. Then she heard him kneel, as he washed first one leg and then the other.

He pressed a kiss to her hip, and the spark of electricity firing out from that spot had her curling her fingers into the wall and almost made her legs give out.

If he didn't stop soon, she thought fuzzily, she was going to have her way with him right here and now.

Before she could turn around and tell him so, he rose and pressed his chest against her back, his arms banding around her waist so his hands rested just below her breasts.

"You are the most gorgeous woman I've ever seen," he growled against her neck, before pressing his lips to her throat.

When his teeth scraped across her skin, and then his tongue followed, soothing the sharp, luscious pain, she had to grab his arms to keep on her feet.

"You're torturing me," she moaned, swiveling her hips against his hardness. "I want you—now."

But he wasn't finished with her.

Letting the cloth fall to the side of the tub, he slid his hands over her body—not gently now, but with the intent to excite already oversensitized skin—until she twisted and shook. With her head back on his shoulder, she whispered and sighed and mewled, trembling on the edge of orgasm.

Then he shifted, effortlessly lifting her into his arms before turning them both under the water and taking her lips in a kiss so hot, so deep, she felt it right down to her soul.

Still holding her aloft, he growled, "Turn off the water."

Leaning down, she did as he demanded, then he stepped out of the tub to carry her out of the bathroom.

"Don't you want to dry off?" she asked against his throat.

"No," he said, nudging a door open with his foot. "I like you wet."

It was on the tip of her tongue to tell him that was a good thing, but they were tumbling onto a bed, and he was kissing her again before the words could come out.

Zach made love as though he were on a mission, and his objective was to make her crazy with desire, then slake that thirst over and over again.

Not that she was passive. Once she realized he was holding himself back, while taking her to new, more thrilling heights with fingers, hands and lips, she decided to return the favor.

But when she tried to roll him over, so as to take control, he resisted, and those dark fathomless eyes snared hers.

"If you touch me, I won't last more than a minute."

His honesty moved her, made her want him even more.

"That would be okay," she said, although she didn't try to wrest free. "I want to make you as happy as you're making me."

Those beautiful lips twisted into what she thought was meant to be a smile but looked more like a grimace.

"When I come, I want to be in you," he said. "I want to feel your body around mine."

The words, so raw and true, made her shiver, and she knew, then, she wanted the same thing.

"Yes," she whispered, lifting her head so her lips were against his. "Yes."

So he took her to the edge of another orgasm, and then went up on his knees to open a drawer by his bed and take out a condom.

Watching him roll it on, Gen shivered in anticipation.

She should be already satiated, but the need she felt was as sharp and hot as ever.

This, she realized, would be different.

Different from anything she'd experienced before, and not just because it was the first time making love with Zach.

But because it *was* Zach, who had already shown her more attention, tenderness and pleasure than any man ever had.

Acknowledging that brought a lick of fear, but it was overwhelmed by an intense wave of desire, which had her reaching for him, pulling him in close to her trembling body.

"Gently," he growled, taking his time, entering her body with all the care he'd shown when he bathed her. "Gently."

"No," she contradicted, tightening her legs around his hips, urging him as close as possible. Wanting—needing—him to let go. Wanting him ferociously, and wanting him as mindless and crazed as she felt. "Not gently, Zach. I need you, now."

He groaned, and, as though her words let loose something wild inside him, he withdrew, then thrust deep, and kept driving home until they both found release together.

CHAPTER NINE

ZACH SCROUNGED THROUGH the kitchen for something to make for lunch, completely distracted by the sight of Gen wandering around clad only in one of his T-shirts.

The shirt was big enough and long enough to cover all of her, but just knowing what lay beneath it, and that she was naked under it, made him hard all over again.

There was a part of him still in disbelief over the fact they'd made love. That she'd wanted him and shared her body with him.

Women like Genevieve Broussard didn't sleep with men like him, unless they had ulterior motives or were slumming. At least in his experience. Yet, try as he might, he couldn't figure out what possible reason she could have, other than finding him attractive.

He had already fallen in with her plan, and surely she knew him well enough by now to figure out he wouldn't back out on her. So there was no need to sweeten the pot, so to speak.

During one of their many nights talking, trying to get up to speed on each other's lives, she'd admitted what she called the sexual revolution had mostly passed her by.

"I've had a few long-term relationships," she'd said. "But I haven't had the kind of extensive experience some of my friends have. No hookups or really brief affairs. They never appealed to me."

Maybe this was Gen using him to catch up? To finally have a no-strings, no-expectations kind of relationship? Having a quick, hot affair with the sort of man she'd never consider for the long-term?

He slapped the bread he was carrying down onto the counter with a little more force than was strictly necessary, his eyes drawn unerringly back to her. She was standing in the doorway, looking out over the view. When she stretched, arms high above her head, it caused the shirt to ride up, revealing the toothsome curves of her bottom beneath the hem. He almost groaned aloud.

Clearing his throat was a necessity before he could ask, "Cheese toasties okay?"

"What're those?" she asked, turning and coming toward him. He had to tear his gaze away from the sway of her breasts, forcing himself to look her in the eyes.

The damned woman was far too gorgeous for his peace of mind.

"Cheese toasties. You know, cheese melted between toasted bread?"

"Oh, grilled cheese sandwiches." She grinned. "Sounds great."

Then, as he assembled the sandwiches, she came around behind him and put her arms around his waist. He hadn't bothered with a shirt, so when she leaned her cheek against his back, the silkiness of her skin had gooseflesh erupting across his torso.

"Is there anything I can do to help?"

Since she was rubbing her hands over his abs and then her lips across his back, all he could do was chuckle, and say, "Perhaps not be so much of a distraction, so I don't either cut myself or burn lunch?"

She giggled. "I guess I can do that."

Then, with a final kiss right between his shoulder blades, she sashayed over to the fridge to take out the pitcher of limeade he'd made that morning.

It was a wonder, he thought to himself, that his eyes didn't just drop out of his head and roll over to her, the way they were so intent on following her every move.

They ate at the table on the back veranda, since the front was in full sun and the day had turned unusually still, making it hotter than blazes. Just as they were finishing up, Zach's phone rang. He was going to ignore it, but Gen said, "Aren't you going to answer that? It might be important."

Nothing could be more important than spending time with her, but he stopped himself from saying so, and instead, went to answer in the kitchen, where he'd left his cell phone.

It was Kiah.

"Hey, cuz, where are you?"

"At home," he replied as Gen brought the plates and glasses into the kitchen. "What's up?"

"Nothing much," Kiah replied, but Zach thought he heard a strange tone in the other man's voice. "I'm off today and wondered if you wanted to come by. I have that Arsenal match on DVR, and I thought we could watch it together."

"Not today," Zach said, his gaze fixed on Gen as she put the dishes in the sink and started washing up. "Have a few things to take care of around here."

That earned him a saucy glance, and she nodded before pointing at herself and mouthing, *me*. Zach had to hold back a chuckle.

"Well…" Kiah drew out the word, making it three syllables instead of one. "You sure?"

"Yeah, man. I'll catch you another time."

"Okay," Kiah said, something suspiciously like amusement in his voice. "Behave yourself. Talk to you later."

As he hung up, Gen was drying her hands on a dishcloth, and her expression had him stalking over to pull her close.

"I was just thinking… You know what you need here?" she asked, twining her arms around his neck.

"What?" He bent to find the spot just behind her ear with his lips, feeling her shiver as he placed a kiss there.

"A bed on the veranda."

Lifting his head, he gave her a curious look. "A bed? Why?"

"I think it would be beyond amazing to make love with you out there as the sun is going down."

She was thinking about places and settings to make love with him.

Somehow hearing her say that had a warm spot opening up in his chest and stole his breath for a minute.

"I'll bear that in mind when I'm redecorating," he replied, his voice a little rough. "Just for you. In the meantime, may I recommend the living room sofa, which is very, very comfortable and also has an amazing view?"

"Mmmm," she said, which he took for agreement when she eased out of his arms and started leading him that way. "Let's check it out."

But Gen had a plan, and Zach soon found himself seated on the sofa, with her kneeling between his spread thighs, doing things to him that he was sure were illegal in several places.

She teased him, taking him so close to orgasm he was sure he couldn't hold back a second more, before easing him back down to where the desire was once more bearable. If only just.

When she stood up and took the shirt off over her head, he growled low in his throat at the sight of her gorgeous body, his fingertips tingling with the need to touch her everywhere.

Straddling his thighs, she said, "We should have brought a condom."

He held on to her waist and flipped her over onto her back in one swift motion, eliciting a squeak of surprise from her.

"I'll go get one in a minute," he said, his lips already around one dark, peaked nipple.

He paid her back for the delicious torment she'd wreaked on him, until she was panting and pleading.

Rolling off the couch was torture, especially when he looked down and saw the glazed, desire-struck expression on her face.

"I'll be right back," he said, unable to resist stroking a hand along one of her long, trembling, outflung legs. "Stay right there."

Taking the front steps from the living room to the floor below got him to his bedroom in a thrice. By the time he'd fetched a condom from the drawer, he heard a sound behind him and turned to see Gen standing in the doorway.

"I couldn't wait," she whispered, as though confessing something slightly shameful. "I want you so very, very much."

Tearing open the packet, he rolled on the prophylactic while walking back across the room to her, already as desperate as she was to be joined together again.

Lifting her, he was about to carry her to the bed, but she put her legs around his waist and wriggled into position with a little cry of pleasure, engulfing him where they stood. So he sidestepped, placing her back to the wall, and tried to hold on to control while she used her thigh muscles and the leverage of her arms around his shoulders to rise and fall.

"Oh!" she cried, her head back against the wall, baring her throat to his ravaging mouth. "Oh, oh, *oh*."

It was too much, and not enough.

Mindless with lust, he dropped his hands to that delectable bottom and took over, driving into her as she egged him on, telling him to go faster, harder, *yes, yes, yes*.

When she came, she arched against the wall, shifting the angle of penetration, and Zach heard himself shout, as bursts of colored lights flashed behind his eyelids, and the top of his head seemed to lift off.

He was still trying to catch his breath, using all his energy to hold her up, locking his knees to keep standing, when she whispered, "Was that a car?"

"What?" he mumbled. "I didn't—"

Then came the unmistakable sound of car doors slamming and voices coming up the path.

The back door was flung open, and a male voice called out, "Zachary? Where are you?"

And as he met Gen's wide gaze, which seemed caught somewhere between amusement and horror, all he could do was whisper, "That's my dad!"

She had to give Zach credit for not dropping her, despite his shock and being galvanized into action. Instead, he carried her quickly to the bed and lowered her onto it, as they heard voices—including one she figured was his mother's—and footsteps going up to the kitchen along the back stairs.

"I thought you said they'd never surprise you like this," she whispered, trying to quell the urge to go into hysterics.

"I never thought they would," he replied, looking around a little wildly. "Where the hell are my shorts?"

"In the living room," she said, stifling a snort of laughter. Then she remembered her bathing suit and cover-up were in the bathroom and bounced off the bed, saying, "Coo-calloo-calloo, I have to get my clothes."

Zach was pulling on another pair of shorts, and said, "Stay here. I'll get them."

He was gone and back quickly, wiping his face with a towel. He handed her the still-damp bathing suit and cover-up, before heading for the door again, pulling a shirt on over his head.

Then he paused with his hand on the latch and looked back at her with a baffled, half-angry expression.

"I'm sorry about this, Gen. I've dropped us both in the soup."

He looked so genuinely concerned, her heart turned over. Caught in the act of untangling her bikini top, she dropped it on the bed and went to him. Putting her hands on his shoulders, she smiled before giving him a soft, quick kiss.

"Nothing to apologize for. And if there is anything, it should be me saying sorry. I started this whole thing, remember?"

"Yeah, but—"

She kissed him again, "Go see your family, before someone comes looking for you and catches me buck naked."

"Come up when you feel like, yeah?" he said, his gaze still shadowed.

"It's the least I can do," she replied, giving him a grin, although her heart was hammering. "Since I seduced you into this position."

And that, at least, made him smile in return.

"Seduction by you is always welcome," he said.

Then he was gone.

In no more than a minute, she heard cries of delighted greeting, and the general hubbub of a successful surprise.

After pulling on her clothes, she made a quick trip to the bathroom, where she looked at herself in the mirror with horrified amusement.

Her hair, although short and usually easy to maintain, was at its unruliest best because of the seawater, ad hoc shower, and, well, several rolls in the hay. Using Zach's brush, she got it somewhat under control, but although she washed her face with cold water, there was no washing off the beard burn on her cheeks.

If she had her own car, she'd be tempted to beat a hasty retreat, but since that wasn't an option, she decided bold insouciance was the next best thing. But first, a quick trip up the front steps to see if she could retrieve Zach's clothes from the living room unseen.

She was in luck, as everyone was on the veranda and out of view, so with shorts and shirt in hand, she slipped back downstairs to put them in Zach's room.

About to go back out, she paused, smiling, as memories of their time together cycled through her head.

She had some answers now. Zach had freckles on his face, but only a smattering anywhere else, and he was an even better lover than he was kisser. He'd fulfilled her every fantasy and left her greedy for more.

But now she had to face the music upstairs, and she couldn't help wondering what his parents would make of her, whether they'd think her good enough for their son. It wasn't that she lacked confidence, really, but just that she now knew exactly how fine a man he was. His parents should want him to have the best, not a lopsided ex–beauty queen who was always doing crazy things.

Although, the crazy stuff she'd done—coming to St. Eustace almost on a whim, asking him to pretend to be her lover—had led her right to this place, so they weren't that insane, really.

Realizing she was shilly-shallying, she forced herself to leave the room and go along the corridor to the back stairs.

Going up and then through the kitchen, she took a deep breath to quell her vibrating nerves. Plastering a million-kilowatt smile on her face, she went through the door and out onto the veranda.

"Hi, everyone," she said, taking in the surprised expressions on Zach's parents' faces, as they turned at the sound of her voice. But it was the double take Kiah gave her that was almost her undoing, and she had to fight laughter as she asked, "Can I get you all something to drink?"

CHAPTER TEN

"A SURGEON, EH, son?"

Zach and his father were walking in the garden, making use of the last rays of the sun, Dad checking on the progress his son and Mass Alex had made on clearing the land.

Not sure what his father's placid-sounding question really meant, Zach just made a noncommittal sound in the back of his throat.

"She's nice enough," the older man continued. "Friendly. Real pretty too."

"She is," Zach agreed, refusing to elaborate any further.

"What happened to her face? Car accident? Stroke?"

"No, Dad. She had a condition called Bell's palsy. It damaged some of the nerves in her face."

"Still look nice, though," his father said. "Never let it stop her either, eh?" Then, as he appeared to examine an allamanda plant beside the driveway, he added again, "A surgeon."

Zach knew what his father was getting at, and he wished he could contradict his father's assumptions.

His dad described himself as a simple man, with simple tastes and needs. Zach understood. He thought of himself the same way. Anything too fancy—or *stoosh*, as his father liked to say, using a word picked up from one of his Jamaican friends—held no appeal.

Usually.

Gen was nice and kind and easy to be around, but there was no getting around the fact that she was, in the final analysis, fancy.

From the way she spoke, with that sweet drawl, to how she carried herself, to the lifestyle she was accustomed to, she was definitely out of Zach's league.

Miles out of it.

Very much as Moira had turned out to be, although Moira never treated his parents with the warmth Gen had earlier.

She'd stepped out onto the veranda like a queen and proceeded to show exactly why the best defense was a good offence. It was pretty obvious what they'd been up to when his parents and Kiah arrived, but Gen handled the whole affair as though everyone had dropped by for tea. And not unexpectedly either.

She'd brought out juice and water, sprinkling good humor and sunshine on all of them as she did.

And everyone just went along with it, although Kiah had looked dumbstruck.

Now that he thought about it, Kiah hadn't mentioned anything to Zach about hearing the rumors about them, nor about Mina clueing him in to what was happening. Or maybe she had, and his reaction was to the newly intimate nature of Zach and Gen's relationship.

Mum had just looked on, seemingly gobsmacked. But when Gen engaged her in conversation, they got on like a house on fire, chatting away about all sorts of topics, from their flight to the weather, to knitting of all things. Everything and nothing really.

Kiah, being in the know about his parents' arrival, had made reservations at a restaurant for the Lewin family to have an early dinner, but when Zach invited Gen, she refused.

"No, thank you," she said with one of those brilliant smiles she wielded with such expertise. "I'm not dressed to go out. Besides, it'll be nice for your parents to have you to themselves on their first evening here."

"I'll drop Gen home," Kiah said. "You're up on Cottage Road, right?"

"I am," she replied, as serene as a forest pool, even though she may well have suspected she was in for a grilling from his cousin. "And thanks. That'll work out well."

At dinner, Mum, in her forthright way, had said, "How serious are you two, Zachary?"

"Not very," he said, even though, for him, things had become infinitely more serious that day. "We enjoy each other's company."

Mum gave him a long look, but didn't say anything more about Gen.

"Let's go for a walk on Coconut Beach," Dad said as they were leaving the restaurant. "I want to watch the sunset with you, wifey."

"Not on your Nellie," Mum replied. "I'm already half-dead from jet lag and just want to put my feet up and have a cuppa. I don't mind staying up so I don't wake up at three in the morning, but I'm not tramping for miles with you in the sand tonight."

"Just as well," Dad said with one of the smiles he reserved just for her. He rubbed his chest as he continued, "I'm a little beat myself."

But even after saying so, he'd insisted on a walk around the garden after they got back.

Zach noticed his father rubbing his chest again, just below the sternum.

"All right there, Dad?"

"Hmm?"

"You're rubbing your chest. Are you in pain?"

"No. No. Just a little indigestion. Airport and then plane food, and being locked up in a shoebox to fly over the ocean would give anybody gas."

Zach was going to tell him to let him know if the pain got worse, but Dad forestalled him by pointing to where Puss followed them, stopping to look for lizards or maybe smell the flowers.

"And since when you get a cat? You always used to want a dog, when you was young."

Zach shrugged. "It just turned up one day, out of the blue. And now she doesn't want to leave, probably because I feed her," he admitted.

Dad smiled. "Sometimes the best things in life come out of the blue, and it's best to hold on to them."

Zach smiled back, the words settling over him like a warm arm around his shoulders.

"Come on up and have some tea, Dad. It should be strong enough for you now."

"Yeah," his father grumbled. "Not like that dishwater your mother always drinks."

They laughed together at the long-standing family joke as they walked back up the driveway, and Zach realized he was happy in a way he hadn't been for a long, long time.

The only thing that could make it more perfect was if Gen were there to share it all.

Yet, he knew he shouldn't even entertain such a thought, much less the attendant longing. Genevieve would be through with him as soon as her mother left.

He was sure of that.

Gen put down her phone on the coffee table and glared at it.

"Coo-calloo-calloo," she said on a huff of expelled air. "It never rains but it pours."

First making love with Zach, then his parents arriving totally unexpectedly, and now...

The phone rang again, and when she saw Zach's name come up, she grabbed it and hit the Accept icon.

"Hey." His low, soft greeting melted her, deep inside. "Just checking in with you."

"I'm fine. Everything going well there?" she asked, lying back on the couch and closing her eyes, just so happy to hear his voice and to know that, even with his parents there, he'd thought of her.

"Yes. They're having tea, trying to stay awake a bit more before they go to bed, although it's obvious they're exhausted."

"Poor souls. Jetlag is a beast."

"That it is."

Taking a deep breath, she said, "I got some news this evening."

"Oh?"

"My mother isn't coming in five days. She'll be here the day after tomorrow."

There was silence on the other end of the line, and then Zach laughed.

Gen huffed, even though the sound of his amusement made her smile too. "If you *dare* to make any smart comments about knowing where my impulsive behavior comes from, I'll be highly upset."

"The thought never crossed my mind," he replied between chuckles. "Why the sudden change?"

"Apparently Daddy's been asked to attend a conference in Addis Ababa, and there's no way Mom would miss the opportunity to go with him. She's fascinated by African cultures, and she's never been to Ethiopia. The conference starts the day before she would have been flying back to the States, so she's moved her trip here up. Shortened it by a few days too. She's just coming for a week now."

After a moment, Zach said, "Changing her flight like that must have cost her a pretty penny."

Gen chuckled. "You haven't met my mom yet, but when you do, you'll realize that by the time she was finished with them, the airline probably gave her money off, if not a free flight for the pleasure of helping her out."

"Ahh, so that's where you get your powers of persuasion."

She ignored that comment, not wanting to go down that road. After all, that was partially what brought them to this point.

Okay, was absolutely what brought them to this point.

"The main thing is—we're going to have both your parents *and* my mom here, all at the same time."

"The plot thickens."

Could it get any thicker? Gen doubted it.

"Right? I'm so sorry I got you into this. I never had any intention of getting your family involved. I hope it doesn't cause you any problems."

"They're curious about you, but I told them we weren't

seriously involved, just enjoying each other, and I think they're okay with that."

He was right, of course, so his words shouldn't hurt the way they did.

But all she said in reply was, "Good." Then a question she'd been pondering all day popped back into her mind. "So, what made your parents decide to come to see you right now?"

"I asked them the same thing, and they said the company Dad works for changed hands, and the new management wanted to clear up all the old, accrued holiday time. They didn't want him to take it all, because then he'd be off the job for months, but offered him three weeks off, plus compensation for the rest."

"So, he ended up with a bit of a windfall, as well as time off."

"Yeah."

"And spent some of it to come see you. That's really nice."

"I'm not sure if my being here was the primary motivation. He's been asking me about the repairs to the house, so I'm guessing he wanted to check up on that too."

"Really?" She infused laughter into her voice. "Silly rabbit, your mom couldn't stop looking at and touching you. They missed you and wanted to see you."

He grunted, the sound so typically male and noncommittal she couldn't help giggling. He didn't comment on her amusement, as though not wanting to get into it.

Instead, he said, "Kiah, that sneaky fellow, somehow got me some time off for while the parents are here, so I'll be taking them around. Do you think your mum would get along with my parents?" He said the last part slowly, as though reluctant to ask.

"My mom gets along with everybody." Then, on further consideration, Gen had to add, "Well, my mom tries to get to know everyone she meets, which drives my father crazy. He's constantly asking her if she *has* to talk to people in the grocery store or restaurant or wherever they are. The thing is, though, people either really like her or can't stand her, so we'll just have to wait and see."

"It would be good if they do get along," he said, still with that hesitation in his tone. "Then we could take them around, all at the same time. Unless you want to spend time alone with your mum."

"That would be great, making one thing of it," she agreed, although she couldn't help wondering what made him sound so unsure. "Do you think your parents would like that?"

"I know Dad would love to have someone new to show off the island to," Zach said, clearly amused now. "And Mum probably would like the company too."

"Perfect," she said, infusing both enthusiasm and surety into her tone. "As soon as Mom gets here, we'll get them all together and see how it shakes out. Agreed?"

"Agreed," he echoed. Then he said, "I hope Kiah didn't give you too much of an interrogation when he drove you home?"

Gen chuckled, but a wave of heat rose into her face, making her glad he wasn't there to see it.

"It wasn't too bad," she lied, not wanting to cause any friction between Zach and his cousin. "He was just curious, because Mina had told him, no matter what else he heard, we weren't really involved. Clearly, he realized we're more involved than they expected."

If by *involved*, she meant having wild, amazing, heart-stopping sex all around his house, and her really, really, wanting to go back for more.

Zach was quiet for a second, and she wondered if he was thinking about what had happened earlier too.

He cleared his throat, then said, "Hmm, I was afraid he'd give you a hard time."

Kiah, like his wife, Mina, had read Gen the riot act and warned her not to hurt Zach. To which she'd rebutted that, since they weren't serious about each other, there was nothing for Zach to be hurt by.

At the rate they were going, though, Gen realized she might be endangering her own heart.

Yet, what she really wanted to know was what had happened to make everyone so protective of Zach?

"No, it was fine."

There was the sound of voices behind him, and a muffled conversation. When he came back to her, he said, "I have to go. But before we hang up—you're off tomorrow, aren't you? Want to come and toodle around with us? I don't know what they'll want to do yet, but you're more than welcome…"

"I wish I could," she replied, genuinely regretful. "But now that my mom's coming sooner than I expected, I'm going to have to clean and figure out some time off too."

"Understood." She wished he sounded upset, but his tone gave nothing away. "Well, 'night, then."

"Yes, 'night. Sleep well."

Just as she was about to lower the phone, he said her name, and a little tremor ran up her spine at the sound.

"Yes? I'm still here."

"I wish you were *here*, with me, right now."

"I do too," she said, her heart hammering, her body reacting as though she were.

"Talk to you tomorrow," he said, and then he was gone, leaving her clutching the phone like a hormonal teenager, considering whether she should call him right back. Get him to say explicitly what he'd do to her, if she were there.

That would be beyond puerile. So, placing the phone back on the coffee table, she resolutely got up to finish tidying the kitchen, which was what she'd been doing when her mom called.

But she couldn't stop her heart giving a little kick when she came back out and saw the message from Zach.

I want you...

CHAPTER ELEVEN

THE FOLLOWING DAY was a whirlwind of cleaning and shopping.

Gen stopped by the hospital on the way to the store to speak to Director Hamilton about the possibility of time off.

"I hate to drop this on you so abruptly, Director, but my mother is a force of nature who defies resistance."

She was profoundly appreciative of the director's laughter-filled understanding.

"I'll be at work tomorrow, as scheduled," she assured him. "And I'd be happy to be on call while I'm off, if you need me to be. And if I plan to take Mom to the other end of the island, or anything like that, I can let you know beforehand, if that will help."

"I think we can manage without you for a few days, but it would put my mind to rest to know you're available, if necessary. John Goulding will be off the island for a few days during that time," he said, still chuckling. "Enjoy your visit with her. Oh, and I guess with Zachary's parents too," he added smoothly, but it was impossible not to notice the speculative look in his eyes. "Things going well between you?"

"Ah, yes. Very nicely." Talk about being put on the

spot! "But I hope you realize that whatever relationship Zach and I have has no bearing on our performance here in the hospital?"

His lips were still smiling, but his eyes suddenly weren't. "I would expect no less, and I'm glad to say I've heard no complaints."

After that, he changed the subject, saying once more how much he hoped she enjoyed the time with her mother, as he rose and escorted her to the door of his office.

By the end of the day, she was tired, having scrubbed the townhouse from top to bottom and done some meal prep for the week ahead. Mom was usually a ball of energy and would probably want to go out to start experiencing the island immediately. But Gen wanted to be ready if next evening she ended up cooking at home.

She showered. Then she went into the kitchen and was trying to work up the enthusiasm to fix a meal when her phone rang.

That had her running back into the living room, and her heart did a little flip when she realized it was Zach.

"Hi," she said, hoping he'd put the breathiness of her tone down to something other than her excitement at hearing his voice. "What's going on? How was the day? What did you do?"

He chuckled. "Slow down, Lewis Hamilton. Before you pepper me with questions, I have one for you. Would you like to come out and have dinner with us? Mum's just getting changed, and then we'll leave. But we can pick you up on the way."

"I'd love to," she said, grinning like crazy. "I'll just need to put on something other than sweats."

Mr. Lewin wanted fried flying fish, so they went to one of the restaurants along a rocky part of the coast that was patronized by locals. It was fairly quiet, and they had the patio mostly to themselves.

Mrs. Lewin had no interest in the local delicacy, but muttered to Gen, "Thank goodness you can always find chicken on a menu. I definitely don't share Hezekiah's obsession with that dish."

"Do you know that Barbados and Trinidad almost went to war over flying fish?" Mr. Lewin asked, drawing groans from both his wife and son.

"Yes, Dad. You've told us a thousand times."

Mr. Lewin's lips twisted to the side as he shot his son a laughing look.

"But I didn't know," Gen said, genuinely curious. "How did that happen?"

"Don't encourage him, dear," Mrs. Lewin said. "Once he gets started on these stories, we can't get him to stop."

"Well," Mr. Lewin began, "cou-cou and flying fish is Barbados's national dish, you know, but the fish started migrating out of Bajan waters—"

"Now you've done it," Zach groaned, but the look he sent Gen was so tender and sweet, she had no regrets.

Mr. Lewin told more stories after that one, but his voice got hoarse, and he stopped just before their meals arrived at the table.

As they were eating, Mrs. Lewin asked Gen, "Are you looking forward to seeing your mum?"

"I am," she replied. "Although she put me on the spot by changing her plans so suddenly. Luckily the director was understanding, and I got the time off I wanted."

"Does she work?" Mrs. Lewin asked next.

"Yes. She's an economics professor, so she's on summer break just now."

There was no mistaking the glance shared between

Zach's parents on hearing that, but Mrs. Lewin only looked mildly curious as she asked, "And what does your father do?"

There was no need to feel self-conscious, but something about the way Zach was gazing fixedly at his plate made the back of Gen's neck prickle as she replied, "He's an astrophysicist."

"Oh, my." Mrs. Lewin's eyes widened for an instant, and then she smiled. "How interesting."

Nothing more was said, as Zach changed the subject to what they had planned for the next day. But later, as Gen got ready for bed, the sense of unease she'd felt at that moment came back.

The atmosphere had seemed to change ever so slightly thereafter, and the entire experience left her on edge.

Her workday seemed never-ending, with several scheduled operations, plus an emergency stabbing victim, who was brought in just as Gen was preparing to start a gall bladder removal. The severity of the penetrating injuries the young man suffered kept her in the OR until not long before she was scheduled to leave.

When she finally was able to check her phone, there was a message from Zach, asking her to call him when she got the time.

She felt a frisson of apprehension as she remembered the somewhat strained atmosphere the evening before.

Had he decided not to come to the airport with her to pick up her mother? Or even intended to tell her he wanted to back out of her plan?

Thinking those things made her not want to call, but she ducked into an empty room and did anyway.

"Hello. How's your day going?"

There was no hint of anything untoward in his voice, and her shoulders relaxed as she smiled.

"Good, so far. I just have a few things to tie up here, and then I'm heading home. How was *your* day? Did you take your parents to the market, like your dad wanted?"

He groaned. "Yeah. He insisted on walking the entire building and bought a whack of stuff we don't need, including veg I have growing in the garden. It was so hot, it tired both of them out, so they came back and napped. But now he's awake again and in the kitchen. He decided he wants to make curry chicken for dinner."

Gen laughed. "Your dad's amazing. I love him."

Zach snorted. "You can love him, because you didn't have to trail after him all over Port Michael Market while he stopped to talk to every vendor. And you didn't have to carry loads of produce for him too. I felt like a Sherpa."

Still giggling at his griping, she asked, "What did you do while they napped?"

"Puttered around," he replied, his voice suddenly deeper, silkier. "Thinking about you, wishing you were here, so we could...nap...together."

Her breath caught, and her heart did a little flip as heat fired out from her core to all points north, south, east and west.

Especially south, as she remembered the thrill of him holding her aloft, the two of them moving together.

She cleared her throat. "I would have liked that too," she said as demurely as she could while thinking about holding him down and doing all things naughty to him. "Although, if I had my way, there wouldn't be much actual napping involved."

The sound he made had a shiver of longing traveling up her spine and made her already warm face grow hot.

"Exactly."

Oh, how she loved that gravelly growl that invaded his voice when he was turned on.

"It's a shame," she said, letting her voice drop almost to a whisper. "Such a shame that with all our family around, there won't be much chance for…napping."

"I think we should try to make time, don't you?"

"Yes…"

Gosh, she sounded as needy as she felt.

"What time are you leaving there?"

"In about ten minutes, give or take."

"I'll meet you at home, yeah? So we can…nap…before picking your mum up at the airport?"

"Yeah," she echoed, her legs already trembling at the thought. "Definitely."

"See you in a few," he replied, his voice rumbling through the phone and into her veins.

It was not surprising that she had to exert Herculean effort to concentrate on what she needed to get done before she could leave the hospital.

Equally unsurprising was that she had to remind herself not to speed as she drove home twenty minutes later.

Turning into the parking lot, her heart skipped a beat when she saw Zach's car already in her visitor's spot, and him leaning against the driver's door.

After she parked and then got out, she knew she should greet him, say something, but her heart was thundering, and her knees threatened to give out, they were so weak.

He walked across to her, but didn't speak either, just put his hand on the small of her back to guide her up the path to her door, and the heat of his palm, even through her clothing, was intense.

It took her two tries to get her key into the lock, and

then they were inside, with Zach shutting the door decisively behind them as she turned to face him in the hallway.

But he stayed where he was, his gaze fixed to her face as he said, "I hardly slept last night, thinking about you."

She nodded, admitting, "I had the same problem."

"This isn't going the way we planned, is it?"

Suddenly, her palms started sweating, and a cold space opened up in her belly.

"No, it isn't. Is it becoming…an issue for you?"

He seemed to consider her question, and from her peripheral vision, she saw his fingers clench and then relax, twice.

"I don't know," he replied with characteristic honesty. "Half of me wants to just go with it and not think. The other bit, though, is trying to make me consider if we are getting in too deep."

By *we* she assumed he meant *you*, and she lifted her chin, determined to let him know she wouldn't try to hang on to him when it was all over.

No matter how much she might want to.

"We set the parameters before we got into this, and although we've taken it further than we first agreed, I don't see why we can't just enjoy what we have. No need to stress about it, is there?"

He didn't reply, just took the one stride necessary to reach her and pull her into his arms.

Then, *oh*, there was no more time to think or to worry, because the blazing passion between them instantly ignited and all she could do was feel and yearn.

They moved awkwardly up the stairs and toward her room, pausing so she could toe off her shoes and shedding garments as they went. Their fitful, almost shambling progress would have been funny if the need wasn't so desperate, the desire so intense.

"I should shower…"

"No," he growled against her throat as they tumbled onto her bed. "I have to touch you. Taste you. Now."

His frank expression of craving only pushed her own higher, and it took only a few light touches to push her over the edge into ecstasy.

Yet, he didn't stop, but feasted on her body as though starved and desperate, until she cried out again, the sound echoing through the room.

"More," she demanded, twisting so they tangled together in an erotic dance and she could touch him, bring him to the same place of longing she already inhabited.

Eventually, when waiting was no longer an option, she took the condom from his hand and rolled it on. Looking up, she saw that taut, ferocious expression on his face and knew he wanted her just as urgently as she did him.

"I want to watch you," she told him, pushing him onto his back so as to straddle his muscular thighs. His groan of acquiescence sent additional heat through her body.

She took him deep, watched as his back arched, the muscles in his neck and shoulders flexed and his eyes closed. He was clutching the sheets in fisted hands as though trying to let her have her way without interference and finding it difficult to do.

As she began to move, his hips powered up to meet hers, and her body tightened, strained, from the delicious sensations firing through her system. When his hands came up to caress her breasts, Gen shuddered, a new layer added to her pleasure.

But she didn't want it to end too soon. Maybe never, ever wanted it to end, really. She slowed, taking her time to swivel and rock against him, and although his strong hands fell to her hips as though wanting to take charge, he didn't try to force her to go faster.

Then his eyelids rose, and the fierceness of his gaze almost undid her.

"Gen. *Gen*," was all he said, his voice a low, needy rasp, but it was all the encouragement necessary.

Giving him what he wanted, she rode him hard and fast, and in doing so was catapulted into orgasm first, her fingers digging into his abs as she wrung every last drop of pleasure from the moment. And the intensity of that pleasure was deepened by the sensation of Zach pulsing inside her and hearing him cry out as he found his own release.

CHAPTER TWELVE

THEY WERE ALMOST late to the airport, but when they arrived and saw passengers already coming out of customs there was no sign of Gen's mother. So they found a spot across from the exit to wait.

Standing beside Gen, seeing some of the passing men—and a few women too—give her the once-over brought out a strange mix of emotions in Zach.

Pride, because she was so amazingly beautiful, but also something akin to possessiveness. When he took her hand, he hoped she thought it was just so her mum would think they looked like a couple, but in reality he was in his own subtle way staking a claim.

He rubbed her knuckles with his thumb.

"Doing all right?" he asked.

"Yes. More than fine." She gave him a sideways glance, redolent with memories of the time just spent in her bed, and her lips quirked with a secretive smile. "Just wondering where Mom is. Knowing her, she's probably chatting with someone and will be the last off the plane."

Zach chuckled. "I'm beginning to think I'm going to start recognizing a lot of you in your mum."

For which he got a glare, although she couldn't keep it up for long.

"Unfortunately, quite possibly so," she answered, shaking her head, smiling once more.

Even holding her hand didn't seem enough, so he let go and put his arm around her shoulders instead, and her snuggling against him with a sigh brought a rush of happiness.

This sense of belonging and possessiveness, he knew, was something he was going to have to contain and stamp out. And the sooner the better.

Gen had made it clear that their relationship hadn't really changed despite their new intimacy. That, in her mind, they were still playacting, although the lines between theater and reality had blurred.

For Zach they hadn't blurred but shifted. He'd forgotten to think of her as a make-believe lover and allowed the attraction and admiration he felt to overtake his better judgment, and he wasn't sure what to do about any of it.

What he knew for a certainty was that as long as Gen was willing to be in his life or to share herself with him intimately, he'd welcome her with open arms.

He didn't want to think about the time when it would be all over and tried to convince himself that, like her, he'd just enjoy what they had for as long as it lasted.

"There she is," Gen said, breaking him out of his twisty-turny thoughts.

Focusing on the exit from customs, he saw a lady waving, a huge smile on her face. Shorter than Gen and with an ample figure, Mrs. Broussard was dressed in a casual light yellow dress that swept her ankles as she walked, accessorized with a necklace made of big blue beads, and matching earrings. There were bangles on her wrist that he could hear jingling even from where they stood, and her hair was braided in an elaborate cane row design.

On her arm she carried an enormous multicolored bag, which reminded him of the tote Gen usually had with her when she went out.

There was something unmistakably elegant in her outfit and carriage, and Zach couldn't help wondering what his parents—both so salt of the earth—would make of Mrs. Broussard.

Gen stepped out from under his arm and walked to meet her mother, and Zach followed a little behind, giving them a chance to greet each other without interfering.

As soon as the gap closed enough, Mrs. Broussard let go of her rolling suitcase and opened her arms.

"ViVi!" she cried, before enveloping her daughter in a huge hug, rocking her from side to side. "Oh, my baby!"

By the time she let go, Zach was close enough to see Gen was blushing, but there was also a beaming smile on her face, and the love between the two women was patently obvious.

"Wow, Mom. I think any cred I might have built up here as a badass surgeon just went out the window."

"Nonsense," her mother replied, in a tone that brooked no argument. "No matter how old you are, you're still my baby, and I don't care who knows it."

Before Gen could answer, Mrs. Broussard turned her light brown gaze his way and said, "And you must be Zachary."

He hardly had time to open his mouth before he, too, was grabbed and hugged tightly and then had a kiss placed on either cheek.

Holding his shoulders, she gave his face a comprehensive once-over and then nodded.

"You're as handsome as ViVi said you were. It's so nice to finally meet you."

"It's a pleasure to meet you too, Mrs. Broussard," he replied, smiling back at her, thinking that although they didn't look very much alike, Gen and her mother certainly had some of the same appealing traits.

"Call me Marielle," she said, her eyes twinkling as she sent a quick sideways glance at Gen. "Or Mom, if you prefer."

"Mom..."

There was a definite warning in the word, but Mrs. Broussard swept right past it, as if she hadn't heard her daughter.

Linking her arm through Gen's, she headed for the exit. "So, where are we going when we leave here? Can I buy you both dinner? I didn't eat on the plane. That food always makes me feel queasy."

"I thought you might like to rest after your flight," Gen interposed, while Zach took ahold of the suitcase and caught up to them at the door.

"Nonsense," came the tart reply. "What is there to do on a plane but rest?"

"My dad's cooking a curry at our place," Zach said as they walked toward where the car was parked. "And he told me to invite you if you'd like to come."

"What a lovely, gracious invitation." Marielle Broussard turned her beaming smile his way, and that was when he truly saw the resemblance between mother and daughter. "I'd love to meet your parents, Zachary."

"Why don't you drop us off at my place, Zach?" Gen had the slightly cornered look of a woman who'd lost control of her life and was trying to claw it back, and it made him want to chuckle. "That way we can drive up and save you having to drive us back later."

"I don't mind at all taking you home after dinner."

Now at the car, he left the suitcase beside the boot and opened the back door for Mrs. Broussard. "It's not a problem at all." As he closed the door behind her mother and then reached to open Gen's, he whispered, *"ViVi."*

"Don't you start," she said, wrinkling her nose and keeping him from opening the door by leaning against it. "With an appropriate last name, I'd sound like a stripper."

He shrugged, raising his eyebrows suggestively. "Maybe that's why I like it?"

"Oh, you…"

But she was laughing as she moved so he could pull open her door and as she slid into the front seat.

Jumping from subject to subject was another trait Gen and her mother shared, and Zach found himself mostly excluded from the conversation as Gen's mother brought her up to speed on family news.

As they turned up into the hills behind Port Michael, Marielle Broussard exclaimed, "What a beautiful place. So unspoiled and green. No wonder you won't discuss coming home, ViVi."

"It is lovely here," Gen replied in that serene voice she used when she had no intention of elaborating further.

"And, I suppose now you've met Zachary…"

"Mom."

No mistaking the quelling tone there, and Zach couldn't help smiling to himself when he heard her mother hum a little tune from the back seat, as though totally unmoved.

When they got to the house, there were a couple of cars already there, and Zach wasn't sure whether to be relieved or annoyed. Trust Dad to turn a quiet dinner into a jamboree.

"That's Kiah's car, isn't it?" Gen asked. "But I don't recognize the other one."

"Probably one of Dad's childhood friends," he replied, glancing at Gen to see her reaction.

"Lovely," she said, sending him a smile. "The more the merrier, right?"

"Yeah," he said, although he wasn't at all sure he agreed.

"I love a party," Mrs. Broussard said happily from the back seat as Zach parked. "One of my favorite things."

Gen chuckled and shook her head. "My mom's a social butterfly," she explained. "Just keep her away from the wine, or she'll be dancing in the moonlight in the garden."

"Genevieve!"

At the horrified exclamation, Gen said, "Sorry, Mom. Too much information?"

"Don't worry, Mrs. B," Zach said as he was opening his door. "My mum might just be dancing with you. She may be a good Scottish lass, but she's a lightweight when it comes to wine."

And they were all still laughing together as they made their way inside and upstairs.

Bless Mr. Lewin, Gen thought a couple of hours later.

"Well, your mum told me I'd cooked too much food, and I thought I'd just invite a few more people to help us eat it," he told Zach when they went inside.

And in doing so, he turned what could have been a stilted, awkward first meeting of their parents into a fun, laughter-filled evening.

Not that Gen was worried, per se, about how they'd get on with her mother. Just that Mom was—well—so extroverted, she could seem a bit overbearing to those who didn't know her. Having a room full of people let her shine without any one person having to weather the brunt of her attention.

However, she greeted each and every person as though they were long-lost relatives, and Gen couldn't help wondering how Mr. and Mrs. Lewin, in particular, felt about being grabbed, hugged and kissed.

Kiah and Mina were indeed there, as well as Kiah's grandmother Miss Pearl, and another couple, Mr. and Mrs. Morris, whom Mr. Lewin had known since school days.

"Where's Charm?" Zach asked Mina as he hugged her and kissed her cheek. "And those two young ruffians of yours?"

"Charm's babysitting for us so Miss Pearl could come along too, without any of us having to constantly keep an eye on them." Mina wrinkled her nose. "And while you might miss seeing the ruffians, I don't mind a night out without them."

"They're a handful, then? Just like their father, yeah?"

She laughed. "Exactly like their father."

"Hey, man. Stop that," Kiah said, giving Zach one of those man-hugs that involved a lot of backslapping. "I'm under fire from all these women enough as it is. I can't wait for Benny-Bop to get old enough to back up his old man. Right now, he's usually in the women's camp."

"As it should be," Mina retorted. "We're always right."

Gen laughed with them but couldn't ignore the little ache around her heart. Once upon a time she'd thought that by now she'd have a child of her own and a relationship as tight and loving as Kiah and Mina's.

Maybe it was time to accept that just wasn't in the

cards for her, but accepting and being happy about it weren't the same thing.

The greeting Gen got from Kiah and Mina wasn't quite as warm, but she tried not to take it to heart. They didn't know that Zach wasn't in any danger of having his heart broken.

He didn't care enough about her for it to be a possibility.

After they'd all eaten, Gen volunteered to wash up, and Zach helped rinse, while Kiah dried. Mr. Lewin turned up the calypso music he'd been playing, and although no one danced, it really increased the fun atmosphere.

"Your mother is amazing," Kiah told Gen as he reached up to put away the plates. "A real live wire."

"That's one way to describe her," Gen laughed. "She really enjoys people and is genuinely curious about their lives, but some people think she's just plain nosy."

He laughed with her and gestured out the kitchen window toward the veranda with his chin. "Well, she might have met her match with Miss Pearl. By the end of the night they'll know all of each other's business. And Aunt Sheila's too, if she's not careful."

Gen and Zach moved to where Kiah was standing to see what he was pointing at, and there they were: Mrs. Lewin, Mom and Miss Pearl, sitting in a little group. As she watched, Gen saw Miss Pearl make a point, emphasized with a wave of both hands, and the two other ladies nodded. Then it was Mom who interjected, which was also followed by sage nods.

"Anyone else getting flashbacks of the *Macbeth* witches right now?" Zach asked, amusement evident in his voice. "I don't know whether to be happy they all seem to be getting along, or afraid."

"You two should be afraid," Kiah said in a dark tone. "Extremely afraid."

And although Gen laughed with them, she was intensely curious about the conversation going on outside.

Who knew what the heck Mom might be telling them about Gen and her life before St. Eustace?

She'd made the determined decision to leave her past behind, as much as possible, when she came to the island. Zach knew her better than anyone else here, and even he didn't know that much. Not the nitty-gritty, down and dirty, anyway.

And she preferred it that way. Then she didn't have to relive any of it or reveal the cowardly, dark corners of herself. The pieces she herself didn't realize existed until after the Bell's palsy and Johan's defection.

Mom knew most but not all of it; more than enough to expose parts of Gen she'd been jealously guarding. Gen didn't think she'd say anything untoward, but who knew?

Wiping her hands dry, she went and stood in the shadow of the doorway, feeling apart from the chatting, laughing group of people spread out before her. Manipulating her eyelid with the tip of her finger, she tried to gather the energy to put on a smile and rejoin the party.

When Zach's arms came around her waist and he placed his cheek against her head, she instinctively rested back against him, tension bleeding away in the presence of his warmth and strength.

"All right there, Gen?"

His breath tickled across her ear, making her shiver deliciously. What was it about this man that one touch immediately had her blood going to a low simmer of desire?

"Yes," she said, resisting the urge to tell him how much better she felt with his arms around her. "But I think Mom's trip is starting to catch up to her. I just saw her hiding a yawn."

"You're tired too." It wasn't a question, but a statement. "Time to get you home to bed."

The way he said it, his voice low and intimate, made her nipples peak and her legs tremble.

"I wish…"

She didn't have to elaborate. Zach's arms tightened, and he pressed a kiss to the spot just below her ear.

"Me too," he growled. Then he let her go, saying, "Go round up your mum, if you can pull her away."

But Mom was willing to concede to being ready to go.

"Hezekiah has a plan for us all to go to somewhere call Northern Cove tomorrow," she said, as she was taking her leave of everyone. "And I need to make sure I get enough rest."

It was a quiet drive to Gen's condo, a sure indication that Mom really was exhausted, since usually she'd be conducting a blow-by-blow review of the evening just gone.

And when Gen led her into the condo and then up to her room, Zach bringing up the rear with her bag, all she said was, "Oh, this is nice, dear."

Then she kissed them each good-night and shooed them out, firmly shutting the door behind them.

Gen and Zach exchanged looks, but he shook his head, then led her down the staircase and to the front door.

"I'm not making love to you with your mother in the room next door," he said, pulling her into his arms and resting his forehead on hers. "I've never made as much noise in bed in my life as I do with you. It's a little embarrassing."

She giggled, but said, "I know what you mean. I've

never been a screamer either, but apparently you're turning me into one."

He sighed, his breath gusting across her face, and she inhaled, taking it into her lungs.

"I don't even think I can kiss you without wanting more," he said in the growly, gravelly tone she loved so much. "But I can't leave without kissing you either. It's a conundrum."

It wasn't for her, so she angled his face with her hand and placed her lips on his, initiating the kiss she was yearning for.

When they broke away several minutes later, Zach shook his head, and she couldn't interpret the expression in his eyes.

"You're addictive," was all he said, before dropping one more brief, hard, hot kiss on her lips.

Then he was gone, leaving her staring at the closed door and pressing her knuckle into the corner of her mouth.

"You are too," she whispered into the empty room.

CHAPTER THIRTEEN

THE NEXT COUPLE of days were a whirlwind of sightseeing, mostly directed by Mr. Lewin.

On the first day, they went to Northern Cove, which was about an hour and a half away. Setting off midmorning, they stopped to have lunch at a very nice restaurant in the hills, with a magnificent view over a valley with a river running through it.

The Cove itself was on a part of the island where the hills seemed to march right down into the sea, parting at the last moment to create a lovely sweep of beach. On the slopes above were dotted a series of large villas, many with steps carved straight into the rock, giving access to the beach.

"Years ago, some of the villa owners wanted to make this a private beach, but the public outcry put pay to the plan," Mr. Lewin said, settling under the umbrella, his slightly smug expression making Gen want to laugh.

"Are you coming into the water, Dad?" Mrs. Lewin asked him, as she took off her caftan, preparing to go into the sea.

But he shook his head. "Not yet. I just want to sit here and take in the scenery for a moment."

Gen saw the narrow-eyed glance Zach gave his father and, from professional habit, gave the older man a long, careful look.

Visually, she didn't see anything to give her concern, but she didn't know Mr. Lewin well enough to discern if he seemed unlike himself.

When they were in the water, she maneuvered Zach away from where their mothers were bobbing in the sea so they could talk without being overheard.

As though it was the most natural thing in the world, he pulled her into his arms, and she wrapped her legs around his waist so he held her aloft. Being so intimately close almost made her forget what she had planned to say, and she had to drag her brain away from wondering if anyone would notice if they made out.

"Is your dad feeling okay?" she asked, and his hands, which had been moving in slow circles along her skin, went still.

"I'm not sure," he replied, looking back to where his father was sitting, his face up to the sky, as though taking in the warmth of the sun. "I've caught him rubbing his chest a couple of times since he came, and usually he'd be in the water now or walking along the beach, but whenever I ask him if he's okay, he says he is."

They both watched the older man for a moment, and Gen said, "I think you might want to keep an eye on him, just in case."

As though aware of their scrutiny, Mr. Lewin suddenly got up and, taking off his shoes and shirt, strolled into the water to join his wife.

"There," Zach said, sounding relieved. "Maybe he did just want to soak in the scenery for a while. It's almost eight years since he's been back home."

Gen wasn't completely convinced but didn't want to belabor the point and make Zach anxious.

"That makes sense," she said, facing Zach and finding his gaze still, nevertheless, fixed on his father for a few moments more. "We should go back and join them. We're starting to drift farther away."

That brought his gaze back to hers, and the look in his eyes stole her breath.

"I know. That's by design. I just want you to myself for a few minutes."

"You're bad," she whispered through a suddenly tight throat, as his hand slipped beneath the elastic at the leg of her bikini bottoms.

"You make me that way," he said, his eyelids getting slumberous, as he found her slick and ready for him. "I just want to make you come, just once. It's become my greatest pleasure, recently."

Glancing back, she realized their parents were now little more than dots in the distance. Reaching between them, she pushed the front of his trunks down.

"Two can play that game," she gasped, her breath already rushing and hitching as he expertly took her closer and closer to orgasm.

And they ended up getting out of the water far down the beach and walking slowly back so the blush of desire satisfied could fade from Gen's face before they got to the others.

The following day found them traveling even farther afield, visiting Lewin cousins who lived at the westernmost village on the island. They were expected, with the outing planned from when Mr. and Mrs. Lewin had arrived, but when Gen suggested that perhaps her mother and herself should forgo it, the idea was dismissed.

"I already told them you'd be coming," Mr. Lewin said. "And they were excited to meet you."

She sent Zach a wide-eyed look, but he just shrugged and shook his head slightly.

So they went, and Gen had to admit she had a wonderful time.

"Wear something cool, dear," Mrs. Lewin advised the night before. "It's hotter than the inside of the Devil's oven there."

And she was glad for the warning, which she also passed on to her mother.

The area was completely different from what she'd seen of the rest of the island, having an almost desert-like climate. And because so many people had been invited to see Hezekiah, Sheila and Zach, the party was held outside.

"It's like a crawfish boil," Mom said when she saw the huge pots over wood fires.

Of course, it wasn't crawfish in the pots, but the food was delicious nonetheless, and with the music blaring and children running back and forth, it was a wonderful hubbub.

They left at about four thirty, over the protests of their hosts, and wound their way back to Zach's house. There they sat on the veranda, some having tea, the others cool drinks, and discussing what to do for dinner, if they even wanted more food that day.

"I'm still stuffed," Mom said with a little groan. "I haven't seen that much food since last Mardi Gras."

Gen was about to agree when a movement down below caught her eye, and she turned to see a teenager furiously

pedaling a bicycle along the road. Turning in through the
gateposts at the end of the driveway, he vaulted off the
bike and started running up toward the house.

Zach and Mr. Lewin were already on their feet, having also seen him.

"That's Collie," Zach said to his father. "Mass Alex's
grandson."

"I thought so," came the reply. "Although last time I
saw him, he was little more than a toddler."

The panting youth came to a halt as soon as he was
within earshot, and called, "Missa Zach, Grandpa chop
hisself with the 'lass, and we caan' stop the bleeding.
Mama send mi come get you."

He spoke so quickly in the local dialect Gen couldn't
follow what he was saying, but she was already on her
feet, and as Zach hurried into the house, she followed.

"What—?"

"Mass Alex, our elderly neighbor, has cut himself with
his machete and the bleeding won't stop. No, Dad," Zach
told his father, who was following toward the steps. "Stay
here. Gen and I will go, and if we need to take him to the
hospital, we'll let you know."

On his way out, he detoured to grab a medical bag
from his room, while Gen hurriedly got into his SUV.
In no time at all they were rocketing down the driveway.

Collie had already jumped back on his bicycle and
was out of sight when they turned onto the main track.

"Age of patient?" Gen asked, hanging on, as every dip
in the road made the car bounce.

"In his eighties, at least. I don't know his medical history, but he told me once that besides some rheumatism,
he was fine."

They flew past young Collie, and then Zach turned

onto another narrower track, this one in much worse condition, but he didn't ease up on the gas, just swerved when he could to avoid the potholes.

Then, on the left, Gen saw an old wooden house and a little group of people standing in the yard, staring at the door.

Zach brought the vehicle to a screeching halt and was out before Gen even got her seat belt undone. She caught up to him as he grabbed the medical bag from the back seat and followed as he skirted the group and went up the rickety steps and into the house.

The old man was on the couch, two women bending over him, and Zach went straight to him.

The women gave him room, but Gen had to say in the firm, authoritative voice she'd mastered, "Let me through. I'm a doctor."

One woman moved, but the other waited where she was, holding a bloody towel against the old man's leg.

"Mass Alex, what happened?" Zach asked, pulling out his blood pressure cuff while Gen took his pulse, which, thankfully, was still fairly strong.

"No so sure," Mass Alex said, his voice calm but quiet. "One minute, mi cutting grass, next mi on the ground, and the cutlass in mi leg. Troycus was with mi, and him pull it out and carry mi home."

"Pulse two-plus," she told Zach, after he'd finished the BP reading.

"Eighty over fifty," he replied.

"Is that the pretty doctor lady your daddy tell mi 'bout the other day?"

Mass Alex smiled at her, but Gen gave him a stern look as she pulled on a pair of gloves.

"None of that flirting right now, sir," she said, even

though she winked as she checked his dorsalis pedis and then the posterior tibial pulses. "Dorsalis fair. Posterior tibial weak," she reported to Zach.

He nodded, looking grim. "Mass Alex, Dr. Broussard is going to look at your leg, and it might hurt, okay?"

Mass Alex nodded and closed his eyes.

The woman holding the towel moved aside then, ceding the position to Gen.

When she lifted it, she realized the severity of the wound.

"Laceration approximately seven centimeters in length, into the lateral gastrocnemius muscle. Free-flowing bleeding makes it impossible to see how deep it is." Putting the towel back in place and applying pressure, she asked the patient, "Sir, are you on any anticoagulants?"

"What's that?" the old man asked, opening his eyes.

"Are you on any medications to stop your blood from clotting?"

"He's not on any medication at all," the younger of the two women in the room said. "Grandpa's always been real healthy."

Zach was pulling gauze out of his kit, and Gen asked, "Do you have a pressure cuff in there?"

He handed her the gauze and cuff, then shifted down to assist her.

"I'm not going to try to wrap it," she told him. "Manipulating the leg too much will induce further bleeding. We'll pad it with the gauze and lift it just far enough to slide the cuff into place. I take it calling an ambulance is out of the question?"

"Quicker to drive him to the hospital than to try to

explain where we are," he replied as she prepared a thick gauze pad.

"We're going to have to figure out why he's bleeding so profusely when we get him to the hospital." Looking at the young woman who'd been holding the towel in place, Gen continued, "Please hold his heel, and when I tell you, lift his foot up, but just a few inches, okay?"

Just the act of removing the towel to place the pad and inflate the cuff brought another gush of blood. But Gen was relatively sure the even, constant pressure on the wound should be enough to get him to the hospital without Mass Alex going into hypovolemic shock.

"Can you put down the back seat so we have more room to lay him down and elevate his leg?"

"Yes."

When he went out to get the vehicle ready, Gen stripped off her gloves and scooted closer to Mass Alex's head.

"How are you feeling?" she asked, touching his face and finding it worryingly cool to the touch.

But the old man grinned, revealing an expanse of gum, within which resided three lonely teeth.

"Better for looking at you instead of that ugly man."

Gen could only laugh softly and shake her head at his nonsense.

"Papa, yuh behave yuhself," the older of the two women said, but her scolding couldn't disguise the worry in her voice.

Gen looked up at her. "Has your father had any issues lately, with bleeding or bruising easily?"

The two women exchanged a glance, and then Mass Alex's daughter replied, "Yes, now I think on it. Every minute I see a scrape on him, and sometimes all three-four days before any little cut him get stop bleed."

There was some banging and shouting from outside, then Zach came in with two other men, one of whom was carrying a narrow door.

"Good idea," Gen said. "And I think a cervical collar for safety, since we don't know what additional damage might have been done when he fell."

They quickly fitted the collar and, with the help of the two other men, Zach and Mass Alex's granddaughter, they eased him from the couch onto the door.

"I need something to elevate his leg," Gen told his daughter, who had tears in her eyes, as she watched her father being carried outside. "Can I take the cushions off the couch?"

"Anything you need," she said, her voice hitching. "Take anything."

Gen took a quick moment to squeeze the woman's arm. "We're going to do the best we can for him, okay?"

The woman nodded. "I called my son, and he's coming here, so I'll get him to carry me to the hospital."

"Good," Gen said, heading for the door when she heard Zach toot the horn. "See you there."

She arranged the cushions on either side of the old man to keep him from sliding around too much and, with Zach's help, elevated his leg on the last cushion. After covering him with an emergency blanket from the medical kit, she sat in the back with him, and Zach put the vehicle, which he'd already turned around, into gear. As they carefully navigated down the hill, Gen kept tabs on the patient's vitals, but she was worried about the clamminess of his skin and the way he seemed to be drifting in and out of consciousness.

As soon as they turned onto the main road, she said, "As fast as you safely can, Zach."

And he put his foot down. Using the hands-free capabilities in the vehicle, he called ahead to the hospital and told them who they were bringing in, and what had happened. Kiah came on the line.

"I'm on duty, and I'll meet you in emerge."

They were still at least ten minutes out when, all of a sudden, a police vehicle pulled out in front of them from a side road and turned on its siren. Zach slowed slightly, but an arm came out of the window, beckoning him to follow, and with their unexpected escort, they made it to the hospital in half the time.

Gen clambered out of the vehicle as soon as Zach opened the back. Orderlies were on hand to lift Mass Alex out and onto a stretcher, and she took that time to update Kiah on her findings and suspicions.

Then the stretcher was being rushed into the hospital, leaving Zach and her outside the door, watching as the team on duty took over.

Zach looked dazed, a little lost, and Gen put her hand on his arm.

"He means a lot to you, doesn't he?"

He nodded, swallowed. "In a strange way, I feel as though he's the last link to my grandad. He's always telling me stories about the family, and how things were even before I was born."

"I think he'll be okay," she said gently, wanting to hold him, but sensing a sudden distance between them she neither understood nor knew how to breach. "They just need to figure out why he isn't clotting the way he should. And he's in great hands with Kiah."

Zach straightened his back and nodded. "You're right.

Let's head back up to the house. His daughter should be here soon."

It didn't feel right—as in, what would be right for Zach in this moment. He was sad and worried, and she understood he didn't want her comfort, but he needed something to make him feel better.

"Wait," she said to his already retreating back, and he paused, almost at his car door, to look back at her. "I need to clean up," she said, gesturing to her blood-stained blouse. "And change. Why don't you stay with Mass Alex until his daughter comes while I run home?"

He gave her one of those unfathomable looks, and she knew he'd completely shut her out when he nodded and said, "Good idea. Just call me when you're coming back, yeah?"

And then he walked into the hospital without a backward glance.

CHAPTER FOURTEEN

ZACH GOT PERMISSION to stay in the room with Mass Alex while Kiah ran tests, but got kicked out soon after. Which, after he'd called to update his father, left him sitting in the waiting room with too much time to think.

Just four more days, he reminded himself, and he could try to get on with his life without this sensation of drowning each time he looked at Gen.

Glancing back in the rearview mirror, seeing the tenderness in her profile as she comforted Mass Alex had his heart turning over and made him realize just how deep in he already was.

She was everything a man could ever hope for, but she wasn't for him, and they both knew it. No matter how explosive they were in bed or how much he admired and was attracted to her, this was just a dream. A fantasy not destined to last.

Perhaps, for her it was purely a matter of enjoyment, but if the last few days had shown him anything, it was just how dangerous she was to his heart.

Now all he had to do was convince himself that once her mother was gone, things could and would go back to normal. That they'd maybe stay friends and be good work colleagues, but this interminable desire he had for her would fade.

After all, he'd been with Moira for more than a decade, had been convinced he'd always love her. Now he realized she'd hardly crossed his mind in the last few weeks. And when she had, it was as a cautionary reminder, rather than the memory reactivating the heartbreak and hurt of before.

Realizing he'd got over Moira was a relief, but it didn't mean he was ready to put his heart on the line again anytime soon, and especially not with Gen. Things were going well while they put on this show for her mum, but he knew he'd never hold her interest for long.

Earlier in the day, her mother had taken his arm and asked him to walk with her down to the salt flat near his cousin's house.

As they stood looking at the shimmering mirages caused by the sun on the surface, she'd said, "Zachary, I know ViVi seems so open and easy to know, but beneath that persona is a complex woman, who's gone through a great deal of hardship and pain. More, I think, than even she acknowledges. It's changed her, and not always in positive ways."

He'd waited, hoping she'd elaborate, but instead she'd patted his arm, and said, "Remember that, please, if anything happens. Now, let's go back before she thinks I'm telling you secrets."

What else could that have been but a warning not to assume things were as they seemed, and that he shouldn't be hurt when things went wrong?

And of course, her mother didn't even know the truth about how their "relationship" came into being.

If you added that in, it spelled disaster for him, should he lose sight of reality.

Leaning forward, he put his elbows on his knees and rubbed his hands over the top of his head, suddenly tired—exhausted from his grinding thoughts.

Why couldn't he be like Gen—seemingly carefree despite the past and able to just have some fun? The consummate actress, making everyone around her believe her performance without losing herself completely in it.

Even he, if he weren't careful, would get sucked in by it and forget it was all playacting.

He wished he knew whether they were in the midst of a farce, a drama or a comedy of errors.

"Hi, man." Kiah's voice brought him out of his reverie. "We're taking Mass Alex into surgery in a little while, and from what I've seen, I'm thinking perhaps vitamin K deficiency as the source of the bleeding, although I'm running further tests to see what's causing it. If it's malabsorption syndrome, then we have to figure out which organ is responsible."

"But you think he'll be okay?"

Kiah's lips twisted to the side briefly. "I believe so, cuz, but you have to remember his age and how difficult rehabilitation may be for him after surgery. Unfortunately, anything is possible, but you know we're doing the best we can for him."

"Yeah, I know it," he replied, looking up to see Doritt, Mass Alex's daughter, followed by what seemed like the entire family. "Here come his relatives."

Just as he was making sure Doritt knew Kiah, and explaining her grandfather was under his care, his phone rang. Excusing himself, he walked away to answer, feeling stupid because his heart missed a beat when he saw Gen's name on the screen.

"Hi, are you ready to go, or do you need more time?"

Taking a deep breath, he strove for normalcy, although he still felt jittery and sad and annoyed, all at once.

"I'm ready. Doritt, Mass Alex's daughter, is here now, and he's about to go into surgery to repair the muscle. Kiah will call when it's over and let us know how it went."

"Okay. Shall I pick you up down by emerge?"

"Yes, please."

"I'm on my way."

Outside, the bustle of the town could be heard in the distance; the honking of horns, the booming bass line of a Saturday night dance. Closer at hand were the sounds of the hospital; chatter and the *clang* of a gate swinging closed. The rattle of a gurney.

All familiar now, but nothing in comparison to London, where the throngs of people, the constant hum of traffic and the bright lights used to exhilarate his soul. There, you could get every conceivable type of cuisine, buy any product, find any kind of entertainment as long as you knew where to look.

Once upon a time, he'd lived for the days when he'd be home from active duty and could experience it all, gorging himself on the hurry and uproar of the city.

Now, as though in response to the mental and emotional upheaval he was experiencing, he realized he no longer craved all those things. He'd found peace, and satisfaction, on St. Eustace, and he might never go back to England to live.

Funny how, when you find yourself at a crossroad in life and think you know where you are, sometimes you're facing in a completely different direction than you imagined.

When he came here, it was with the idea of having a quiet place to lick his wounds and the opportunity to help Dad out by getting the house repaired. He'd never entertained the thought of staying permanently, and he wasn't quite sure why he was contemplating it now. Yet, it felt right.

And it made his decision to try to keep his head on straight when it came to Gen even more important. She was a big-city girl, here just for a while. Not only could he not hold her interest, but he suspected St. Eustace wouldn't either.

Even her mother seemed to think the same and was anticipating having her daughter back in New Orleans.

"Hey you." Gen's voice startled him, and he was surprised to realize she'd driven up and he hadn't even noticed. "What're you doing?"

He saw her reach for the seat belt, and said, "I was just woolgathering. Do you mind driving up?"

"Sure," she said, snapping the buckle back into place. "Jump in."

As they drove along he tried to ignore the sweet vanilla scent emanating from Gen's side of the car, even though it filled his head and made his body tighten. To keep his mind off it, he relayed all the information Kiah had given him and heard her sigh.

"I hope he makes it through okay. He's a sweet old man, and I know how much he means to you."

When she swung into a small strip mall, he asked, "Why are we stopping here?"

"I ordered some Chinese food, just in case anyone's hungry. If not, we can have it as leftovers tomorrow."

As she said it, his stomach grumbled loudly.

Gen paused, half in, half out of the vehicle, and looked back at him.

"Good idea, I guess?"

And the amusement on her face chased the last of his worries to the back of his mind as they shared yet another laugh together.

Zach was still a little withdrawn when she picked him up at the hospital, but since he seemed to snap out of it, she put it down to worry about Mass Alex.

Different people dealt with stress in different ways, and maybe withdrawing was his?

She also had to remind herself that theirs wasn't the type of relationship where they shared their deepest secrets or expressed emotions to each other.

Which was just as well, really, since she didn't want to get to the point where she was so comfortable with him—or anyone else—that she left herself vulnerable. She knew all too well where that could lead and had no interest in that kind of pain.

Once in a lifetime was more than enough.

At the house, as she parked, Zach said, "Thanks for driving. I just didn't feel up to it."

As the dome light came on, she could see lines bracketing his mouth and the tired set to his eyes, and she replied, "I'll call a taxi to take Mom and me home."

He shook his head, reaching for the door handle. "I'll be okay once I have a chance to relax for a little. I had a bit of an adrenaline dump at the hospital."

"Understandable."

They met up at the path, and Puss let out a *murp* at

them as they passed by on the way to the door, but didn't get up.

"Is it my imagination, or is that cat getting lazier by the day?" she asked.

As if in response, Puss yawned, and Zach chuckled as he gave the cat a little tickle under her chin.

"I think you got your answer right there."

Mrs. Lewin met them at the top of the stairs.

"Dad was that worried about Mass Alex, I'm afraid he's got into the rum."

Mother and son exchanged a glance, and then Gen saw Mrs. Lewin's gaze slide her way for an instant before she continued, "Marielle's entertaining him, but I'm not sure…"

There it was again, Gen thought, that unfathomable expression on Zach's face she'd yet to learn how to interpret.

He shrugged and bent to kiss his mom's cheek.

"It'll be okay, Mum. Gen's pretty much family now, aren't you, love?"

Then he strolled off, carrying the bag of food, leaving both women staring at his back.

Shaking her head, wondering what he was up to, Gen turned to Mrs. Lewin and said, "If you prefer we leave—"

"I'll take you home after I've eaten," Zach interjected. "And, in case you're worried, Dad's not a violent drunk. He just gets maudlin and talks too much."

"Oh," Gen said weakly, not sure what else *to* say.

Mrs. Lewin pursed her lips, her gaze going from her son to the door leading outside, then back again. She sighed and shook her head.

"If you say so, Zachary. But he'll be working himself up to singing *Danny Boy* soon."

Zach grunted, taking down a plate. "Won't that be a treat."

A little annoyed at him for the way he'd dismissed his mom's concerns, although knowing he'd had a hard evening, Gen turned her back on him and gave his mother one of her best smiles.

"Well, if he needs a companion who also talks too much, he couldn't have found a better one in Mom."

That, at least, made Zach's mother smile.

Outside, though, Gen realized why Sheila had been worried. Her husband was in full spate, sounding as though he was already beyond worked up.

"We're simple, hardworking folk, but some don't think much of us—me a bus driver, Sheila looking after old folk. But our daughter has two degrees—two—and works for the foreign office. And Zach, he would have been a doctor, like your girl, if he hadn't got caught up with—"

"That's enough now, Dad." Sheila's voice cracked like a whip, making everyone, even Mr. Lewin, jump, and leaving Gen wondering what, exactly, he had been about to say. "I'm sure Marielle doesn't give a fig for any of your nonsense, and Zach wouldn't thank you for talking about his private business."

"No, I wouldn't." Zach came out with a plate in his hand. "There's some Chinese takeout inside, if anyone wants some."

His tone seemed aimed at putting an end to the entire conversation, but Gen couldn't leave it there. Not when it was clear Mr. Lewin didn't appreciate his son's accomplishments.

"For the record," she said quietly, keeping her gaze fixed on Mr. Lewin's, "Zach's not only one of the finest nurses I've ever worked with, if not the best, but I'm here to tell you that in an emergency, I'd want a nurse to help me, over most of the doctors I know."

"Leave it, Gen," Zach said. "He doesn't care."

"He *should* care." Frustrated, Gen waved her hands for emphasis. "Nurses like Zach are…are…" She searched for an appropriate analogy and came up with, "They're like Ginger Rogers. She did everything Fred Astaire did, but she had to do it backward and in high heels. The doctors get the glory, but it's the nurses that really keep everything together and running smoothly."

"No, no, I proud of him." Mr. Lewin's South London accent suddenly seemed to fall away, replaced with the St. Eustace vernacular of his youth. "But we work so hard, him Mum and me, to make sure him have a better life…"

"That's what we all want, isn't it?" Mom said, as Mr. Lewin's voice faltered. "What we all try so desperately to achieve. Making sure our children do better than their parents. My grandmother had that same dream. She was born in the backwoods of Louisiana, and she moved to New Orleans and became a maid. Years later, my mother, bless her, used to try to fancy it up and tell her church friends Nanoni had been a housekeeper.

"And Nanoni would say, 'Ah weren't no housekeeper, Delphina. Your mama was a *maid*.' But through her hard work my mom got to go to school and became a teacher."

Gen smiled at hearing her mother so faithfully recreate her great-grandmother's drawl, which she remembered from her early childhood. When she glanced at Zach, his gaze was fixed on her face, and heat trickled down her spine.

Then he looked back at his plate, and the connection was lost.

"I'm proud of my son," Mrs. Lewin said, in an almost defiant tone. "I'm proud of all my children."

"I am of mine too," Mom said, sending a little smile Gen's way. "None homeless or in jail, all gainfully employed. What more can a mother ask?"

That made them all laugh, although the fraught conversation still hung between them, like smoke.

"Just one more," Mr. Lewin said, trying to lever himself out of the low chair he was in and failing. Slumping back, he waved his glass and said, "Son, fix your old man a rum, nuh?"

"Oh, no, you don't," Mrs. Lewin said, getting up and plucking the tumbler out of his hand. "It's bedtime for you."

"Need a hand, Mum?"

"If you don't mind, on the steps."

With Mrs. Lewin on one side and Zach on the other, Mr. Lewin departed for the evening. And Gen and her mother exchanged a laughing look when a strained, falsetto rendition of *Danny Boy* came wavering up the staircase.

"I wonder what Mr. Lewin was about to say?" she mused aloud. "About what stopped Zach becoming a doctor."

"Does it matter, ViVi? Whatever decisions Zachary made back then can't be changed, can they?"

"No, but—"

"Either you accept him as he is, or you don't. It's really that simple."

Her curiosity had nothing to do with accepting him, since she thought he was amazing just the way he was. Rather, she wanted to know everything of importance about him, to understand him better.

But before she could say so, the man in question stepped out onto the veranda and said, "Let me take you ladies home before it gets any later."

It was a quiet trip back down to Gen's condo, and, once there, Zach walked them to the front door but made no effort to come inside.

"Are we still on for the botanical gardens tomorrow?" she asked after he'd said good-night, and was turning to go.

He glanced back and shrugged. "I'll let you know in the morning. I have a feeling Dad might want to go visit Mass Alex in the hospital."

"Okay," she said, wondering at his coolness and the lack of even a kiss on the cheek. He'd resumed his walk to the car, when, unable to leave it alone, she called, "Zach, is everything all right?"

He stopped and turned to face her, bland expression firmly in place.

"Yeah. Why wouldn't it be?"

Then, not waiting for a reply, he lifted a hand in fare-well and left.

CHAPTER FIFTEEN

THE NEXT MORNING Zach awoke at the usual time, but lay in bed for a few minutes, trying to shake the mood he'd gone to bed with and that still lingered like a sore tooth.

Last evening had been an exhausting debacle. As if poor Mass Alex's injury and Dad's tirade weren't enough, hearing Marielle Broussard tell Gen she either had to accept him as he was, or not at all, had felt like the last straw.

He hadn't heard the first part of the conversation, but he'd heard enough to be angry.

Gen really was the consummate actress, wasn't she? Defending him to his father in a way that made Zach feel like a giant, even while secretly disdainful enough that her mother noticed and took her to task.

The simmering anger he felt was, he knew, ridiculous under the circumstances.

She had the absolute right to view him however she pleased, especially since it was all a big hoax anyway. For all he knew, Gen was setting the scene for their eventual "breakup."

But no matter what her motivations, it still rankled.

He could have sworn she wasn't the two-faced type, and everything he'd thought he knew about her made her speech to his father ring completely true. Yet, he'd be the first to admit his track record on accurately judging character was poor.

There was no use lying around, thinking about a situation he had very little control over, so he threw off the covers and sat on the edge of the bed.

What he could control, though, was how much further he allowed the physical side of the relationship with Gen to go. As fantastically amazing as making love with her was, it would be best, especially for him, if they didn't do that anymore. He had come to realize he couldn't easily separate physical attraction from emotional, and each time he was intimate with Gen drew him closer to falling for her.

He chuckled grimly, acknowledging he was already there. If he weren't already emotionally involved, none of this would matter, yeah? She could say whatever she wanted, think whatever she wanted of him, and it wouldn't hurt. But, just as it still hurt to hear Dad express disappointment at his career path, knowing Gen, too, thought less of him because of his job was definitely painful.

Both hurt because of the people involved.

Enough.

Pushing off the bed, he quickly dressed, the restlessness of spirit driving him to do something other than go into the garden. While he often found solace in the quietude of mornings among the plants, today he needed more physical activity to help get his whirling brain calmed down.

His parents weren't up yet, so he left a note on the kitchen counter and went for a run through the fields near the house.

It was the perfect blend of flat and undulating topography, which allowed him to vary his pace and forced him to think about how he expended his energy. Normally he ran for about an hour, but this morning he let the meditative rhythm of his strides carry him farther than usual before turning for home.

About a hundred meters from the driveway, he slowed to a jog and then used the walk up to the house as his cool-down exercise.

To his surprise, he could see his mother and Mrs. Broussard on the veranda, and when he got to the back of the house, Gen was sitting under the gazebo, a cup of coffee in hand. She was wearing shorts, exposing her long, toned legs, and an off the shoulder top in a peachy color that made her skin luminous. Just the sight of her had his heart rate going back up and his fingertips tingling with the urge to touch, and he silently cursed himself for reacting that way.

Drawing closer, he realized she was wearing what he thought of as her beauty queen smile, used as either shield to hide behind or weapon for fending others off.

Impossible to know which one it signified this morning.

"You're here early," he remarked, as he headed to the tank to get the hose, needing something to do with his hands. Something to focus on, other than the beautiful, infuriating woman still smiling so broadly at him.

"Your mom called to ask if I'd heard from you since she couldn't find you and was getting worried."

"I left her a note." Untangling the hose, he turned on the spigot. Adjusting the stream of water, he began misting the plants, watching as the droplets formed rainbows in the sunlight.

"Yes. It had blown off the counter. I found it under the table when I got here."

"Well, sorry for her bothering you so early." He knew he sounded churlish, but it was in an attempt at self-preservation. There was something about Gen that was impossible to resist, but he'd do his damnedest to keep his distance—both physically and emotionally.

"I didn't mind," Gen said. "We were already up, and I got worried too. It wasn't like you to just disappear like that, without telling someone where you were going."

Both her false solicitousness and assumption that she somehow knew him, after so short a time and considering their faux relationship, made his temper start to simmer. Reining in the words on the tip of his tongue, he gave a noncommittal grunt instead.

"I called the hospital," she continued. "Since Mass Alex had a bad night, they're limiting visitors to family, but so far the prognosis is still good."

"Okay, so we're on for the gardens?"

"According to your father, yes, we are."

"Right. I'll finish up here and go shower, then we can head out."

He was trying to take a leaf out of her book—be calm, and smile—but it wasn't easy. Then it became more difficult when she got up and stood next to him.

Immediately, her scent surrounded him, filling his head, reminding him of how it felt to hold her, touch her, give her pleasure and receive ecstasy in return.

"Zach, are you still annoyed about what your father said last night?"

His first impulse was to pretend he didn't know what she was talking about, but while that type of deflection might work with some people, he knew it wouldn't work with Gen.

He shrugged. Even got the corners of his lips to curl upward, as though amused by the whole thing. "Dad didn't say anything last night I haven't heard a hundred times before."

"Doesn't mean it doesn't hurt to hear it again."

If he didn't know better, he'd swear the compassion in her voice was real, but he knew better. He'd known better from the beginning, but had lost sight of reality when he took her in his arms and gave in to the attraction.

He walked away from her, striving for control, hoping she'd let the whole thing drop.

"It all happened a long time ago, and I'm over his disappointment, even if he isn't. So, don't worry about it."

Glancing back, he saw her pressing her knuckle into the corner of her mouth, but she had on dark glasses, so he couldn't gauge her thoughts.

Strange to realize he'd come to depend on her eyes to tell him things her facial expressions wouldn't.

He'd turned off the water and started rolling up the hose when she said, "What really stopped you from becoming a doctor, Zach? And don't tell me it was the finances or you were bored. I'm not stupid. I know there's more to it than that. What did you get mixed up in that changed your plans?"

Taking a deep breath, he tried to rein in his knee-jerk reaction to her soft words, biting his tongue to stop himself from saying things he shouldn't.

Hanging the hose back on its hook, he told himself to let it go. Let it pass. But now it was her hypocrisy that made his blood boil, and he couldn't resist walking back to stand right in front of her, getting up close and personal.

They were almost nose to nose when he said quietly, "You made the rules about this fake relationship, and they didn't include me blabbing my business to you, yeah? You don't need to know every little thing about me to fool your mother into believing you're doing all right, so don't expect to get more than you're willing to give."

Her breath hitched, and her lips parted, but no words came out.

Zach nodded. "Right. I'm not stupid either, Gen. We both have pasts we don't want to talk about, so don't push me to tell you mine, especially when you have no interest in reciprocating."

Then, because those gorgeous lips were right there, and he was far thirstier for them than he should, he kissed her, hard.

But if he'd set out to punish or make a point, by the time her arms went around his waist, and his hands were cradling the back of her head, he knew the only one in purgatory was him.

And if he could stay there forever, he would.

Finally, he pulled back, trying to get his breathing under control, glad to hear the air rushing in and out of her lungs too.

"I'm going to shower."

Despite his best efforts, the words came out as a rasp, and it took every ounce of willpower to let her go and walk away.

As Gen watched Zach walk toward the house, she pressed trembling fingers to her lips and had to admit he was right.

This whole mess was her idea and she'd made the rules. Even when the physical aspect of their relationship changed, they'd agreed not to get emotionally involved.

At least, *he'd* made it clear that it would be unwise for her to get emotionally involved. Now that she had, she had only herself to blame.

But most importantly, what he'd said about her holding back, not being willing to talk about her own past, hit her like a blow to the solar plexus.

No, she didn't want to tell him about her past; about the dark place she'd gone to, revealing her weaknesses and fears.

Opening herself up to the pity she'd faced before.

Yet, she'd expected him to let her into *his* past life. Hoped that somehow, someway, there might be an opportunity to build on the mutual attraction and make what was fake, real.

But do it without revealing her own vulnerabilities and shame.

Shaking her head at her own temerity, she picked up her coffee mug and made her way inside, stopping to scratch the top of Puss's head just outside the door. Since Zach had started feeding the cat, she'd put on a little weight and become friendlier, but it was clear her feline heart belonged to Zach.

"Don't blame you, at all," she told the cat, who narrowed her eyes in seeming superiority. "He is rather irresistible, isn't he?"

Upstairs, Mom was sitting out on the veranda, sipping her coffee and looking out on the view. Mr. and Mrs. Lewin, she said, were getting ready for their day out.

"Although poor Hezekiah does look a little the worse for wear," she whispered with a smile.

Gen dug up an answering smile, but she knew she hadn't fooled her mother with the effort when Mom reached over and patted her hand.

Shaking her head in response, glad she had on her glasses so the moisture in her eyes wasn't visible, she leaned back in her chair, brain whirring.

It was easy to admit to herself how much she cared about Zach, and even how she craved him physically. Equally simple to entertain the thought of their relationship becoming a true one—but to what end, when she wasn't willing to reveal all the parts of herself that were unlovely and unlovable?

If her past experiences had taught her anything, it was the necessity of being honest, no matter what the relationship. Yet, here she was, caught up in a huge lie just to appease her mother, rather than standing up for herself and speaking her truth.

Before getting to know Zach, she hadn't wanted a relationship, not even a casual one. How do you dare trust again when two of the people you had utmost faith in betrayed you, publicly, and at the time when you needed them most?

When the experience left you feeling as though you'd entered some alternate reality, because nothing felt safe or solid or even recognizably normal. Not for a long, long time, with the aftereffects of the cataclysmic shift echoing for months and years afterward.

Oh, she'd acted as though she'd gotten over it, once past the initial seismic shock and attendant reactions, but instead she'd pushed it all down, deep inside, where it festered. Her ability to discern truth from fiction, her worth, her value as a woman, a lover or a friend were all now uncertain.

Work, her talent and medical ability, became her one solace.

Here was something she controlled, and no one but her could cause to be called into question. Yet that focus on work to the exclusion of most everything else caused its own problems, and the overload to her system had taken her within inches of burnout.

St. Eustace had given her a place to decompress and start over, but through her own machinations, she was endangering the peace and happiness she'd found.

If she were going to make it right, she needed to come clean, starting with her mother.

And there was no time like the present.

"Mom, there's something I need to tell you—"

"We're ready to go." Mrs. Lewin stepped out onto the veranda, her bag in one hand, a sun hat in the other. "Zach and Hezekiah are already down at the car."

As they rose, Mom said, "Can it wait until later, ViVi?"

"Sure. There's no rush."

There was even that cowardly part of herself that, dreading the fallout, hoped the conversation could be put off forever.

CHAPTER SIXTEEN

THE ST. EUSTACE BOTANICAL GARDENS were only about fifteen minutes outside of Port Michael, but on the opposite side of the town from the Lewins' home. Located on a twenty-acre site, it consisted of a large grassy area with multiple flower beds and a bandstand, surrounded by terraced fields and trees going up the hillsides on three sides. Walking paths wound through the various sectors, which were dotted with sculptures and plaques describing the history and provenance of the plants and artwork.

It was a perfect day to visit—hot, yes, because it was summer after all, but with a lovely breeze blowing up from the sea, which made it bearable.

After the excitement of the day before, Gen thought it would be nice to have a leisurely stroll through the lush grounds, except her unsettled spirit refused to allow her any peace.

In her all-or-nothing style, she'd wanted to get her talk with her mother over with as soon as possible, but fate, or karma, or whatever was afoot didn't give her a chance. All the parents, seemingly in some kind of pact, stuck together like glue.

Mr. Lewin was in his element.

"One of my uncles was a sculptor, and some of his

work is on display here," he said, casting a narrow-eyed gaze around the gardens. "One near the bandstand and others up higher, toward the lookout platform at the top of the terraces."

They were strolling through the lower gardens, where the beds were a mass of vivid color, the summer flowers blooming in all their glory.

"It's a shame there are so few people here," Mr. Lewin said, as they made their way toward the bandstand to look for the promised statue. "It used to be crowded on a weekend."

"Well, it is summer, Dad," Zach said. "Most people are at the beach, yeah?"

"It was different in my day," his father replied. "Saturday we could gallivant, as your grandmother called it, which included going to the beach or even a picture show if you'd made a little money that week doing work on the farm. But Sunday—now, that was for church, a big lunch and then coming to the gardens to hear a band play."

"I find we don't have family traditions anymore, the way we used to," Mom said. "Or, more importantly, rites of passage, leading us from one stage in life to another."

"It's hard to maintain a lot of those rituals now," Mrs. Lewin agreed. "There are too many distractions."

And as the older folks commiserated with each other about the decline of civilization, Gen and Zach exchanged a laughing glance, the first one for the day. It raised her spirits and sent a familiar tingle of awareness along her spine.

Then he looked away, and the connection was broken, leaving her bereft.

The statue was a minimalist depiction of the indigenous Kalinago people, who had inhabited the island long before Europeans even knew it existed.

"Our family has Kalinago blood," Mr. Lewin told them. "And my uncle was fascinated by their culture and place in St. Eustace's past. He led an initiative to include Kalinago history in the school curriculums. That was your gran's brother," he added, speaking to Zach. "He died when I was a young man, though, so you never had a chance to meet him."

"You should write all this down, Dad," Zach said. "So we can pass the information on and it doesn't get lost.

Mr. Lewin laughed and shook his head. "I'm no scholar. Just thinking about writing sixty-odd years of stories down makes my head hurt. Let's go up toward the lookout, see if we can find Uncle Erwin's other pieces."

Behind the bandstand was a sloping ramp leading to the interconnected pathways, and they all went that way, Zach and Gen falling behind their parents. As they walked, Zach slung his arm around her shoulder, and Gen cursed herself for the way her awareness of him was dramatically heightened by his closeness.

He'd been cool and distant since their run-in that morning, but although in her head she was thinking she should maintain some emotional distance, it made no difference to her body. It reacted in a way that told her, no matter how things ended up between them, these weeks of being with him would be indelibly imprinted on her brain.

And heart.

Should she tell him she was going to confess to her mom first, or wait until after she had?

It was hard to make a decision when her brain kept short-circuiting because his scent filled her head and their bodies moved in perfect synchronicity as they walked. It reminded her of other times they'd moved as one.

Intimate times.

Yet, even with him right beside her, the chasm that had opened between them over the last two days felt wider than ever. In the past they would have been talking and laughing together, but what had started out as a caper had turned serious so quickly, she was at a loss as to how to handle it.

Feigning interest in a mermaid statue, she paused, letting the parents go farther ahead, knowing in her heart what she needed to do.

She already knew the only way to make any of this right was with honesty, but while she'd thought to start with her mom, she should really begin with coming clean to Zach.

She touched Zach's wrist, where it lay over her shoulder. "You don't have to pretend to be into me anymore, if you don't want to. As soon as I get a chance, I plan to confess to Mom what I did, so you'll be off the hook."

He stiffened, his arm going rigid. Then, before she knew what he was planning to do, they were off the main path, with him steering her into a small thicket of trees. Deeper in, until they were hidden from sight of the trail.

When he turned her to face him, his lips were tight, and anger came off him in almost visible waves.

"You're a right little madam, aren't you? Just wanting to do whatever you want without a thought for anyone else."

Shocked, she stared at him, trying to figure out what he meant. "Why are you so angry? I thought you'd be pleased to end this farce."

The sound he made was feral. A guttural negation of her words.

Before she could say anything more, he was kissing her, his lips fierce. Punishing at first, then, as desire spiked and she kissed him back just as ferociously, it devolved into a passionate frenzy of lips and tongues.

His hands swept the elastic neckline of her top down, and his thumb dipped beneath her bra, sweeping over her nipple, tightening it to an aching peak. He bent his leg, bringing one thigh up between hers, and Gen bit back a moan of need at the contact.

"Does this feel like a farce?" he demanded as he bent to suck her nipple into the damp, erotic heat of his mouth.

She couldn't answer, too lost in the moment and the sensations firing along her nerve endings.

Who knew how far they would have gone if they hadn't heard hurrying footsteps on the main trail and her mom calling their names?

Zach straightened, and although she couldn't see his eyes because of his dark glasses, she could feel his gaze boring into hers.

"We'll finish this later," he growled as she tidied her clothes with shaking hands. "We're here," he replied, as Mom called out for them again.

"Hurry," she said. "Your father's unwell."

Zach froze for a moment, and then they were running back through the trees to the path and in the direction her mother was pointing, everything else but Mr. Lewin's well-being forgotten.

As they rounded the next corner on the trail, Zach saw his dad sitting on a bench, Mum beside him, trying to get him to put his head between his knees.

"Stop," Dad said, batting her hand away. "That hurts."

Zach had left Gen in his dust and skidded to a halt to drop to one knee beside his father. "What's going on, Dad? Where hurts?"

He automatically took his father's wrist between his fingers, habit taking over, as Dad replied, "Nothing for you lot to be going on about. Just felt a little light-headed for a second."

"He almost fainted," Mum said, her voice wavering. "Looked set to topple right over."

"Nonsense." But Zach heard the breathless nature of his father's voice. "Just a bit of a turn."

Gen was there, and she began examining him, peppering him and Mum with questions about Dad's medications, whether he'd taken them that morning and what other symptoms he'd been experiencing.

Dad seemed disinclined to cooperate, actually sounding rather surly as he kept reiterating there was nothing wrong. Zach was about to take him to task when Gen beat him to it.

Putting her hand on his father's shoulder and looking him directly in the face, she said, "Your heart rate is elevated. You're short of breath, and your skin is clammy. Over the last couple of days, I've seen you periodically rub your chest as though suffering discomfort. Whether you will admit it or not, there's something going on, and we need to figure out what it is."

Dad just stared, apparently gobsmacked by seeing Gen in full Dr. Broussard mode.

"You listen to Genevieve," Mum said, looking as though she couldn't decide whether to hug Dad or smack him. "Tell her what she wants to know."

Then, and only then, did Dad admit to intermittent

discomfort below his diaphragm. "Not pain, though, just an achy feeling."

"We're taking you to the hospital," Gen told him, and her no-nonsense tone left no room for discussion. "Zach, I don't want your father walking back down to the car, so call an ambulance, please."

He'd been so caught up in what was happening, he hadn't thought to do so and was kicking himself for that as he got up and stepped to one side to make the call. By the time he'd explained where they were and got the ambulance dispatched, Gen had come to stand beside him.

"They're on their way," he told her, suddenly realizing he felt unsteady, as though his head was about to float off his body. She put her hand on his arm, and the warmth of it steadied him, although there was nothing anyone could do to decrease his anxiety. He lowered his voice so it wouldn't carry to where his mum and dad sat. "Heart attack?"

She rubbed the back of her neck. "Could be, but I can't make a definitive diagnosis here. Once we get him to the hospital, we'll have a far better chance of getting to the bottom of it."

He looked over at his parents, saw the fear in his mother's eyes, even as she tried to keep a stiff upper lip, and his father's bravado as he attempted to look as though nothing out of the ordinary was happening.

"We'll take care of him, Zach." Gen sounded brisk. The voice of a woman in complete control. "Maybe you should go down to the road and make sure they know where to find us."

Not wanting to leave, he hesitated, but she put her hand on his cheek, and when he looked at her she gave him a soft, reassuring smile.

"I'll be here, keeping an eagle eye on him. Go on. The longer it takes them to find us, the longer it will be before we can figure out what's going on with your dad."

She was right, of course she was, but it didn't make it any easier. And not even the kiss she gave his cheek helped. Only the little shove on his shoulder finally got him moving, and he sprinted down the path, his ears straining for the sound of the siren coming in the distance.

He should have known something wasn't right with Dad since that first night when he was rubbing his chest and complaining about indigestion. As a nurse, he'd seen too many people die who'd assumed what they were experiencing could be cured with antacids, when they were, in reality, having a heart attack.

But he'd been too wrapped up in Gen, in the charade they were playing and his growing feelings for her. Too busy trying to guard his heart and his ego from being smashed again to pay proper attention to what was happening with his father.

Guilt racked him, as he looked back up the hillside, although the group was out of view.

This was the wake-up call he needed.

He'd been angry when Gen said she was going to confess to her mother. Not just because it meant what was going on between them would be over, but because he dreaded being embarrassed in front of his parents when it came out their relationship was a sham.

Dad and Mum had seemed so happy, even relieved, that he'd found someone. He hadn't wanted them to look at him the way they had after Moira's defection: with worry, and worse, pity.

Yet, none of that mattered now.

The only thing of importance was Dad's health, and keeping his mum on an even keel while they figured out what was happening.

"Thank God," he muttered as he heard the approaching siren and strained to see the ambulance turning into the gardens.

Then he was waving like a crazy man to get their attention, putting everything else aside in the push to help his father.

CHAPTER SEVENTEEN

GEN RODE IN the ambulance with Mr. Lewin, monitoring his vitals along the way. Ambulances in St. Eustace weren't the fully equipped conveyances she was used to. In fact, they were fairly basic, with a gurney that locked into place and a minimum of medical supplies, mostly just what was needed to staunch bleeding and administer oxygen.

Since Mr. Lewin was still suffering some shortness of breath, she put him on oxygen and used the BP monitoring system to track his blood pressure. She also took the opportunity to examine him more fully and ask additional questions, which he seemed more willing to answer when the rest of his family weren't present.

When they got to the hospital, she reluctantly handed Mr. Lewin over to Dr. Carmichael, the ER doctor on duty, but gave him her considered opinion before he went into the examination room.

"Blood tests will tell if he's had a series of mild myocardial infarctions," he said. "But I'll schedule him for the ultrasound, as you recommend."

She had to be content with that, but as she made her way to the waiting room, her worries about Mr. Lewin's condition stalked her along the corridor. Stopping at the nursing supervisor's office, she inquired which surgeons were on duty that afternoon.

"Dr. Cutler is here on-site," she was told. "And Dr. Langdon is on call."

"What about Dr. Goulding?"

"He's gone to Jamaica to attend an orthopedics conference and won't be back for another two days."

"And who's in charge in radiology?"

"Dr. Figueroa."

"Thank you," she said, now more worried than before.

If Mr. Lewin needed surgery, of the two options available her choice would be Kiah. But he was too close to Mr. Lewin for him to undertake the task. Omar Cutler was young and quite inexperienced. Gen had also found him far too cocky for comfort, not wanting to take advice or direction. Depending on the diagnosis, he might never even have performed the necessary procedure, but probably wouldn't hesitate to do it anyway.

At least Dr. Figueroa was head of radiology, so if he were needed, that aspect of the situation was covered.

When she walked into the waiting room, Mrs. Lewin got to her feet, her hand over her heart.

"It's okay," Gen said, going to hug her. "They're examining him now and will come and tell us when they have something to report."

"I thought you'd be looking after Hezekiah," she told Gen.

"She's a surgeon, Mum, and not even on duty right now. But don't worry. Dr. Carmichael is a good diagnostician."

"He really is," Gen agreed. "We just need to give him some time to do his job."

So they waited, and Gen could see Zach's anxiety

level rising, although anyone else looking at him would think he was calm. She saw it in the way his fingers clenched and seemed to have to be forced to relax, and in the periodic joggling of his leg as his pent-up energy sought release.

It was long past lunchtime, and Gen started worrying about her mom, who'd been recently diagnosed with prediabetes, having something to eat. Yet, she was loath to leave Mrs. Lewin, wanting to be there in case she could be of help.

Finally, thinking it might do Zach good to have something to do, she asked if he'd take her mother to get some food and suggested he bring something back for his mom too.

He started to object, but his mother, who'd been all but silent, said, "That's a bonny idea, Zach. Gen can keep me company until you come back."

Her tone was such he didn't dare argue, so, with obvious reluctance and the demand that they call him right away if they got any news, he left.

As soon as it was clear he and Mom were probably out of the hospital, Mrs. Lewin said, "You know what's wrong with Hezekiah, don't you?"

Gen bit her lower lip, and then admitted, "I think I have a pretty good idea, but the tests will tell if I'm right or not."

"Will he need an operation—if you're right?"

"He will need surgical intervention, if I'm right." That was the most she was willing to say.

"And this…surgical intervention, is it something you can do?"

"I wouldn't be the best choice," she admitted. "But

unfortunately, they don't have the type of specialist who would usually perform the surgery on staff here right now."

"But you can do it?"

Mrs. Lewin was unrelenting, and Gen reluctantly nodded. "I've done a few, but…"

The older lady's hand on her arm stopped her from continuing.

"If Hezekiah needs the operation, I want you to do it. I know he'd want that too."

"I can't promise, Mrs. Lewin. It might not be up to me."

That got her a shake of the head. "I know that if you put your mind to it, you'll find a way."

Then the other woman changed the subject, asking if Gen could call Zach and ask him to go to the house and get her knitting. Stepping out of the room, Gen wandered just outside the outer doors, wanting a breath of air, but staying where she could watch the entrance to the waiting area.

"Hey," she said when he answered. "No word yet, but your mom is wondering if you'd stop by the house and get her knitting for her."

"I can," he said. "But I want to be there when they tell us what's happening with Dad."

"I know," she replied, her heart aching for him.

Then he sighed. "At least you're there with her."

"It won't take too long to get what she wants," she said, trying to reassure him. "And it'll keep her hands occupied, hopefully calming her down some."

"Okay. We've got food, and I'm heading to the house, so I should be there in about twenty-five minutes or so."

"All right. Bye."

Hanging up, she stayed where she was for a while longer, contemplating what Mrs. Lewin had asked of her.

It could be tricky, getting the powers that be to agree to her operating on Zach's father, simply because they'd done such a good job of convincing everyone she and Zach were a couple. But if it were at all possible, she'd do it.

For Mrs. Lewin, and for Zach.

She couldn't allow doubt to cloud her mind, but she'd have to be superhuman not to realize whatever she and Zach had would shatter into ten thousand pieces if she operated unsuccessfully on his father.

"Coo-calloo-calloo," she muttered, but not even her favorite curse word was sufficient.

When Zach and Mrs. Broussard got back to the hospital, it was just in time to hear what Felix Carmichael had to say.

"Your husband has an abdominal aortic aneurysm, Mrs. Lewin. That's an area in the wall of the main artery running through his belly that's become weak and is swollen, like a balloon."

Zach expected his mother to look to him for clarification, but instead, she looked at Gen, who nodded slightly.

"What can you do about it?" Mum asked, twisting her fingers together.

"Well, it measures just about six centimeters, and depending on some of the other test results, he should be a candidate for endovascular stent grafting. If the surgeon determines the endovascular surgery isn't the right choice, then he or she will want to do a conventional repair."

As Carmichael explained the different procedures to

his mother, Zach was watching Gen, who was pressing her knuckle into the side of her lip and staring out the window. When Felix finished, he asked Mum if she had any questions.

"Which one will be best for Hezekiah?"

"The surgeon will have to make that determination, Mrs. Lewin. There are a lot of variables to consider and to talk over with your husband before a decision is made."

After that, Mum went quiet, seeming not to have anything else she wanted to ask, but Gen did.

"EKG results look…?"

"Very good, actually."

"And will you do a stress test?"

"That will be up to the surgeon."

"And who that will be?"

"I contacted Kiah Langdon, but although he's on his way in, he said he'd be unable to do the surgery because of his close relationship with the patient. I have a call in to the director for his input before I hand the patient over to a surgeon."

Zach was going to interject and ask who else was available, and why it was taking so long for the decision to be made when Gen's mother touched his arm and pointed.

His mum was silently crying, looking down at her lap, probably in the hope no one would notice. Zach knelt beside her and hugged her, stroking her back and whispering reassurances. By the time she'd calmed down, both Felix and Gen were gone.

Leaving Mum with Mrs. Broussard, telling them he had some questions of his own for the doctor, he tried to find them, eventually hearing Gen's voice from one of the consulting rooms.

The door was ajar, and he was in time to hear her say, "...Two choices. You let me operate, or you fly Mr. Lewin to Trinidad for the surgery, and I wouldn't suggest the latter. Considering the swift onset of symptoms, the abdominal pain and the size of the aneurysm, if you delay the surgery you're risking rupture. And you don't want that to happen at twenty thousand feet."

It sounded as though she were in battle mode, and Zach was about to knock and join the war when he heard another voice—that of Omar Cutler—and paused.

"I'm the surgeon on duty, so it's my responsibility to do the surgery."

"It would be your responsibility *if* you were assigned the case and were qualified to perform the procedure."

"I am qualified..."

"How many endovascular repairs have you performed? How many conventional open repairs?"

"I've assisted on..."

"Assisted isn't doing." Her voice was cold, cutting. "How many have you *done*, yourself?"

"Listen, don't get up on your high horse with me." The anger in the young doctor's voice was patently clear. "You can't do the surgery because you're sleeping with the patient's son, and it would be an ethical violation. Everyone knows it, so don't try to deny it."

"What does that have to do with anything?" Gen's voice was amused, dismissive. "Whatever Zach and I have going on isn't serious enough or important enough to make any difference. And, as for the patient, I've only known him for a few days. There's no attachment there either."

No attachment there either?

Zach stepped back from the door, hearing the rise and

fall of the continuing argument coming from behind it, but no longer listening.

...*isn't serious enough or important enough to make any difference.*

Him. She was talking about him, and the words cut through him like her scalpel.

Turning on his heel, he walked away.

Was this how boxers felt when they left the ring after a knockout? As though their brains had been scrambled, and nothing made sense anymore?

He'd told himself whatever there was between he and Gen didn't matter in the grand scheme of things, but hearing her dismiss him so easily, so *casually*, gave lie to that idea.

Somewhere, deep inside, he'd held on to some stupid hope that they might, just might, become a real couple. That she would realize she felt as deeply for him as he did for her and want to make a go of it.

He'd known better, faced the disparity in their lives and expectations and reminded himself she was out of his league over and over, but that hadn't stopped his stupid heart from getting involved.

Yet, wasn't it better to hear it like this, than to have her spell it out at a later date?

No. That was a lie too. No matter how he heard it, the grinding agony, the heartbreak, would be the same.

It was too much to deal with, and the part of his brain that controlled emotion, that was screaming with agony, shut itself down, recognizing his priorities.

Making sure Dad got the best treatment.

Holding Mum together as she watched her husband of almost forty years undergo a potentially dangerous surgery to repair a defect that could, if left alone, kill him.

It wasn't the first time he'd had to lock shame and anger away, to pretend everything was fine and make it through from one day to the next.

He'd done it before and come out on the other side, and he could, he *would*, do it again.

"Zach." Kiah's voice came from behind him, and Zach squared his shoulders, put on a mask of impassivity to greet his cousin. Kiah grabbed him and hugged him hard. "Man, why you never call me right away?"

"It all happened so quickly." How could his voice sound so normal, when his entire face, even his lips, felt numb? "And then…" He shrugged, at a loss to explain.

"I get it. I really do. What's happening now? Have you been in to see Uncle yet?"

"Not yet. I was just going to find out if I could take Mum in to see him."

"Come on," Kiah said, slapping him on the back. "I know one or two people around here, so I think I can get you past the guards."

Zach felt his lips curl, although of their own volition, and knew he'd survive it all intact.

Or as intact as a man with a shattered heart could be.

CHAPTER EIGHTEEN

GEN GOT HER WAY. Director Hamilton gave her the go-ahead to perform the surgery, but she knew now, more than ever before, she was under intense scrutiny.

Especially from Zach, who, from one instant to the next, had turned into a cold, somehow forbidding stranger, making her wonder if he doubted her ability to perform the operation.

Yet, they'd worked together so many times, surely he knew her well enough to realize she'd never endanger his father's life? That if she thought it was best for his father, she'd medically evacuate him to Port of Spain, where they had vascular surgeons on call?

The only people who were happy about the turn of events were Mr. and Mrs. Lewin.

When she'd gone in to see Mr. Lewin, who was yet to be transferred out of emerge, it was to find an almost party atmosphere in the room, mostly instigated by Kiah.

"Okay, everyone except Mrs. Lewin, out, please." She tried to catch Zach's eye, hoping to give him some kind of reassuring signal, but he avoided all eye contact and walked away without a word.

That was something to be dealt with later, she told herself, even though the slight hurt horribly.

"I knew you could do it, dear." Mrs. Lewin sent her a sweet, grateful smile, before explaining to her husband what she'd asked Gen to do.

He seemed equally appreciative. "Zach told us you're one of the best surgeons he's worked with, so I'm glad it'll be you working on me."

"Do you want Zach in here while I explain the differences in the procedures?"

They exchanged glances, and then Mr. Lewin shook his head. "No. I know you'll do right by me, and I don't want Zach involved. If anything were to go wrong, he'd blame himself."

Gen nodded, understanding and believing that to be true. Zach was exactly that type of man. The kind who would shoulder any burden for those he loved and take the blame if things went awry.

Just the type of man any woman with sense would love and want to have at her side for all of life's ups and downs.

But now wasn't the time to consider why knowing that caused her heart to ache. She had an important job to do.

One that she was determined to succeed at—for all their sakes.

Having gone through Mr. Lewin's test results and looked at his scans, she told the older couple what she'd found.

"Either surgical option will work for you, and I checked to make sure that both are approved back in the UK, so follow-up shouldn't be a problem."

After she'd explained the advantages and drawbacks of the procedures, Mr. Lewin decided on the endovascular repair, mainly because of the quicker recovery time.

"I don't mind that I'll have to get regular checks to

make sure it's still in place. I don't want to be laid up for weeks recovering from surgery if I don't have to be."

He'd been a bit upset when she told him she was admitting him to the hospital rather than sending him home, but she didn't sugarcoat it.

"From everything you've told me, and from what I've seen in your scans, this is a fast-growing aneurysm, and I don't want to take any chances on a rupture. Keeping you here, instead of having you go home, is just my way of making sure the chances are minimized, and also that if a rupture should occur overnight, you can get immediate care. Not that I think that will happen," she hastened to add when Mrs. Lewin's eyes widened. "I'm just being extra cautious."

She scheduled the surgery for midmorning the following day, after consulting with the Chief of Radiology to make sure he was available and ordering the necessary CT scan for that evening.

Then, she went looking for Zach and her mom, only to find Mom had driven herself back to Gen's place while Gen had been talking to his parents.

"We got your car at the same time I picked up Mum's knitting, and it didn't make sense for her to have to stay here waiting for you when we didn't know how long you'd be."

His words were innocuous, even polite, but the tone was cold enough to make her shiver. Then she remembered his anger earlier and decided now wasn't the time to get into any of it. Not with his dad about to have surgery, which she was going to perform.

No, best to let things ride and deal with it afterward. If he were willing.

"Would you mind taking me home, then?" she asked.

"Although I can take a cab, if you want to stay with your dad until visiting hours are over. They should be moving him to a room soon."

"No, I'll run you home," he said. "I just need to let Mum know I'll be back in a mo."

There it was again. Perfect courtesy, wrapped in a block of ice.

The drive to her place passed in silence broken only by the radio.

When they got to her condo, she took a leaf from his book, and said, "Thank you. No need for you to get out. I'll see you in the morning."

Then, with all the dignity she could muster, she got out of the car and walked up the path.

Her mom was in the living room watching TV when she got inside, and Gen's stomach rumbled at the smell of food emanating from the kitchen.

"I knew you were the only one who hadn't eaten," Mom said. "So I came back to put something together for you."

Gen showered and ate, keeping the conversation light. Her overwhelming need to come clean to her mother had faded, both in light of Mr. Lewin's illness and the confusion over Zach's behavior.

If he continued to treat her that way, there'd be no need to tell Mom anything. She'd be able to see for herself that the relationship had imploded.

"I'm sorry part of one of your last days will be spent by yourself, Mom. I'm going to sleep at the hospital tonight, just in case Mr. Lewin's aneurysm ruptures, and then I'm operating in the morning. Once I'm sure he's out of the woods, I'll come home, and we can do something together."

Mom just smiled. "I'll be fine. Do what you need to."

Gen called to make sure Zach and his mother had left for the night before she drove back to the hospital, not wanting another frosty encounter with her patient's son. Putting her bags down in the doctor's lounge, she went up to check on Mr. Lewin, finding him still awake and sitting up in bed.

He looked surprised when he saw her.

"I though Zach said you'd gone home."

"I did. But then I came back," she said casually, picking up his chart and looking at the notations.

"Well, I'm glad you did," he replied. "I wanted to talk to you alone, and wasn't sure I'd get the chance before the surgery."

Smiling, she put down the chart and walked over to the side of the bed.

"What did you want to talk about?"

He hesitated for a moment and then said, "I know you said the surgery tomorrow shouldn't be dangerous, but hearing you have a bomb in your belly waiting to explode makes a man think."

She held up her hand. "Don't start getting maudlin on me, sir, and talking about dying."

"No, no." He shook his head. "I trust you to make sure I get through okay, but, as my good friend from Jamaica always says, 'Any card can play.' No one knows what tomorrow will bring, so I wanted to tell you now—if anything does happen to me, take good care of Zachary. He's a good, good man, and he deserves to be happy, especially after what Moira did to him."

He said the name as though she should know who he was talking about, and she had to bite her cheek not to ask who that was and what she'd done. To do so would alert

Mr. Lewin to the fact he'd said something he probably shouldn't have, and she didn't want him upset in any way.

So, instead of letting any of the questions flying around her head out of her mouth, she smiled and said, "I'll do the best I can, but you'll darn well be around to see it as long as I have any say in the matter, that is."

Later, lying on a cot in the doctor's rest room, trying to relax enough to sleep, she realized she didn't really care who Moira was. Although knowing the story would help her understand Zach better, the most important question of all was: had he gotten over this Moira woman, or was there no place in his heart for anyone else?

Someone like her?

Despite the heat of their passion and the honest emotional connection she felt to him, was she just kidding herself to even think he'd want to be with her long-term? His recent coldness seemed to say she was, especially since she couldn't figure out why he'd suddenly seemed to turn completely away.

The sensation of being rejected brought back harsh, painful memories. It had happened before, in the most devastating of ways, and she knew the damage lingered, even now. Was that what she was facing again? Should she try to pursue a lasting relationship with Zach? Was she willing to open herself up to that type of pain again?

Yet, she couldn't get away from the fact that lying there in the dark, all she longed for was his arms around her, his voice in her ear. Zach had always made her feel safe, accepted and wanted, even though he knew she hadn't been completely open and honest with him about her past.

Now she faced the trap she'd set for herself.

If she told him about Johan and what had happened

after the breakup, would he view the story as her trying to guilt him into giving their relationship a chance?

And if she didn't tell him—keeping her shame to herself, protecting her ego—would he think her reticence a sign that she didn't trust and love him?

Heart heavy and eyes damp, Gen called on years of discipline and closed her eyes, starting the relaxation technique she'd mastered to help her sleep on the worst of nights.

Mr. Lewin and all his family deserved to have her very best self in the OR in the morning.

Everything else, no matter how important to her, would have to wait to find resolution.

Zach made sure to take his mum to the hospital early enough to see his father before the surgery, and they found him in good spirits, although Zach wasn't sure if that was just an act for Mum's sake.

"There's mi darlin'," he said, with that cheeky look he reserved just for her, and they held hands until Nurse Monroe came to kick them out to prep Dad for the operation.

Gen had already been in and out of the room several times, once with Dr. Figueroa, and another time with the anesthesiologist. Mum had greeted her as though she were one of her children, but besides a brief "good morning," Gen and he hardly exchanged a word.

When the nurse told them it was time to go, there was a round of kisses and hugs, but after Mum stepped out, Dad called Zach back and asked the nurse for a moment with "his boy."

"Some 'boy,'" Nurse Monroe teased, looking at her watch and heading for the door. "You can have five minutes, but no more. Dr. Broussard is always punctual to the second."

"Zachary, your Gen tells me I'm going to pull through this and be fine, but if I don't—"

"Dad—"

His father held up his hand. "Son, nothing in life is certain, so I want you to know I love you, and I'm prouder of you than I can ever say. You're a fine, accomplished man, and I know I don't tell you that often enough, so I wanted to make sure I said it now."

"Okay, Dad." And although he tried to make his voice impatient, he knew he'd failed and that his father saw the tears gather in his eyes. "I love you too."

"Don't be afraid of love, Zachary," his father said, seemingly out of the blue. "I know it hasn't always been kind to you, but I think you've found something special now. Something like what Mum and I have. You should hold on to it, you hear?"

Before he could answer, Nurse Monroe was back, saying, "That's it, Zachary Lewin. Out. Unless you want the job of prepping your own daddy for surgery."

It was a long morning. Sitting in the waiting room outside the theatre wing gave him more than enough time to think all kinds of horrible, crazy thoughts.

Dad had opted for general anesthetic instead of an epidural. Suppose they gave him the wrong dosage or he was allergic? He wanted to ask Mum if Dad had ever had an operation before, but she looked so peaceful, sitting there with her knitting, that he didn't want her to start worrying.

What if the stent was the wrong size, or Gen tore the

artery, or it ruptured before they could get the stent in place, or…or…or…

Realizing he was starting to go a little insane, he got up.

"Mum, I'm going to nip down to the canteen for a cuppa. Do you want one?"

"Yes, thank you, dear."

He was heading for the stairs when he saw Mrs. Broussard coming toward him carrying a beverage tray with cups in one hand and a paper bag in the other.

"Morning. I brought you and your mom some tea and pastries. I know you probably wouldn't want a full breakfast or might have already eaten."

Taking the tray from her hand, he bent to kiss her cheek. "You're a lifesaver. I was just going down to get tea."

She smiled slightly, then sobered. "Any news?"

"Not yet. It'll be a little while yet, I think."

"Did you see ViVi at all this morning?"

"I did." He opened the door with his hip and held it for her to precede him into the waiting room.

"I hope she got some sleep. She always complained during her residency that the cots in the hospital were so terribly uncomfortable, and I doubt the ones here are any better. Ah, Sheila, how are you doing?"

As the women greeted each other, Zach let the fact that Gen had slept at the hospital sink in.

"Doing well, thank you," Mum said, accepting Mrs. Broussard's hug and returning it in kind. "I know Hezekiah is in good hands. Our Gen will take care of him."

Our Gen.

Mum said it as though Gen was one of her children, and Mrs. Broussard was smiling and nodding, as though it was quite fine with her too. Coupled with his father's advice the night before, Zach came to the inescapable conclusion that, like him, his parents had fallen head over heels for Gen.

It was a shame all of them were going to be disappointed when things fell apart.

Still restless, and unwilling to sit there and listen to the two ladies sing Gen's praises, he put the tray of drinks on the table, and said to them, "I'm going to walk around a bit."

His phone pinged as he left the waiting room and paced closer to the doors leading to the operating theatres. It was his sister, texting to ask for an update. He sent her a reply, saying Dad was still in the OR, and paced back the other way along the corridor again.

Ping.

The blasted phone again. He wanted to throw it against the nearest wall, even while acknowledging his role as the family's point of contact. Just as he got to the other end of the corridor and was reaching to take the phone out of his pocket, he heard the door to the operating wing open, and he spun on his heel.

Gen came through with Chief of Radiology Dr. Figueroa beside her, the two speaking in low voices, the radiologist shaking his head. Gen had her head down as she pulled off her surgical cap, and then she rubbed at the back of her neck.

Zach was frozen in place, watching them come toward him, ice slipping and sliding through his veins, filling his belly. He couldn't read their postures. Couldn't even seem to think or reason.

Then Gen looked up and saw him, and the most beautiful smile he'd ever seen spread across her face.

"It went perfectly," Dr. Figueroa said, grinning too, as they got to his position. "Picture-perfect."

"Thank you," Zach said, but he only had eyes for Gen and her smile, which made all his previous anger, doubts and fears seem irrelevant.

He wanted to hold her, to take strength from her, find solace in her arms. And that rush of need was almost as terrifying as sitting in the waiting room while Dad had his operation.

"Let's go tell your mother," she said, putting her hand on his arm. At the tenderness of her touch, his legs, which moments before had threatened to give out, regained sensation.

As though struck by a bolt from the blue, he knew—acknowledged—that he'd never be complete without her in his life. That the emotions he'd fought so hard could no longer be denied and the warmth rushing through him, heating every muscle and sinew, was love.

Plain and simple.

But there was no benefit to telling her how he felt, no future stretching ahead of them. So all he said was, "Yes. Let's go."

Hiding this new pain, so no one would see.

CHAPTER NINETEEN

Mr. Lewin was ambulatory by the day following the operation and back up at the farmhouse that evening. Gen monitored him in the hospital and kept in touch with Zach once he was released, but most of the time was spent with her mother.

They went up to visit with the Lewins on the day of Mom's flight, and watching the older folks, Gen realized a real bond had been formed between the three of them. There were addresses exchanged and promises to keep in touch and open invitations to visit extended. Zach was quiet through it all, not contributing much to the conversation, busying himself with drinks and food, and making sure his Dad was comfortable.

To Gen, the way he avoided touching her was marked, but if any of the parents noticed, they were too polite to say.

"We've extended our trip by four days," Mrs. Lewin told them. "And then Zachary will fly with us to Port of Spain so we have someone to help with luggage and Dad's wheelchair. Then Cameron will meet us at Heathrow and drive us home."

"I wanted to just convalesce here," Mr. Lewin said,

giving his wife a baleful glance from the corner of his eye. "But she decided she wanted to go home."

"I want him to be seen by our family doctor, so she knows what's happening," his wife interjected. "And besides, I've had enough of this heat."

Amused at their banter, Gen looked at Zach and found him staring at her in a way that made her insides melt. But as soon as their gazes clashed, he turned away and her heart sank. Seeing the fondness with which Mom took her leave from Zach, kissing his cheek and whispering something to him, just increased her pain.

After she and her mother got back from the Lewins' house, they sat outside on the patio, enjoying a final glass of lemonade before Gen was to take her to the airport.

"What's happening between you and Zachary?" Mom asked abruptly when there was a lull in the conversation. "I know you said the relationship was going slowly, because of his past experiences, but seeing you two together, I thought things were going well, until recently."

She'd shelved the idea of confessing the lies to her mom, and Gen had no intention of going back on that decision now, so she replied, "I'm really not sure, Mom. He just…went cold on me, but he's had so much on his plate, it's not surprising, is it?"

Her mother took a sip from her glass, seemingly lost in contemplation for a moment or two. Then she sighed.

"Did he tell you what happened to him in his last relationship?"

"With Moira?"

It was a calculated stab in the dark, but it hit home.

"Yes. That was her name."

"Not in a lot of detail."

Mom slid her a shrewd glance. "And have you told him about Johan and Loren and what you went through?"

Oh, she felt the trap then, but figured she might get away with the same prevarication she'd used before. "Not in a lot of detail."

Mom snorted and shook her head. "So, neither of you have told the other about the pain you carry and the fears you must have about going into another relationship. Baby, without trust, the relationship will never work. So, if you can't see your way clear to move forward in honesty, it's best you don't see each other anymore."

Those words stayed with her long after she'd dropped her mother off at the airport that evening.

Mom was right, of course, and Zach had said it too. Gen hadn't had the courage to be honest with him, afraid to open herself up to disdain or ridicule.

Afraid to trust again and have that trust thrown back in her face.

But was he that type of man? Could she see him doing what Johan had done?

Or was the fear a knee-jerk reaction on her part, an instinctive attempt to protect herself at all costs from something that felt so huge and important?

She couldn't decide, and in the face of her uncertainty, couldn't act. This was no longer a romp or a game, and the seriousness of it paralyzed her, forcing her to think rather than simply react, as she often did.

Hard enough to admit to herself she loved Zach, much less to consider admitting it to him and perhaps have him laugh. After all, hadn't he warned her not to get attached, and she'd agreed? It wasn't his fault she couldn't keep up her end of the bargain, and she didn't think he'd even want to know how she felt about him.

Yet, there was a part of her pushing to do something, anything, to come to a decision. Zach was, as his father had said, a good man—and kind too. Even though she internally cringed at the thought of his possible rejection, did she really think he'd be cruel?

No.

That wasn't the type of man he was.

And wasn't he worth risking everything—her ego, her heart—for?

He was, if she could just find the courage to be honest.

Still racked with hesitancy, as well as feeling ineffably lonely and needing something to do, she went up to the guest room and stripped the bed. Gathering up the sheets, along with the towels her mom had used, she carried them downstairs just as her doorbell rang.

When she looked through the peephole and saw Zach standing there, her heart flipped and her mouth went dry. Shoving the dirty linens under the hall console table, she opened the door, plastering one of her best and brightest smiles on her face, although it felt as if it would crack her skin wide open.

"Hi." He looked so stern, it took everything she had to speak and keep her smile in place. "What's up?"

"I have to ask you something. When you were talking to Carmichael, before you were assigned Dad's surgery, was what I heard you say the truth?"

"I don't remember what I said, Zach." And she really didn't. All she remembered was her promise to his mother and being determined to keep it. "Do you want to come inside?"

He rubbed his hand across the top of his head, his narrowed gaze never leaving hers, and didn't respond to her offer for him to come in, and just said, "You told them what was happening between us wasn't important, and there was no *attachment* to me. Was that true?"

She stepped back, hanging on to the door, realizing this was it, the moment she had to decide whether to trust him or to let him go without him knowing she loved him and wanted him for her own.

"It wasn't," she admitted. "I'd made a promise to your mother to be the one to operate on your dad, and I knew I was the best person out of the surgeons available. I honestly don't even remember saying those things. I just remember being determined not to let your mom down and trying to make myself the obvious choice. I couldn't let my feelings for you get in the way."

He stepped through the doorway so they were only a foot or so apart.

"What feelings?" His voice was gravelly and demanding, and she had no intention of denying him an answer.

Yet, still she hesitated, realized she was pressing her knuckle into the side of her mouth when he captured her hand with his, and electricity zinged up her arm.

"I'm in love with you," she confessed, the words coming out soft and wobbly, revealing the vulnerability she couldn't hide anymore.

Then she couldn't continue speaking, even if she'd wanted to, because she was in his arms, and he was kissing her as though she were air, and he'd been drowning. That was how she felt too—alive again, when for the last couple of days she'd felt dead inside.

Zach kicked the door closed behind him, and Gen linked her arms around his neck, letting him know with the tightness of her embrace that she didn't ever want to let him go.

He drew back, just far enough that she could feel his breath rushing across her face. "I want you, Gen. But I want to sort this out between us, before we make love again. Every time I touch you, I fall a little deeper."

She shivered at the gravelly admission, but didn't release her grip.

"I want you to fall all the way, like I have," she told him. "You're all I want. All I could ever need. So make love with me. I've missed you so much."

And when she led him upstairs, Zach made no further objections.

Making love with Gen once more blew his mind, ecstasy heightened by their confessions of love.

Afterward, she lay curled against his side, her head on his chest, and they finally got around to unraveling each other's mysteries.

"The Bell's seemed like the beginning," she told him. "But truthfully, what finally happened had started a long, long time before."

His heart ached for her as she told him about the series of blows that came one after the other. Bell's palsy endangering her career, her fiancé's admission that he wasn't attracted to her anymore because of the nerve damage.

"The real kicker, though, came when I found out he'd got engaged to the woman I considered my best friend in the world. They livestreamed the engagement party, and Loren knew I'd be watching because she was the one who sent me the link."

"What a pair of bastards." Zach felt as if he could throttle them both if they were nearby.

Gen snorted. "That's one way to describe them. I was back at my apartment by then but…" Her voice faltered, and he heard her take a deep breath. "I lost it. Thank goodness my sister was there with me and stopped me from destroying the place, and perhaps myself too. It just felt like the last humiliating straw, and I was sure my life was better off over. Dad wanted to send me to a psychiatric hospital, but Mom took me home instead and pretty much nursed me back to normal."

"I'm so sorry, love." He was sorry and livid and oh, so grateful. "I'm glad you didn't hurt yourself. I'm so thankful you're here now, with me."

She rolled over to rest her chin on the hand she had on his chest, bringing them face-to-face. Her gaze was searching, and he wondered what she was looking for.

Then she asked, "That doesn't scare you?"

Confused, he replied, "What doesn't scare me?"

"I had a mental breakdown, Zach. No one in my family even talks about it, out of shame or fear—I don't know which."

"Or maybe out of a desire not to hurt you by bringing it up?"

She blinked and pressed her knuckle into her lip.

"I guess that's a possibility too," she conceded.

"They're probably waiting for you to mention it first. And to answer your question, no, it doesn't scare me in the slightest. You were under immense stress, and worse, had been treated with the worst kind of emotional cruelty. I'd be more surprised if you were completely unaffected."

Her eyes filled with tears, and she placed a kiss right over his heart. "I told you Mom was worried because she thought I was suffering the aftereffects of the Bell's, but it was all the other things that she was concerned about. My mental and emotional health, and the way I'd lost my ability to trust and wasn't sure I'd ever get it back again."

"I'll earn your trust, every day, until you have no more doubts," he vowed, using his finger to wipe away her tears.

Then it was his turn, but Gen forestalled him, saying, "You don't have to tell me about Moira tonight if you'd rather wait. Just tell me you've gotten over her, so you have space for me in your heart."

"My heart belongs to you," he told her honestly. "But I'd rather just tell you now, so we can move on."

Talking about it didn't hurt anymore. It still stung, but it was a muted pain and only residual anger.

At least on his part.

Gen bounced up to sit cross-legged beside his hip, scowling more ferociously than he'd ever seen her do before.

With narrowed eyes, she said, "She dumped you, after ten years of you supporting her so she could go to law school? After you gave up your own ambitions to help her achieve hers?"

He shrugged. "That about sums it up."

"Wow. Talk about trust issues. Yours must be pretty serious too."

He contemplated her words. "Yes, but different. Moira thought she was better than me, because she came from a middle-class family who lived in a nice village, and I was born and raised in South London. She was always trying to 'improve' me, making it clear I wasn't good enough the way I was. When you and I met, I convinced myself you'd never be interested in me long-term because we come from two different worlds."

Gen shrugged. "You heard my mom talking about her grandmother, and my dad is only where he is today because he's smarter than should be legal, and had mentors who guided him in the right way. Sure, we're affluent, but it doesn't make us stuck-up, because we know where our roots lie."

"Not everyone stays grounded that way," he said, before telling her what Moira had said before she left, about being embarrassed by him.

Gen literally slammed her fist into her other palm as she listened, clearly livid.

Zach found himself fighting back laughter, and she turned that furious gaze on him.

"How can you laugh, Zachary? You're the finest, most wonderful man I've ever met, and she has the nerve to say something like that to you? I want to grind her into pieces right now."

In between chuckles he told her, "I've never seen anyone do the Hulk smash into their own hand in real life. It was cute."

"Cute?"

She was trying for outrage, but amusement was getting the better of her, and he couldn't resist tugging her back down, then rolling so he was above her, and they were face-to-face.

"Incredibly cute," he teased, feeling light and free in a way he couldn't remember ever experiencing before. "Like kitten cute."

"You better stop while you're ahead, Zachary Lewin. Remember I wield a scalpel for a living."

But the threat lost most of its potency, her breathy voice betraying anything but anger.

"Tell me again," he demanded.

She knew exactly what he needed, as she lifted her head so her lips were soft against his.

"I love you, Zach. Just the way you are, and forever."

And that was all he needed to know.

* * * * *

TAMING THE
HOT-SHOT DOC

SUSAN CARLISLE

MILLS & BOON

To Debbie.
Thanks for your friendship and support.

CHAPTER ONE

Dr. Shay Lunsford hurried up the short hallway to answer the insistent rapping on the front door of the Delta Medical Clinic. Would she have an emergency to deal with first thing in the morning? The clinic didn't open for another twenty minutes. She looked through the full glass door of what had once been a dress store in a strip mall.

A man with dark hair styled in the latest cut and sporting a closely clipped beard on his square jaw stood there. Surrounded by all that shading was a beautiful full mouth. Her attention drifted to his green eyes watching her so intently.

"We're not open yet." Shay would've said she knew everyone in Lewisville, a suburb of Jackson, Mississippi, but she'd never seen this man before. She would've remembered him. That mouth.

"I'm Dr. Matt Chapman. Didn't Dr. Warren tell you I was coming?"

Huh? What was the name of the doctor her Uncle Henry had called to say was on his way to help her? This guy must be him. He'd give her a few weeks of assistance until she found more permanent help. Her clinic had grown so fast in the last eight months she couldn't handle it on her own any longer.

She'd been in the middle of stitches on a man's hand when the receptionist, Sheree, had told her to expect new help on Monday. With a nod, Shay had continued her work and forgotten the details, like his name. She studied the guy before her. "Can I see some identification?"

The man's movie star mouth thinned into a line as he dug into the back pocket of his well-worn jeans. She watched as he pulled a square out of his wallet. With the card facing her, he plastered it between the glass door and the palm of his hand.

It was a California driver's license. He was one of the few people who could take a good license picture. She met his look, turned the lock and opened the door. "Okay. Come in."

As he moved past her, he smelled of lemony aftershave. Everything about him made him stand out from the average men in the area. His shirt appeared carefully pressed and his khaki pants were a brand that she recognized as one of the best. The brown shiny loafers on his feet screamed they cost money.

He shoved his wallet into his back pocket and murmured, "I'm not used to being carded to get into a public medical clinic."

She flipped the lock closed again. "We have to be careful here. We keep drugs that some people would break in to get."

He pursed his lips and nodded. "So, I look like a drug addict? Good to know."

Shay shook her head. "That's not what I meant."

That put a slight smile on his lips.

"I'm cautious when I'm here by myself. I worked too hard to get this clinic up and running to have it fail because I wasn't careful. Let's start again." She extended her hand. "I'm Shay Lunsford. You'll be helping me for the next six weeks."

The doctor took her hand, dwarfing it inside his larger one. He shook with a firm and confident grip with a nominal amount of movement and time. Is that how he would handle patients? Short and sweet? She hoped not. Could a simple handshake tell her that much about someone? If so, what had hers said?

Relieved to have her hand returned to her, she said, "I appreciate you coming. I can use your help. Our patients will start lining up in a few minutes. I'm gonna warn you, you won't get much downtime."

"That's the way I like it."

She chuckled. "Says a man who's never worked at the Delta Clinic before. Come on, I'll give you the ten-cent tour before we open the doors." She started down the hall. "Obviously, this is Reception and Waiting." She waved a hand around them at the tiny space with only six chairs. "Most of the waiting is done outside. We hope to one day find a larger space, but that's not happening anytime soon."

Shay continued on, warming to her subject. The clinic wasn't much to look at, but she was proud of it. Having it had saved her sanity after her marriage and husband died. "The clinic is associated with Jackson Medical Hospital. We get everything including trauma cases. The nurses are from the hospital and rotate in and out by the week. They're a good group. This is a patient-centered clinic and I treat them like family. I expect my staff to do the same. We do have a regular receptionist. Her name is Sheree Boyd. She should be here in a few minutes."

She glanced at Dr. Chapman. He looked around with interest. Shay continued, "We have six exam rooms, three on each side. And this one—" she pointed to the last one on the left "—we use for trauma cases.

"Here's our supply room and drug cabinet. You and I'll be the only ones with keys. The next room is our office. We have to share. Actually, it's more of a room with a table and two chairs. There's also a small bathroom with a shower off it."

"Noted."

She continued down the hall. "The last room's our break room slash storage space or whatever else we need."

He nodded. "Got it."

There was a knock at the back door ahead of her.

"That'll be Sheree." Shay walked to it and looked through the eyehole before opening the door to the woman with dark hair and skin. "Good morning."

"Hey, sweetie. They're already lining up outside." Sheree stopped in midstride and gave the new doctor a long look. "And who do we have here?"

"This is Dr. Matt Chapman. He's our help for the next few weeks."

Dr. Chapman offered his hand. "Nice to meet you."

"You too. I think you're not from around here with that Mister *GQ* look about you."

He shrugged. "I've been living in Los Angeles."

Sheree continued with a grin, "You do have the look of a movie star. I'm glad you're here." She directed a thumb toward Shay. "This girl has been working herself to death. She needs some time for a social life."

And there came the age-old argument between her and Sheree. Why didn't Shay go out more? "Okay, Sheree." Shay gave the words a sharp note. "When you're ready we'll take the first patients." She looked at Dr. Chapman.

His focus remained on her as if she were a virus under a microscope. She swallowed hard. "Your exam rooms are on the left-hand side. If you have any questions just ask."

Matt shook his head. Coming to Lewisville, Mississippi, and working in a small clinic was like stepping into a surreal world he had no idea existed. Where he had been used to a modern glass-and-chrome hospital, he now walked out of a tiny examination room created by plaster walls in a space that had once been a business.

He looked down at the chart of his next patient. Before arriving here he'd seen one or two patients a day as an orthopedic surgeon, and most of that time they had been asleep. He'd now made a complete turnaround in the way he spent his day. Just this morning he'd seen fifteen patients so far. Yep, he had made a drastic change. Not one he'd anticipated but one he had to accept. He'd done the right thing by standing up for a patient even if the repercussions hadn't been what he'd expected.

He glanced toward the waiting room and out the large picture windows along the front of the clinic. He saw a line just as Dr. Lunsford said he would. Apparently, she hadn't been exaggerating about the number of patients the clinic saw.

Over the next few hours, he cared for people who had coughs, an infected toe, a boil—and the list of everyday complaints went on. The sort of issues he'd not seen since medical school. Here he was out of his treatment element as well.

Working at the clinic appeared nothing like the high-pressure, trying-to-get-ahead world he'd just left. He'd have to downshift some to fit in here. It was just as well he wouldn't be staying long. Being used to an adrenaline rush at least once a day, he would soon miss it. At least he had an exciting job waiting for him in Chicago.

But hadn't that fast pace been part of why he had to make a change from a job where he was becoming the bright and shining star to one of starting over? He'd questioned one of the senior surgeons' decisions in the OR and that had been the end of it. In Chicago, he would have his chance again. The surgeon in LA's influence didn't stretch all the way across the country, thank goodness. In Chicago Matt could regain what he'd lost.

He passed Shay Lunsford between exam rooms and she smiled at him. "How's it going?"

"So far so good." She had a nice smile. One that showed in her eyes. It made her go from attractive to pretty. She'd pulled her dark hair up on her head, and it was long enough it fell to her shoulders. Wearing a knit shirt and jeans, she looked more like a college student than a doctor responsible for a bustling clinic. She came up to his chest in height but the authoritative air around her suggested she stood much taller.

"Good to hear. Let me know if you have an issue." She knocked on an exam room door and entered.

As he continued to work through his patient list, his nurse, who had arrived while Shay had been showing him around, kept the rooms on his side of the hall filled.

The next time he passed the doctor he asked, "Is every day like this?"

She grinned, her eyes twinkling as she headed up the hall with the words flowing over her shoulder. "I thought you were used to busy?"

At noon the clinic doors closed for a thirty-minute lunch. Matt followed his nurse to the back room and took a seat at the table. He had to admit he'd worked every bit as hard here as he had in Los Angeles. The cases were just different.

The others had brought their lunches and started unpacking them.

Shay took the only empty seat, the one beside him. She sighed. "You weren't told to bring your lunch?"

He received only the basics when Dr. Warren had called and told Matt that his grandniece could use his help while he waited to start his new position. As his mentor in medical school Matt felt he owed the man. The old doctor had express mailed Matt keys and directions to his boyhood home for Matt to live in while working in Lewisville. "Nope. I thought there might be a restaurant or drive-thru nearby. I can see I misjudged that."

"Don't worry about it. We'll share." Each of the women pushed something from their lunch toward him. Shay offered half of her sandwich.

Sheree chuckled. "We can't have the new doctor going hungry."

Hungry and not wishing to embarrass himself, he accepted the sandwich and bit into it. "I'll return the favor sometime. Maybe order pizza."

"Don't worry about it. We're just glad to have your help. How did it go?" Sheree tore open a package of cheese.

"Pretty good. Nothing I couldn't handle. Thanks to Marie." He nodded at the young dark-eyed nurse who'd assisted him. "I was able to find supplies without looking like I didn't know what was going on."

"This was a good day for you to start on, it's been fairly slow." Shay took a sip from her drink can.

"What do things look like when they get faster?" He took a bite of sandwich. It wasn't his usual lunch fare, but he was glad to have it. He liked to order from a gourmet café.

All the women laughed.

Shay said, "We can have almost twice as many. If we have a major case, then it can cause a backup to deal with."

He nodded. "Good to know."

Sheree pinned him with a look. "So, what brings you to Lewisville?"

He shrugged. "I'm just here to help out for a few weeks. I'm on my way to a position in Chicago."

All the women's attention remained on him.

Matt continued. "I'm an orthopedic surgeon. I'm between jobs for a few weeks and Shay's uncle knew she could use some help. He asked me and I agreed."

"That your Uncle Henry? The one who's the professor up north somewhere?" Sheree asked Shay.

"Yeah. He checks in a couple of times a month. During one of his calls, I told him how busy we were." She turned to him. "I have to admit I'm glad he sent you our direction."

Matt nodded. "Glad I could help." He looked at Sheree. "Dr. Warren was one of my professors at Northwestern."

Sheree's eyes widened. "I get it now. Small world."

As quickly as the group had sat down for lunch, they all cleaned up and returned to work. Shay didn't linger either.

So far Shay had been pleased with how well the fill-in doctor had worked out. She'd had her doubts at first, but she found Matt efficient and intelligent. Even better than those traits, the patients seemed to like him.

She'd also heard no complaints from her staff. He and Sheree had quickly bonded.

The afternoon had been running smoothly until Sheree hurried down the hall toward Shay. "We have an emergency."

Behind Sheree came Mrs. Clayton supporting her husband as he held one of his hands wrapped in a bloody shirt.

"Bring him back here." Shay moved to the door of the trauma room.

The couple had just entered the door when Matt stepped out of an examination room. He glanced at the blood drops on the floor.

"Dr. Chapman, I may need your assistance." Shay followed the couple into the room.

"Sure. Right behind you."

Shay helped Mrs. Clayton to seat her husband on the exam table. "Tell me what happened, Mr. Clayton."

"I was working on the car and got my hand caught in one of the belts. I didn't pull it back fast enough."

In a gentle voice Matt said, "You'll be fine. We'll take good care of you."

Shay glanced at him where he stood beside her. "This is Dr. Chapman. He'll be helping me take care of you."

Mr. Clayton gave Matt a suspicious look before he turned white and his eyes rolled back in his head.

"Lay him down before he passes out," Matt said as he placed a hand on the man's back and lowered him to the table.

"Rachel, we need a blanket here and to treat for shock." Shay pulled out the extension on the table, took the man's feet and laid them across it.

"Dr. Lunsford, do you mind?" Dr. Chapman nodded toward the man's hand. "I have experience here."

"I want Dr. Lunsford."

Shay placed a hand on Mr. Clayton's shoulder. "Dr. Chapman cares for this type of injury more often than I do. Trust me, he can help you."

"Jim, let him do what he knows best." Mrs. Clayton's eyes held tears.

To Dr. Chapman, Shay said, "Go ahead."

With gentle movements, Matt started unwrapping the dirty material covering the hand. He said to no one in particular, "I need a pan, saline. This needs to be cleaned so I can see the damage. Set up for an X-ray."

He had gone too far. "Dr. Chapman, may I speak to you."

"Right now?" His disbelief filled his voice.

"In the hall, please." She stepped outside and to her relief he followed.

The gloves on his hands came off with a pop then the trash can top dropped with a thump after he threw them in. He pulled the door closed behind him with more force than necessary.

Shay faced him. "We're to stop the bleeding and transport. The rest will be handled at the hospital."

Matt gave her a piercing look. "I know what I'm doing. This is my area of expertise. Let me save this man's hand. If he has to wait, he might lose the use of it."

Shay vacillated between agreeing and standing her ground.

"Trust me."

She huffed. "You better be as good as you think you are."

"I won't disappoint you." Without another word he returned to the room. Pulling on gloves again, he finished removing the wrapping and examined the hand.

Rachel had already laid a paper pad on the table beneath Mr. Clayton's hand.

Shay intended to take some control back in her own clinic. To Rachel, Shay said, "Hold the pan under his hand while I pour the sterile water over it."

Matt stood close, watching as if making sure she did it correctly.

Her chest tightened at the sight of the skin peeled back showing severed ligaments and broken bones. She compressed her lips to prevent the hiss from coming out.

Matt spoke to her with complete authority. "You should call the hospital now and tell them to have the ortho and vascular guys standing by. Mr. Clayton will need to go straight to surgery."

"They'll want to make that decision." It wasn't his place or hers to call the shots.

"You need to make them listen. If they don't, they'll have lost precious time. Even a chance to save the use of his hand. He needs to be started on IV antibiotics right away."

Shay glanced at Mrs. Clayton. A tear rolled down the woman's cheek. Matt and Shay didn't need to argue in front of her or their patient. Shay finished emptying the container over the hand. Matt picked up the hand to examine it more closely. He worked with focus and confidence. His were the actions of the practiced surgeon he said he was.

Shay spoke to Mrs. Clayton. "Is Mr. Clayton allergic to any medicines you know of?"

"No," the woman answered.

"I'll take care of the call and get the antibiotic." Shay

exited the room. By the time she returned, Matt and Rachel had their heads together as he continued to clean the hand.

Shay went around to the other side of the table. Matt glanced at her. Her attention went to placing a needle in the man's arm and attaching a bag of glucose and adding the strong, broad-spectrum antibiotic through the fluid.

"I need the largest gauze pads available, a cloth and a large bag of ice."

"I'll take over." Shay took the pan from the nurse.

"When will the ambulance be here?" Matt asked.

"Thirty minutes at best." Her response came out as level as his tone.

"That's an hour round trip. That's not acceptable. One of us will have to meet them."

Her head jerked up. "What?"

His look locked on hers. "The latest studies show surgery done under a three-hour ischemic time have the best success."

She didn't blink. "Then I should go. I know the way."

"Agreed." His attention went to the supplies Rachel had placed on a metal instrument table she'd pulled over beside him. He picked up the gauze.

"I'll do that." Shay took the roll from him. She started wrapping Mr. Clayton's hand from the fingertips down.

"It doesn't need to be too tight." When she finished, Matt said, "We need to pour the water over it." She did so. "Then wrap it in the towel."

She took care of that.

"A plastic bag goes over the hand. Then tape it at the wrist. Rachel, we'll take that bag of ice." Matt placed the hand into the bag of ice.

Shay secured the bag.

"This is the best we can do here." Matt looked around briefly, appearing disappointed.

"I'll get my purse and let the hospital know I'll be meeting the ambulance. We'll take him out the back door. Rachel, please ride with me. Mrs. Clayton, you can meet the ambulance at the hospital."

The nurse nodded.

Matt snapped off his gloves. "I'll see to things here."

Shay had no doubt he would. The mild-mannered guy had turned into superdoctor.

CHAPTER TWO

MATT HEARD SHAY'S voice in the hall. She'd returned. She'd been gone a little over an hour and a half. He hurried into the hall. "How did it go?"

"Fine. I met the ambulance as planned." She walked by him on her way to the office. "It looks like we've a few more patients to see."

Thankfully it was almost closing time and the waiting room had open seats. He'd been busy while she'd been gone. More questions would have to wait. An hour later he'd seen his last patient and joined Shay in the office to tie up loose ends from the day.

When he entered, she stood and walked around her side of the table, resting her butt against the edge. "Close the door, please."

He did as she said. What was going on?

She stepped close to him and bit out, "Don't you ever get high-handed with me again and take over one of my cases."

Matt looked behind him, questioning who she spoke to. "I'm sorry. I don't know what you're talking about."

"The high-handed way you handled Mr. Clayton's case. This is my clinic and we have agreements with the hospital and protocols."

His jaw hardened. Was she like the surgeon he'd dealt with in LA? He sure hoped not. "I did what needed to be done. Weren't you interested in the best care for Mr. Clayton?"

"Of course, I was! I am."

"Then I was the one who needed to take the lead on the case. It was as simple as that."

She pointed a finger at his chest. "Maybe so but that still doesn't give you the right to start ordering me around when we have a tough case."

He looked down at the slim finger pressed against him then into Shay's snapping blue eyes. His fingers gently pushed her hand away. The softness of it registered before his fingers slipped away from hers. "I don't like having people pointing fingers at me physically or figuratively."

Shay's eyes widened. Her jaw jutted out at a determined angle. "And I don't like people countermanding me in *my* clinic. No matter what they think they might know. We discuss things here, not order each other around. I have the final word—always."

Matt had to admire her directness. He couldn't remember the last time someone spoke to him that way. Used to running his operating room, he had a tendency to take control. "Agreed. I'm sorry. I'll do better in the future."

Someone knocked on the door.

Shay stepped back, putting space between them. She pushed at her hair and called, "Come in."

Sheree stuck her head though the opening. "Good work today, you guys. I'm out of here. See you in the morning."

"See you," Shay called.

"Thanks, Sheree." Matt moved around the table and slumped into a chair.

She sat back in the one she'd been in when he came in and studied her tablet.

When he'd seen the clinic, he'd questioned if they would be as up-to-date with technology as he'd been used to, but had soon been given a tablet for keeping up with patient charts. It cut down on the amount of paper pushing he'd be required to do. He wasn't very good at tedious chores. More than one time he'd heard complaints about his inability to keep his charting in order.

Shay started typing, seeming to take no notice of him. He went to work as well. Silence surrounded them except for taps on the screen.

"Matt?"

"Mmm?" He looked at her with a raised brow.

"Is there anything about any of the patients you saw today that I need to know?" She watched him.

"Not that I can think of." Was she being conscientious about her patients or did she question his thoroughness?

"Other than Mr. Clayton's case how did it go for you today?" She crossed her arms and leaned on the table. He liked having her full attention. Jenna, his ex-girlfriend, hadn't been able to give him that even when they had been on a date. Thinking back, she'd spent more time on her phone than she had talking to him. Why hadn't he recognized that? They had been two people caught up in their careers who complemented each other.

"Pretty well. I do have to admit I was busy."

"Yeah. It can get intense around here. Today was about average." She swiped the page on the tablet.

"Then it'll be interesting to see what it's like on a busy day. I did need to ask you what I should do about referring a couple of the patients I saw to a specialist. One needs a general surgeon and another an orthopedist."

"Make a note of their names and I'll check their charts and take care of referrals first thing in the morning."

"I don't think you need to review my work." He pushed the paper he'd written the names on toward her.

"Maybe not, but the patients seen in this clinic are ultimately my responsibility."

Matt's mouth tightened. He generally ran his world. He wasn't used to other doctors or people questioning his decisions. The idea of someone monitoring his work made his skin prickle. He stood. Now he understood how Dr. Walters had felt when he'd questioned his decisions in the operating room, but in that case Matt had been right. Walters had been endangering the patient. In this one, Matt knew he had done the right thing for the patients, not trying to cut corners.

"I'd like to hear how Mr. Clayton's doing. Have you heard anything?"

"No, but I'll call." She pulled out her phone. Seconds later she spoke to the hospital. When she ended the conversation she said to Matt, "He's still in the OR. Otherwise he's doing well."

"That's good to hear. Will you be calling to check in on him later this evening?"

"Of course." She sounded insulted he'd had to ask.

"Would you mind letting me know his status?"

She nodded. "I'll make sure you have an update."

Glad she seemed to have gotten over her anger with him, Matt said, "Great. Let me have your phone and I'll program in my number." His fingers touched hers as she handed him the small device.

She jerked back.

Had it been an overreaction to being touched in general or by him in particular? Matt entered his number and set the phone on the desk. "Why don't we call it a day? I think we've earned it."

She sighed. "It has been an adrenaline-driven one. I have a few notes to make, then I'll be ready to go."

He watched as she double-checked the front door had been locked and checked all the exam rooms on their way to the back door. Shay watched over the simple clinic like it was her baby. What would it be like to have someone care that much about him? His mother had, but his stepfather certainly hadn't. The hospital had sided with the wrong doctor because of Dr. Walters's status. His girlfriend hadn't cared enough about him to move with him even when he'd offered marriage. Such devotion eluded him.

In the parking lot behind the clinic she said, "I'll see you tomorrow."

"Okay."

"By the way, in the morning you can park in the back, knock on the door and I'll let you in."

He stopped on his way to his car. "What time do you usually get here?"

"Around seven. That gives me an hour before opening to take care of supplies, extra charting and referrals. Even a little cleaning sometimes."

"Then I'll see you at seven. I can help out with those." He normally arrived at the hospital at 6:00 a.m. Arriving at seven would feel like sleeping in to him.

"It's not necessary."

"Maybe not, but I'll be here anyway. You can use my help or not. After that lecture this morning you shouldn't be here by yourself."

"I'm used to being here by myself." Opening the door to the car, she looked at him.

"That doesn't sound like a safe plan."

She glanced at him. "Well, up until you no one's even noticed."

"They should have. I'll hang around out in my car, then, if you'd rather I not come in, but I'll still be here at seven. Good evening, Shay." He started toward his car again.

She smiled. "I was glad to have your help today, Matt. The EMTs were impressed with how Mr. Clayton's hand had been secured."

He returned her smile. "You're welcome."

"See you tomorrow." Shay gave him a slight wave and climbed into her family-size sedan.

Matt continued along the side of the building to his navy sports car. He waited until Shay turned into the road before following her into the traffic. He hadn't been sure what to expect at the Delta Clinic. The one thing he was confident about was he hadn't expected the dynamo that was Shay Lunsford.

His drive home was uneventful with the exception of one missed turn. He traveled through well-established neighborhoods past shopping areas into the Jackson University area where Dr. Warren owned a 1950s bungalow he usually rented to students. Thankfully, it had been available for Matt. With white clapboard siding, large shrubbery and a small front porch it looked much like the rest of the houses on the tree-lined street with sidewalks on both sides.

He pulled into the paved drive and climbed out. The older woman who lived next to him stood at the end of her drive talking to another woman about the same age. She waved at him. He gave her a fixed smile and quick wave, then hurried into the house. In the places he'd lived, people rarely paid any attention to the others living around them. For the last ten years he'd lived in transit communities. Neighbors who would be gone in three months to a year wouldn't have been worth the time to meet, even if he'd had the time to meet them."

Gladys—he believed she'd said that was her name— had already been over to introduce herself and had even brought him a pie. Never had he had a neighbor bake for him. She'd totally taken him off guard. She'd done much of the talking and had asked him a number of questions about himself. The type of interest she showed made him a little uncomfortable. He'd hurried her on her way with a thank-you. At first, he'd been unsure about eating anything someone he didn't know had prepared, but one bite of Gladys's apple pie and that concern had flown out the window.

After popping something in the microwave for dinner, he got a drink and settled in front of the TV. Watching television had been a change for him. He'd rarely turned it on prior to coming here. He sank into the recliner, exhausted and grateful that Warren's house included furnishings. In Chicago, Matt would have to hire someone to handle furnishing his apartment. Matt looked around the room with a sigh of acceptance. It was nice to live in a house instead of an apartment, even for a short time.

He'd finished his meal and was reading a medical journal when his phone rang. "Hello."

"Matt, it's Shay."

She had a nice voice. "Hey."

"Is this a bad time?"

"No, no. What's up?" He sat up in the chair.

"I was just calling to tell you that Mr. Clayton is out of the OR and in a room. The doctors believe he's going to get back the full use of his hand. They praised how you took care of it."

"You had a part in it as well."

She paused. "Thanks for pushing. If you hadn't insisted…"

"It was a good day's work for both of us."

"I'm glad you were there." She sounded as if she meant it.

Why did it matter to him so much to have her praise? "I'm glad I could help."

"See you in the morning, Matt." She hung up.

He wished they had talked longer. He would've enjoyed her company even if it was over the phone.

The next morning Shay turned into the parking lot and drove to the back of the building. As Matt had promised he waited in his car. She had to admit it was nice to have someone there when she entered and exited the building. Even though she knew most of the people that lived in the area it still bothered her to go into the clinic alone.

When her husband had been alive and left for his first deployment she hadn't been wild about staying by herself, but she'd learned to deal with it at home and thought she would at the clinic as well.

Shay smiled at Matt as she stepped out of the car. He walked toward her. "Good mornin'."

"Good morning." He offered her a slight lift of his mouth.

She couldn't get over how sensual his lips were. No man had the right to have such a sexy mouth. She'd felt nothing for a man for so long it made her wary of him noticing something so personal. She didn't make a habit of paying attention to a man on that level…but for some reason he drew her. She wanted to know more about him. That was a new sensation. Maybe it was just curiosity because he was a stranger. "Did you get some rest last night?"

"I did. Much-needed rest." He fell into step beside her as they walked to the door.

Shay chuckled. "You didn't find anything exciting to do?"

"Nope. Didn't even go looking for something."

That surprised her. Somehow, she'd gotten the impression he wasn't a homebody type.

The rest of the week continued much the same way. She had to admit she looked forward to finding him waiting for her each morning. It had been a long time since someone had shown that type of concern for her. She missed it. Best of all Matt worked every bit as hard as she did and to her even greater surprise hadn't questioned her authority since the first day.

Friday evening Shay started out of the clinic parking lot when she noticed Matt hadn't started his car yet. She waited, watching in the rearview mirror for him to back out of his parking space. Instead, he stepped out of the car shaking his head.

She reversed her car and rolled down the passenger-side window. "Need a ride?"

Matt shook his head with a look of disgust on his face. He slammed the car door closed. "Yeah, it looks like I do. As skilled as I might be as a doctor, I have zero mechanic skills."

"Can't be good at everything. Come on, I happen to know someone who has great mechanic skills."

He climbed into her passenger seat, making the space feel much smaller. "We'll stop by Ralph's and ask him to come tow it to his place. Ralph's is the local garage in town. He's actually very good."

"Ralph's it is. The car is brand-new. I don't know what could be wrong."

"It's nice. We don't see many of those around here." She drove out of the parking lot. His attention remained on the road as if it made him nervous being a passenger.

"Is your husband or boyfriend going to say anything about you riding around with some man?"

"My husband died three years ago and there's no boyfriend."

"I'm sorry. About your husband, not the boyfriend. That didn't come out right."

Shay giggled. She rather liked Matt being flustered. It was nice to know he could be after seeing him always so sure of himself. "It's okay."

As they reached town, she pulled into the lot of an old gas station. Cars lined the area.

Shay got out of the car. "Ralph should be around here somewhere."

Matt joined her as she strolled through the wide and high roll door. Inside she called, "Ralph?"

"Yeah." The muffled sound came from the back of the building.

She followed it. "Ralph, where are you?"

"Shay, is that you?" came a gruff voice.

Matt shook his head. "Do you know everyone?"

She grinned and shrugged. "Around here? Mostly. That's what happens when you live in the same place all your life." She continued around a car until she could see legs sticking out from under it.

Ralph rolled out on a dolly he lay on and looked up at her. "Shay, girl, how're you doin'?"

"Great, Uncle Ralph."

"Uncle Ralph?" Matt murmured beside her.

Ralph scrambled to his feet, picking up a rag and wiping off his hands. He eyed Matt suspiciously, studying him closely. "And who is this? I hope he's better than that last guy."

"Uncle Ralph! This is Dr. Matt Chapman. Uncle Henry asked him to come help me out for a few weeks while I look for another doctor for the clinic. His car wouldn't start. It's parked at the clinic. Do you think you could go and check it out? Tow it in if you can't get it started."

"Sure thing. It'll be a couple of days before I could get to it if it needs a part."

Matt pulled a face.

Shay turned to him. "Don't worry, I'll pick you up and take you home each day."

Matt crammed his hands in his pockets. "That seems like a lot of trouble. I can just rent a car."

She briefly placed her hand on his arm. "I don't mind giving you a ride. It's the least I can do for a visitor."

"Thanks, I appreciate that. I hate to put you to so much trouble."

Shay smiled at him. "Hey, that's what we do around here. Help friends out."

A baffled look came over Matt's face before he fished around in his pocket for his keys. "I appreciate that."

"Thanks, Uncle Ralph."

"Sure, Shay, girl." He turned to Matt. "You better be nice to Shay. She's a special one."

Matt looked taken aback. "Uh…yeah, sure."

Shay colored pink with mortification. There was nothing like being overprotected. She'd lived through the humiliation of being the topic of conversation when the town had found out about what John had done. Over time it had turned to protecting her. They wouldn't let her be hurt by anyone again.

Back in her car, Shay turned out of the gas station and headed through town.

Matt looked back at the station with a perplexed frown. "What was that all about?"

"I'm sorry about that. It's old history. Nothing to do with you." He glanced at her. But thankfully he changed the subject.

"Where're we going?"

She glanced at him. "I'm taking you home."

His brows rose. "You didn't even ask me where I live."

Shay smirked. "I've been to Uncle Henry's hundreds of times."

"I forget you are family."

"How did the two of you become such good friends?" She shifted lanes and headed toward the university.

"I think he recognized someone eager to learn who needed a father figure."

What an odd statement. She looked at his profile for a moment before she had to turn her attention back to driving. Not sure how to respond, she said, "Uncle Henry is a nice guy."

"He made a real difference in my life. Still does."

Shay glanced at him. "How do you find living in Jackson?"

"I like it. I can get around much quicker than I'm used to. Or at least I could until my car wouldn't run. Less traffic I have to admit is nice. Even the pace at the clinic is slower, even though we stay busy. There's a different feel."

"It's nice to know we have some charms." She grinned.

"Charms. That's a nice way of putting it. I've lived all my life in one large city or another. I've never thought of them as having charms."

"Every place has good attributes and bad, I'd guess." She made a left turn.

He looked at her. "And what would you say Lewisville's attributes are?"

"Love and acceptance." She'd had them, then questioned if they were gone, to soon learn they had never left.

"That's nice." A sadness filled his voice.

Her eyes met his. Had he not had love and acceptance in his life? "I'll say that living in the same place from childhood means that people know more about you than you might want them to."

"I'm not sure I'd like that. It makes me uncomfortable to know people know where I live without me even telling them. Do you mind so many knowing your business?"

She'd lived the last few years feeling humiliated as the center of gossip. It wasn't until she'd started devoting her time and energy to building a clinic in the Lewisville area that she'd started hearing less about her past and more about the good she was doing. "It shows that the townsfolk of Lewisville care about each other."

"You didn't exactly answer the question and I won't push. Even with the good and bad it's nice to know someone cares."

Had he felt unwanted in some place by someone?

A week later Matt looked out the car window as Shay made a right turn onto his street.

"Tell me, have a Ms. Gladys and Ms. Adriana been fighting over you?" she asked.

He'd had a few women aggressively come after him,

but his seventy-something neighbors had taken it to a whole new level.

"I wouldn't exactly call it fighting over me, but I'll say I've got a freezer full of casseroles."

Shay chuckled. He liked the sound. "I'm not surprised. There's always been competition between the two of them. I think they've been competing for the same boys since they were in elementary school. Uncle Henry eats it up when he's home. Says it's good for a bachelor's soul to still have women after him."

"And here I was thinking I was special." He'd not always felt that way. Most of his life he'd worried if he had been good enough. Apparently, Jenna hadn't thought so. His stepfather had made him feel the same.

While Shay drove down the street, he studied all the well-kept yards. All of them looked neat and tidy except for his. He winced. He never before felt a need to keep up with his neighbors. But at this moment, shame filled him. Hell, he hadn't even known any of them before coming to Jackson.

"Apparently, we've been keeping you so busy you can't get your grass cut."

His chin lowered to his chest. "Something like that. In my defense it has been cut once since I moved in, but I didn't do it. I just came home, and it was done. No one left me a note or bill."

Shay laughed. "It's our way of saying welcome and also to remind you to take care of your yard."

"Sort of like a backhanded compliment."

"Something like that." She pulled into his drive. "Do you not have a lawnmower?"

He gave her a chagrined look, not meeting her eyes.

"It's more like I've never mowed grass before. I don't know anything about a lawnmower."

She brought the car to a jerking stop and turned to look at him with her mouth open. "You've never mowed a yard?"

He winced. "I'm not sure whether I should be ashamed or glad, but no, I haven't."

Her eyes were wide with pure disbelief. "How's that possible?"

Both his brows rose. "If you pay to have it done, or don't have a yard."

"You've really lived a sheltered life." Shay shook her head. "I guess if you lived in an apartment all your life you could have never mowed grass, or if you were rich enough to pay someone. Which are you?"

"Mostly living in an apartment."

"Around here, we have to cut grass." She pulled farther up in the drive. "Would you like me to show you what to do?"

"I would be grateful. I think my neighbors would be as well." He should have been embarrassed, but for some reason he liked the idea of Shay showing him such a skill.

"Today, Dr. Chapman, you'll learn something new. You'll have an experience to talk about when you leave Lewisville." Pride and humor filled her words.

He studied her pert nose and sparkling eyes. Matt suspected he'd remember more than how to mow grass when he got to Chicago. "I guess I will."

She turned off the engine. "Where's the mower?"

"I saw one in the shed." He climbed out of the car.

Shay followed him to a small building behind the house. He opened the door and pulled out the push mower. She stepped up beside him like he had done during the emergency. Here she had far more confidence than he did.

"Pay close attention," she instructed. "I don't want you to miss anything, Doctor."

He moved in closer. "Shay, you're enjoying this far too much. I do have a fragile ego."

"I doubt that. I've just never known someone who has never mowed grass, not even once."

"I can't be that rare." His ego in some areas could be weaker than he might let on.

"Okay, now I may be making fun of you." A silly grin covered her mouth.

I'd like to kiss that grin. Wow. Those thoughts were better left alone. "Thank you for at least seeing it my way." He shoved his hands in his pockets.

Her look turned serious. "Let me start over. Would you like me to show you how to start the mower and how to use it?"

He looked around at the calf-high grass then at the other houses' yards. "Please. I think Ms. Gladys and Ms. Adriana would appreciate it if I learned."

Shay smiled before she turned back to the machine. "Okay, the first thing we need to do is check to see if there's enough oil. You never want to run the engine without there being enough oil in it." She opened a little top and looked inside before closing it.

"Oil. Got it."

"Now we need to see if there's enough gas." Shay turned another top and checked inside. "There's plenty of gas." She looked around in the shed and pointed. "There's a can if you need more gas."

He cocked his head locating the red plastic can. "Okay."

"The next step is to start it. This can be tricky if it

hasn't run in a while. Pump this." She pushed a button in three times. "This is the choke. Now pull this bar up and hold it. Then pull the cord." She reached over.

He stopped her and pulled the cord. The machine coughed. Matt let the cord go back in and pulled again. The mower roared to life. He stepped close to her and said into her ear, "I think I can take it from here."

Shay stiffened.

He held the bar down. Shay stepped away from him sweeping an arm out, indicating for him to go to it. He made one pass around the yard and came back to her.

As the mower rattled to a stop, he grinned. "Nothing to it."

"Says the man who didn't mow his grass 'cause he didn't know anything about a lawnmower."

He nodded. "Point taken."

"I think you've got it from here, so I'd better go." She glanced at the house next door where the curtain had been pulled back and Ms. Gladys watched them. "You might get a cake out of this."

He gave the older woman a wave and the curtain dropped back. "I guess I'll be the talk of the street because you had to show me how to start the mower."

She placed a hand on his forearm. "You'll survive. You've already become a hero around here anyway."

"How's that?" Matt met her gaze.

"The word gets out. By now everyone knows of your work at the clinic. I bet they can all tell you about what happened with Mr. Clayton."

His eyes narrowed. "How would they know that?"

"One of Ms. Gladys's nephews works at the hospital. I'm sure one of the nurses has reported back."

"Oh." He glanced toward Ms. Gladys's again. "Anyway, thanks for the lawnmower instructions and not making more fun of me than you did. I've rarely felt so inept in my life, but I did about the mower. I'm also indebted to you for taxiing me around. Hopefully your uncle Ralph will have my car done next week."

She smiled. "Not a problem. I'm glad I could help. I hope your self-esteem is still intact."

"It has been shaken but I think I will recover."

Shay grinned. "If you get really good at mowing and you like doing it you can always cut Ms. Gladys's and Ms. Adriana's yards as well as the other neighbors'. They'll love you forever. That'll help rebuild your ego."

After the beating it had taken over the years, he could use some of that admiration. What would it be like to have a close relationship with his neighbors? With Shay?

CHAPTER THREE

On Thursday afternoon of the next week, Shay stepped out of the examination room of the clinic in search of Matt. She could use his expertise with this case. Looking one way then the other, she spotted him at the reception desk talking to Sheree.

He must have sensed her need because he looked in her direction. As she started toward him his forehead wrinkled and his appearance darkened with concern. He spoke to Sheree and walked toward Shay. "What's wrong?"

"I'd like to get your opinion on a patient."

His shoulders eased. "Sure. What's the issue?"

"Joey is eight. He had a broken arm last year. Now he's complaining of aches and pains. I thought with your background you might have some ideas." Shay sure hoped so. She was out of them.

Matt's voice lowered. "Have you considered abuse?"

Shay shook her head. "I've known his mother, Beth, all my life. She would never abuse him."

"What about the father?"

Shay stiffened. "Him either. I don't want to go down that road until I have exhausted all other ideas. Something else has to be going on."

Matt gave her a firm look. "I have to warn you I will do what has to be done if I find out differently."

"You won't, but if abuse turns out to be the issue, I'll handle it. I know the law and my duty."

"Okay then, let's see the patient." He stepped back so she could open the door to the examination room.

Shay entered and Matt joined her, closing the door behind them.

"Beth, this is Dr. Chapman. He's an orthopedic surgeon."

Shay's petite blond friend quickly stood. "Surgeon? Joey doesn't need surgery, does he?"

Stepping forward, Shay laid a hand on Beth's arm. "No, Dr. Chapman's here helping me. He just happens to be an orthopedic doctor so I thought he might have some ideas about what's causing Joey's problem. There's nothing to worry about."

Matt moved to Joey, who sat on the examination table. "Hello, Joey. I'm Dr. Chapman and I'd like to have a look at you, would that be okay?"

The eyes of the boy with the white-blond hair widened as he gripped the edge of the table. He looked at his mother. Joey's fearful look eased as his mother sat down in the chair. "I guess so."

Shay watched as Matt bent his long frame until he came to eye level with the boy. "Can you show me where it hurts?"

"All over." The boy pointed to his thighs and arms.

"Not in any one spot?" Matt's voice remained even while his manner remained intent.

Joey shook his head.

"Good," Matt said with a nod. "I need to touch you. Will that be all right?"

Again, Joey nodded.

Matt proceeded to run his hand over the boy's legs from his feet upward. "I hear you broke your arm. What were you doing when that happened?"

"I fell while I was playing a baseball game."

Matt glanced back at Shay as if to say maybe she was right about there not being any abuse.

He continued to run his hand confidently over the boy's limbs. "What position do you play?"

"Shortstop," Joey said proudly.

"That's an important position."

Shay couldn't help but admire how Matt put the boy at ease. She'd overheard other patients when they were leaving the clinic talking about how much they had liked Matt. She could see why. He had a way with people.

"Joey, do you mind if we take some X-rays of your arms and legs? I know you must've had them done when you broke your arm. They don't hurt. The nurse will take you down the hall for the pictures while I talk to your mom for a minute."

Joey looked at his mother. She nodded and he slid off the exam table. He winced when his feet touched the floor.

Shay stepped to the door and opened it. Her nurse waited there. "Lucy, will you take Joey for X-rays of his legs and arms."

As they walked down the hall, Shay returned to Matt and Beth. The two women's attention focused on Matt. He leaned his hip against the examination table and faced them. Shay swallowed, unsure she'd like what he had to say.

"I think Joey has what is called fibrous dysplasia. It's a rare disorder."

"Oh, my." Beth's hand covered her mouth.

Shay placed a hand on her friend's shoulder. Shay looked at Matt. "I thought it might be."

He gave her a wry smile and spoke to Beth. "We'll be able to confirm it with the X-rays. It can't be cured, but it can be controlled. Unfortunately, it'll require some surgery. Shay can give you the name of a doctor here in Jackson who can oversee Joey's case. Or if you wish, I'll be glad to—but you'd have to travel to Chicago."

Beth took a deep breath. "What do we need to do now?"

Shay stepped away from her. "Beth, why don't you take Joey out for an ice cream on me and I'll let you know what the X-rays show. You and Luke can talk about this. I can get names together for who to see. I'll see that Joey has the best care he can receive."

Matt stood. "And I'll do all I can to help as well."

Shay looked at him and mouthed *thank you.*

He nodded. "Then I'll go."

Shay watched him quietly slip out the door. She hated giving bad news but somehow it had been easier with Matt's support.

That evening, Matt rode home with Shay with a heavy heart.

"I checked the X-rays and I'm confident Joey has fibrous dysplasia. His bones look like ground glass. A sure sign. Let me know how I can help."

Shay looked over at him. "I'm just glad you were here to confirm what I suspected. You were really great with Joey. Especially for a surgeon."

A wrinkle formed on his forehead. "What exactly does that mean?"

"Surgeons aren't known for having great bedside manners since most of their patients are asleep."

"I think I've been offended. I have to meet with them before and after surgery. They're awake then. So, I do have some skills."

Shay grinned. "Touchy, are you?"

In that area of his life, he was. He'd worked so hard to make his stepfather proud of him and never felt he hit the mark. It was nice to hear he had done well in Shay's eyes. "Maybe, a little bit. I've not always been great with people."

"That's hard to believe. I've heard nothing but good things about your interactions with patients."

"That's good to know. It doesn't come natural." He'd too often let his feelings toward his stepfather bleed over into his interactions with people, fearing they would treat him the same as his stepfather did. Jenna had more than once accused him of closing himself off. Maybe he did.

Shay's phone rang. She punched her hands-free button and spoke into the speaker. "Hello."

"Hey, Shay. It's Billy. I'm not gonna be able to play in the game Sunday. Addison called to tell us she's on her way to the hospital to have the baby."

"Oh, wow. I understand, Billy. Give Addison my best. Be sure to send pictures. Don't worry about the game." She gave Matt a pointed look with a gleam in her eyes. "I'll find someone to replace you."

What were they talking about? Shay's look and her tone of voice didn't bode well for him. He'd seen it in other women's eyes when they wanted something.

With a slight lift to her lips Shay said, "I think I already found a replacement. You go on and give that new grandbaby a kiss from me."

"Thanks, Shay. I hate to miss one of the highlights of the year."

"There's always next year. Take care, Billy." Shay punched the button ending the conversation.

Shay didn't immediately say anything to him. The conversation hung between them. She was good, he'd give her that. His curiosity finally got the better of him. "What was that about?"

"I've got to find a replacement for Billy on my softball team." She continued to focus on the road.

"You play softball?" Matt shouldn't have been surprised, but she'd never mentioned it.

"Only once a year."

Matt turned so he could better see her. "That's interesting. Why once a year?"

"I organize a community game to raise money for the clinic. We play Sunday afternoon at two. Now we're short a team member. It'll be pretty hard for my team to win if I don't have enough players." She glanced at him.

"Why haven't you mentioned this game before?"

Shay shrugged. "I don't know. I figured you wouldn't be interested."

Her tone made him feel guilty. Of what he wasn't sure. He felt he should defend himself.

"Would you help me out and take Billy's place? Please."

His chin dropped and he narrowed his eyes. "Are you begging?"

"It's something I don't like to do, but in this case I'm desperate." Her tone sounded serious, but she grinned.

"*Desperate.* Interesting word." Matt pursed his lips and nodded. He had started to enjoy this. "So, I'm better than nothing."

"That's not exactly what I was saying."

He put a hurt tone in his voice. "Sure sounded like that to me."

She sighed. "Come on, Matt, will you help me out?"

He chuckled. "I'll do it."

A bright smile covered her face. "Great. Thank you so much. Have you ever played softball?"

Her obvious jab made him glad he'd agreed. "A couple of times, but I'm much better at baseball."

"Why am I not surprised? I think you'll have a good time."

He'd started to think he might enjoy anything he shared with Shay.

"I'll pick you up around one o'clock unless you'd like to go to church with me. We've a covered dish meal afterward, then we'll go to the ballpark for the game."

Overwhelmed, he wasn't sure he should sign on for all of that. "I don't know."

"Come on, Matt, live dangerously. You might be surprised." She grinned. "You afraid?"

He'd take her challenge. "Okay. What time should I be ready?"

"I'll pick you up at ten thirty."

As Shay drove away from his house Matt questioned if he was wading in too far. He liked being a part of this slower pace of life, but he shouldn't get used to it. Or being around the intriguing and full-of-surprises Shay.

Shay shifted closer to Matt to give Mr. and Mrs. Griffin room to join them on the church pew on Sunday morning. Having to sit pressed against Matt hadn't been in her plans. The church buzzed with talk of him attending with her. Maybe she'd gone too far by inviting him. Gossip had been what she'd been avoiding for the last few years. Not that she'd been able to after letting it be known that John had been planning to divorce her. Bringing a man to church with her would only start the tongues going again.

The side of Matt's solid, warm body pressed against her made her want to forget the fact that they were the topic of the day. She should have known better. It had been a long time since she'd been so close to a man. She glanced at Matt. He acted unaffected.

Grateful the service had begun and for having to stand to sing, which gave her space away from Matt, the distance didn't last long when he shifted to look over her shoulder to see the hymnal. As disconcerting as she found being near him there was something about it she found desirable, like having someone special in her life. A man who stood strong beside her.

Now her thoughts had turned to those of a sad widow woman desperate for attention, interested in the first handsome man who came along. He hadn't even shown any real interest in her and here she sat daydreaming of would-haves and could-haves.

Even if he was interested, what could they have but a fling? Matt had no plans to stay in Lewisville. His destiny was Chicago. She never planned to move. This was her home, where she belonged. But how many times would someone like Matt come along? For once in a long while she felt alive again.

She had no idea of what the sermon was about. Her head remained full of Matt and what-ifs. She moved as far as she could away from him, but when she did, he swallowed up the space with his leg coming to rest against hers once more. He appeared to be contently listening with no idea of the conflict he created in her. Not soon enough for her the service came to a close.

Matt let her step out into the aisle in front of him when the service was over. They were immediately stopped by Mrs. Lyles.

"Shay, I haven't met your visitor." The woman who had taught Shay in grade school studied Matt.

"Mrs. Lyles, this is Dr. Matt Chapman. He's helping me at the clinic for a few weeks and playing in the softball game. Matt, this is Mrs. Lyles."

Matt gave the woman a warm smile. "It's nice to meet you."

"And you too." Mrs. Lyles smiled in return. "You know Shay is very special to us."

He looked at Shay with a raised brow then turned back to the woman. "I'm figuring that out."

Three more women came up behind Mrs. Lyles.

"We want to meet this handsome man," Mrs. Smith said.

"Yes. Is this the doctor we've been hearing all about?" another in the group asked.

Shay introduced the women to Matt, who suffered through the introductions with a polite smile on his lips, before they were interrupted by the pastor who introduced himself and engaged Matt in conversation.

Knowing she'd had enough of the inquisition and that Matt no doubt wanted to run, Shay took his arm at the first break they got and headed for the front door. She led him down the steps, not stopping until they were alone under a large oak tree. "I'm sorry about that."

"I haven't been to church in years," he said, sounding breathless and relieved. "I'd forgotten what it was like to be the new guy."

She chuckled. "It's a weekly occurrence without fail here. Sorry about the horde wanting to meet you."

"No problem. I guess it's better than no one noticing."

"I wouldn't know, but I think I might like experiencing that sometime." She looked around at people still mingling in front of the church.

"Are they always so…um…protective of you?"

"I'm sorry if they pried." It would be a long time before she brought another man to church with her. Even for an innocent reason.

"Hey, we're good. I think it's nice that you're so loved and appreciated. Nowhere have I lived that I've had that.'

At one time she wouldn't have seen the close attention as welcome. She'd felt like a disappointment to them for so long. "Have you recovered enough to go under the microscope again?"

He rolled his shoulders. "I think I can handle it."

She grinned and tugged on his arm. "Then let's go get something to eat. I promise the food will be worth the pain."

They walked around the side of the white shiplap building with the high steeple.

Matt stopped. "Wow. This is amazing. I've heard of people doing this, but I've never seen anything like it."

Shay looked at the long tables set up end to end underneath the large open pole shed under the hundred-year-old oaks. Ladies worked like ants as they arranged food on one table while others brought it out from the back of the church. Other church members circled around waiting for them to finish their chores. More tables were covered in thin plastic tablecloths and had folding chairs beneath them waiting for hungry people who were already lining up to fill their plates.

Shay watched Matt. His eyes were wide and bright in anticipation. "Yeah, it's almost like you can hear the tables groaning in pain."

"I've never seen so much food in one place. And I've been to a number of fancy banquets." His awe hung in the air.

He'd just confirmed they were from two different worlds. The nicest event she'd attended had been her own wedding reception held inside the church. "All I can say is welcome to the South. Where we do believe in eating."

They moved over to where the line had formed and took their places. People continued to come up to speak to her, but they were really interested in Matt.

He whispered in her ear, "Does every new person in town get this kind of treatment?"

"They're just curious." She handed him a plate and grinned. "Enjoy filling it up."

Shay went down one side of the table while Matt moved down the other. She glanced over to see the food piling up on his plate and smiled.

When he joined her at the end of the table, he looked at his plate. "I have no idea where I think I'm planning to put all this."

She chuckled. "You afraid your eyes are bigger than your stomach, Doc?"

"Yeah."

"And to think you haven't even seen the desserts yet."

He looked around as if searching for that table. "And sweets are my weakness."

"Come on, let's find you a place to sit down so you can get started on all that." Shay looked out over the sea of people. Her mom waved and pointed to two empty chairs across from her and Shay's father.

"Brace yourself, you're going to be eating with my parents."

He hesitated a moment. "I look forward to meeting them. Will they ask a lot of questions about why I'm with you?"

"Maybe. But I'll handle them."

He met her gaze. "I can take care of myself, Shay."

"Okay. Just don't say I didn't warn you."

They took their seats. Before she had a chance, Matt smiled at her parents and introduced himself. He skirted her mother's questions by digging into the food and making sounds as if he had found nirvana. Shay couldn't help but laugh.

"This has to be the best potato salad I've ever eaten. And this chicken—" he held up a chicken leg "—is so crispy."

"The potato salad is mine," her mother said. "I'm glad you like it. What did you bring, Shay?"

"I made my lemon ice box pie."

"Matt, you'll have to try a piece. Shay makes the best pies."

He looked at Shay as if she'd been keeping something valuable hidden from him. "I didn't know that. Is that what you handed the lady as we were going into the church?"

Shay nodded.

After that he started asking her mother and father about them and Lewisville, along with the Jackson area. He seemed interested in their remarks.

"Shay, you need to bring Matt to dinner one night. Let him have a good home-cooked meal," her mother suggested.

"Thanks. That sounds nice," Matt responded.

Shay wasn't sure how she felt about that. That sounded as if Matt might be getting too involved in her life. She didn't want to become overly attached to him.

Together they went to the dessert table. Matt filled his plate, making sure he took a large slice of the pie she'd prepared.

Back at their seats, he raised a fork full of the pie. "This is wonderful. Ms. Gladys will have to step up her game."

Shay couldn't deny the pleasure that filled her at Matt's praise. John had never said anything kind about her cooking or anything else for that matter. In hindsight she could see where he'd been far more interested in himself.

With their plates cleared away, Shay said, "We need to be getting to the ballpark."

They said their goodbyes to her parents and started toward the car. Shay said, "We'll change here. It's much nicer than in the ballfield restrooms."

When they arrived at the ballpark one of her team members was already busy handing out new team T-shirts. She grabbed hers and Matt's. As soon as he had his, he stripped out of the shirt he wore. Her mouth went dry as she stared at his toned chest before it disappeared behind the T-shirt.

"Shay, aren't you going to change your T-shirt?" Matt stuffed his shirt into his bag.

She blinked. "Yeah…uh… I'll run over to the restroom."

As she walked across the parking lot, she saw Matt on the field warming up with the other players. He looked supersexy in the T-shirt just tight enough for her to make out the valleys and dips of his chest. His sports shorts highlighted a nicely rounded butt while allowing her glimpses of thick muscled thighs and calves down to sports shoes. He'd pulled on a ball cap.

This had to stop. She refocused and headed for the field. As she joined the others tossing the ball, she called to Matt, "Hey, where'd you get the glove?"

"I found it out in the shed, which seems it has a little bit of everything in it." With a smile on his face, he pitched the ball to her.

She caught it. Her heart fluttered when he grinned at her.

CHAPTER FOUR

MATT HAD MISSED THIS. He threw the ball to second base from left field.

Before his mother remarried, he'd been on a baseball team. After that his stepfather had said that Matt playing ball was a waste of time and money. That had been the end of his ball career.

He'd liked being part of a team, the camaraderie. Most of his childhood, he'd been on the outside of the family. His stepfather had made Matt feel as if he wasn't as important to him as his own son and daughter. In college, medical school and afterward, Matt had made a point not to get too close to anyone. Except Dr. Warren who had been his mentor and friend, but even from him Matt had held his relationship with his family back. As good as Dr. Warren was to him their relationship still remained professional.

In an odd way Matt felt more a part of a community today than he ever had. He never thought he had time for this type of activity before. He had always been studying or putting in overtime at the hospital to get ahead. Where had that gotten him when it had been his words against a senior doctor's? Without a job and starting over.

Maybe when he got to Chicago he'd seek out a place

to play some ball. Yeah, like he'd have time for that. He had a whole new learning curve ahead of him.

Shay pulled their team into a circle to give them a pep talk. "I want you to play fair and have a good time." She looked around the group and grinned. "But I want us to beat these guys. We can't go home again in defeat this year. Everyone in on it?"

Those in the group whooped and hollered. Matt wasn't shocked she was such a competitor. He'd seen some of that character at the clinic. He liked that about her.

She stuck her hand out and the other men and women put theirs on top of hers. Matt joined them. "On three, say win. One, two, three."

Everyone raised their hands and shouted before they trotted out onto the field.

Matt took his position in left field while Shay went to center field.

"You okay over there?" Shay called.

"Yeah."

She grinned. "Good. Thanks for helping us out."

"You're welcome."

Matt hoped his very rusty skills didn't fail him. He survived the top of the first inning, and they went in to bat. That part of the game became problematic for him when Shay stepped into the batter's box. He watched her hips sway as she adjusted to get a good foot position. He swallowed. He shouldn't notice her that way. They were colleagues. The only problem was the longer he stayed around Shay the more difficult it became to ignore her appeal.

At the bottom of the fifth inning with their team down by one run, his turn to bat came up with bases loaded.

The team called encouragement as he stepped up to the batter's box.

Above all the noise he heard Shay's voice yelling, "You've got this, Matt."

He wasn't so sure about that, but he wanted to make her proud. Looking around the bases, then over his shoulder at the crowd and then at his teammates and Shay in particular, he settled his nerves by swinging a few times. Not since his solo surgery had he been this nervous.

The first throw he let go over the plate.

"Strike," the umpire called.

Great. At this rate he'd humiliate himself. If he just managed a hit the game would be tied or maybe they'd go ahead.

This time the throw went wide.

"Come on, Matt. You've got this." Shay's voice stood out among the others.

He swung at the next ball. With the pop of the bat against the ball, he ran for first base. The ball hit just behind second base and rolled toward the outfield. As the players scrambled, Matt ran for second base.

Cheers went up. He stopped and watched Shay jumping up and down just outside the dugout. Their team was up by two. Gorgeous in her excitement, she jerked her cap off. Her hair flew around her face. Her shirt flipped up, revealing a tanned and fit-looking swath of skin.

Shifting his focus back to home plate and the next batter, he waited for the man to make a hit. He did and Matt ran, glad for all those regular runs he made. When he crossed home plate, Shay waited for him. Her arms circled his neck as his arms wrapped her waist.

Wiggling against him in her joy, she said into his ear, "You're our secret weapon."

The other team members joined in the celebration.

In that moment his chest swelled. It felt good being a part of something outside of the operating room. He'd known a part had been missing in his life but had no idea what. Was it possible to have this feeling more often?

By the bottom of the seventh inning, they were still holding the lead. The best player on their team, he'd soon learned, was up to bat. The pitcher threw the ball. Their man gave the ball a solid shot and it became a line-drive at the pitcher.

Seconds later the ball hit the pitcher and he stumbled forward, landing on his face.

At a run, Shay followed Matt out of the dugout. She yelled over her shoulder, "Dad, call 911 and get my bag out of my car."

Matt slid to his knees beside the man. Before he could get words out Shay joined him. Together they rolled Gil onto his back and pulled his shirt up out of the way. A discolored spot the size of a softball showed over his heart.

"Gil, it's Shay. Gil." She shook him. The man didn't answer. His lips had turned blue.

Matt snapped, "He's in commotio cordis. The ball hit him just in the right place at the right time. We have to start CPR." Matt placed one hand over the other, beginning chest compressions.

"Someone get the AED machine," Shay shouted to the crowd. She took her position at Gil's head. Leaning his head back, she checked his mouth for any obstructions. Inhaling deeply, she pinched off Gil's nose and sealed her mouth around his and breathed into him until his chest rose.

Matt continued his efforts. Not soon enough for her the

crowd parted and the portable AED machine in a lime-green box was placed on the ground beside her.

One of the EMTs who had been playing for the other team joined Shay and Matt, but on the opposite side of Gil. With quick, sure hands, he opened the box and placed the sticky pads on Gil's chest.

She and Matt moved away from Gil as the machine beeped and the electric shock went into his body. Shay picked up Gil's wrist and took his pulse. "Nothing."

The EMT reset the machine.

Her father set her bag beside her. She opened it and pulled out her stethoscope.

Gil's body jumped again at the shock.

Matt picked up his wrist this time.

With the ends of the stethoscope in her ears, she placed the bell over Gil's heart. Was that a flutter? She slid the bell to the left. Yes! She looked at Matt for confirmation. His face filled with concentration and eased as a soft smile came to his lips. He nodded.

She looked around the crowd. "We've got a beat. Does anyone know how much longer on the ambulance?"

"In ten minutes," someone called.

She looked at Matt. "We have to prevent shock. We need a blanket here and something to put under his feet."

A sports bag was passed their way. Matt took it and placed it under Gil's feet. A picnic blanket appeared, and he pulled it over Gil.

Shay continued to listen to Gil's heartbeat. Thankfully it had grown stronger. They closely monitored Gil's vitals until the ambulance EMTs took over.

She and Matt saw Gil settled in the ambulance then walked over to join the crowd still lingering near the field.

"Way to go." A number of people patted them on their backs.

Matt looked as humble as she felt.

"I think we've both had enough excitement for the day. Are you ready to head home?" she asked Matt.

"Sure."

They picked up their belongings and started for the car.

Less than an hour later, Shay drove up Matt's drive.

He turned to her. "I have to say that was one of the nicest and most interesting days I've spent in a long time. Thanks for inviting me."

Shay nodded. "It was a good day. I could have done without Gil getting hurt but…"

"Will you let me know how he's doing when you hear?"

"I will."

Matt opened the door. "Thanks again. The day was one to remember."

He stood in the drive and watched as Shay drove away. He'd never met someone so completely dedicated to her work and her community. Shay gave them her all. The more he got to know her, the more he wanted to know about her. Where he'd once thought her ordinary, now he recognized her beauty inside and out. Her love hung in her voice when she talked about any of her patients. She considered them all equally important. What would it be like to live under Shay's umbrella of care?

Later that evening the phone rang. Matt expected it would be Shay letting him know about Gil, but instead it was his mom.

"Hey, sweetheart. I haven't heard from you in a few weeks and wanted to see how you're doing."

He hadn't wanted to tell her and his stepfather that he'd had to leave LA until he'd settled into his new position. He didn't want them to worry about him—or worse, be disappointed he left his job. It was important they were proud of him. "I'm fine, Mom."

"That's good to hear. How's Jenna? We'd love to meet her sometime."

His lips tightened into a line. He'd planned to marry Jenna and hadn't even introduced her to his mother. What had he been thinking? Jenna deserved better and certainly his parents had. "We broke up."

"Oh, sweetheart, what happened?" Her disappointment and concern sounded clear in her voice. His mother wanted him to have someone who loved him, to share his life with. She felt he worked too hard and didn't give enough attention to finding the right person to settle down with. Maybe that was why he'd misread Jenna.

"I decided to move to Chicago, and she didn't want to come with me."

"You're moving to Chicago? When did you decide to do that?" His mother sounded perplexed, concerned and disappointed. "Why am I just hearing about this now?"

A tinge of guilt pricked him. Was he unfair to his mother just because he didn't want to look bad in the eyes of his stepfather? He feared it was true. For years he'd worked to make the man proud. "I would've when I got there."

"You're not there now? Where are you? Matt, why do you insist on treating me, us, as if we don't care about you? As if you don't have family who love you?"

It had started when he hadn't felt like he measured

up to the standards his stepfather set. He wanted to. Just once he'd like for his stepfather to say Matt had done well. "I'm in Jackson, Mississippi. I'm staying in Henry Warren's place and working in a clinic until it's time to go to Chicago."

His mother sighed heavily. "Will you tell me what happened in LA?"

"I reported another surgeon for a decision that could have killed the patient. He had more clout than me. I saw the writing on the wall and left before I was fired. The upside is I have a good position in Chicago waiting for me." Matt didn't even want to think about what his stepfather would say when he heard the explanation. He would probably think Matt should have stayed and fought for his job.

"You'll be closer to us." Excitement filled her voice. "We'll be able to see you more often. Will you come see us soon? It's been over a year since you've been home. Your brother and sister ask about you every time they call."

Every time they spoke his mother begged him to come home. He always put her off. How could he face them after telling her that story? After he gave it some time, then maybe. "I'll see about coming before I start work in Chicago."

"I'd like that." The expectant note in his mother's voice made him feel only guiltier.

"I have to go, Mom. I'll call you soon."

"I love you, Matt."

"I love you too. Bye."

Matt looked at the phone. He hated hurting his mother, but he couldn't change the years of feeling inadequate. In truth, he'd worked so many long hours for so many years he'd really had a good excuse not to visit more often. But now… He just didn't want to face them until he had his act together once more. He would go to Chicago, settle in and feel better about what happened in LA before visiting with his family. Then there might be a chance he could handle it.

He envied what he'd seen between Shay and her parents. Shay and the people she knew. Could he find that?

Moments later his phone beeped. He had an incoming text. Shay.

Gil is stable. They are keeping him overnight to be careful. Thanks for your help saving his life.

He typed back, We made a good team.
Shay returned with, We did. Good night.

Why did the tension in him ease just by receiving a text from Shay? She had a way about her that just made him feel better about himself. He wanted more of that in his life.

Midafternoon Monday, he received a call from Ralph saying his car had been fixed.

As he and Shay walked out to her car that evening, he said, "My car's ready. Do you mind dropping me off at Ralph's?"

"Sure, I'll be glad to."

He slid into the passenger seat. "I'll finally be out of your hair and you can spend less time being a taxi driver."

"I haven't minded."

"I've appreciated it." Now that he'd have his car back, he'd miss their time alone before and after work. He enjoyed their talk of anticipating the day and sharing their day after work. It had been just their time.

He hopped out of the car when they arrived at the garage. "See you in the morning." Before he could close the door, he asked, "I'd like to take you to dinner Friday night to say thank you for all your help."

Her mouth dropped open. Had he surprised her? "Uh...no thanks are necessary."

"Come on, Shay. I get tired of eating alone even when the casseroles are good."

Both her hands gripped the steering wheel and she looked out the front window. "I don't date."

"As in me or in general?" He watched her.

"I'd say both."

He leaned his head farther into the car. "Could we maybe make it a business dinner between colleagues? Not call it a date, if it bothers you that much."

Her gaze returned to him. "I haven't been out with a man since I got married."

"How long ago was that?"

"Six years," she said quietly.

His forehead wrinkled while disbelief rang in his voice. "You haven't been on a date since your husband died?"

She glared at him. "Yeah. I know that sounds pitiful, but you make it sound like I have some type of rare virus."

"I'm just shocked. I figured a woman as attractive, intelligent and loved in the community as you are would have plenty of men wanting to take you out."

"I didn't say I hadn't been asked. I just haven't been interested," she said softly.

"How about making an exception for me? If you're afraid of being seen with me then how about we go to Natchez?"

Shay thought for a minute. She let go of the wheel and smiled. "No. Jackson has plenty of good restaurants."

"Then it's a date. I mean dinner get-together."

She raised her chin as if she had made a major decision. "I think I'd like to call it a date."

He suddenly felt excited about life for the first time in weeks. "A date it is."

On Friday evening Shay opened her front door to Matt with a drumming heart. She refused to admit to herself or anyone else how much she'd looked forward to the evening. Sheree had asked more than once why she wore such a smile.

She'd glanced at Matt one too many times at lunch and had gotten caught. Sheree had winked at her and grinned. Just before Sheree had left for the day, she'd popped her head in the office and looked around.

"Okay. What gives between you and the hunky doctor?"

"Nothing."

"Those looks you keep giving him isn't nothing." Sheree pinned her with a look.

"He invited me to dinner to say thank you for driving him around is all." Shay sounded defensive even to her own ears.

"If he just wanted to say thank you he could've bought you a card. It's way past time you started living again. This is a good time to do that. And a great guy to do it with."

Shay went hot, embarrassment washing over her.

"I'll want to hear all about it on Monday. Every little

detail. Have a good time. Don't do anything I wouldn't do." Sheree chuckled.

Over the next few hours Shay built the evening up into more than it should be. Now she was confident it couldn't live up to her imagination.

"Come in." She opened the door wider for Matt. "All I need to do is get my purse."

Matt stepped inside and closed the door. "Interesting."

Shay looked around the room trying to find what brought on that remark. "What?"

"This isn't at all what I expected. It doesn't look like you at all."

"How's that?" She looked over the space at the brown sofa and black leather chairs with the plaid pillows. Chrome tables sat at each end of the sofa and a large one served as a coffee table. It looked as it always had.

"I just thought you'd—" he shrugged "—have floral pillows all around. I've seen you in a number of shirts with flowers on them. Even the dress you are wearing has them."

He'd paid that much attention to her clothing? "This is what my husband liked."

Matt shook his head as if disappointed. "You haven't changed it in all this time?"

Outside the entrance to the restaurant, Shay watched as Matt walked around the front of his car to open the door for her. He looked so handsome dressed in his green plaid collared shirt, navy jacket and tan pants. Even his confident walk of a man who knew and understood himself drew her attention. She'd bet wherever he went he had no trouble finding dates.

He opened the door for her. "Ready?"

She nodded. Something about being with Matt built her self-confidence, which had been demolished by John's defection.

He placed his hand at her back and directed her toward the doors of the building. It felt nice to have personal contact. She'd missed it. For a long time, she'd kept to herself. Fearing she couldn't trust her judgment where males were concerned. Still, she should be careful not to read more into the evening than it was. A friendly meal between friends.

Matt said close to her ear, "You look lovely."

Shay had tried to suppress her excitement over the evening, but despite that she'd taken great care to look nice, wearing a dress she'd been saving for a special occasion. The simple, flowing material with little flowers everywhere flattered her. The fact he'd noticed made her feel good. She shouldn't have been surprised because she'd noticed his attention to detail when seeing patients. He'd taken special pains with Joey. "You look nice too."

He stroked his beard. "I did take the time for a little trim."

"I like it." His lips continued to draw her attention. Right now, they were lifted in a sexy grin that joined the twinkle in his eyes. The man knew he appealed to her. That kind of exposure made her uncomfortable. She had kept those emotions locked away for a long time. If she couldn't trust a man she'd known most of her life, how could she possibly trust one she'd known for only a few weeks?

She wasn't surprised Matt hadn't picked a simple café but instead had chosen a restaurant with white tablecloths and flickering candles, located beside the Pearl River. It fit his personality more than a diner. "This is a nice place. I've never been here before."

"Let's hope it's good. Ms. Gladys said it was the best place in town."

She grinned. "Ms. Gladys, huh?"

He shrugged. "It seems she reads all the restaurant reviews. Who would have thought?"

"You never know how people can surprise you."

His gaze shifted away. "I guess you don't. I have to be honest I double-checked it on the internet, but she was right about the reviews."

"Then I'm looking forward to my meal." Shay had already been anticipating spending time with him. Too eagerly.

Matt looked out the large picture window. "This area fascinates me. I've never lived in a place that makes you want to slow down and appreciate life."

"Where have you lived?" She saw his wince as if he'd made a mistake. Did he not want to talk about himself?

"Mostly in the Midwest. A few places in Indiana. My stepfather had to move a couple of times for his job."

Crossing her arms on the table and looking across at him, she leaned forward. "I think, Dr. Chapman, there's more to you than is obvious."

"Isn't that the case with everyone?" He relaxed in his chair. "But I am flattered you're so interested in me."

He made that sound as if she wanted to know about him for personal reasons. Shay narrowed her eyes. "Let's just call it Deep South curiosity."

Matt quirked a brow. "That's all?"

"Yeah. Growing up and living in the same area most of my life, I'm used to knowing about everyone."

The waiter came to take their drink order. Afterward Matt said, "I'd like to know a little more about you."

"A little is all you'll probably get. Almost anyone you ask in Lewisville can tell you about me."

"Have you ever lived anywhere but Lewisville?"

"I moved to Houston, Texas, to go to school."

He watched her as if absorbing every word. "Did you go to the University of Texas Medical School?"

"I did."

The waiter returned with their drinks and took their food order.

Matt took a sip of his drink. "I don't think I've said this before, but I think you're a really great doctor. What you're doing at the clinic is admirable. The staff respect you and the patients adore you. More than one has acted disappointed when they had to see me instead of you."

Warmth flowed through her. She worked hard to make the clinic successful. His praise mattered. "Thanks. I wish we could do more. It's a shame a person needing medical care has to come stand in line all day to be seen. I need at least one more doctor if not two. In fact, I have a couple of doctors interviewing next week. I want to have one in place before you leave. I'm sorry. I've obviously forgotten how to act on a date, talking about work."

"You're fine. There's nothing wrong with being passionate about your work. I certainly am."

"Yeah, but there are other things in life."

"I don't take much time for those. I haven't even been out to explore Jackson since my car was in the shop. It's the capital and I haven't seen the sights. My family used to count off the state capitals we visited." His thoughts seemed to leave their space and time for a moment. "You know I've not thought of that in a long time."

"Then you should see it. I'm ashamed I haven't offered to show you around. I was taught to do better." Why hadn't she? Because she had been too afraid to take a chance on being with a man? "Why don't I make that up to you tomorrow afternoon."

"Tomorrow?" He sounded surprised she'd offered.

"I have a garden club meeting in the morning, but I could do it tomorrow afternoon around one."

"Garden club? That sounds interesting." He grinned.

Shay's eyes narrowed, daring him to say more. "Don't be laughing at me. I'm trying to learn something new. I don't exactly have a green thumb."

He raised a hand as if to ward her off. "Tomorrow afternoon sounds great."

"I'll come get you. It's easier for me to drive because I know the way and don't have to give you directions." She picked up her napkin and placed it in her lap.

"Sounds like a plan. I look forward to it."

The waiter returned with their meals. They spent a few minutes quietly eating.

"How's your pasta?" Matt asked as he cut a slice of his steak.

"Very good. How's your food?" Shay looked over at his almost clean plate.

"Good." He grinned. "I'll have to let Ms. Gladys know."

She leaned toward him as if she were going to tell him a secret. "You do know everyone in your neighborhood knows by now that we're having dinner together."

"Really?" He looked around as if he would see someone he knew.

"Really. Ms. Gladys and Ms. Adriana are known as the biggest gossips in the neighborhood."

Matt groaned. A low sound that came from deep in his throat. It made her shiver as her blood heated. What would it be like to hear it as he nuzzled behind her ear? Her fork rattled to her plate. She really was making more of this dinner than would be healthy for her emotions.

"Is everything okay?" Matt's concerned gaze went from her face to her plate and back again.

Shay picked up her fork holding it tighter than necessary. "Fine. Just fine."

Matt watched her closely for a few moments and returned to his meal.

She had to get her equilibrium back. "Did your neighbors say anything about you mowing your grass?"

He grinned and raised his chin like a conquering hero. "Let's just say I got a banana cream pie out of it."

"They're going to have you fattened up before you leave for Chicago. Uh, not that you don't look great as you are." She wanted to drop through the floor. Not since John had she ever been so fixated on a man. "I'm sorry that didn't come out exactly right."

"I knew what you meant." The lines at his eyes became more prominent and those lips she liked so much quirked up at one corner. "Not that I don't like that you noticed."

Heat washed through her as she tried to focus on her meal.

"Would you like to have some dessert?" Matt asked.

"I'm so full I don't think I should."

"Why don't you share some of mine?" Matt picked up the menu the waiter had just put on the table. He didn't wait for her answer before he said, "We'll have the Mississippi Mud Cake. It sounds interesting."

The waiter left them.

Matt looked at her as if asking for confirmation of his decision. "I hope I don't regret that."

"I promise you won't."

The waiter soon brought him a large slice of chocolate cake with thick chocolate pecan icing.

"This looks wonderful. *Mud* in the name is misleading." Matt took a forkful and placed it in his mouth.

Shay watched with rapt attention as his sensuous mouth closed around it. A look of pleasure came over his features.

He looked at her. "This might be the best thing I've ever eaten. Don't you want some?"

Shay laughed. "I'm afraid to take any. You might fight me if I do."

"Here." He scooped up another forkful and offered it to her. "This is too good to miss."

She hesitated a moment then took the offering. "It is good."

"Good is an understatement." He ate more cake.

"Do you have someone special who bakes for you?"

"No. I don't have a great track record where my personal life is concerned. A number of ex-girlfriends. No wives or children. Which is just as well. Let's not ruin this delicious dessert by talking about that."

An interesting answer. There was more to Matt than he let on. Had he been as hurt as she?

Soon after they were on their way home. Shay couldn't get away from what Matt had said about having a personal life. She might have known a deep heartache, but she still dreamed of having a forever relationship. Along with that she wanted children, to have a family of her own. From Matt's glib answer he had no interest in those. For some reason that made her sad.

Matt took her away from her thoughts by asking, "Will you tell me about your husband, Shay?"

She didn't want to do that. If he wasn't going to share why should she? Because she wanted him to understand why she'd not been on a date in so long. Maybe if she shared, he would too, eventually. More than anything she wanted to know more about him. "What do you want to know?"

"Where did you meet him?"

That question surprised her. She fully expected him to ask her how John died. "We were high school sweethearts. You know…the hometown hero quarterback and the head cheerleader love story. We won the state championship our senior year. We were the golden couple." They had been. She'd been so wrapped up in that ideal she couldn't see anything else.

"There's a lot to live up to in there."

Matt seemed to see what others never had, including her parents and especially not John's. A note in his voice implied he understood from experience. "Yeah, a whole lot. We went off to the University of Texas together. Him on a football scholarship and me on an academic one. Our parents were not only proud of us, but all of Lewisville seemed invested in us. We were the couple who couldn't fail."

Matt said nothing, but she had no doubt she had his complete attention. His profile remained intent on the road, but he looked at her every chance he got.

"Since I had more school to be a doctor, John decided he'd go into the US Marines while I was in med school. I would finish and he would get out then we'd come home and start building our life together. When we married John had one more year to serve. The entire town was at the wedding. Afterward John left on his first overseas deployment."

"No honeymoon?"

"One night in New Orleans." It had been a wonderful night. Life looked bright and wide-open back then. "He returned six months later but went back. He didn't return."

Matt reached over and took her hand, giving it a squeeze. "I'm really sorry."

Could she tell him the entire sordid story? She removed her hand. "The town is talking about putting up a statue in his honor."

"Oh, wow. That's an even harder cloud to live under. Forever being the wife of a hero. How do you feel about that?"

"He earned it. John saved men's lives fighting for his country." He didn't earn hero status in other parts of his life, though.

Matt pulled into her drive and turned the car off. After studying her a moment, he said, "I hear a *but* in there."

Shay sighed. She shouldn't make such a big deal out of telling him. Everyone knew. Someone would eventually tell him. She took a deep breath. "He'd been having an affair. He told me to expect divorce papers on the day he left."

Matt didn't say anything for a few moments.

Even with the years that had passed she still couldn't believe how John had humiliated her by having an affair. Her heart still hurt. Well, she'd managed to put a cloud of gloom over the end of the evening. She opened the door. "I just dropped an egg on a good time. Sorry. Thanks for the evening out."

Shay made it halfway up the walk before Matt caught

her. He cupped her elbow, stopping her. "You know it was his loss. You were, are, too good for him."

She gave Matt a sad smile. "Thanks for that. You'd think after all this time I wouldn't let it upset me."

His hand slipped down her arm to hold her hand. "Rejection is rejection. No one likes to be on the receiving end. We carry the pain around with us."

Matt sounded like he understood better than most. Shay's eyes found his. "You're a nice guy, Matt Chapman."

"You're not bad yourself." He studied her for a moment. His focus dropped to her lips.

Was he going to kiss her? Did she want him to?

He stepped back. "I had a really nice time tonight. I'm looking forward to tomorrow afternoon."

CHAPTER FIVE

MATT STOOD IN the yard talking to Ms. Gladys when Shay turned into his driveway. He had walked over to help the older woman pull her garbage can back to the house. The woman's interest in his comings and goings he found a little disconcerting, but she was nice enough. He put it down to loneliness.

"I have to go, Ms. Gladys. Shay's going to show me Jackson's sights. Hey, I appreciate your suggestion of a restaurant. It was every bit as good as you said it would be."

He glanced over to see Shay coming toward them, a flowing dress dancing around her legs. She wore all that silky hair down. Clips held it back near her ears. She looked as fresh and lovely as a clear brook did to a thirsty man.

He'd wanted to kiss her last night. She'd looked so sad. Wanted to reassure her she was desirable. But that wasn't the only reason. He was attached to her, liked her. Yet he shouldn't start anything with Shay. He'd just ended a relationship where he thought he would marry. Shay would want more than he could offer. The timing, the place, the needs were all wrong. It was best he kept his distance.

Shay wrapped Ms. Gladys in a hug. "It's so good to see you. It's been so long."

"It has been a while, honey. How's your uncle doing?" She continued to hold one of Shay's hands.

"Uncle Henry's doing great. I'll be sure to tell him you asked about him."

The older woman's cheeks pinkened.

Matt grinned. Did Ms. Gladys have a thing for Henry Warren? Matt finished pulling the can to the house and returned to the women.

Shay looked at him. "We better get going if we're going to see everything I have planned. I hope you've got your walking shoes on."

He pursed his lips in thought as if acting unsure about going with her. "So, this is going to be sightseeing and an exercise class. This may be more than I bargained for."

Shay grinned. "Yeah, we're going to do a walking tour."

"You two have a good time." Ms. Gladys waved and headed inside her house.

Shay drove them the short distance downtown.

"I'm not known for sightseeing," Matt said as he looked around as they moved through a business district. "My family did do some while I was growing up. I got out of the habit when I started college. Medical school didn't leave me any time. When I had some hours off all I wanted to do was sleep."

"Well, today, I'm going to wake up your sleeping tourist."

"So where are we headed?"

"We're gonna start down by the capitol. We don't have time today to go into the museums, but we'll just have to settle for a good overview."

Shay continued down what he did know was the main street. She took an open parking place. "Okay, this is where the walking part of the tour starts."

They joined the other people on the wide sidewalk. They strolled past small businesses and large department stores toward the huge four-storied official-looking white building, which was obviously a government building, surrounded by a green lawn.

Shay raised her hand like a TV game hostess. "This is the capitol building of Mississippi. It was built in 1903. If we were here on a weekday, we could go inside, but today we just have to appreciate it from out here. Let's go this way."

"You really do like history, don't you?"

She stopped and looked at him. "Am I boring you? Please tell me if I am."

"No, I'm enjoying this." More than that he enjoyed spending time with her.

"If you'll look right over there—" she pointed across the street "—you'll see that we have our own clock tower and gargoyles just like Notre Dame. My favorite is the one on that corner."

"Have you ever been to Paris and seen the real Notre Dame?" Matt looked at the angry-looking animal squatting on the corner of the building.

"No. But I'd love to go sometime. Right now, all my focus is on the clinic. Maybe one day." Her sigh lingered in the air.

"I've never been either. I always thought I'd like to see the city."

"Now, over in this direction is my favorite building in town. The old capitol building. It was built in 1846."

The box-shaped building with a green dome did have a simple authority to it that appealed. "It's nice."

"We can go in here. You need to see the rotunda. It's gorgeous."

Shay's eyes lit up. He couldn't imagine the rotunda being more beautiful than her at that moment. She had started to put a spell on him.

They walked up the wide steps and through massive doors. Inside, round columns created a rotunda with the dome allowing light in from above.

Matt watched as Shay walked around the area enthralled.

"Can you imagine what it was like to come here in your finest dress and be waltzed around this beautiful room?"

Matt chuckled. "I had no idea you were such a romantic."

Shay looked at him. "I haven't thought about it, but I guess I am. Kind of sappy, isn't it?"

"Charming is what I was thinking."

She looked at him as if she saw something she hadn't before. "Thanks for not making fun of me."

Did people question the softer side of her often? "And thanks for sharing something special with me. I'm honored."

She smiled. "Come, we have a little way to walk to our next stop."

When they had to cross a busy road, Matt took her hand. She glanced at him, but didn't pull away. Back on a sidewalk he kept her hand firmly clasped in his. Soon her hand relaxed in his.

They walked in silence for a while. As they came up to a grand house Shay announced, "This is the governor's mansion. It was built in 1842 in the Greek Revival style.

And you have the sum total of my knowledge. I went in it when I was in the fifth grade on a field trip, but I don't remember much about it other than it was big."

"You never wanted to dance here?"

She thought for a minute. "Nope. It's always been at the old capitol building. Now I think it's time for the tour guide to give the tourist a rest and treat him to an ice cream."

"That sounds good."

"On the way to LeFleur's Bluff park we'll pass Eudora Welty's house—she was one of Mississippi's great literary authors."

He knew that name. "I had to read one of her stories when I was an undergrad. I liked it better than most."

Shay's chin came up proudly. "I've read everything she wrote."

Matt shook his head. "Why am I not surprised."

She tugged on his hand. "Let's go get that ice cream." At the cart outside the park, she bought them each a cone. Handing one to Matt she said, "Only a small one this time. We have to save room for dinner. There's a bench over there that's empty. Let's go get it."

Matt licked the cream before it ran down the cone as they sat down. "You sounded just like a mother a minute ago."

"I hope to be one someday."

"I'm surprised you aren't already." He had stepped into an area that wasn't any of his business.

"I wanted to be. John said we needed to wait until he was out of the service." Her voice turned bitter. "But apparently with the right woman that didn't matter. It turns out the woman he was having an affair with was pregnant."

Matt put his arm around her shoulder and gave her a

gentle hug. There were no words to fix the hurt in her voice. When he eased his hold she slid away from him.

They watched families and couples go by on the walking path along with a few individuals out for a hot afternoon run.

Finally, she said, her tone having returned to normal, "Can you name a superfamous singer who's from Mississippi?"

He thought for a moment. "No."

She laughed. "Elvis."

"I thought he was from Memphis, Tennessee."

She sat straighter. "I'll have you know he was born in Tupelo, Mississippi."

"My stepfather used to dance my mother around the kitchen to Elvis's love songs." He would give credit to his stepfather for one thing—he did obviously love Matt's mom. "Do you like Elvis?"

"Yeah. Of course, I do. I've even seen his movies."

The sky rumbled. It had darkened while they had been sitting there.

"I think we should be heading back. If we don't, we might get wet." Shay stood.

On their way out of the park they threw their garbage in a can. He took her hand again. At the next roll of thunder big drops of rain started to fall.

"We better find some cover," Shay squealed.

At the next storefront with an indented entrance Matt pulled her into the space. The building was dark. It was just the two of them when the sky opened up and the rain fell full force.

As the wind picked up, he tugged her closer to the door, gaining more protection.

"This shouldn't last long." Shay shivered.

When she shook again, he took her into his arms putting himself between the worst of the weather and her. She accepted his help and snuggled into him. It felt right to protect her, to have her in his arms.

Shay's shoulders shook.

"Are you laughing?"

Her gaze met his, her eyes shining with humor. "This reminds me of those 1940s movies where the couple runs in out of the rain and the guy…"

"Kisses the girl?"

For a moment, they simply stared at each other. Shay's fingers curled into his shirt as he lowered his head, as his lips found her warm damp ones. A soft sigh floated from her. Her arms tightened, bringing her snugly against him. His tongue traveled the seam of her mouth and to his great satisfaction she opened for him. He took her invitation and found heaven.

The honking of a car horn made them jerk apart.

He looked into Shay's eyes. Uncertainty filled them. It wasn't what he wanted to see.

She looked beyond him. "Uh… I think the worst is over now. We can start walking again."

Shay started down the street, giving him no choice but to follow. He wanted things to go back to the way they had been between them. The easy friendship. Had he ruined that by kissing her? Shay had been enjoying it. He certainly had.

"Thanks for showing me around this afternoon. I have to say, it's been nice to gather my thoughts and rest."

"That's good to hear, but once you get to Chicago are you planning to pick up where you left off?"

He shrugged a shoulder. "I'll have to pick up my pace

compared to here if I plan to get back to the same position I held in LA and eventually to the head of the program."

Shay looked at him. "Why's that so important?"

That was a good question.

Shay wasn't sure why she had been peppering Matt with questions. Maybe it was to cover up the effect his kiss had on her. Her knees still felt like jelly. She shouldn't have kissed him. Where could something between them go?

What she needed to do was get over it and move on. It wouldn't happen again. Why did the thought of that being true make her sad?

When Matt would have kept walking, she grabbed his arm, but quickly let it go. "Hold up. This is where we're going to get supper."

She pulled the diner door open. "This place is famous for its tacos and tapas. I love to have a chance to eat here." She smiled at him. "And you've given me that opportunity."

Shay spoke to the hostess about needing a table.

"Why don't we eat outside under the awning?" Matt suggested. "That way you won't get cold in here in the air-conditioning."

"That's a good idea." Had John ever been that considerate of her? Not that she could remember. They followed the waitress out to the patio. The rain had only made the air more sauna-like than cool.

They were shown to a wood-and-chrome table off to themselves. The restaurant had started filling up for the evening. They ordered their drinks.

"Thanks for thinking about this," Shay said. "It's much nicer out here."

They both looked at the menus the waitress had left.

She soon returned with their drinks and they placed their order.

Shay crossed her arms and leaned on the table. "Why did you leave LA? From all I can tell you were successful there. I did look you up."

Matt leaned back in the curl-backed chrome chair that matched the table and watched her for a moment. Was he deciding if he should tell her? Trust her? "I had a disagreement with a senior surgeon."

"Disagreement, huh?"

"It was a little more than that. We were in the middle of a procedure and he was making an incision that would endanger the patient and I said so."

She winced. "I bet that didn't go well."

"It didn't. I had to report him to the medical board."

She hissed in a breath.

"Yeah. Before the hearing he used his clout with those he could, and his word stood over mine. The board sided with him. I was the new kid questioning the senior surgeon. I knew my time there was limited even if I was right. I'd been approached about a position in Chicago last year so I called to see if they might still be interested in me."

"That must've been tough." Wow. This wasn't the average man.

"Yeah, but the patient always has to come first." He picked up his drink and took a swallow.

"I agree, but I still admire you for standing up for what was right when it couldn't have been easy. To disrupt your entire life and career to stand by your convictions is asking a lot. I know many who wouldn't. It takes a special man."

He fingered the moisture on the side of the glass. "I

don't know that I did anything special. I felt I didn't have a choice. It's what I was taught to do."

A man with principles, and humble too. If his kiss hadn't gotten her, what she'd just learned about him would've. The more she knew about Matt the better she liked him. Not a good thing. Her heart could get in trouble. "Your parents did a good job with teaching integrity."

He said nothing for a moment as if he was deep in thought. "I guess they did. My mother is a good woman who has integrity, but it was my stepfather who insisted I admit when I had done something wrong. When there was a kid in the neighborhood being bullied he said it was important to take up for those who couldn't take up for themselves. I've not thought about that for a long time.

"The problem was that I had basically called my boss out. In the three seconds it took to say something my career went into a tailspin." Sadness filled his voice.

"I'm sorry that happened to you. Still, I'm impressed you did the right thing. Others might not have in that situation."

His gaze met hers. "I bet you would have. My mom has been begging me for years to move closer. She'll be pleased to have me in Chicago."

"You never say anything about your father."

"He died when I was three. Mom remarried when I was eight." His words were flat.

By his facial expression and tone of voice she'd save any discussion about that for later. "At least your moving closer to home is something good coming out of bad."

Matt sat straighter and looked directly at her. "Has something good come out of bad for you?"

How like him to turn her words on her. "Yeah. Because of what John did and the gossip and sad looks, I throw myself into building the clinic."

"You've done a great job with that, but what have you done for yourself?"

"I don't know. I'd like to travel. See the gargoyles on Notre Dame, the Swiss Alps. One day have a family."

Matt leaned back again and watched her for a moment. The waitress bringing their food changed the atmosphere between them. As they ate, their conversation turned to movies they had seen, and TV shows they watched.

Later, Shay pulled into his driveway. It had just turned dark enough for the streetlight to come on.

"Would you like to come in? Watch some TV for a while?" Matt watched her.

Shay hesitated a moment before saying, "No, I better be getting home. It's getting late anyway."

"I really enjoyed my afternoon and dinner. Thanks for showing me around. If you ever want to give up medicine, you'd make a great tour guide." He grinned.

Matt really did have the best smile. "I enjoyed it too. It has been too long since I visited those places."

"Shay, about that kiss—"

"Don't worry about it. We both know it wasn't a good idea."

The back of his hand brushed her cheek. "Why?"

"I don't... I don't think we need to start something that neither one of us can finish. You're only gonna be here for a few more weeks and the last thing I need is another heartbreak."

His eyes held an earnest look. "I don't plan to break your heart."

"I'm sure you don't, but that doesn't mean it won't happen." Shay knew herself. She could so easily fall for him.

Matt leaned closer. His warm, musky scent filled her nose. "You like me that much?"

Shay closed her eyes and swallowed, hard. All she had to do was lean forward just a little and her lips would touch his. "Yeah."

"Will you look at me, Shay?"

Shay shook her head. If she did, she'd disappear into his eyes.

"Please."

At his pleading tone, she opened her eyelids. "I like you too, Shay. I can't offer you more than here and now but that doesn't mean I don't care about you."

A lovely warmth washed through her.

"Think about it." He kissed her forehead. "See you Monday at work. Good night."

Shay drove away with hands shaking and a flutter like a hummingbird flying in her middle. How would she survive being around Matt for the next few weeks? Did she really want to resist him?

CHAPTER SIX

MATT HADN'T RESTRAINED himself this much since he'd been a teenager and wanted to yell at his stepfather. He'd wanted to take Shay into the house and show her what it could be like between them. Just from their short kiss he had no doubt it would be powerful.

Sunday he'd resisted calling or texting her to give her room to think. It had made for a long day. On Monday she'd acted as if nothing had happened between them and he followed her lead, yet he caught her watching him more than once. She wasn't as immune to him as she seemed. He could be patient—for a while.

Tuesday at lunch Shay said to the table in general, "I have a couple of doctors coming in for interviews this afternoon."

"Anyone we know?" Sheree asked.

"I don't think so." Shay picked up her sandwich. "A Dr. Stevie Brown and a Dr. Kurt Willis."

"I know Dr. Willis. He's a nice guy. Really good," one of the nurses said. "Really cute too."

Shay grinned and said flippantly, "Which is always important for patient care."

"It's nice to know what's considered important to you

ladies. Not all the years of training," Matt groused before he finished his leftover casserole.

"Hey, what're you complaining about," Sheree said. "You certainly qualify in the looks department." She stood. As she did, she placed a hand on his shoulder. "We just need to find one as fine as you."

"Thanks. But I'm not sure I feel any better."

Shay grinned at him as if she were enjoying his discomfort. "Seriously, your skills will be hard to replace."

Why should it matter to him that Shay was trying to find a replacement for him? That had been the agreement all along. He shoved his lunch bowls into his bag. What he didn't want was some guy coming in and gaining Shay's interest as well. Why not? He had no hold on her. She would move on when he was gone. The idea left a bad taste in his mouth.

Between patients he saw Shay showing around a woman. So, Stevie was female. Later he saw her with a tall blond man that even Matt had to admit had better than average looks.

Sheree walked up beside him wearing a teasing smile. "He looks like he might fit in here perfectly."

Matt snarled and walked off with the sound of Sheree's laughter following him. Jealousy wasn't something he was familiar with. He'd never felt one ounce of it with Jenna. He wasn't in any real relationship with Shay and jealousy was running wild in his blood. Would this blond doctor be the man that opened the world up again for Shay?

Matt hated the idea but what could he say or do? Soon he would be leaving. They would be living hundreds of miles away from each other. He'd be spending countless hours trying to build his career. Matt glanced at Shay and the doctor. Maybe it was just as well. Anyone would be a better choice for Shay than Matt. Most of all he wanted her happiness.

He knocked on the exam room door with more force than necessary. There were patients to see.

Wednesday afternoon he and Shay were on their way to see patients after lunch when Sheree met them in the hallway.

"Matt, Mr. Clayton is here requesting to see you."

He looked at Shay. People didn't request to see him. They usually asked for Shay. "Who? Oh, yeah, the man who hurt his hand the first week I was here."

"Yes, that's the one." Sheree pointed to exam room two. "He's in there."

"I'll see him right now."

"I'd like to see him too, if it's all right with him," Shay said from behind Matt.

"I'll ask and see. Make sure it isn't something he'd rather see a male doctor about." Matt knocked on the door and entered.

Mr. and Mrs. Clayton stood with wide smiles on their faces. "We wanted to come by and say thank you."

"Thank you?" What were they talking about?

"For saving my hand." Mr. Clayton raised his bandaged hand.

"You're welcome." Matt couldn't help but be impressed they had stopped in just to see him. "Dr. Lunsford would like to see you too if that's okay?"

"Sure," the man said in his deep, gravelly voice.

Matt went to the door. "Come in. They're just here for a friendly visit."

Shay entered. "It's good to see you, Mr. Clayton. How's the hand doing?"

"Dr. Roper says it's doing great thanks to Dr. Chapman. They tell me I might have lost it altogether if it hadn't been for Dr. Chapman."

Embarrassment filled Matt at all the praise. "Do you mind if we have a look at your hand, Mr. Clayton?"

"Not at all."

Matt sat on the rolling stool while Mr. Clayton took a seat on the exam table and Mrs. Clayton took the chair. Shay stood beside him. She handed him a pair of scissors.

As Matt removed the bandage he said, "Your surgeon has kept us posted on how you have been doing. He's pleased with the results." Matt finished taking the gauze off and dropped them in the garbage can.

Gently, he took Mr. Clayton's hand in the palm of his and studied it. Shay stepped close behind him and looked over his shoulder. The mangled skin would be scarred but otherwise the hand looked as if it would recover well. "Can you move your fingers for me?"

Mr. Clayton moved the tips of his fingers. "I've been told it'll need some physical therapy but that I should get the majority of the use back."

"That's wonderful to hear."

Shea put her hand on his shoulder and gave it a squeeze.

"It does look good. I'll get the supplies and get this wrapped up again for you." Matt pushed back from the exam table.

"I'll do that," Shay said. She went to the cabinet and started pulling out what was needed.

Mrs. Clayton picked up a large basket filled with fresh vegetables that had been sitting on the floor and handed it to him. "These are for you as a thank-you. They're from our garden. Jim is known for his tomatoes."

Matt had received casseroles and pies but for some reason this simple gift meant more. This was the first time he'd ever had a patient bring him a gift for doing his job. With a lump in his throat Matt said, "Thank you. These look wonderful."

A few minutes later Matt, with Shay beside him, watched the Claytons walk toward the front door. Shay squeezed his upper arm. "Nice going, Dr. Chapman."

He looked at her. "That's the best patient visit I've ever had."

"You deserved it."

Shay had just gotten home from having dinner with her parents and changed clothes. She'd thought about going by Matt's, but stopped herself. It would have been sending the wrong message if she had. She'd drawn the boundaries and she should live with them. As Matt had been. As much as she would've liked for him to kiss her, he'd been a gentleman.

She smiled at the memory of the look on his face after the Claytons' visit. He'd been overwhelmed. Shay feared he'd not had enough admiration in his life. Matt was the type of doctor, and man, that deserved it. It was good he'd received it while working here.

Her phone rang. She picked it up.

She recognized Matt's voice even though it was little more than a groan. "I need help."

"I'm on the way." Shay scooped up her purse and ran for the car.

Twenty minutes later, of what was usually a thirty-minute trip, she pulled to a jerking stop in Matt's drive and ran for the back door. She raised a hand in Ms. Gladys's direction where she stood near the street talking to a neighbor. Not bothering to knock, Shay entered the house. "Matt, where are you?"

"In here." His voice came as little more than a painful moan from somewhere deep in the house.

She found him sprawled on a bed with a sheet over his hips and the rest of him bare. Shay swallowed hard. Then she saw his ankles and legs and the rest of him was forgotten. They were a deep red with small marks dotting them. One calf had swollen to a painful size. Matt's arm lay across his face covering his eyes.

Her heart went out to him. "Matt, what have you done to yourself?"

He didn't remove his arm as he spoke to her. "I just mowed the grass. Some kind of ant did the rest. My legs are on fire."

"Yeah, that's because you stepped in a fire ant bed. They don't like that at all."

He raised his arm just enough to glare at her. The pain showed clearly in his eyes. "I learned that the hard way. All I did was push the mower over a mound of red dirt. The engine bogged down and quit. I was trying to restart it when something stung me. I looked down to see my shoes and ankles covered in red ants. They swarmed me. No matter how much I stomped they hung on."

"They'll do that." He sounded so pitiful Shay couldn't help but feel sorry for him.

"I ran for the house pulling my clothes off as I went."

"I bet Ms. Gladys liked that," Shay murmured.

"It didn't matter. I had to get those things off me. I wore my shorts into the shower. The water was the only way to get them off. Hot water only made things worse, so I ended up with a cold shower. That didn't help much. Then I called you."

Shay put her bag on the bed beside him. "I'll see if I can make you more comfortable. It looks like you're allergic to them. Are you having any trouble breathing?"

"No."

"If you do start having trouble, we'll need to get you to the emergency room. I'll give you an antihistamine and some pain medicine and see if that helps."

His arm went back over his eyes again. "I doubt that's possible. This is embarrassing but I'm so miserable I'll take any help I can get."

"I'm sorry. You really must be in pain." She squeezed his hand. "I'll have you feeling better in a few minutes." Shay dug through her bag and found the medicine. "I need to get you some water to take these with. Don't move."

"Like I could," Matt grumbled.

She went to the kitchen and soon returned with the water. She handed Matt the pills and he quickly swallowed them.

"I don't have any steroid cream with me. I'm going to ice your legs. If your leg swells any more then I'll have to go to the clinic and get the cream. For now, I'll wait and see. Do you have any freezer bags?"

"What?" he muttered.

"Then I guess not. I'll see what I can find in the kitchen." She'd be surprised if there was much in the house based on what she'd seen so far. "I'll be right back."

The house wasn't much different than the last time she'd been in it. All the same furniture, mostly secondhand stuff. There were two other bedrooms along the hall but there wasn't any furniture in them. Uncle Henry must figure his renters would want their own bedroom furniture.

In the kitchen she checked the freezer of the refrigerator and found no bags of frozen vegetables. At least the ice tray was full. Pulling out drawers and looking in the cabinets, she found a couple of plastic bags from the grocery store. She filled them with some ice, tied them closed and returned to Matt.

From the bath, she grabbed a towel and draped it over his legs then placed the bags on his legs, arranging the ice so that it covered as much of his skin as possible.

Matt made a moan of pleasure. "Thanks."

"Better?"

"Yeah. At least you put the fire out for a while," he murmured.

She pulled the sheet farther up his chest and brushed his hair from his forehead. He had a fever. "Get some sleep. It'll help."

His hand caught hers and held it for a moment. "Thanks, Shay."

"Not a problem. I'm just sorry you feel so bad." When his breathing turned even, she pulled a stuffed chair from the corner and positioned it beside the bed. She would stay with him as long as he needed her.

There was a knock at the door. Shay hurried toward it, not wanting the person to wake Matt. Halfway there she realized what she wore. At Matt's call she hadn't thought to change clothes in her urgency to get to his house. Now she realized she wore a knit tank-top with no bra and very short cutoff jeans she'd pulled on to get comfortable.

Running back to Matt's room, she shook out one of his dress shirts lying on the chest of drawers and pulled it on, tying it at her waist and rolling up the sleeves.

Another insistent knock had her dashing to the door. Ms. Gladys stood on the other side.

"Is everything okay? I saw you running in a while ago. I got worried."

"Matt stepped into a fire ant bed and didn't know what they were. Turns out he's allergic to them."

The old woman sighed. "I should've known. The lawn-mower was left out in the yard. He's been so good about mowing the grass lately."

"He's eaten up pretty badly and running a fever." Shay hoped to placate the woman, so she'd soon leave.

"Is there anything I can do?" Ms. Gladys moved forward as if she planned to enter the house, but Shay blocked the doorway.

"Right now, I think we're fine. Matt's sleeping."

"You let me know if you need me. Matt's a nice guy. I've become fond of him."

So had Shay. Too much so. "Thanks, Ms. Gladys. I need to get back to Matt right now. He doesn't need to be alone until his fever is gone."

"All righty, I'll go." The old woman slowly walked away.

"Hey, Ms. Gladys."

The woman turned to look at Shay. "Yes?"

"I bet Matt would enjoy some of your soup when he's feeling better."

A bright smile came to the woman's mouth. "I'll fix him some."

Shay had lived with this type of helpful yet some-times nosy neighbor situation her entire life. There was a time when it bothered her, but it had nice aspects as well. Being cared for by others mattered.

Returning to Matt, she found him resting easy. His legs were still bright red and swollen. The fire ants had really done a job on him.

Shay touched his forehead. The fever remained. That

concerned her. She'd hoped it would be gone since he'd had medicine to bring it down. Matt slept soundly enough as she hadn't woken him with her touch. She didn't feel good about leaving him yet. She'd stay a little while longer. Thankfully she kept a book in her purse for times like these. With it in hand she settled on the well-worn sofa to read.

An hour went by before she heard Matt stir. He went into the bathroom. At the sound of him coming out she moved down the hall calling out, fearing he wasn't back in bed yet. "Hey, how're you feeling?"

"Awful. My legs are on fire."

She entered his room. He'd returned to the bed and was in the process of adjusting the towel and ice on his legs. The sheet collected low on his hips just covering his groin. Shay made herself look away. She was a doctor. She'd seen naked men before. But this wasn't just any patient.

"Lie back and I'll do that." The words came out harsher than she intended.

To her amazement, he did as she asked without argument, indicating how uncomfortable he must be. Thankfully, he pulled the sheet up to under his arms as she went about seeing to his legs. "I need to get some more ice. Are you hungry?"

"Yeah, I guess so. What I really am is thirsty."

"Then I'll be right back with ice and something to drink." She headed out the door.

"Hey, Shay."

She looked back at him. "I like those sexy shorts and you look cute in my shirt."

Matt grinned for the first time in hours. A flush of color came to Shay's cheeks at his observation. He liked it when he got the best of her. She appeared so self-assured all the time but when he made any suggestion of attraction between them, she acted all shy as if she didn't want to think about the spark between them.

He settled back, waiting for her to return. He hated that she had to take care of him, but even he realized he'd messed up when he'd gotten into that ant hill. As bad as he felt, it didn't mean he was unaware of Shay's charms, especially those unbounded breasts she covered with his shirt.

Soon Shay returned with ice in bags and a large drink in her hand. She handed him the glass and fussed around his legs. He checked his phone while she left briefly; then she returned with a slice of chicken potpie for him. Thank goodness for neighbors. Sitting up, he leaned back against the headboard, making sure his waist remained covered. She handed him the plate then took a seat in the chair.

He picked up the fork. "Thanks for taking care of me."

"You've already said that." She watched him as if ready to jump in to help him.

"I mean it. Tell me about these fire ants. Who knew ants could be so vicious?"

She leaned back as if settling into a subject she was comfortable with. "Hundreds of years ago they rode into America on a banana boat from South America. They got off in New Orleans or someplace on the coast and started their march north."

Matt grinned. "You make them sound like a human army."

"They're more destructive." She pointed at his legs. "You should know. I've seen small children hospitalized from being bitten by fire ants. They're awful. Haven't you seen the mounds of dirt one or two feet high in the fields?"

He swallowed. "Yeah, but I didn't know what they were."

Shay gave him a wry smile. "I bet you do now."

"That I do. Who was at the door earlier?" He finished off his potpie.

She grinned and took his plate. "Ms. Gladys. She was concerned about her favorite neighbor."

He raised his brows. "Was she?"

"She would've come in to see you if I'd let her." Shay placed the plate on the dresser.

"She might have seen more than she wanted to." Matt adjusted the sheet.

Shay grinned. "Knowing her, she wouldn't have minded."

"Still, I'm glad you didn't let her in." He paused for a drink.

She moved to stand.

He grabbed her hand. "Stay and talk to me for a while."

She settled on the edge of the chair. He didn't like her being skittish around him. He thought they'd gotten past that. "Tell me about your family. I met your mother and father, but do you have any brothers or sisters?"

"I have a brother who lives in Memphis. He and his wife have two children—who are the best, by the way. They come down when they can but it's not often enough for me, Mom and Dad. How about you? Brothers and sisters?"

He could tell by the look on her face and the sound of her voice she loved them dearly. He was sure he didn't have those tones when he spoke of his family. "Both. I have a half brother who lives in California and a half sister who lives in St. Louis. I haven't seen either of them in years."

Her eyes widened and she leaned forward as if she didn't believe him. "Oh, wow. That's awful."

How like Shay to say exactly what she thought. "I've been busy."

"I'm never too busy for people I love." Her mouth turned down in horror. "I shouldn't have said that."

Shay wouldn't be, but then she knew what it was to meet their expectations, to make them proud. He didn't. Despite him being a doctor, he never felt he'd been enough in his stepfather's eyes. The issue in LA and changing hospitals wouldn't improve on the situation either.

Shay stood. "Let me check and see if you're still running a fever." She pulled her electric thermometer out of her bag, placing it on his forehead. When it beeped, she looked at the instrument. "It's low-grade but still there. I'll take this—" she picked up the plate "—and get you more to drink, then give you another dose of medicine. You should sleep. By morning you'll hopefully be better. I'll be here if you aren't to take you to the hospital."

"You're going to stay?" Surprise filled his voice.

"Yes. I don't want you to get worse and no one know it. I can't have you going into anaphylactic shock with no one around." She gave him a stern look.

She did care. He watched her tight behind in those short shorts as she left the room and wished he felt better.

The next thing he knew he woke to a dark room. A light came from down the hall, but the house remained quiet. He was cold and his legs itched like the devil. Climbing out of bed, he made his way to the bathroom.

When he came out Shay stood in the doorway. He should have put some shorts on but didn't have the energy to look for them. In the dim light she couldn't see much.

"Hey, how're you doing?"

He got back into bed. "I'm freezing and my legs itch. Other than that, I couldn't be better."

She walked to the side of the bed and touched his forehead. "You were sleeping, and I decided to wait to give you medicine. I should've woken you."

He pulled the sheet up to his neck. Shay draped the blanket over him. "Do you have any other bedcovers?"

"No." His teeth chattered as he closed his eyes.

Shay woke against a warm body. Matt lay at her back with his arm across her waist. A ripple of shock went through her. What was she doing here? All she planned to do was help keep him warm until he settled. Heavens, she had fallen asleep. In bed. With Matt. It did feel good to have a man holding her close. It had been so long. Yet she couldn't stay here.

Heat no longer radiated off him. At least his fever had broken. She'd removed the bags of ice, gave him pain medicine trying to make him as comfortable as possible, but he still pulled into a ball and shivered. She'd found an extra blanket in the closet, but it had done little good. He continued being miserable. Unable to sit by and watch him in misery, she'd crawled under the covers and wrapped her arms around him, intending to stay for only a few minutes.

Now here she was in bed with Matt hours later. He shifted, and she took her chance to move away, but his arm tightened. His breath was but a soft whish across her cheek. She had to get out of bed before Matt really woke. What would he think about her sleeping with him?

Matt's breathing changed. He nuzzled her neck. "Mmm…"

"Matt?" she whispered.

"Uh?"

She'd been tempted to move her head, giving him better access to her neck. His lips against her skin had her thinking and feeling things better left alone. "I need to get up."

"I like you right here," he grumbled, but his arm moved off her waist.

She slid out of bed, then looked down at him. "I, uh… didn't mean to go to sleep."

He watched her too closely. "I didn't mind."

"How're your legs feelings?" She needed to get this conversation going in another direction.

He grinned. "Better than other parts of my body."

She shivered. "Really."

He rolled to his back, the covers showing more of his chest than she would have liked. Then again, she would have liked to see more. She needed to get out of here before she got herself in trouble.

"Better I think," Matt answered.

"I'm glad to hear it. I need to go, but before I do, I should check your legs."

Matt lay back on the pillows. She pushed the covers up to reveal his calves, and he watched her as she went about examining his legs. She felt his attention as if it were a hand resting on her. The muscles in her middle quivered. Why didn't that bother her? Instead, she wanted to get back in bed with him.

Why wouldn't she let go and take what she wanted? What she believed Matt would be willing give. Because she wanted forever, and Matt wouldn't be that.

CHAPTER SEVEN

SHAY MADE IT through an unbelievable day—barely. It had been difficult on two levels and all because of Matt. Without his help she'd been busier than usual and when she wasn't seeing a patient she walked around in a haze of what-ifs.

She wanted to say that fog had to do with the long stint she'd gone without sex, but she feared it had more to do with Matt in particular. Being wrapped in his arms that morning had been enough to whet her appetite.

Having a fling wasn't like her, but she wanted to, badly. Her life stayed under a microscope. She had an obligation to the town who had expectations of her. Still there was nothing like the feeling of being desired. Matt had given her that as no one else had. Her and John's relationship had been about youth and dreams and being comfortable. With Matt it was about being mature, of knowing what she wanted; and the fact Matt made her uncomfortable in a good way. *It has been too long since you've been held in a man's arms, much less been kissed into oblivion.* It was a heady experience. She could so easily get drunk on need.

That morning when she'd come out of the bathroom, he'd still been in bed. The temptation to join him had almost taken her control. Instead, she'd gone into doctor mode and cared for his legs. "I'm going to ask Ms. Gladys to check on you."

"You're going to do what?" He sat up in bed. "Are you trying to punish me?"

She narrowed her eyes and pursed her lips as if talking to a child. "Someone needs to check on you. To make sure you aren't running a fever."

"I'll go to work. I can make it." He grabbed the sheet as if planning to flip it back.

"No, you won't. You need to stay off your legs for the day. Without you at the clinic I can't get away to see you." Her look bore into him. "That leaves Ms. Gladys. And if I know her, and I do, she'll see that you are fed. I already have her bringing you soup."

Matt groaned and leaned back.

"I'd suggest you get a shower now." She glanced down at his hips barely covered by the sheet. "And put on some clothes because ten minutes after I talk to her, she'll be over here."

He glared at her much like he had the night before. "You're enjoying this, aren't you?"

Shay grinned. "A little."

He gave her his best wolfish look that made her eyes widen. "You do know I'll have to get you back for this."

"I'm not the one who stepped in the fire ants." She stepped back toward the door.

"You can be a cold woman, Dr. Lunsford. How're you going to handle the clinic by yourself? Why don't I come in after lunch?"

"I'll deal. You need to stay off those legs *all* day. Keep in mind I'll be asking Ms. Gladys for a report this evening when I stop by to see how you're doing. Now, I've got to go, or I'll be late."

Shay called at lunchtime to check on him.

He growled, "I'm fine and I'm going to get you for this. Ms. Gladys is killing me with kindness. Come save me."

She couldn't help but laugh.

As soon as she locked up the clinic she headed to Matt's. Her heart beat faster as she drove closer to his house, yet her mind pushed down the excitement. She had no business getting involved with a man who wouldn't be around after the next two weeks.

When she arrived at Matt's house, Ms. Gladys met her in the drive with her mouth pinched with worry.

"How's the patient doing?" Shay climbed out of the car.

The older woman placed her hands on her hips. "He told me he was going to take a nap and locked me out."

Shay put her arm around Ms. Gladys's shoulders and gave her a gentle squeeze. "I appreciate your help today. I know Matt will tell you he's thankful when he's feeling better. I'll check on him, but he should be able to take care of himself from here on out. I'll call you if we need you."

"Please do, dear. His legs really are a mess." Ms. Gladys shook her head and started toward her house.

The lawnmower still sat in the yard and Shay went after it, pulling it in under the carport. She knocked on the door and waited patiently. On his bad legs it would take Matt a while to get to the door, plus she had no doubt he was hiding out from Ms. Gladys.

Finally, she saw the curtain move and an eye peeking out. The click of the door soon followed. It was quickly opened.

"Get in here," Matt snapped, looking around frantically. "Hurry."

Shay stepped inside the house, barely controlling her laughter. "Aren't you being a little dramatic?"

Matt glared at her. "You aren't the one she threatened to bathe!"

Shay burst into laughter. She held her waist as tears rolled down her face. Matt gave her a look of disgust and hobbled off. Working to get the merriment under control, she followed him into the living room.

He plopped into the recliner and pulled the footrest up. His legs looked awful. Soon they would start to itch without mercy. He wouldn't like that either.

"You have no idea what I've endured today and now you're laughing at me. Is this your idea of a good bedside manner?"

She couldn't help but huff at that. Which had him glaring at her again. "I'm not at your bedside. I'm making a house call to check on your legs. Do they hurt? It looks like the swelling has gone down."

"It has. I started feeling better this afternoon. The only problem was that I couldn't convince Ms. Gladys of that."

Shay chuckled, covering it with a cough. She glanced around the room. "You know if you'd open some of these curtains and get some sunlight in here it would help your feelings." She stepped toward a window.

"Don't open that. I like watching TV in the dark, plus I'm afraid Ms. Gladys will look in the windows."

She dropped her hand to her side. "Now you're just being silly."

"I know she's just being nice, but I'm not in the mood."
He reached down and scratched his leg.

"Don't do that. I brought you some aloe to put on it to
keep down the itching." She went to the kitchen where
she'd left her bag on the table. Opening it, she pulled out
the plastic jar with the green gel and returned to Matt.
She handed it to him. "This should help. I also have a
couple of allergy pills for you to take. You should be able
to return to work on Monday." She took those out of her
pocket. "I'll check on you tomorrow."

"You're leaving me?" His disappointed look fed her
ego.

"I am. I have a committee meeting tonight."

His mouth turned down. "Thanks for coming by, then.
I'll be fine." His attention returned to the sports on TV.
"I'll see you at the clinic."

Shay left feeling like she'd done something wrong.
Had he been upset with her for not wanting to stay with
him? Being around Matt outside the clinic only increased
her chances of heartache. She had enough of those for
a lifetime.

But she liked him, like no other man in a long time.
Matt intrigued her. Kept her on her toes. Excited her. All
of that had been missing in her life. She felt invigorated
being around him. She'd been going through the motions, the same old actions, for so long it was liberating
to break out of the mold.

By the time Saturday afternoon rolled around, Matt had
had enough of being the invalid. His legs were much better but looked awful. He would recover. Having become
desperate for company, he answered the door when Ms.
Gladys had come over to see how he was. She'd brought

him lunch. He'd had mercy on her and been civil, but the person he really wanted to see was Shay.

He picked up his phone and called her. She answered on the second ring. "Matt, are you all right?"

"My legs are fine, but I'm bored out of my mind. If I order in pizza will you join me? Stay and watch some TV. I promise to behave myself. Just a friendly night in." She took so long to answer he feared she wouldn't do so.

"Sorry. I already have plans."

Disappointment washed through him. "Okay, I understand. See you later." He prepared to hang up.

"Matt?"

"Yeah?"

She hesitated a moment. "If you want to go with me you can."

His blood quickened. "I'll be ready when you get here."

"You don't even know where we're going." Surprise filled her voice.

Desperate to get out of the house, and a chance to see Shay, it didn't matter where they were going. "I don't care. I just need to get out."

"All right. Dress casual and bring a change of clothes."

"Now, that does sound interesting." Where could they be going?

"Don't get any ideas. I can change my mind," Shay said.

"I promise to be a gentleman."

"I'll be there in fifteen minutes."

"Don't bother coming to the door. I'll be watching for you."

Shay chuckled. "You really are wanting to get out."

"And I'm looking forward to seeing you." He was, too much.

"Matt." Her voice held a warning.

"Understood. See you in a few." He ended the call.

Good as her word she pulled into his drive minutes later. He was out the door before she stopped the car. He glanced over to see if Ms. Gladys stood at the window. He didn't see her. Opening the passenger door, he threw his bag in the back seat and climbed in. It was one thing to have his neighbor concerned about him, another to have her in his business all the time. "Let's go before Ms. Gladys comes out and starts asking questions."

"In a hurry?" Shay grinned as she backed out of the drive.

As she left the city limits, he asked. "Where're we going?"

"To my farm."

"I didn't know you had a farm."

"I don't talk about it much. It's my hideaway. The one place where I can be me."

He looked at her. "Be you?"

"Yeah. Not the doctor. Not the daughter. Not the daughter-in-law, not a hero's wife. Just plain old me."

"I didn't know you minded being all those things." He'd thought Shay was happy being all things to the town.

Her mouth thinned. "I don't mind most days, but others it's a burden. So sometimes I need to get away."

"You still haven't really answered to where."

She turned and headed out of town going west, putting the sun in their eyes. "We're going out to my grandparents' homestead. I bought it from my parents a few years ago."

"Your mother's or father's side?" As they left the regular stores and businesses of the city and the homes of the suburbs the scenery turned into flat farmland with rows of cotton and corn. Occasionally there would be fenced-in fields with cows grazing.

"It belonged to my grandparents on my mother's side. She inherited it. There isn't much to it, but it's mine. I've spent any extra time I have fixing it up. I had a few things I wanted to do this weekend and you happened to call as I was going out the door."

"How far away is it?"

"About forty-five miles from your place. A little closer from mine."

"You ever thought about moving out there?" He looked out at the rich delta dirt.

"About every day."

He glanced at her. "Then why don't you?"

She pulled up the corner of her mouth. "I don't know. I guess because it's easier to stay where I am."

"Really? Forever? So when you remarry you'll want to live where you and your ex-husband lived?"

She shrugged. "I've never really given it any thought."

"Which one? Remarrying or where you would live."

"Either."

Matt looked at her in complete disbelief. "As smart, vivacious and beautiful as you are you don't think someone would want to marry you? You'd be a real catch. Perfect, in fact."

Shay narrowed her eyes. "Are you offering?"

He gulped. It had sounded like that. "No, I uh…was just saying. Maybe we should change the subject."

"You know I was kidding you about the offer of marriage."

This wasn't what he wanted between them. He'd gone

too far. "I'm sorry, Shay. I said more than I should. It's not my business. I should use my manners. I'm your guest on this trip."

Her body relaxed. She made a right turn down a dirt road. Dust billowed up behind them as they traveled. Soon they drove into an area with fenced grass fields on either side of the road. She made a turn up a drive with grass down the center of the lane.

"This belongs to me." Shay waved a hand at both sides of the drive.

"How many acres do you have?" Matt watched as they approached an area with trees. Among them he could just make out the corner of a white clapboard building with a red tin roof.

"There's twenty acres left, but I did manage to save some along the river. Even though it's at the back of the property. The house couldn't be too close to the river because it might flood."

As they drew closer, he could tell the trees were a cluster of large oaks. Shay drove onto a grassy area then around one of the trees and pulled to a stop in front of the house. A porch ran the length of the front. On either side of the door were a set of red rockers with yellow pillows in them. Between the chairs sat a white table with a red flowering plant on it.

Everything about the place looked like peace and tranquility. It couldn't be more different from the house Shay had shared with her husband or his apartment in LA.

"I know it's not much, but it's mine." Pride filled her voice.

"I like it. It looks like you."

Shay smiled, obviously pleased with the idea. She had the best smile. It reached her eyes, made her face glow.

"Come inside. I'll give you the grand tour of all four of the rooms."

He followed her onto the porch and held the screen door while she unlocked the wooden door with a glass panel across the top. She pushed it wide and they stepped inside. The walls of the room were painted white and the wooden floor gleamed. An overstuffed sofa sat at an angle in the far corner. Two matching chairs faced a fireplace with a large footstool in front of them. A small desk and bookcase had been positioned against another wall. Thin white curtains hung on each side of the two windows in the room.

"Obviously the living room." She moved to a doorway off the living room. "This is your bedroom."

A regular-size bed with a high wooden headboard and matching footboard filled the small space. A bedside table and a chest of drawers were the only other furniture. A braided rug lay on the same type of flooring as the living room.

She directed him down a short hall to a room to the left. It was a kitchen which looked to have been recently redone in a retro look. Even the refrigerator was a sea foam green. A farmhouse sink faced one of the windows. The small wooden table had two mismatched chairs.

"My bedroom is across the way." She pointed to a door but didn't stop. "The bath is back here."

It was a small room with all the basics. The large two-person claw-foot tub was the showpiece of the room. What he wouldn't give to share that with her. *Stop those thoughts. You made a promise.* "Nice tub."

"Yep. The shower is out back." She remarked it as if she knew exactly what he'd been thinking and wanted to remind him of his place.

"Got ya. You said you had a few things to do. How can I help?" He moved to a window to look out. There were two outbuildings behind the house.

"I didn't bring you out here to put you to work." She fussed with a towel near the sink.

He met her gaze. "Why did you bring me?"

She shrugged. "You sounded desperate to get out and I happened to be coming here. I thought you could rest and see something different than the four walls of your living room. It's also a good idea for someone to keep an eye on you for another day and make sure you've fully recovered."

Matt put his hands in his back pockets and gave her a quizzical look. "Are you sure those are your only reasons?"

Shay turned away. "Yes, that's it. You don't believe me?"

Matt grinned. He made her nervous. She wasn't as unaffected by him as she acted yet she made sure she held him at arm's length. "Unfortunately, I do. Now tell me what you want done."

Shay looked as if she wanted to say more, but she didn't. "I need the yard mowed."

He winced and looked down at his legs. "I'll take care of it with my new knowledge in hand. I know how to stay out of the ants' way now. Where's the mower?"

"It's in the smokehouse. The larger building out back." She pointed out the back door. "If your legs start bothering you, stop."

"Yes, Doctor."

Matt had the yard half-finished when he pulled off his shirt and wiped his face with it, then slung it over the wooden fence. He had made a few passes around the yard and he'd looked over to see Shay outside beside the window she'd been repairing. Instead of working on it she stood with a screwdriver in hand watching him. He waved and she quickly turned away.

Exactly why had Shay brought him here? He wasn't her type. She wanted hearth and home while he was all about ambition and work. How could they ever find common ground?

Shay gulped. Matt had removed his shirt. She couldn't help but stare. The last time she acted this muddleheaded about a man with a bare sweaty chest she'd been a teen. Actually, it hadn't been this bad when she'd been high school crazy about her eventual husband. Where Matt was concerned, she'd lost her sense of perspective.

He smiled at her on his next round.

She pursed her lips and turned her attention to the window. The worst part was that he recognized her desire. After giving him time to make a turn so his back was to her, she looked at him again. He stayed fit. That she would give him. Shay went back to scraping the window seal. With little enthusiasm, she planned to paint before he turned to come back her way. She refused to be caught ogling him.

By the time he had finished cutting the grass, she had gone inside to prepare their evening meal. At the slam of the car door, she guessed Matt had gone after his bag. Not long after the shower started running. That only added to her agitated nerves. The thought of naked Matt standing under the water had her hands shaking.

Subconsciously, had she had an ulterior motive for bringing Matt to her hideout? Was she that desperate? How pitiful. Especially after she'd told him to keep his distance. Why couldn't she just admit she was attracted to him? That she'd liked having his attention even for a little while.

"Hey."

She jumped at the sound of Matt's voice. Had what she'd been thinking been written all over her face? He'd changed into a T-shirt and jeans, but his feet remained bare. His hair stood out, messy and damp. Sexy would be how she'd describe him, if asked. "Hi."

"What're you up to?"

"I'm preparing our supper." She held a bowl in her hand.

He leaned against the door casing as if he hadn't a care in the world. Like he spent every weekend at a woman's home. "You've done enough for me already. I should take you out to dinner."

"No way. Coming out here is about getting away." She forced her hands not to tremble.

"Okay. I can live with the rules." He stepped farther into the kitchen.

"I thought if you didn't mind, we'd have a picnic. The weather's great." She pulled the large hamper off a shelf and placed it on the table.

"That sounds nice. What can I do to help?" He came close enough she could smell the soap she'd left in the shower rack. He wore it well.

"We need a quilt. There's one in the bottom drawer of the chest in your room. If you would get it." She put the bowl on the counter. It rattled to a stop.

"I'm on it. By the way, I brought your bag in and set it by your door."

"Thanks." As he left she called after him, "You might want to bring a jacket or sweatshirt if you have one."

By the time Matt returned, she had the hamper and small cooler ready to go. He'd put on tennis shoes and had a sweatshirt in hand. "What do I need to carry?"

"If you can get the cooler off the counter, I think we'll be ready." She picked up the hamper.

"Where're we having this picnic?"

"There's a nice spot down by the river. While we're there I need to check on a dying tree my neighbor told me about."

"Dying tree? I've never had to check on one of those before. Shay, you do have fascinating ways of entertaining a man." His heated gaze locked with hers.

Her heart pumped faster. "Come on, we need to load the four-wheeler. It's in the shed."

"Now that sounds like fun."

"Have you ever ridden on one?" She led him to a small shed and unlocked it.

"Nope. But I've always wanted to."

She set the hamper on the ground beside Matt's feet. "I'll back out then we can load the food."

When she had the four-wheeler out, they strapped the containers on a rack behind the seat. Shay climbed on and Matt got on behind her. She put the machine in gear, and they headed down a path she used to the river. She hadn't anticipated how intimate it would be to ride with Matt's thighs pressed against hers or his hands at her waist.

A couple of times she stopped for large limbs that had fallen in the path. Matt quickly climbed off and removed them. The nicest thing about him was that she didn't have to ask him to help. He knew what needed doing and did it. She'd forgotten what it was like to have someone as a partner.

He asked close to her ear so he could be heard over the motor, "Are all these trees yours?"

"They are. They were so close to the river they weren't cleared for farming land. I'm lucky to have them. Most landowners don't have any. Over the years the river has changed course."

"They're amazing."

"They're one of the reasons I love this place so much." She continued driving over the pine needle bed and down into a dry creek and out again. She slowed as she came to a stand of trees. Stopping, she turned off the four-wheeler.

"This is where the tree is supposed to be." She looked up, studying the tops.

Matt came to stand beside her. "What're we looking for?"

"Some indication the tree is dying. See the top of the tree is turning brown." She walked to the tree.

He followed.

She pointed to a mass of sap running out of the tree. "This shows where the bugs have been boring into the wood."

Matt reached as if to touch it. Shay caught his arm, stopping him. "You don't want to get sap on your hands. You'd have a devil of a time getting it off."

"What's the big deal about bugs in one tree?"

"The bugs will spread. In no time they would kill a number of these trees. I'll have to have this one removed and spray the others. These trees have been around too long to lose them now."

"I've never thought about trees or tree-eating bugs." He put his hands in his pockets and looked up.

"I don't guess there's a big call for concern about either in Chicago."

He continued to look at the tree. "There isn't. But who knows, one day that might change and now I know what to look for. Once again, I've learned something from you. Knowledge is always a good thing."

Shay smiled and continued walking as she studied the trees. "I've learned a few things from you too."

"That would be?"

"That I need to stop and listen when someone offers learned help. That there are people who are willing stand up for what's right even if it may hurt them." She grinned at him. "That Uncle Henry has good taste in friends.

"What I don't know is why you don't talk about your family. I've not heard you say anything about your stepfather. What's the deal there?"

By the look on Matt's face, she may have ruined the entire day. His jaw tightened and his lips thinned.

She touched his arm. "Hey, you don't have to talk about him if you don't want to."

"It's no problem." He shrugged. "My stepfather is a man with a well-defined list of what life should consist of. He believes in doing the right thing. That we have to protect those who can't take care of themselves. We should always be the best at what we do."

"He sounds like a good man."

"Yeah, I just wished I recognized that sooner. It took me growing up to understand him better. By then there was such a distance between us I don't know if we will ever find common ground now."

"It's never too late to try." Shay's soft suggestion held hope.

"Maybe so. But I been so busy since I left home and seen so little of them I feel more like a stranger than a family member."

"I can't imagine that ever happening with my family. But everyone makes time for what they want to do."

Matt winced. "I guess I'm just making weak excuses for being a jerk."

Shay touched his arm again. She didn't want him to think she was criticizing him. "I didn't mean to make you feel bad. I know your work takes dedication, but family and our friends are important as well."

He continued to look at the trees for a moment before he said, "Are you ready to go? I want to see the river."

They climbed back on the four-wheeler.

Shay understood Matt better. He'd seen his family so rarely in the last few years that he feared he didn't fit in anymore. She hated that for him. His family must miss him. He needed them and didn't realize it.

CHAPTER EIGHT

MATT WATCHED WITH interest as they continued down the path. They broke out into open land on a bluff with the river beyond. He made an effort not to think about what he'd revealed about himself to Shay. How he'd treated his family. They all deserved better. How had he convinced himself it was a good idea to stay away? Because of his hang-ups he had hurt them. That only made matters worse.

He climbed off the four-wheeler, then helped Shay off. They stood looking out over the river with its steady current flowing to the south.

"Damn, this is amazing. I know the Mississippi is a huge river just from the few times I've driven over it, but this is unbelievable."

"It's impressive, isn't? Wait until you see it against the sunset." She nudged him with an elbow.

"And this spot," Matt said with awe as he looked around them.

"Yeah, it's my special place." And she'd chosen to share it with him. He felt honored.

"You brought me to your special place, huh?" He didn't look at her, instead letting his voice let her know what that meant to him.

"Hey, don't let your head get too big. I had planned this trip before I let you tag along."

"Okay, you have now put me in my place."

"It wasn't intentional. This spot always calms me. Makes me feel better. After John died, I spent a lot of time here. I wanted to have our wedding ceremony here. Just John and me, our families, but it wasn't large enough for John, and the town wouldn't have been happy if they weren't invited."

"You had the wedding that he wanted." It was like the relationship had swallowed her up and taken her over. Where had the Shay he knew been then?

"Yeah. I guess I did."

"Not to speak ill of the dead, but he sounds like he was a pretty self-centered guy."

"I didn't realize that then, but I can see it now." It sounded as if she had just figured that out.

"Have you ever wanted to marry?"

"I thought I did. I had a girlfriend and even asked her to marry me but she turned me down."

Shay turned to face him, sympathy on her face. "Why did she do that?" Her eyes widened. "Forget I asked that. It's not my business."

Matt hesitated a moment. Did he even understand enough about the why to answer? "I'm not proud to admit it, but I guess I was selfish too. I thought she was the one. We were both into our careers. When I realized I had to move I asked her to go with me. I hadn't thought how doing so would affect her career. She said no. I didn't think I could stay. I guess I didn't care enough about her to stay. It's taken me a while to figure that out."

"That still had to have hurt when she said no."

He shrugged. "It did, but I know now that it wasn't meant to be."

"I can't say that the way John treated me doesn't still hurt. We spent too many years together. What I will say is that I learned to be happy with myself, but it took a long time."

Matt winced. Could he say the same about himself? He'd messed up his relationship with Jenna, expecting her to give up everything for him. Then there was his job situation. Could he have handled it differently to preserve his position? And his family? They deserved better than his avoidance. How had his life become such a twisted rope of *wish I had, could I have and can I.*

He couldn't deny that it all hurt. Matt put his arm around Shay's shoulders and gave her a quick hug. "Enough of all that. Tell me what you know about the river."

"Are you sure you want more of me expounding on history and stuff? Haven't you had enough of that?"

"I can never get enough." He took her hand. "Expound away."

Shay cleared her voice as if she were about to present the knowledge of life. "It's the lifeline around here. The Mississippi is the second largest river in North America. The Native Americans called it the Great River. It flows into the Gulf of Mexico. I've heard you can step over it where it begins. I'd like to do that sometime. I can't imagine that since it's so wide down here. Oh, there are only five bridges across it. The main ones are at St. Louis, Memphis and New Orleans. Which means you have to drive a long way around to get to the other side depending on where you want to go."

Matt chuckled. "I certainly hit on the right subject."

She gave him a mortified look. "I told you."

"Hey." He waited until she looked at him. "I liked hearing all of that. I found it interesting."

He stood behind her and put his arms around her waist, holding her securely. His cheek rested against the side of Shay's head. She leaned back against him. They stood like that for a long time. Somehow being with Shay eased his burdens. It had felt good to share his pain over his family. To have her know all of him. The good and the bad.

At his stomach's rumble, Shay giggled. "Let's have dinner before your stomach complains more."

They unloaded the four-wheeler and laid out their meal. Each took a side of the blanket with the food between them. Shay served their plates.

When they were done Shay said, "I bet you think we don't have bright lights like you do in the big city, but I'm going to show you different."

His blood ticked up a notch. "That sounds interesting. What do you have in mind?"

"Help me clean up this food and I'll show you." A hint of humor filled her voice.

A few minutes later they had everything packed away and secured on the four-wheeler.

Shay returned to the quilt and sat down. She patted a spot beside her. "Hurry. You don't want to miss it."

Matt sat close, but not touching her.

"Now watch." She pointed to the west where the sun hung low on the horizon.

He took her hand as they watched the bright yellow sun, then the burst of light turning orange and pink as it fanned out and slowly slipped beneath the land. "That was amazing. You win on the best light show."

"Hey, we're not done yet. The next show is coming up." She pointed toward the river. A barge with lights burning slowly moved up the river. A few minutes later another came by going the other direction.

They watched in silence for a while.

"It's so peaceful and calm here that it makes me not fear anything for just a little while." Her voice was but a whisper, as if she spoke as much to herself as to him.

"What do you fear?"

She sighed. "Sometimes I worry that I'll end up like Delta Dawn in the song. Wandering around town thinking about what was and not living in the 'what is.'"

He wanted to take her in his arms and tell her that wouldn't happen to her. But how could he say that? He wouldn't be around to help make it any different for her. He didn't want to hurt her. She'd had more of that than she deserved. Shay needed someone who would give her security and the assurance that she was the center of his world. He couldn't even bring himself to see his family. He was in the middle of seeing where his life would go, and he had no right to involve Shay in the mess it had become. He wasn't in any position to make promises.

"How about you? What do you fear?"

"That I'll never have another night like this."

Shay watched him for a moment, then leaned toward him and cupped his cheek. "That was the nicest thing that has been said to me in a long time and I needed that." Her lips touched his.

They were as sweet and plump as he remembered. And he wanted more.

Shay's arms wrapped around his waist as she moved closer, her soft body pressing against his. His heart went into overdrive as his blood heated. She felt so good against him. She opened her mouth to him. Matt invaded, taking and giving. Shay returned the need.

Thunder rolled and Shay pulled back. "We've got to go. She jumped up and Matt followed.

"It looks like we're going to get a third light show that I hadn't planned on. This time of the year the thunderstorms can be dangerous. We especially don't want to be in the trees when it comes over us. It can get scary out here quickly."

Fighting his disappointment, Matt grabbed up the blanket into a wad and took her hand. "Then let's move."

Soon they were making the return trip to the house. They had made it out of the trees when the first drop of rain hit him. The wind bellowed against them and a couple of times Shay had to work to keep the four-wheeler steady. The lightning flashed with too much frequency and too close for his taste. He leaned over Shay in an effort to protect her from the pelting rain. With great relief, she pulled up under the shed.

"Leave this stuff." She indicated the items strapped to the back of the four-wheeler. "We'll get it in the morning. Run for the front porch. That'll be easier than trying to go in the back. We can take off some of these wet clothes before we go in the house."

Hand in hand they raced across the yard. Lightning flashed again and Matt saw a smile on Shay's face. Now that they had made it to safety, she was enjoying the experience. When they got to the end of the porch, he picked her up and placed her on her feet under the roof into the dry then he stepped up beside her. Shay had left a light on beside the door.

"This is some weather. Not here one minute and then on top of you the next."

She shrugged. "I warned you."

He grinned. "That you did."

Shay pulled off her shoes and windbreaker. "Turn around."

"Why?"

Her hands went to the hem of her shirt. She gave him a challenging look. "Because I'm going to take off these wet clothes before I go into the house and get us towels."

"You do know I'm a doctor, don't you? I've seen bodies in underwear before."

Her look didn't change. "That may be so, but you've not seen mine."

"Not because I don't want to."

Her eyes widened.

"I'm sorry. I shouldn't have said that." He shouldn't be thinking it either. Hadn't he already decided that he wasn't what Shay needed in her life? That they were traveling down two different roads? He should be keeping his distance instead of making suggestive remarks. Kissing her. "I'll be a gentleman and turn around."

He waited for the door to close before he stripped off his shirt and dropped it with a plop on the wooden boards. How was he going to stay here with Shay and not act on his attraction to her especially after their kiss? While she talked as if she didn't want to get involved with him, she'd brought him to her special place and kissed him. Was she as confused by what she felt as he was?

Shay returned wearing a large T-shirt that covered her to the top of her thighs. He swallowed hard. She'd never looked more amazing or vulnerable. Her focus left his eyes and dropped to his chest.

"Shay?"

"Mmm."

"Can I get a towel?"

"Oh, yeah." She threw him a towel. He used it on his hair.

"When you're done leave the wet stuff out here and we'll see about them tomorrow."

"Is this a new way to get me naked? If it is, I like it."

Shay looked away from him. "No. I just don't want my floors sopping wet. I worked too hard on them to see them ruined." She began toweling her long hair.

"Let me help you." He stepped close behind her, taking the towel from her.

"I can do it."

"I know that, but I'd like to."

Her gaze met his for a moment, then she dipped her head toward him.

Matt gently rubbed the top of her head then started on the ends of her hair, putting sections between the terrycloth and rubbing it together. What was happening to him? He'd never given another woman this type of care. Shay had a way of bringing out the tenderness in him.

"That feels so nice." She moaned and looked at him.

"Shay, don't look at me that way."

"How's that?"

He sighed. "As if I were a man worthy of you."

"Who said you weren't?" She came up on her toes and kissed the corner of his mouth.

"Shay, think about what you're doing. If we take this further, I want you to know I can't make any promises. I don't want to hurt you."

"I'm a big girl. I know the score and what I want. I can take care of myself. Right now, at this minute, I want you."

The towel joined his shirt in a pile. His hands cupped her shoulders as he felt her warm, sure hands at his waistband.

She released the button on his jeans. "I told you these had to come off."

His breath caught. This he hadn't anticipated from Shay, but he sure liked it.

With a deliberate tug, she lowered his zipper. "I can't have a guest who won't mind."

His mouth found hers. Her hands roamed his chest. She shivered. He pulled her against him.

When he broke the kiss, she said, "I want you to make love to me. I need... I just need."

Shay had no idea what had come over her. She'd never acted like this before. That had been one of John's complaints about her: she wasn't aggressive enough. Here with Matt, it hadn't occurred to her he wouldn't welcome her attention. With John it had been all about him. With Matt he gave more than he took. She'd seen him do it in so many ways.

She pushed at his pants, the wet material making it difficult to get them off. He chuckled. He took a pace back and finished the job, stepping out of his jeans. His length stood tall and proud behind his knit boxers. She could hardly remember the last time she'd been desired so obviously. It was empowering.

Matt brought her against him. She basked in his warmth, her hands circling his waist and kneading his back.

He kissed her forehead. "I need you too."

She took his hand, leading him inside and down the hall to her bedroom.

He stopped in the doorway. "I believe this is the most feminine room I've ever been in."

She'd chosen to do it in a pale blue with plenty of pillows. A quilt made of pastel flowers covered the brass bed, with its high headboard and a footboard. It sat catty-corner to the door, making a statement in the space. A French provincial dresser with a large mirror was stationed against one wall. She'd positioned an overstuffed chair next to a window with a floor lamp behind it. The ruffled curtains in white with a hint of blue dots finished the look.

"This is all me."

Matt stepped around her and looped his arm loosely at her waist. "I like 'the' you. And I like your bedroom. I like you in your feminine bedroom even better."

"You don't think all this—" she waved a hand around "—will hurt your performance?"

He grinned. "Why don't you let me know what you think in the morning. By the way, the room suits you." His fingers were featherlight as they trailed down her arm. "Soft, sweet and sensual."

She shivered, her nerves alive from Matt's touch. Shay liked that description of herself. For too long she'd had to act strong and resilient. Be what others expected of her.

He teased the hem of her shirt. "I think we should get under the covers where you can be warm."

The storm still raged outside. Rain tapped against the window. The light in the kitchen flickered and went out.

"There went the electricity. Wait here a second." She went to the dresser and opened the top drawer and found the matches she kept there. On the next flash of lightning, she lifted the glass chimney of the oil lamp sitting on top of the dresser. She lit the wick. Light flickered softly around them.

"I'm glad you lit it. I want to see you. To appreciate all of you." He tugged off her shirt then kissed her. As he did, he reached around her and unhooked her bra. His hands brushed the straps down her arms. It fell to the floor between them.

Matt cupped a breast in each of his hands. He lifted them as if testing their weight. "Perfect."

The way he whispered the word with such reverence made her believe it. He kissed the top of one just above the nipple straining for his touch. Moving to the other breast, he placed his warm mouth over the nipple and sucked. She shuddered. Her center clenched. Biting her bottom lip, Shay stopped herself from moaning her pleasure as her fingers fed through his hair.

As his devotion continued, Matt's thumb hooked into the elastic of her panties at her hips. He tugged them down to her knees, then let them drop to the floor. Standing, he held her hand as she stepped out of them. Backing away to arm's length, his gaze started up her body.

Shay moved to cover herself. Matt stopped her, taking her hands. "You are breathtaking. Please let me admire you. Just so amazing in the lamplight." His eyes locked with hers. "You're amazing all the time."

She loved hearing that from him. Over that past few years, she hadn't felt as if she were amazing in any area of her life. At the clinic she been giving back to the community that had supported her, while knowing the man who had been her life for so long no longer wanted her. Not just that, but had replaced her with another woman. She needed someone to see her. Matt did.

He walked backward toward the bed, bringing her

with him. Pushing pillows to the floor, he jerked the quilt back. He turned her around, so she stood with her back to the bed before he picked her up and placed her on it.

As she watched, Matt removed his boxers. He then lay on his side next to her. He propped his head on his hand. His other came to her belly, his finger drawing small circles on her skin. She sucked in air as her core heated.

She reached to touch him. He stopped her. "No, stay still. Just feel. I want to enjoy you. We have all night."

Shay wasn't sure she could remain immobile. Her body tingled all over. Her blood roared through her veins to her center, creating a throbbing pool. Matt asked the impossible.

His fingers left a hot then cold trail as they traveled up to her breasts. He brushed a finger over her nipple. Her middle contracted. She squirmed.

"You liked that." Pure satisfaction hung in his voice. He gave her other breast the same caress before he leaned over and took it into his mouth.

She moaned, her hips flexing. She reached for him.

"Not yet." He placed her hand on the bed again then returned to loving her breasts. His tongue twisted and tugged. Her breasts went heavy with need. She closed her eyes, soaking in the sublime sensations flooding her body.

Matt's hand continued to work its magic as his mouth left a path of sweet nips along her neck. Her hands fisted in the sheet. Not soon enough for her, his mouth claimed her in a feverish kiss making her think of nothing but him. The need built like the storm outside into something out of control.

His hand left her breasts and skimmed down her ribs, across the plain of her stomach, and brushed her curls before cupping her between the legs. He didn't have to ask her to open for him. She had moved well past the point of no return. The want had taken over her mind. She wanted...had to have him now.

Matt's finger slipped into her ready center. She lifted her hips to meet the push and pull of his hand. Nerves at a heightened pitch tumbled over each other and grew, curled into themselves until she exploded with the fury, and experienced honeyed pleasure.

Matt continued to kiss her as if she were the most precious person in his life. He eased away and dropped a kiss on her shoulder.

Shay opened her eyes to find him watching her. A smile curved his gorgeous lips. She cupped his beard-covered cheek, brushing her thumb across his lips. "You've the most beautiful mouth."

He chuckled. "I like yours too. If I leave you for a sec you promise not to move?"

"I couldn't even if I wanted to."

He tapped her on the end of the nose with a fingertip and stood in all his nude glory. His manhood rose straight and thick in front of him. He headed out of the bedroom door giving her an amazing view of his tight butt. Matt was the best specimen of a man she'd ever seen. He soon returned with a foil package.

"Let me do that." She sat up and took the square from him.

As he stood before her, she slowly rolled the protection over him. Finished, she kissed his stomach.

"Shay," he hissed.

She took his hand and tugged him to the bed. He came down over her, his hot body covering hers. His length pressed her entrance.

"Are you sure, Shay?"

She gave him her best seductive smile. "Oh, I'm sure."

Matt, unable to control his craving any longer, slowly entered her. He paused to appreciate the softness and acceptance of Shay. Her heat welcomed him. Nothing had ever felt this good, this right. His mouth found hers as he pulled back, then moved forward again.

Shay clung to him. Her legs wrapped around his hips, pulling him to her. He pumped deeper, faster, harder. She tensed. Her fingers bit into his back.

With control beyond any he could have imagined, he sank into her once more.

Shay shuddered beneath him as she keened above the noise of the storm. "Matt."

With a final thrust, he joined her in a release that shook him to the core. He buried his face in her neck and moved to lie down next to her, weak from pure fulfilment unlike any he'd ever experienced.

As his breathing eased, he reached for Shay's hand, brought it to his lips and kissed the back of it.

Under control once again, he nudged Shay to him and shifted around in the bed until his head lay on a pillow. He pulled the covers up over them.

She placed her hand in the center of his chest and caressed the patch of hair there. Soon her breathing turned even in sleep.

By the time he woke, the storm had become a steady rain. The side where Shay had been had gone cold. Where was she? If anything, he didn't want her to regret what they had shared. Too many times he'd disappointed others. His mom, his stepfather, Jenna, even the board members in LA. Himself. He didn't want to do it again with Shay. Particularly with Shay.

He climbed out of bed. Cool air washed over him. Looking into the hall, he could see light coming from under the bathroom door. He knocked lightly, then gave the door a gentle push. What he saw took his breath and shook his manhood into instantaneous attention.

A multitude of candles glowed around the room. Shay, with her hair piled on her head, sat in the large footed tub with bubbles surrounding her. Her face looked flushed from the heat but the sparkle in her eyes was all about a woman well loved.

She grinned. "Hey, there. I was wondering when you'd show up. Close the door. You're letting the heat out."

He kicked the door closed and walked toward her. Placing his hands on the rim of the tub, he leaned down and kissed her. She returned it. Standing, he released the towel and let it drop to the floor. "Is there room for one more?"

A teasing glint twinkled in her eyes and she moved her legs to the side. "Only for a very special person."

With a grin, he stepped into the tub, sinking under the warm water as he faced her. His legs went to either side of her hips. She lay her legs across his thighs.

"Hey, you're splashing out the water," Shay protested.

He ran a hand along her calf across her knee and started up her thigh before he came down again. "Is that really what you're worried about?"

She lightly splashed the water in his direction.

"Now who's spilling the water?" He found her foot beneath the water and brought it to his lips and kissed her instep then nipped at her ankle bone. At Shay's quick inhale of breath, he smiled. He had her. Letting her foot go, it slid under the water. Her foot caressed the inside of his thigh. He reached for a breast peeking out of the bubbles, cupping it in his palm.

He grinned at her wickedly. "I'll scrub you if you'll scrub me."

Her lips went pouty and she looked away from him as if not interested. "I washed up before you took over my bath."

"Then you can concentrate on me."

Her gaze met his, holding it as she came to her knees. "I can do that."

Matt grinned as she moved toward him. Apparently, Shay no longer cared about water on her floor.

Her hand rested on his thigh and skimmed up it. "Is there any particular part you'd like me to start with?"

Red-hot desire shot though him. He grabbed her, pulling her along him as his mouth found hers. What had he done to deserve Shay?

CHAPTER NINE

MATT LEFT SHAY sleeping when he slipped out of bed. He pulled the bedroom door closed behind him as he headed to what was supposed to have been his bedroom. Picking up his bag off the floor, he found shorts and a T-shirt and pulled them on. He wouldn't call himself a cook, but he could put together breakfast.

Putting his hands above his head, he stretched. When was the last time he'd felt this good about life, or been so at peace? He couldn't say. Over the years he'd been with his share of women, but none had touched him like Shay. He'd never experienced such depth of caring even with Jenna. As awful as he thought being turned down by her and his work issues were, in an odd way they'd been a blessing. He'd come to Jackson and found Shay.

Yet he'd added another strand to his already-twisted life. He could become dependent on Shay. He'd feared she might want more when he should've been worried about himself. Would Shay consider a real relationship with him? A long-distance one? Why would she? Hadn't she had that with her husband? That had turned out bitterly. Hadn't his past proven he wasn't good with letting people in? Shay wouldn't accept half measures. She'd be nuts to take a chance on him. He sure wouldn't. But if he were different…

What if he slowed down? Realigned his priorities. Faced his insecurities. Could he capture this feeling forever? Maybe deserve Shay and happiness.

Going into the kitchen, he located what he needed to get a meal together. Even being in this simple home with its history gave him a sense of satisfaction, belonging. This world, the pace, was light-years different than his norm. It soothed his disappointments and fears. Just like the Mississippi River he and Shay had picnicked by, his anxieties had eased under the slow flow of living where people cared and showed it. Getting ahead wasn't everything here: people mattered. He would soak this up while he could, then hold on to it as long as he could in the days ahead.

He flipped the frying bacon and put bread in the toaster, then he sensed he wasn't alone. Turning with spatula in hand, he found Shay dressed in a thin housecoat standing in the doorway watching him. The soft smile she wore punched him in the gut. He was falling for her.

She held her nose up as if sniffing the air. "Hey, I had no idea you cooked. What you have in your kitchen certainly doesn't show that."

He held up the spatula. "I wouldn't make fun of the man fixing your breakfast. He might not share."

"I wasn't making fun. I was just surprised to hear you in here." She walked toward him.

"Did I wake you? I didn't mean to."

"No. I've been awake for a few minutes. It's nice to hear someone else in the house. It's usually too quiet."

"So, what you're saying is I'm being too noisy?"

"Not at all." She stopped just short of touching him. "What I'm telling you is it's nice to wake up knowing *you* are here."

Matt moved the pan off the burner and set the spatula on the counter. He turned back to her and scooped her into his arms, giving her a tender kiss. She had no idea what it meant to him to feel like he was enough just as he was for someone.

Shay clung to him as he slowly let her down to stand on her own feet. Her gaze locked with his. Warm contentment filled her eyes. They stood there for a while just looking at each other. Something had happened between them last night that he couldn't put a name to or maybe didn't want to. Whatever it was would bind him to Shay forever even after he had gone. Suddenly his new job and his life ahead didn't hold the same appeal they previously had.

Yet he'd made a commitment to the hospital in Chicago. There was his career to consider. How could he be the best if he didn't work in a major metropolitan city with a well-respected teaching university hospital affiliated with it. What he'd wanted and dreamed of was elsewhere. Everything but Shay.

Real life couldn't and wouldn't include Shay and mornings like this. That thought shook him. He looked away and stepped out of her arms. "I better get you fed."

Looking perplexed, Shay pulled the belt on her robe tighter as if protecting herself. He hadn't intended to hurt her. He just needed a minute to process his shaky emotions. He smiled. "Want to help?"

Her expression brightened. "Sure."

Together they finished preparing the meal and sat at

the table as sunlight streamed in on them. The scene was almost too perfect.

With their food eaten, Shay said, "Leave the dishes. Let's go out to the front porch and drink our coffee. This is the best part of the day."

Matt wasn't sure how she determined that. Any time of the day with her seemed wonderful to him.

For the next half an hour, they rocked and sipped from their mugs. He'd never done something like it before. None of the women he had been interested in would have settled for something so sedate. Hell, he wouldn't have. Shay and her world brought serenity to his.

Shay couldn't be more beautiful. She'd half pinned her hair up on her head. The other half fell down around her face in the most appealing way. She still wore only the robe. One foot she had tucked under her, while with the other she pushed the rocker with her big toe.

"I've been meaning to ask you how your legs were feeling?"

When he didn't say anything, her gaze met his. Her eyes widened slightly in question.

He must have looked like a lovestruck sap. Love? Was that what he felt? His chest tightened. Loving someone would make him vulnerable. Not having Shay's love could crush him. Did she or could she love him? Did she want to? He wouldn't go there. Instead, he'd enjoy what they had here and now and not expect more. If he did, he might be disappointed. For so long he'd felt he didn't measure up. It would destroy him if he disappointed Shay.

"I haven't thought much about them. I've had other things on my mind."

She smirked. "How about thinking about them? Do they itch?"

"After our hot bath I noticed them. The aloe helps."

She stood, took his hand, leading him into the house and to the bedroom that had started out as his. "Come in and lie on the bed so I can give those ankles a good look."

He flopped back on the bed, bringing his legs up so she could see them.

"There doesn't seem to be any more swelling." Shay studied the welts and gently touched a few spots.

"They don't hurt anymore." He waited until her gaze met his.

"You must've had good medical care." Her eyes twinkled.

"Tell me, Doctor, is this the kind of care all your patients receive?"

Shay stepped closer to him and said in a syrupy voice, "Oh, no, you're special."

He took her hand and tugged her down on the bed beside him. "That's good to hear. I'd be upset if it was for anyone else but me." He lightly brushed her breast and was rewarded with a catch in her breathing. "I'm thinking I might need more special attention."

Shay giggled. It sounded sweet, like a breeze through a wind chime. Despite what life had handed her she still looked forward to the possibilities ahead. She hadn't become bitter as he had. He admired that about her.

She smiled that special smile he'd seen her give only him. The peace she created in him settled over him again.

"We could stay here." She brushed her hand up and down his arm. "But I was thinking we could go swimming."

He hadn't seen a pool. The river wouldn't be wise. "Where?"

"In the pond."

"The pond?"

She stood and pulled on his hand. "Sure. Why not?"

"I've never swum in a pond before."

"Then you haven't been hot enough to swim wherever you can."

He grinned suggestively. "Oh, I've been hot enough."

A touch of pink rose in her cheeks. "You say things like that to get a reaction out of me."

Matt shrugged. "Maybe so but the reward is getting to see how cute you look when I tease you."

She gave him a quick kiss. "Let's go for that swim. It's almost noon and plenty warm enough." Shay popped off the bed.

"I didn't bring my suit," he called as she left the room.

"Who needs a suit?" She let the screen door slam.

Matt laughed. *Yeah, who needs a suit?*

Shay wasn't sure what had gotten into her. She had never been known as a free spirit. The idea of going skinny dipping, especially with a man in broad daylight, had gone way beyond her usual comfort zone. But it had felt so good. Liberating. How long had she lived under the expectations of others? Or those she put on herself? Far too long.

To make matters worse she'd had sex under the sun beside the pond. She'd taken all that repressed sexual desire and let it out into the world as if it were confetti. Now she stretched across her bed. Matt lay sleeping on his stomach next to her. They'd returned to the house and had a simple lunch and decided on a nap. That had turned into slow, sensuous and spine-tingling sex before sleep took them.

She would have never imagined how much her life

would have changed in just a few weeks. It was as if she'd been a firefly captured in a jar, blinking and living, a part of a group of other captured fireflies, then along came Matt, who opened the top and let her out into the world again. She wouldn't be going back into that jar.

Brushing her hand over Matt's back, she watched as the one eye she could see opened. "I hate to wake you, but it's getting late. We need to head to Jackson."

Matt moaned. "Do we have to?"

"We do." She kissed his shoulder and climbed out of bed.

An hour later they drove out the drive toward the main road and beyond the bubble of pleasure they'd created for them alone. She'd always had a sense of sadness when she left the farm. This time it was deeper. Her hours there had been perfect. The old house where her grandparents had been happy now held the same memories for her.

Somehow, she'd found herself again. Or maybe found the person she was meant to be. Matt had made her feel special. Not for being the head cheerleader, who became a doctor, who married the town hero, but cherished for the woman inside. Matt had given her a rare gift. One she would forever treasure.

Carrying around the knowledge that John, who she'd believed for most of her life would always be her one and only, then to learn she wasn't enough for him, had colored her entire world. Matt appreciated everything about her. He'd become her lover, but more importantly he was her friend.

He had only a few more weeks with her and she planned to make the most of them because it might be all the time they ever had. They might be from different worlds, yet they had collided and created something wonderful for a time. She intended to snatch every precious second while she could and hold it tight.

Even though her life remained under a microscope, she wouldn't give up Matt while she could have him. If a fling was what she could have then a fling would be what she would accept. There was nothing like the feeling of being desired. It had been so long since she had been, that the idea she was, and by someone as wonderful as Matt, had her dreaming of more. For too long she'd not been held in a man's arms much less kissed into oblivion. To have that now was a heady feeling. One she wasn't willing to give up until she had to.

Matt placed a hand on her shoulder, his fingers sliding under her hair to caress her neck. "Shay, when we get back to town, I'll understand if you want to keep what happened between us quiet. I know things sort of got out of control between us. I never want to hurt you."

Her chest tightened. "Is this your great sex but I'm moving on speech? If it is, save it. I'm a big girl. I can see about my own heart."

His fingers stilled. "Hell, that's not at all what I'm saying. Don't put words in my mouth."

"Then what *are* you trying to say?"

Matt sighed. She held her breath, waiting for him to speak.

"What I'm saying, poorly apparently, is that I care about you and that I want to see you as much and as often as possible until it's time for me to leave. Then I'd like for us to still see each other when we can."

Shay let her breath go. She looked at Matt in the dimming light of the day as her heart flew. "I want that too."

Matt smiled and returned to rubbing her neck.

She looked back at the road, then braked sharply.

* * *

Matt's look jerked to the road. Ahead of them a large piece of farm machinery lay half in the ditch at an odd angle with two of its wheels in the air. It was the only bump in the flat, wide field filled with white cotton hanging on the plant.

"Something's wrong." Shay's voice sent a sense of foreboding down his spine.

"How do you know?"

"I don't see anyone. No one would leave a cotton combine resting like that. They're top-heavy especially when full. We need to stop and make sure everything is all right."

She pulled quickly to the shoulder where the exposed underbelly of the machine showed it was still running. They both got out.

She cautiously moved forward, yelling above the sound of the engine. "Hey, is anybody here?"

Matt started around to the other side. Shay caught his arm. "Careful, this monster is really leaning."

Making a wide circle around the machine beside Shay, he studied the ground around the machine for a body. A large clear door hung open with a corner stuck in the ground.

"Matt," she gasped as she gripped his arm. "There's someone under it. Rick Stokes, is that you?" There was no answer. The machine creaked. She started forward then came to a stop. "If this falls it'll crush us all."

Matt paused a moment to think. The guy needed their help, but they'd be no good to him if they got hurt. "Move the car parallel to it on this side. If it starts down, it'll be supported by the car, leaving us space to get out."

She looked unsure for a moment as she studied the

situation but left him without a word. Moments later she pulled her car off the road near where he stood. He directed her into position.

Shay left the headlights on and turned on the emergency lights. Red flashed around them. Seconds later she was out of the car, carrying her medical bag. She hurried to the young man. "Rick?" She went down beside the man.

Matt joined them, reaching inside the cab and finding the key to turn off the machine. With that done, it became eerily quiet.

"Help." The word was but a whisper from the man on the ground.

A whoosh of air came from Shay. "Rick, how long have you been here?"

"I don't know. I wanted to get home before dark."

Matt went down on his knees beside Shay. A least that news was positive. Rick hadn't been there too long. Time would make the difference between saving the man's legs and having to remove them.

"Shay. Help me. My legs are caught."

"I'm right here. Just stay calm and keep talking to us."

Matt moved in closer to her. The ground was damp at Rick's hips. Matt feared his leg had been cut. Too much blood loss could mean the loss of the leg. He said to Shay, "You call 911. You know where we are better than I do. Tell them we need leg braces. Something to lift this machine off him."

Shay started punching numbers on her phone.

"Rick, I'm Dr. Matt Chapman, I'm a friend of Dr. Lunsford. I promise we won't leave you. I'm going to check your heart rate and pulse." Matt picked up the man's wrist and found the slow but steady movement of blood. He told those numbers to Shay who relayed them to the EMTs. "Tell them to call in Life Flight."

"They'll want to make that call," Shay stated.

Matt's eyes locked with hers. "Trust me. Tell them there isn't time to waste. He needs to get to the closest trauma one hospital in the next hour or lose his legs."

Turning back to the patient he said, "Rick, can you wiggle your toes?"

"No," he groaned.

"Try. Any movement is important to know." Matt worried Rick's blood flow had been cut off too long.

"I can't."

"Okay." Matt patted his shoulder. "More help will be here soon. Hang in there."

"Life Flight is on the way." Shay joined Matt on the ground again with the phone line still open. "And a wrecker."

"Rick, can you tell us what happened?" He had to keep the man aware. They'd need him to tell them what he was feeling when they got him out.

"I decided to drive over the ditch instead of going all the way down the field to the road. I wanted to save time." He took a deep rattling breath.

Matt looked over at Shay's concerned expression. They needed help soon or they might lose Rick. Not just his legs.

"The ditch was deeper than I thought. A tire came off the ground. I got out. Had to see if I could get unstuck. While I was looking at the tire the combine leaned more. I slipped trying to get away. It caught my legs."

Matt looked at his watch for the umpteenth time. *Where was that emergency crew?* All they could do was wait. Precious time was passing. With relief he heard the whine of sirens in the distance. The noise grew louder by the second.

"I hope the wrecker isn't far behind." Shay looked in the direction of the noise.

She'd voiced his fear. Without it there wasn't much they could do.

"I'll go meet them." Shay didn't wait on his response before she crawled out of their protected space.

The noise became deafening, then suddenly stopped. Matt took a moment to retake Rick's vitals. They weren't what they should be, but they were holding steady. That wouldn't continue much longer if they didn't get him out from under the combine.

The EMTs joined him with Shay right behind them.

One of the EMTs said, "What's the situation?"

Matt relayed the necessary information. He moved out of the way and let the paramedics go to work. Soon there was an IV line in Rick's arm.

"Where's that wrecker?" Matt called to no one in particular.

A male voice outside yelled, "It just pulled up."

"As the wrecker pulls the machine off him pressure needs to be applied to his legs as the pressure of the machine is release. Another person needs to pull him out while one more handles the IV. We need the board in here and leg braces."

"Doctor, we can handle this," the paramedic stated in a firm voice.

Matt met his look. "I appreciate your authority but the medical care he receives right away will make a difference whether or not he walks again. I'm an orthopedic surgeon who specializes in that care. Give me a fighting chance to give Ricky his legs back."

The paramedic waited a moment before he said, "Okay. We'll do it your way. They told me you were some big-time doctor."

The *beep-beep-beep* of the wrecker backing into position on the opposite side of the cotton picker drew their attention.

"Let's get that board in here," the paramedic called.

The backboard was passed through the opening. They worked to position it into place under Rick's head and shoulders.

A man from outside called, "Y'all are going to need to come out here while the picker is being lifted."

"No way," Matt announced. "I'm staying here. Applying pressure is too important. The ground is already damp with blood. Seconds could mean the difference. The car will protect me."

"We aren't willing to take a chance like that," one of the EMTs said.

"I'm not asking you to," Matt snapped.

"I'm staying too."

Matt gave Shay a narrow-eyed look of displeasure, but didn't bother to argue with her. By the look of determination on her face he'd never change her mind. He moved to Rick's head.

Slipping his arms under Rick's shoulders and clasping his hand over his chest, Matt prepared to pull him out. To Shay he said, "Be ready to apply pressure the second you can."

The EMTs hovered outside of the little tunnel created between the picker and the car.

The metal of the machine groaned and rattled then shattered as it was being lifted. It moved only an inch. Finally, the big piece of equipment shifted far enough

Matt could pull Rick out. Seconds later Shay applied pressure to the wound on the left leg while Matt settled Rick on the board.

The EMTs quickly joined them.

Matt moved around to Rick's right side and began running his hands over his leg. Rick winced when he touched his upper thigh. It was broken. "Rick, move your feet for me." Matt watched for the slightest movement. Relief washed through him when Rick's right foot relaxed slightly.

"Good," he told Rick. Matt then turned his attention to Shay. She still applied pressure to the other leg.

Shay met his look. "It's a compound fracture."

Matt nodded. "Let's let these guys do what they do best, get him ready to be transported. The leg needs to be cooled down."

"We have the ice packs waiting," one of the EMTs said as he took over for Shay.

"Don't remove his boots. We need them to slow down the swelling," Matt ordered.

Shay backed out of her side of the tunnel, and he did the same out of his. He walked around the car and joined her near the road.

The encouraging sound of the *whop-whop* of the helicopter could be heard in the distance.

"What do you think?" She glanced to where Rick lay.

Matt's lips thinned. "I won't really know until we get to the hospital. He has major injuries."

They both turned as the Life Flight helicopter set down in the middle of the road.

Matt touched her arm briefly. "I need to go talk to these guys. I'll be right back."

Soon the EMTs passed her with Rick secured on the board and ice packs around his legs.

Matt returned to her at a lope. "They have room in the copter for me. I'm going with Rick. I'll let you know how he's doing."

"Okay."

Matt didn't have time to say all he needed to or wanted to. He gave Shay a quick kiss then ran toward the helicopter.

Pride filled Shay at the work she and Matt had done. The EMTs had commented it had been the most amazing example of heroism they had ever seen. They couldn't get over her and Matt insisting they stay under the machine while the combine had been moved.

She watched as the helicopter lifted off until there was nothing but dim flashing lights and a hum of the engine. The noise of people moving around her and the slamming of doors said she needed to get going.

One of the guys working on the wrecker helped her back out onto the pavement. She headed for the hospital to check on Rick and to give Matt a ride home. By the time she arrived Rick was already in surgery. Matt had been invited into the OR to watch only because he didn't have privileges at the hospital. Shay waited in the doctors' lounge with the understanding a nurse would let Matt know she was there.

When she grew tired of her own company, she went out to the waiting room to look for Rick's parents. She ended up spending the rest of the time sitting with them. Late in the night, the surgeon who had done Rick's surgery with Matt beside him walked out to speak to the parents.

Dr. Roper, the best orthopedic surgeon in the city, introduced Matt. "This is the man that saved Ricky's legs. Without his initial care there wouldn't have been anything for me to work with."

Matt moved over beside her. "Dr. Lunsford was just as involved."

It was nice to have him remember her. John wouldn't have been so inclusive in sharing the limelight.

The surgeon continued. "Ricky will need another surgery that we've planned for the end of the week. I've asked Dr. Chapman to assist me."

She would see if she could find someone to cover for him at the clinic. Ricky needed Matt's skills. His talents were being underused at the clinic. She'd known that from the first week Matt had been there. He should be where he could do the most good.

When Dr. Roper turned to move away, Matt touched her arm. "I'll be right back."

She nodded.

Matt and Dr. Roper stepped to the side and spoke quietly. They shook hands and Matt returned to her. "I'm beat. Let's go home. I'm not used to seeing a case from start to finish. I usually come in at the middle."

"Pace kind of picked up around here, didn't it?" She yawned.

Matt put his arm around her shoulders and pulled her in close for a hug. "I think you are making fun of me."

"Who, me?" She grinned.

Less than half an hour later she pulled into Matt's drive. "I'll see you in the morning."

He didn't immediately get out. It was one of the few times she had seen him looking unsure.

"You know when you have a night like tonight it reminds you that you need to appreciate the time you're given."

"It does." What was he getting at? It wasn't like Matt not to say what he meant.

"I'd like you to stay with me."

"I thought you'd never ask." She opened her car door and pulled her bag out of the back.

After a shared shower, they climbed into bed. Matt pulled her back against his chest and curled around her as if he wanted to protect her. He kissed her temple. Soon his breathing evened.

She followed him into sleep.

CHAPTER TEN

ON WEDNESDAY MORNING, Matt finished up with a patient and stepped out into the clinic hallway.

"Mrs. Dobbs, it was nice to meet you. Be sure to make an appointment with Dr. Lunsford for the week after next. I won't be here."

"Oh, I'll just wait until you are," the middle-aged woman said.

"I'm sorry, I'm moving to Chicago."

She shook her head. "I hate to hear that. It's hard to find a doctor you like. I was hoping you'd be around for a long time."

"I think you'll like Dr. Lunsford. I can personally vouch for her." In more ways than he could say out loud.

"I'll come back and check her out."

Matt watched the woman leave out the front door of the clinic. He'd miss this interaction with patients, but it had been invigorating being back in the OR the other night. He'd not actually gotten to do the surgery, but he'd watched and even offered help when asked. Many surgeons could be territorial, but Dr. Roper had been aware of Matt's skills. It didn't hurt that Dr. Roper had also seen Matt present a paper at a conference and had read a number of articles he'd written.

"I see you've been charming the female patients, Dr. Chapman." Shay came up beside him with a grin on her lips.

He winked at her. "I'm only interested in charming one woman."

"Then you can consider that done." That special smile formed on her lips.

"How's the new guy working out?" Shay had hired the blond doctor, Dr. Kurt Willis.

"I think he'll work just fine. I'm glad he could start today since you'll be gone tomorrow."

"Sorry to have put you in a bind."

She placed a hand on his arm. "You should be in the OR. I'm glad the hospital board gave you privilege. I know you can help Rick."

"Thanks for the vote of confidence." It was nice having someone in his corner and he didn't doubt for a minute Shay supported him.

The new doctor came out of an exam room and looked toward them.

"I better go." Shay headed down to meet Kurt.

Matt moved to the next exam room door. He glanced at Shay. She and Kurt had their heads together, looking at the tablet. His chest tightened. Matt didn't like that scene at all.

He'd already begun to worry about how he'd handle it when he had to say goodbye to Shay. Maybe he would get enough of her soon, but he didn't think so. In fact, with each day and night that passed it was becoming more difficult. He had to continue to remind himself that text, phone calls and airplanes did exist, but it wouldn't be the same as touching her.

Neither of them had discussed what they'd do when the

time came. Yet he'd seen Shay looking off with a tightness to her lips and a sadness in her eyes. What had he done? The last thing he wanted to do was hurt Shay. He couldn't even begin to describe how much he'd miss her.

Shay would never agree to leave Lewisville. This was her home, her clinic, the place she was passionate about, her life. He studied her. Her beauty held him. Shay had outside beauty, but she was even more beautiful on the inside. That was what really captured him. He felt honored she'd shared even a small part of her life with him.

The next evening at her house, he slipped into bed beside Shay. She made some changes in her bedroom, putting a bright cover on the bed and adding pillows with large flowers. New curtains lay over a chair ready for hanging. Pride filled him at how she'd embraced making changes. He pulled her into his arms appreciating her warmth and softness.

"Hey," she murmured. "You're later than I thought."

"I wanted to stay until Rick was settled in ICU." He rubbed his cheek against her hair.

"How's he doing?"

"Okay. He'll have a few more surgeries but he shouldn't have but a small limp."

Shay rolled over and huddled into his chest. "Because you're so wonderful."

He chuckled. "I like having a fan club."

She kissed his chest as her hands came up around his neck. "I'm your biggest."

Friday morning Shay stepped into the office to get some papers to give Sheree. Matt was there on the phone. His brows drew together in concentration.

"Yes, yes," he said.

She quietly picked up what she needed and wiggled her fingers at him as she left.

He gave her a weak smile that didn't make it to his eyes and said into the phone, "I should be able to make that work. I need to check on a few things and I'll get back to you. I'm looking forward to it."

As she came down the hall after speaking to Sheree she saw Matt standing in the doorway of the office. His lips formed a line.

Worry filled her. What was going on? "Is everything okay?"

"Can we talk a sec?"

Her heart thumped harder. She didn't think she'd like what he had to say. "Sure."

Shay entered the office and Matt followed, closing the door.

"What's going on, Matt? You're starting to scare me." She stood facing him.

He took her hands. His thumbs rubbed the top of them a little harder than necessary. "It's nothing like that. That phone call was from Chicago. They'd like me to come up as soon as possible. Monday, if I could."

Shay's hands tightened on his. She'd known this day would come, but it shouldn't be this soon. Or hurt this much.

"The situation has changed up there. The other doctor is leaving a week early and they're backlogged. They need me now."

The note of excitement surrounded by sadness in Matt's voice tugged at her heart. She'd heard it before when he talked about being in the OR with Rick. He missed his job. His skills were wasted at the clinic. "Then you should go."

His brows drew together. "I don't want to leave you in the lurch here at the clinic." His gaze met and held hers. "I don't want to leave you."

"But you have to. I understand that. We knew this day was coming. You should go on. If they need you to come early then that means they can really use you. You have to go."

"At least Kurt is working so you won't even miss me."

Miss him? She'd miss him with every fiber of her being, but she would survive. She'd changed since he'd come into her life. This time she wouldn't get stuck and not move on with her life. Shay fortified herself to say, "Of course you'll be missed, but you have to do what you need to. We'll be fine here. I want you to be happy."

Disappointment filled his eyes as he squeezed her hands. "I'll have to leave in the morning to make the drive. That means it'll mess up our plans to go to the farm."

Shay's chest tightened, making it hard to breathe. She'd get through this. Just like that he would be gone. "I understand. You need to pack. I'll get you some snacks together for the road."

"I was really looking forward to spending the weekend with you. But I should go. I need to get off on the right foot."

She forced a smile. "I agree. It's important to make a good first impression. You're only leaving a week early."

"But I would have spent that week with you. Maybe we can get together for a weekend soon. You could come see me."

That was a nice dream, but she knew in reality that probably wouldn't happen.

"I'm sorry about this. You know this isn't how I would

have planned my leaving, don't you?" Concern still filled his eyes.

"Hey, I understand it's life. We just have to deal." She would take what it dished out and meet it. No more hiding for her. Still it hurt to have Matt leaving.

"Then I'll call and tell them I'll be there Monday." He pulled her to him. "I want to take you out to dinner tonight to help make up for messing the weekend up."

"I'd rather us just stay in. I'll cook something easy and we can watch a movie after we get you all packed. Now, we should see some patients so we can get out of here on time this afternoon."

He gave her weak smile. "I won't miss working for such a demanding boss."

The problem was she'd miss everything about him.

That evening Matt settled on the sofa at his place waiting for Shay to join him after their meal. When the word had gotten out that he was leaving, Sheree had arranged an impromptu going-away party during lunch. She ordered in sandwiches along with cake and ice cream. He'd worked in LA six years and not had that type of attention when he had left. This small group of people, even those who rotated in and out, had become his family in such a short while. Shay had worn a smile while everyone laughed and told stories about his first few days in town, but it hadn't reached her eyes. He sensed she was going through the motions.

As excited as he was to work in an OR again, he hated having to leave her.

Shay joined him on the sofa but left some distance between them. "How did it go with Ms. Gladys?"

He raised his chin with pride. "She said she'd miss me

and if I was ever in town, she expected me to come for a visit. She's bringing over an apple pie in the morning for me to take with me."

"You made a real friend."

"I'm pretty sweet on her too. Which comes as a big surprise to me." It had. After he stopped holding back, he appreciated people more.

"People around here can grow on you."

He took her hand, tracing her fingers with the tip of his. "You certainly did on me. Shay—" he waited until she looked at him "—I don't want this to end here. I know it'll be difficult, but I want to see you every chance we get. I'll come down for long weekends, vacations, holidays. I'm not ready to give you up."

A wry smile came to her lips as she looked anywhere but at him.

"What's wrong?"

"I don't know if it's such a good idea to make plans that we may not be able to keep. I've done the long-distance relationship stuff and it didn't go well. Let's just enjoy tonight and what may come without too many promises that might be broken. That way if it works out it'll be great."

"You do know that I'm not your ex-husband."

"I do. It's not just that, it's where we live. The pace of life we live at. What we want. Enough of that. Let's just watch the movie then go to bed."

He pulled her into his lap. Maybe Shay was right. If she was, he wanted to make sure when she thought of him it brought a smile to her face.

"I was thinking about skipping the movie and moving on to the bed." His lips found hers.

She returned his kiss.

He tenderly made love to her, trying to express all his emotions, including his fears. Was he wrong to suggest they might continue a long-distance relationship? Was he thinking more about what he wanted than what Shay needed? He had no plans to offer her forever and if he hung around, she'd never find that person she deserved. It was past time he thought of others' feelings instead of just his.

With Shay, could he be repeating his past mistakes? Jenna had seen their relationship had turned one-sided. Would Shay soon realize that as well? He couldn't have her think of him as Jenna and his family did. It was important Shay remembered him well.

During the night Shay woke him. This time she showered him with attention. It was as if they were both trying to take and hold tight to all they could for the days ahead. He'd wanted to put his imprint on Shay so she would think of him every night. The problem was he feared she'd done the same to him.

He'd made a commitment to the hospital in Chicago. He had to go. For years, he'd studied and worked for an opportunity to join a world-class hospital where he could be a part of advances in medicine. He couldn't give that up. He had skills that needed to be used to help patients. The adrenaline rush was addictive as well. He'd be lying if he didn't admit to enjoying the notoriety. He'd made a commitment he needed to keep.

As the sky lightened, he loved Shay again hard and fast.

They were putting the last load of his things in the car when Ms. Gladys walked over in her housecoat with a pie in her hand. Matt placed it carefully in the car. He hugged the older woman—something he would've never done a few short weeks before. She returned it. He let her go to find her eyes watery. When had someone last cried for him?

Ms. Gladys said, "You take care of yourself." She glanced at Shay. "Remember some things are more important than others. Sometimes you just have to figure that out." With that, she started back to her house.

He and Shay stood there looking at each other. She blinked a number of times, but there were no tears. "I'll be in touch. Call me anytime."

Shay just watched him, saying nothing.

"I better get going." He pulled her into his arms and gave her a gentle kiss.

She clung to him. When he released her, she stepped back, giving him room to get in the car.

Minutes later he drove down the street, fearing he had just left his heart in Shay's hands with no hope of getting it back.

Pulling into her garage, Shay turned off the car and closed the large door before she lay her head on the steering wheel and let all the misery she'd been holding in flow out. Matt was gone.

She knew better than most what that meant. Hadn't she lived this all before?

With no tears left, she headed inside and went through the motions of living. Finally, she gave up. Fully dressed, she crawled under the bedcovers. She pulled Matt's pillow against her, inhaled deeply and moaned.

She'd brought all this sorrow on herself. Hadn't she known better than to get involved with Matt? He'd made it clear from the beginning he'd be leaving in a few weeks. That his destiny was elsewhere. His leaving this morning had only proven that. What had made her think he would stay for her? She shouldn't be acting this way. Yet, here she was wallowing in grief.

She would give herself today to fall apart then she'd move on. Isn't that what she'd learned to do in the last few weeks? That she needed to move on. Not hang on to what had been. If she saw Matt again great, if not she'd have sweet memories. What she wasn't going to do was stop living the life she wanted.

Matt called that evening, but he sounded tired and they hadn't talked long. He called again on Sunday when he'd arrived in Chicago, but he soon ended the call, saying he needed to get ready for the next day. The distancing she'd expected had already started.

Monday morning, she drove into the clinic parking lot after a long, lonely and listless weekend. Matt not being there waiting for her brought more pain, but she refused to let it control her. She had work to do. A clinic to run. People who depended on her.

Matt had gotten past that wall she'd built and made her care for someone again. What she hadn't anticipated was how hard it would be to let him go. Nothing had come close to this pain before.

At Sheree's knock on the back door of the clinic, Shay let her in.

Sheree took one look at Shay and pulled her into a tight hug. "Aw, honey, I wanted you to let yourself go but I didn't want this for you. Still, that man opened you up again. That's a good thing."

Shay backed away from her. "Was I really that bad?"

Sheree nodded. "Yeah, you were that bad. Now, let's go to work and try not to think about how much we all will miss him."

* * *

Shay didn't hear from Matt on Monday. She figured that would be the case. He had to have been busy learning his way around the new hospital and meeting people.

Before Matt left, he'd made arrangements for Rick's transport to Chicago. He and Dr. Roper had agreed Rick needed the advanced care University Hospital could provide for his next surgeries. Rick's surgery had been scheduled for Wednesday. Shay used checking on Ricky as an excuse to call Matt.

His phone rang a few times before it went to voice-mail. She savored hearing his voice even though it was a recording. The next day Sheree said there was a call waiting for Shay from a doctor. She went to an office to take the call. When Shay answered a woman on the line said, "Hold for Dr. Chapman, please."

Shay's heart fluttered and her palms turned damp just as they always did in anticipation of talking to Matt.

Seconds later he said, "Shay?"

"Yes." The word came out as little more than a squeak. She couldn't believe how nervous she'd become.

"Hey. I'm sorry I didn't call last night. They have me covered up with surgeries. Rick is doing well. He made the flight fine. We're going to try a new procedure designed for people with Rick's injuries. He'll have another surgery next week. We're hoping since this is a new procedure there'll be no charges for the family. We need the practice."

"That's all good to hear." Why did they sound like strangers giving each other reports? "Somebody so young and who makes his living farming needs his legs."

"They're really doing great work here, Shay. People like Rick are walking again."

There was an awkward pause. She wanted to say all the things she'd been thinking and feeling over the last few days, but that wasn't what Matt needed to hear. He was happy. Excited. That was what she wanted most for him. "It sounds like you're where you should be. I know you'll help a lot of people."

"I hate it, but I've got to go. They're paging me. I'll call soon." It was quiet on the line for a moment. "Shay." His voice had lowered, became intimate. "I miss you."

Matt disconnected before Shay had a chance to respond. She spoke into the silence. "Take care of yourself. I love you."

She did. With all her heart.

Over the next two weeks they played phone tag more than spoke to each other. Shay kept busy by redoing her house. She'd hung the curtains in the bedroom. Sacked up the pillows in the living room and donated them to a local charity. She'd even started to remove a wallpaper border in the kitchen to prepare for painting it. Slowly, but surely, she'd started changing her life. She'd taken some suggestion from the garden club about flowers to plant near the front door. The few adjustments she'd made in the house lifted her spirits. Made her feel more in control of her life.

She'd hoped she and Matt could have a long talk on the weekend, but he texted that he'd had an emergency and didn't know when he would have a chance to call. The next weekend she was busy with a community event she'd volunteered to help at and couldn't pick up when he called.

They were already drifting apart, and she didn't know if she could hold on.

Matt had been busier than he'd ever expected. When he'd had a moment free, he'd been dead on his feet and fallen into bed. He hadn't been so tired that he didn't miss having Shay curled up beside him. Somehow, he had to figure out how to get time off to see her. Even the phone calls he'd been so sure would happen between them had been too few. The last had been so terse the fear they could never find their way back to how it had been niggled him. The fast lane he once lived in and thrived on had gone into hyperdrive. This time he didn't care for it, yet didn't know how to get out of it.

Finally, with an afternoon off he took a long hot shower then flopped back on the bed in the hotel that was his temporary home. He hadn't had time to look for an apartment. He'd get a few hours' sleep then call Shay and have a long overdue conversation. One not interrupted by him being needed elsewhere.

Matt woke to the alarm he'd set on his phone. Eager to talk to Shay he pushed her speed dial number.

"Hello."

Peace washed over him just at the sound of her voice. He'd missed her. Far more than he imagined he would. It had taken the joy out of his new job not having her to come home to.

"Hey, Shay. It's so good to hear your voice."

"Matt."

He loved the way she said his name as if it was the best in the world. "How are you?"

"I'm fine."

He sighed. Where was the easiness that had once been between them? They sounded like strangers. He didn't want that. When he'd been with Jenna they'd gone long amounts of time without seeing each other, but he'd never had this pain in the center of his chest like he had from missing Shay. "I'm sorry I haven't called you. It's been busier here than I dreamed it would be."

"I understand. What you do is important. Demanding. I read the press release about you coming to the hospital up there on the internet. It said you're an up-and-coming star."

He chuckled. The first time he'd done so since leaving Jackson. How pitiful was that? "I think they say that about everyone they hire."

"Don't say that. You're great at what you do. I've seen you in action."

"I love being in the OR again." It was a part of him he couldn't do without. "But I really miss you."

Shay's soft sigh made him want to reach out and touch her. If he only could.

"You sound happy. I'm glad." Her voice had a strength in it he'd not heard before. Was she already creating a life that had nothing to do with him?

"I am except for one thing. You're not here. I need to see you. Will you come see me? I'd love for you to move up here."

There was a long pause before Shay said, "I won't do that."

Matt didn't blame her. He couldn't offer her what she wanted—marriage. He felt for Shay what he hadn't for any other woman, but the last few weeks had proven he wouldn't be good husband material. His devotion to his job overtook everything else. He didn't even have time to call her. More than that he wasn't sure he'd be a good father and she wanted children. His relationship with his family proved what a poor risk he was. What made him think it was a good idea to ask that of Shay? He already knew she would say no before the words were out of his mouth. "I'm sorry. I shouldn't have asked you that. It wasn't fair."

"No, it wasn't." Shay's words were filled with sadness and a touch of anger. "I knew this long-distance stuff wouldn't work."

He hated to admit it, but she was right. He couldn't even find the time to meet her halfway for a weekend together. "Shay—"

"Matt, I'm not going to give up my life, my work at the clinic to move to Chicago to see you whenever you have time for me. I won't do that to myself. I deserve to be the center of some man's life. I've been the extra, on the sidelines showpiece already. Never again. I want more. I deserve more and I won't settle for less."

Matt couldn't blame her. He wished he were there so he could pull her to him and hold her, reassure her that she was all of that to him. But was she? He certainly hadn't treated her that way in the last few weeks. It had been all about him. "You make it sound like what we've shared meant nothing to me. That's not true. I've felt more with you than I ever have for anyone. Even my family."

"From what I can tell, you shared as little as possible about yourself with your family as you have with me these last few weeks. I think family and friends is everything. You act like yours are just people you have to deal with. I don't want to be another one of those. I'm not surprised you have an issue with commitment since you refuse to work through your problems with your stepfather. You've been running from them too long. You're looking for a place to belong in all the wrong places. Of course, you live for your job. It's easy to have a relationship when the other person is asleep and when they're awake they revere you for saving their life. True relationships require attention and honesty between both persons—with themselves and each other."

He flinched. "You don't know anything about me and my family. What it's like to never feel like you measured up."

"Have you ever thought you might be part of the problem? I know you don't give them, especially your stepfather, a chance now. Did you ever?" she snapped.

Was she right? Anger boiled up in him at the idea she might be. "Like you have a right to say anything about how I handle my life. Look at you. Up until recently you've lived in a house that looked more like your good-for-nothing husband still lived there than you do. You're so involved in the community you haven't taken time to do something for yourself like travel. It's past time for you to make decisions based on what you want—not on what you think looks good to the people around you."

Shay's voice turned tight. "Thanks for that insight into my life. For your information I've made changes, am making them, but you haven't had time to hear about them."

That statement certainly hit him in the gut. This conversation, which he'd believed would be a happy one had taken a horrible turn. How had they gone from what they had shared to slinging accusations at each other? "Shay, I didn't mean—"

"It doesn't matter what you meant. It was going to be over when you left anyway. I should have been strong enough to say it then. We want different things out of life, want to live in different places, value different stuff. We just didn't want to admit it. Thanks for helping out at the clinic and especially with Ricky. It's been nice knowing you, Matt. Bye."

The line went dead as he said, "Shay, listen—"

He'd lost Shay. He felt physically sick. Here he was almost a thousand miles away where he couldn't touch or hold her or try to convince her they could make it work. But could they?

His chest constricted, making it hard to breathe. Maybe Shay was right. Their relationship had been slowly dying, which made it far more painful than a clean break. He wasn't the man Shay needed anyway. She deserved better than him. Shay need someone who would put her first. Always. He couldn't make that promise.

But all that intellectual knowledge didn't make the ache in his chest ease. For once he'd found a woman who accepted him, cared about him, loved him. He liked the feeling. Shay filled the empty hole in him. Loneliness had been so much a part of his life he'd no longer recognized it until Shay had come into it. For once he started to feel as if he were a part of something special, worth fighting for. Now he'd destroyed it.

A few minutes later his phone rang. It had to be Shay. She must be calling him to tell him she'd changed her mind. She'd give them another chance. He jerked the phone off the bedside table. "Shay?"

"Hey, Matt. It's Mom. Who's Shay?"

"Mom." He didn't even try to keep his disappointment out of his voice.

"What's going on? Are you all right?"

How like his mom to care. No matter how he treated her she still loved him. He had treated her badly. She didn't deserve it.

"I'm fine." He sighed. "No, Mom that's not true."

"Tell me. Even if I can't help, I can listen."

Hadn't his mother always listened when he'd given her a chance? When had he stopped giving her that opportunity? Too long ago. "There's this woman I met. Her name is Shay. She's one of the most amazing, selfless, caring, funny people I've ever met. She has this old family farmhouse she's redone. When her community needed a clinic, she'd started one. There's nothing she can't do."

"It sounds like she's a special person. Someone you really care about."

Or someone he loved. "I do care about her. A lot.

"She has her clinic and I have my work here. I don't see how we can make it work." Matt groaned. "And I messed up what we did have. Worse, I'm up here and she's in Jackson."

"Are you not at the clinic in Mississippi any longer?"

"I'm in Chicago. I came up here three weeks ago."

"Matt, why do you insist on keeping us at arm's length? We care about you and want to know where you are and what you're doing. I worry about you." His mother's disappointment and hurt rang clear. She sounded too much like Shay. Had he been treating Shay the same way he'd been treating his mother and the rest of the family all these years? Everything one-sided. And that being *his* side.

"I'm sorry, Mom." He hated always having to say that to her. To feel as if he was failing her. That had to stop.

"All you have to do is open up to us." His mother gave him a moment to let that sink in. "Are you liking your work?"

"I do. I thought this would be a great place to build a career." Why didn't that interest him as much as it used to? Because he feared he'd left the truly important part of his life back in Mississippi.

"But not so much now?" she asked softly and with concern.

"I don't know. What I wanted and what I can have seem to be two different things."

"That's life, son. Sometimes it doesn't go the way we planned. Life has to be about more than work. Having someone you care about and can grow old with matters as well."

"Like with Dad?"

There was a pause before his mother said, "Yeah. But we can change directions and make something different, just as good maybe even better."

Had his mother been as lonely as he when his stepfather, Michael, had come along? Matt had never really thought about how his mother's life had changed when his father had died. Once again, he'd been more focused on his life than hers. That had worked when he was a boy, but as a man he should know better.

"I know you and Michael haven't ever seen eye to eye. I know you've always thought it was his fault, but some of it has been you. It was difficult for you to accept him into what had become our life. By the time Jane and Ben came along, Michael gave up and focused on them. I saw how that hurt you, but you never gave him a real opening. But that doesn't mean he doesn't care about you. You are a part of our family. We all love you."

In the background Matt heard his stepfather ask, "Is that Matt? I'd like to talk to him." A few seconds later Matt's stepfather's gruff voice came on the phone. "Hey, Matt. Your mother told me what happened in LA.

I wanted to let you know I'm proud of what you did. That took guts. It was the right thing to do."

Matt swallowed hard. Shock shook him. If his stepfather had ever said anything like that to him before, Matt didn't remember. "Uh...thanks."

"How did the patient do?"

"Great. He has full use of his leg." The strain in Matt's shoulders relaxed.

"All because of you. And come to see us when you can. Here's your mom."

Matt wasn't sure what dimension he'd gone into, but he liked it. He was speechless. Shay had pointed out more than once that his stepfather had set a good example. Matt just didn't want to see that.

His mother continued, "The reason I called is your brother and sister are coming for a visit in a couple of months. I want to get on your calendar. It's been too long since we've all been together. I wondered if you would try to come too?"

Suddenly, he wanted to reconnect. See if he could find common ground with his stepfather. To do his part. "I can't promise anything for sure right now, but you have my word that I'll really try. I'm not just saying that."

"That's all I can ask for."

Matt didn't miss the note of joy in his mother's voice.

"And Matt...about Shay. You need to think long and hard about what you really want. Think about it. Sometimes we don't get a long time with the ones we love."

"Thanks for loving me even when I've not been very lovable."

"What are mothers for? Others will love you too—you just have to give them a chance. I look forward to seeing you soon. Bye now." His mother hung up.

She'd given him a lot to think about. It was time he started thinking beyond himself. To look at how other people saw and felt about things. Like Shay. He had to decide how he wanted to live his life, and with whom.

He paced across the small room that he was learning to hate.

Was he trying to fill a void with his work that was no longer there because he'd had Shay? Had he been using the adrenaline rush of surgery and long hours to cover his inability to face people he cared about? He did good work, he didn't doubt that, but did medicine fill his need to be needed? While Shay used medicine to care for others.

He stopped to look out the picture window to the busy city far below.

She'd accused him of wanting her to make all the sacrifices. Hadn't he? Was that what he'd wanted from Jenna as well? He'd not treated her with any more respect than he was treating Shay. What did it take for him to learn his lesson? He'd treated his parents the same way. He was an intelligent man who should have seen the pattern before now. He'd been thinking only of himself for so long that he couldn't view life any other way. Until Shay pointed it out. He'd have to work at it, but he'd start acting differently. Figure out some way he could be worthy of Shay.

CHAPTER ELEVEN

OVER THE NEXT two months Shay poured all her efforts into her work, community activities and clubs. If she stayed busy, she wouldn't think about how much she missed Matt. Or how really happy she had been when she had Matt in her life.

She couldn't believe he'd think she'd just pick up and come join him in Chicago. He hadn't even offered her any commitment. Her life was here. At times she'd felt her community had expected something she couldn't give them, but still this was her home. People depended on her. She couldn't just dump it all so that she could be there when Matt had time for her. Didn't he know her better than that?

If she had let him, he wouldn't have treated her any better than John had. Those days were gone. She would have all of him or none. Never again would she be second in the life of the man she loved. Where she couldn't speak up for herself before, she had to with Matt. She wouldn't be an afterthought. She deserved better than that. And would see to it she got it.

Yet, she'd found something with Matt she'd never experienced with John. It made it even harder to lose Matt because he had seen her. The real her.

Everything she did seemed surrounded by memories of Matt. He'd ruined the peace she found going to the farm because all she wanted was him there with her. At her house she started sleeping in the guest bedroom because she didn't want to sleep in the bed they'd shared without him. The joy of working at the clinic had been taken away. Patients came in and asked about him all the time. Each time it happened it was like another reminder of what was gone.

On a Wednesday evening, she pulled up to her parents' house and parked. They had been inviting her to dinner more often. They didn't say it, but she could see in their eyes that they worried about her. She'd lost weight. Sleep came only after many long hours of tossing. Her parents weren't the only ones who had noticed. Sheree, who usually teased Shay out of a mood, had given that up. Shay got more hugs instead.

"Hello," Shay called as she entered her parents' house through the kitchen door.

The design of the house looked much like hers except it sat in the center of a large farm. A fence surrounded it, creating a spacious yard with a few trees near the house. Shay had always loved her mom's kitchen. So much so she'd patterned much of the farm's kitchen after her mother's.

Shay inhaled the smell of cooking roast beef and potatoes. Her mother had made one of Shay's favorite meals. Matt would like it. Why did everything go back to him?

Her mom stood at the kitchen sink washing fresh fruit.

"Hi, Mom."

"Hi, honey."

Shay put her purse down on the empty chair by the

door. The calmness and familiarity of the atmosphere eased her tight nerves.

Her dad came into the room and gave her a hug. "How's my girl doing?"

"I'm all right."

He studied her a moment. "Staying busy at the clinic?"

"Yeah. The new doctor is working out great."

"Is he as good as Matt?"

Her mother cleared her throat, and Shay's father looked at her.

No one was as good as Matt. "Dr. Willis is good. The patients like him."

"Supper is ready," her mother announced almost too brightly.

During the meal their conversation went to the weather, an issue at church and one of the families in town whose son planned to marry. Shay had the sense her parents were talking around what they really wanted to say.

Her father put his fork down on his empty plate and set his napkin on the table before he reached across and touched her arm. "We're worried about you, honey."

This was why Shay had been asked over. Her father wore the same concerned expression he had when what John had done exploded around her. His forehead wrinkled as he watched her.

"We're concerned you're making yourself sick. We love you and want to help," her mother said.

The words hung in the air thick and stifling. Shay couldn't look at her parents. She could hear her heartbeat in her ears. "I'm fine."

Her mother said softly, "I know you really liked Matt. I saw the way you looked at him. It was so nice to see you start living again. We understood why you threw yourself into starting the clinic, but that wasn't the same as having someone you cared about. The clinic helped you to heal, but Matt made you light up again."

Her father gave her arm a gentle squeeze.

"The clinic is a worthy cause, but it isn't the same as having someone to love and come home to. We know you and Matt were spending a lot of time together before he left," her mother continued.

There was the gossip again, but it didn't bother her. She had liked Matt. In fact, she loved him. That was the problem.

"How can we help you?" her father asked.

"This is something I have to work through myself."

"If two people really care for each other there's always a way to compromise," her mother said softly.

Shay wasn't sure that was true where she and Matt were concerned.

"Do you ever hear from him?" her mother wanted to know.

"I did for a while, but he was super busy, and the calls got fewer and fewer. It wasn't working so I broke it off."

"Honey," her father said. "You need to figure out what'll make you happy. Then figure out how to make that happen. Not worry about what others think you should do."

"I wish it was that easy." She feared what she wanted had already been lost.

"What you lived through with John wasn't easy. But you did it." Her father patted her hand. "Nothing worth having is ever easy."

How like him to speak the truth practically.

He smiled. "Think about it."

Half an hour later Shay drove up in front of her house. Despite the changes she made she didn't want to go in. That part of her life was behind her. Without giving it any further thought she continued on and headed for the farm. It wasn't that much farther to drive to the clinic from there.

She had to pull out of this Matt-induced stupor and take control of her life. Her parents were right. She'd wallowed long enough. Shay refused to continue to live in the land between what could be and what wasn't.

At the farm she sat at the kitchen table with a pad of paper and wrote "Changes to Make" across the top. Sell house. Move to farm. Set up schedule at clinic where she wasn't doing everything. Create a come in early/late schedule for the doctors. Form a fundraising committee for the clinic that she didn't head. Give up all civic clubs except for the garden club. Start going to the small church near the farm. Call Matt and see if she was still invited for a visit.

Shay felt better about herself than she had in years. Now she could start building her future. Hopefully with Matt in it in some way but if not, she'd be living the way she wanted. Not in the way she always had.

Tomorrow she would call the real estate agent about selling the house. On the weekend she would start sorting and moving her belongings. She was determined to start working her list as soon as possible. She had a plan and for once in a long time she liked herself.

Matt pushed the OR doors open. The case had gone well and for that he was grateful, but something still didn't feel right. He wasn't as satisfied with himself as he should be. It had been a tough surgery and he wanted to share his success—with Shay. Yet she wasn't there for him to do so. It was time he faced it. He wanted to be elsewhere.

He missed Jackson and the way of life he had for too short a time. The pace of the place. Looking at the stars. The grandeur of the Mississippi River. The pine trees. The farm. The people.

He pulled off his surgical garb and tossed it in the dirty bin with more force than necessary. The truth was he'd never been lonelier in his life. He missed Shay. His and Shay's conversations over the phone, despite being brief, had eased the frantic pace of his life that living in Chicago had created while they lasted.

He wished for the contentment Shay's simple farm house gave him when he returned to his sterile box hotel room. It had been months and he still hadn't found an apartment. Each one had something that didn't suit him. He huffed. What didn't suit him was Shay not being in them with him.

Was this what he wanted for his life? Did he want to live like this? The demand on his time might slow down, but what would he have then? An apartment someone else had decorated, a great view of a busy city, and no one to share it with.

He walked down the highly polished floor of the hallway toward his office. At one time none of that might have bothered him, but after what he'd experienced in Jackson, he wasn't sure he'd be satisfied anymore. He wanted to sit on a porch and drink coffee while he rocked. Wanted to skinny dip on a hot day. Wanted to eat a homemade apple pie. Most of all he wanted to see Shay smiling at him and to pull her to him for a kiss.

He'd not been pleased with what had led him to Jackson and Shay, but he was grateful for it. Because of what had happened in LA he'd had a chance to experience what his life could be like. He'd unearthed a place where he belonged. Hadn't that been what he'd been searching for? His mother was right. Having someone special in your life was the most important thing. He'd found it, then shoved it away for position and money and lost Shay and the tranquility she brought to his life. With her he had found home.

Would she take him back? If she would, he'd open his heart and feelings to her without reservations. He couldn't correct the mistakes of his past, but he could vow to never knowingly keep her closed off from how he felt—like he'd done with his family or in his other relationships. He would offer her his entire life, his devotion and most of all his fidelity. Shay would be his all. In all things he would consider her first.

He picked up his phone. It was time to accept that he'd made a mistake. He would start correcting it right away.

Matt's nerves were about to get the best of him. He was finally back in Jackson. After giving notice two weeks ago, he'd sold his car and bought a truck and headed south. His boss at University Hospital hadn't been pleased with him, but Matt had given him two names of surgeons who would be glad to fill Matt's empty position. He'd even called them to make sure they would relocate. That had eased the displeasure some.

Shay had phoned, but he'd miss the call. He hadn't returned her call, wanting to talk to her face-to-face. He desperately needed her to see his sincerity on his face, in his eyes. He didn't want her to misconstrue anything he had to say. He could be making a mistake by surprising her, but he'd take his chances.

Matt drove straight to Shay's house when he'd arrived in Lewisville. There was a for sale sign in the yard, and she wasn't home. He saw a neighbor in the yard and asked if they might know where Shay was. The woman said she now lived out at her farm.

He drove toward Shay's farm. While he'd been gone the leaves had turned and there was a nip in the air. Would Shay have a fire burning? The bigger question was would she let him in the house.

Making the turn down the lane to the farmhouse, he took a deep, fortifying breath. His life, his happiness hung in the balance. What happened in the next few minutes could change his world for better or worse. A petite, strong-willed woman held it in her hands. He'd brought this situation on himself and he planned to humbly pay his dues. Whatever he had to do to fix things between them.

With relief, he saw her car parked in front of the porch. He pulled slowly around and up beside it.

Shay stepped out of the house. She wore an oversized sweater, which she pulled tight around her and crossed her arms over her chest. Her hair hung free. Matt winced. Not the most welcoming stance. To his deprived eyes she'd never looked more beautiful. He continued to study her closely. She'd lost weight. Because of him?

Her focus remained on his truck as if trying to figure out if it was familiar or not.

Climbing out, he closed the door and stepped to the front of the vehicle.

The shock on Shay's face made him unsure of his decision to surprise her. He smiled.

She grabbed the top of the closest rocker. "Matt. I hadn't expected to see you."

The sweet sound of his name on her lips filled him with warmth. His smile grew.

"You didn't have to go to this much trouble to return my call."

How like Shay to find the humor in a situation. "I was in the neighborhood."

She looked at the wide-open land for a moment and shook her head. "I don't think so. If you come here, you mean to."

"You got me. I came to see you."

"From Chicago?" Disbelief filled her voice.

"Yes. I need to tell you something." He stuffed his hands in his jean pockets to keep from pulling her into his arms.

"What?" Concern filled her eyes as she tugged her sweater tighter.

"I decided the job in Chicago doesn't work for me."

Her eyes went wide. "Why?"

"Because it isn't what I want anymore."

"You don't?"

"No. I've joined Dr. Roper's practice. We both think it's a good fit. He likes doing the routine stuff and I'll be doing the complicated work."

"You're moving back here?" Shay said the words slowly as if having a difficult time understanding their meaning.

"Yeah. I have all my worldly belongings right here." He patted the hood of the truck.

"You bought a truck." Wonder surrounded the statement.

"Somehow it's better suited to life here. I may even buy a four-wheeler."

Shay just looked at him in disbelief.

Matt cleared his throat. "Can we talk? Would you invite me in?"

"I guess I can do that. Would you like to come in?" She turned toward the door.

He grinned. "I would like that."

Shay stood in front of the fireplace where a gentle blaze burned.

Matt took one of the chairs. His gaze met hers as he patted the arm of the other chair. "Will you come sit?"

She sat in the chair still looking unsure about what was happening.

Matt turned so he could see her clearly. "I went by the house and saw the for sale sign."

"Yeah. I decided it was time to move on."

"I'm proud of you. Not so much of myself. I've spent too much time thinking about what I thought I wanted without any consideration of others' feelings—especially yours. When I left here I didn't understand that this land, this world, these people were ingrained in you, making you who you are. I didn't grasp what it was like to have those types of connections because I've never had them until you showed me they existed. I became a better person by knowing you. I have discovered where I want to be, to belong. Please tell me you'll forgive me and will give me another chance. If you don't want a future with me, I'll remain your friend. I think Jackson is large enough that we don't have to see each other if we don't want to." Matt took her hand and she allowed it. "But I'd rather you take pity on a misguided surgeon and take him back into your life."

Her face brightened. "I think I can do that."

"Just think? Would it help if I said I love you?"

"That would make it a sure thing." She flung herself into his arms and kissed him.

Matt's heart soared. Shay smelled fresh and healthy. All that he remembered and more, better.

"I love you too," she said against his lips.

Her kiss was honey to a hungry man. "Even though our lives have been driven by different ideas I want us to move forward together."

Shay blinked then blinked again. "You do?"

"Of course, I do."

"That's not what it sounded like during our last conversation."

"I think I was too scared of my feelings to admit them to myself, much less you. I've spent so much of my life pushing people away I didn't know how to let you in. I thought you could never really care for me. That there was too much for us to overcome to have a future. I promise that I'll work to make up for all the pain I caused you over the last few months, even if it takes the rest of my life."

She cupped his cheek and stroked his beard. "You don't have to make up for anything. I needed to make some changes in my life too. You forced me to see that. I've lived too much by what had happened in the past. I needed to be my own person. My parents were worried about me and confronted me about what I wanted out of life. Truthfully, they were worried about me moping over you."

"You moped over me?" He grinned, but it pained him to think about what he'd put her through.

"Hey, don't get too full of yourself."

His arm tightened around her waist. "I'm really sorry I hurt you."

"I needed to hear what you said. I'm selling the house which should have been done years ago. I'm living here where I belong. I've given up clubs and committees I was doing just to be doing. I told the committee wanting to put up a statue to John that they were welcome to it, but that I'd not participate. Believe it or not I've given up some control at the clinic. I was even planning a trip."

"You have been busy."

He grinned as she raised her chin in satisfaction. "I've never felt better in my life. Until now. You were right. I needed to do it. It's like having a weight lifted off me."

"I'm proud of you. You're a brave woman. Where are you going on your trip? Could I maybe come with you?"

Her gaze met his. "I was coming to see you."

"In Chicago?"

She nodded. "I was waiting on you to return my call. I wasn't sure you'd want to see me."

Matt kissed her deeply. "I'll always want to see you. More than that, I want you. That's not exactly right either. What I want is you if you'll have me."

"I'll have you." She whispered into his neck.

He kissed her not with the hunger he would've imagined he would have, but with the tenderness of knowing he'd almost lost her. And that it would've been his fault. He poured his feelings into caressing her lips, her cheeks, her eyes, and nibbling at her ears.

Shay returned his affection with enthusiasm.

They broke apart, breathing heavily.

"I have missed you so much." Matt gave her another quick kiss. "But I have something more to tell you. I've made some changes too. I went to see my mom and step-father on the way down here. It wasn't easy, but it had to be done. My stepfather even said he was proud of what I had done in LA."

"I know that meant the world to you to hear him say it." Shay hugged him.

"It did. I don't know where things will go from here, but I know I've tried. I can't fix years of hurt feelings overnight, but I've made a step forward and it feels good."

"I'm proud of you. That had to have been difficult."

"It was, but worth it. I've only been more scared when I drove down your drive not knowing what reception you'd give me. After having you in my life I understand why my mother married again. Why finding true love is important. Maybe I was responsible for closing my stepfather out, but I'm doing what I can to open that door again."

Shay cupped his face and looked directly into his eyes. "All you can do is try. I'm not worried that he won't recognize what a special man you are, just as I do. Are you sure you'll like living here and working with Dr. Roper? I want you to be happy too."

"I promise I'll be happy here. I want to be here. I think I can build a real and successful career here. Best of all you'll be here beside me."

"I don't want you to regret leaving Chicago for me. Ever."

"Are you trying to get rid of me?"

"No, no, no." She kissed him. "You'd just had your heart set on someplace bigger."

"That's because my heart didn't know what I really wanted and needed. I found myself in Jackson, with you."

"I just want you to know that I'd leave here for you. I wouldn't like it, but I love you more than any place or person."

"That's good to know. But I'm staying right here. Just so you understand, I'm not giving up anything, I'm gaining everything. I had nothing before finding you. You're my present and my future. The past doesn't matter. This is me happy. And in love with you."

She kissed him from the depths of her full heart.

"I do have to leave in a few weeks. I told my mom I'd be at her house when my brother and sister plan to be at home. Will you go with me?"

"Of course, I'll go with you. I'd love to meet your family."

"Great. I think it's a good idea for them to meet you as soon as possible. I don't want them to get to know you for the first time at our wedding."

"You're pretty sure of yourself, Dr. Chapman."

He grinned and kissed her. "I'm not letting you get away."

"I'm glad to hear it. I promise I'm not going anywhere without you."

EPILOGUE

SHAY STEPPED OUT of the SUV with her father's help. She picked up the front of her wedding dress and let it drop, then fluffed it out. She felt like a princess in the boat-neck dress with capped sleeves and a tight bodice that fell into a full skirt. Her mother's pearls encircled her neck.

She looked at the glimmering ring on the finger of her left hand. It sparkled in the late-afternoon light. It had been the one Matt's father had given his mother.

Matt had said, "Now everyone will know you are mine."

Shay liked the idea of being his.

Taking her father's arm, they walked together toward the river. The setting sun had turned the sky to pink and orange. The horizon made a picturesque backdrop to the handsome man with the beautiful smile waiting for her. Dressed in a dark suit, Matt stood at the end of the aisle created by their families, including his stepfather and a handful of their friends. Matt had issued a special invitation to Ms. Gladys, who was providing the apple pies instead of a groom's cake.

Matt stood tall and strong and steady. Shay didn't doubt he would be there for her during the good times and the bad. She'd always know his love and support.

He'd already shown her that in so many ways. She could count on him.

Shay would continue her work at the clinic, but with two additional doctors, not just one. Soon she would start the process of expanding. But for now, enjoying time with the man waiting on her would be her focus. They planned to travel to see all the places they had talked about. Their first stop would be Paris for their honeymoon.

They had agreed to live at the farm. When they had children, they'd build a home somewhere on the property, but the farmhouse would remain their private getaway.

Her gaze locked with Matt's. Those green eyes never wavered. She gripped her bouquet of daisies tighter. She would soon be joined with him forever. He would soon be all hers. Not the town's, not the country's, not the world's—but hers.

Shay had never been happier in her life. Her smile broadened as she approached her future. Matt returned it with a twinkle in his eyes. Her father kissed her cheek and left to stand beside her mother.

Matt took Shay's hand. "I love you. When I'm with you I'm home."

"And I love you. Where you are is where I belong."

Together they turned to the preacher.

* * * * *

COMING SOON!

We really hope you enjoyed reading this book.
If you're looking for more romance, be sure to
head to the shops when new books are
available on

Thursday 19th
August

To see which titles are coming soon, please visit

millsandboon.co.uk/nextmonth

MILLS & BOON

MILLS & BOON

THE HEART OF ROMANCE

A ROMANCE FOR EVERY READER

MODERN

Prepare to be swept off your feet by sophisticated, sexy and seductive heroes, in some of the world's most glamourous and romantic locations, where power and passion collide.

HISTORICAL

Escape with historical heroes from time gone by. Whether your passion is for wicked Regency Rakes, muscled Vikings or rugged Highlanders, awaken the romance of the past.

MEDICAL

Set your pulse racing with dedicated, delectable doctors in the high-pressure world of medicine, where emotions run high and passion, comfort and love are the best medicine.

True Love

Celebrate true love with tender stories of heartfelt romance, from the rush of falling in love to the joy a new baby can bring, and a focus on the emotional heart of a relationship.

Desire

Indulge in secrets and scandal, intense drama and plenty of sizzling hot action with powerful and passionate heroes who have it all: wealth, status, good looks…everything but the right woman.

HEROES

Experience all the excitement of a gripping thriller, with an intense romance at its heart. Resourceful, true-to-life women and strong, fearless men face danger and desire - a killer combination!

To see which titles are coming soon, please visit

millsandboon.co.uk/nextmonth

MILLS & BOON

Coming next month

SECOND CHANCE WITH HER GUARDED GP
Kate Hardy

'In London, I never really got to see the sky properly,' he said. 'Out here, it's magical.' He turned her to face him. 'You make me feel magical, too, Gemma,' he said softly. 'And, right now, I really want to kiss you.'

'I want to kiss you, too,' she said.

He dipped his head and brushed his mouth against hers, and her lips tingled at the touch.

'Sweet, sweet Gemma,' he said softly, and kissed her again.

It felt as if fireworks were going off in her head. She'd never experienced anything like this before, and she wasn't sure if it made her feel more amazed or terrified.

When Oliver broke the kiss and pulled away slightly, she held his gaze. His pupils were huge, making his eyes seem almost black in the twilight.

She reached up to touch his mouth, and ran her fore-finger along his bottom lip,

He nipped gently at her finger.

Suddenly, Gemma found breathing difficult.

'Gemma,' he said, his voice husky. 'I wasn't expecting this to happen.'

'Me neither,' she whispered. And this was crazy. She knew he was only here temporarily, and he'd probably go back to his life in London once his locum job here had finished and his twin had recovered from the transplant. Was she dating him purely because being a temporary colleague made him safe – she wouldn't be reckless enough to lose her heart to someone who wouldn't stick around? Or would it be like the misery of all those years ago when her parents had moved and left her behind?

'We ought to be heading back,' she said. Even though both of them knew there was no reason why they couldn't stand on the cliffs all evening, just kissing, the unexpected intensity of her feelings scared her.

Continue reading
SECOND CHANCE WITH HER GUARDED GP
Kate Hardy

Available next month
www.millsandboon.co.uk

LET'S TALK
Romance

For exclusive extracts, competitions
and special offers, find us online:

f facebook.com/millsandboon

🐦 @MillsandBoon

📷 @MillsandBoonUK

Get in touch on 01413 063232

For all the latest titles coming soon, visit
millsandboon.co.uk/nextmonth